Chapter One

Camberwell South East London

'1933'

'Georgie' shouted Annie Powley, leaning half of her five foot two frame out of her upstairs front room window. 'Georgie Powley get yourself back here now.'

'Oi, Annie, do you 'ave to shout so loud? Me old man's trying to get some kip, I bet they can hear ya, down the Old Kent road.' Annie's next door neighbour, Dolly Bell, who was black leading her front door step, called up to her.

'Sorry, Gel, I fought your Arfur was back on day's this week'

'Yeah, well he should a bin but that lazy old so and so, Jim Wise, is pulling a fast one agen, says his wife's ill and she needs him there at night, to see to their young, Billy.'

'More like so's he can go down the pub, eh, Doll?'

'I feel sorry for her though. He was out of work for all that time and she, the fool, took in washin' and ironin' and did her little cleanin' job at the Duke. You wouldn't catch me doing that for nuffing,'

'Nor me, Gel. Look at her now, after havin' had, what is it, three miscarriages? The poor soul's first child to live, has got a weak heart, it's not fair is it?'

'My, Arfur, says, that if the crafty bugger don't pull his socks up, he'll be out. There's 'undreds just waiting to take his place.'

'Where would that leave his, Ivy, though? She couldn't go back to doing what she used to. I know he don't give her much out of his wages but at least she gets by, what with the little bit of help her mum and dad give.'

Annie was enjoying this gossip with her friend and neighbour, Dolly, so much, that she had forgotten why she was hanging out of the window in the first place. Her twelve year old son Georgie hadn't though. When he heard his mother calling his name for the second time, he ran across the playground of the Avenue school, opposite to where he lived with his mum, Annie, and dad, George. The playground was at the back of the school, his mum knew only too well he'd be there, he spent nearly every day after school and weekends on the school's chalked out football pitch. When he arrived at the front gate of the school, Georgie looked across the road to see his mum and Dolly from next door, nattering away ten to the dozen.

'Good ole, Doll' Georgie said to himself, 'I should get a least anuvver ten more minutes football', so he ran back round to the pitch where he'd left his mates, Siddy, Joey and Bernie, who were still kicking the ball around.

'Thought you had to go 'ome?' called Siddy, the same age as, Georgie.

'Na, ma's yakking to Doll, got time yet to show you how it's done'

The three other boys shook their heads at Georgie's cockiness. Yet at the same time knowing that what he said was true. He was a very good footballer and held the record in their street for being able to keep the ball in the air the longest, without it touching the ground, by using his feet, knees and head to do so.

'When's your next match for the 'amlet then, Georgie?' asked ten year old Joey, who looked on Georgie as his hero.

'Next Sunday. We should've had a match tomorrer but the other team are two players short.'

'Couldn't you take the points then? It ain't nuffink to do with your lot if they ain't got a full team?' put in Bernie, the eldest of the four boys, at fourteen..

'Nah, we wanna win the cup this year, well we should win it at any rate, cause we've got loads more points than any of the other teams. When we do win it, we don't want anyone saying that it was given to us by teams that had to cancel. We've told them to arrange another meet as soon as they're at full strength.'

'Can I come and watch yer next week then, Georgie?'

'I don't mind taking you wi' me, Joey, but this time make sure your mum and dad know about it.'

A couple of weeks ago, young Joey had taken himself off to Ruskin park to watch Georgie's team play a match, trouble was, he had a penny, that his granddad had given him, to pay his bus fare on the way but didn't have any money for the return journey. It took him over two hours to walk the four miles or so home. Poor Joey was a bit slow for his age, other kids at school took advantage of him and bullied him into doing things that would upset the teachers. Had he told someone where he was going that Sunday, his dad might not have reacted in the way he did.

When by seven o clock, and Joey hadn't been seen since dinner time, half the street were out searching. They questioned Georgie on his return, but Georgie had not noticed Joey at the match. Brothers Siddy and Bernie, were with their parents paying their weekly visit to their nan and grandad for Sunday dinner. Then, in the distance they saw a weary little figure walking down John Ruskin Street where they all lived. Joey's dad rushed down the road taking his belt off as he went and before Joey opened his mouth to speak, his dad took a swipe at his backside, Joey screamed out in pain as the buckle hit him on the back of his legs. Little Joey ran as fast as his legs would carry him. He ran straight into his mum's out stretched arms. His dad chased after him but when he reached Joey, some of the other mums including, Annie stood in his way.

'Come on now, Dan' Annie had said, 'leave the poor little lad be, can't you see he's frightened out of his wits?'

'This ain't nuffink to do with you, Annie Powley, so keep yer bleedin nose out of it'

Just then Georgie's dad appeared.

'Don't you talk to my wife like that, Dan. You know by tomorrow you'll regret it if you do the boy any harm.'

'He's right, Dan' joined in Joey's mum. 'Where you bin Joey? We've bin worried out of our lives.'

'Sorry Mum, Dad' Joey tried to explain through his sobs 'I only wanted to see Georgie play football but I didn't 'ave enough money for the bus fare 'ome. I took a short cut that we used once, Dad, when you took me to Ruskin Park.... and I, and I, got a bit lost'

'Right, well get indoors and don't you ever go off like that agen. You 'ear me?'

'Yes, Dad.' cried Joey.

As every one started to disperse to return to their homes, Annie turned to young Georgie.

'You sure you didn't see little Joey up the park?'

'No. honest, Mum, if he had told me he wanted to come, I'd've taken him with me. Cor his dad didn't half give him one, poor little sod.'

'Oi you, don't let me or your mother ever hear you swear like that again.'

'Sorry Dad.'

That little episode was over two weeks ago but little Joey, as everyone calls him, still bore the scars to remind him.

The four boys continued on with their game. Georgie needed to practice headers in front of the goal, being the youngest player at the Dulwich Hamlet F.C and the shortest boy in the team, at five foot four; he felt he had got to prove himself, even though he was the highest goal scorer so far that season. So, his best pals were more than happy to help him. Over the last few months, Georgie had painstakingly, taught little Joey, how to take a good corner kick, while the other two try to beat Georgie to the ball, by jumping as high as they can. Both Siddy and Bernie, are taller than Georgie, so he really has to work at jumping higher than them to reach the ball and head it in the net.

'Thanks you lot. Been a good session, but I'd better go home, me mum and Doll must have run out of breath by now. See yer this afternoon?'

'Yeah, me and Siddy'll come and knock for yer about two'

'What about you, Joey?'

'I've got to 'elp me mum take some stuff to pawn, Georgie.'

This was a common occurrence in Joey's house. There was never enough money, never enough food, or decent clothes and shoes for Joey, or his five younger brothers and sisters. His dad works for the council as a dustman and spends most of his wages as soon as he gets them on a Friday, down the Rose and Crown. Georgie felt sorry for Joey, he was a nice kid.

'Well, Joey, we'll have a kick around here until you get back. Maybe we could all go to Kennington Park then. Look I gotta go, see yer later.'

'Okay, Georgie, see yer later'

Georgie found his mother sitting in the back room, smoking a cigarette.

'Bout time too. Didn't you hear me calling you?'

'No, when was that, Mum?'

'Oh it don't matter, you're here now. Go in the kitchen and get the jug out of the cupboard for the liquor. You should still be there and back before your dad gets in from work.'

'How many pies shall I get?'

'You ask that every week. You get the same as usual, greedy little beggar, one's plenty enough for you. Give me, me purse over.'
Annie took the right amount of money from her purse and handed it to Georgie.

'Don't forget to take me shoppin' bag with you, they charge extra if you ain't, I mean haven't, got your own.'

When young Georgie was born, Annie and her husband George, decided there and then, that they would try to teach him to speak better than they did, they wanted the very best for their son and were prepared to work hard to give it to him. They wanted him to make something of his life and be successful. The way they saw it, was that, only those that spoke good English, succeeded in this hard life. There was just one thing that Annie desperately wanted to do, and as yet had not succeeded in, that was to stop smoking. Lately, she had started to feel a little breathless whilst she was at her cleaning jobs. Annie was up by six thirty, six mornings a week, ready to walk to the other end of John Ruskin Street, to clean and prepare Doctors McMannus' Surgery before the arrival of his patients. At the end of each school day, Annie then went across the road to the Avenue, where she scrubbed and cleaned the classrooms, halls and toilets. George, her husband had managed to stop smoking more than a year ago. He never stopped telling her, how he felt so much healthier.

'Well if what my George says is right and that it's the fags making me lose me breath, well, I'm gonna do it. If you wanna be around to see your boy grow up, gel, then you've got to pack it in' Annie scolded herself. ' I don't want my boy to start it up, watching all his money go up in smoke. Nope, I'm gonna make a promise to meself, by this Christmas, I'll have stopped.'

Georgie ran down the stairs, smiling to himself, knowing full well, that his, mum had given him an extra penny, as she did every Saturday. So, as usual he could have a bowl of mash and liquor in the pie and mash shop, before putting his order in for, four pies and mash with the liquor being poured into the jug, from home.

'Hello, Georgie, love, same as usual, Boy?' The lady behind the high counter at Arments, the much frequented pie and eel shop down the Walworth road, greeted Georgie.

'Yes, please' He answered, handing over the bag with the jug inside and the money. He eagerly awaited the arrival of his treat of the week. Georgie took his bowl of mash and liquor from the assistant, smacking his lips together. He made his way over the sawdust covered floor to one of the marble topped tables with bench seats that were so tall, when he sat down you couldn't see the top of his head. He sprinkled lots of vinegar over the piping hot food, Georgie liked what he called, the real vinegar. On the table stood two large bottles, one was Georgie's favourite and the other had, to Georgie's eye, little worms floating in it and it didn't taste like proper vinegar to him at all. When he had scraped every last drop of the rich green liquor from the bowl, he collected the bag from the assistant and rushed back along the Walworth Road to his home. His mum had lit the oven and inside the dinner plates were warming. How he loved Saturdays. After finishing his early morning job of helping set up 'Old Pegs' market stall, it was a couple of hours of football, then pie and mash for dinner, that was after his treat of course, then back out with his mates in the afternoon.

'Come on, Georgie' pleaded Siddy. 'We can't wait all afternoon for, Joey; his mum probably won't let him come out agen t'day'

The boys have been waiting in the school playground, for more than an hour for little Joey.

'Yeah, come on, otherwise we won't 'ave time to go up the park before tea' Bernie was impatient to be off.

'Ok, you two, but lets just give him a knock on the way'

Grudgingly Siddy and Bernie walked off with Georgie to Joey's house. Joey's mum answered their knock on the door

'Hello, Mrs Smiff, can Joey coming up Kennington Park with us?'

'No, sorry, Georgie he can't come t'day.'

'Oh, alright is he then?'

'Yeah, course he is. But, well, fings ain't bin too good this week see. Y'know I bought him that smashing pair a' shoes a couple a' monfs ago, off old Peg's second hand stall down the lane, well, it's like this, he won't be having them for a few days, 'til I get fings sorted like.?'

'What about school on Monday, Mrs Smiff?' Georgie asked, knowing full well, that until Mrs Smith had the money to get them out of the pawn brokers, where they obviously were, Joey would have to stay away from school.

'Can't be 'elped can it. Anyway, it's not as if he learns much, fick as two short planks my Joey.'

'We'll be off then, Mrs Smiff.' Georgie was keen to get away before he told her in no uncertain terms that her son was not, as thick as two short planks. He kept his voice calm.

'Tell Joey I'll come round tomorrow morning to see him'

As Sally Smith closed her front door the boys walked away, heading for the Park, with Georgie, feeling very sad for his little friend Joey.

'Wish there was some way we could 'elp' Bernie said to his mates.

'Not much we can do though is there? We ain't got enough money to get them out of the pawn shop' his brother, Siddy, answered.

'Who says we need money' Georgie was looking down at his shiny boots. His dad had been saving for ages to buy them for him as a special treat, he gave them to Georgie when he got into the Hamlet's first team.

'What d'yer mean, Georgie?' Siddy was keen to know.

'Well, I don't wear my old boots no more, they don't fit properly anyway. I'll have a word wiv me mum and see if she'll let me give 'em to Joey.'

'Be a bit big though, won't they?' Added Bernie.

'That won't matter, he can push some old newspaper down the toes.'

The boys felt that they had accomplished something good, their mood changed from feeling low to feeling proud of themselves. They carried on to Kennington Park with a swagger in their walk.

'Cor, Georgie, these boots of yours ain't 'alf comfortable, they fit even better than my new shoes do.'

'What even with the toes stuffed with paper?'

'Yeah, honest, I ain't just saying it cause they're yourn'

The two boys were walking back from the bus stop, returning from the football match that Georgie had just played in.

'When's your mum gonna get your shoes out of pawn?'

'Dunno, me dad says she should leave 'em there. Now that I've got these.'

'But they won't last too long, Joey, the soles have got a coupla little holes in them. My dad had mended them loads of times before buyin' my new ones.'

'No look, see what me dad's done' Joey lifted one of his feet up, to show Georgie the underneath of his boot. 'See?'

'But that's cardboard, it'll soon fall to bits, especially if it rains.'

''E's put some on the inside a'nall. And if it looks like it's gonna rain, then 'e say's I gotta stay 'ome.'

Georgie shook his head. Not for the first time did he thank his lucky stars that he had a caring mum and dad. Georgie was an only child, although he sometimes wished he had brothers and sisters, well brothers mainly. He knew that it was because some kids came from big families they had so little money and then that, made them unhappy so the parents argued a lot. In little Joey's case it was that when his mum and dad married, Joey was already well on his way. His mum, Sally, so Georgie had overheard when his mum was talking with the neighbours, was just seventeen when Joey had been born, now aged twenty nine, she had six kids. Neighbours in John Ruskin Street, remember Joey's birth, and how his father shunned him. He did then and still does, blame everything that goes wrong for them, on the fact that he had to get married, and give up the easy going life of womanising and boozing he had enjoyed before little Joey arrived. Sally had been a pretty, happy go lucky girl, until the night when a drunken Dan had enticed her to go back to his empty house. She was flattered that the handsome, as he certainly was, older man by some seven years, had taken a fancy to her. It only takes once and in this case it did. Sally, now, could not afford to have any pride, she had learnt the hard way, that life for her and her children was not going to be easy, and that if she had to accept handouts and charity to survive, then she would do so. Annie expected no thanks, the day she and Georgie gave the old pair of boots to Joey. Annie had even put a bit shoe polish on them, to give the dull old worn leather a bit of a shine.

'Coming back to my house, Joey for a drink and a biscuit?'

'Yeah, ta Georgie. Will yer dad be there?'

'He should be back from the pub by now. Why?'

'Cause I can tell him all about that goal you got, bloody brilliant that header was.'

'Well, that's thanks to you, Siddy and Bernie, for all that practice you've been doin' with me. Just one thing though, Joey.'

'What's that then, Georgie?'

'No bloody swearing in front of me muvver' this made Joey fall about with laughter.

Annie and George, were enjoying a quiet cup of tea, when the boys burst in on them. While Annie went to the scullery to make the boys a cold drink with a couple of rich Tea biscuits to go with it. Little Joey gave Georgie's dad a running commentary on the football match.

'Cor, you should 'ave seen him, Mr Powley, he had their defence runnin' round in circles'

George smiled at the open enthusiasm Joey showed towards his son. But he had a secret, only his wife Annie knew about. He wanted to say to Joey that he had indeed seen it; he didn't though, because Georgie had said to his dad that after a hard week's work, he deserved to go for a drink with his mates on a Sunday afternoon. He would tell his son soon though, for he wanted to join in with recalling the game with Joey. Instead he said. 'That's my boy. Annie, in a couple of years we might be living with a top class footballer. Which team you gonna choose to play for, Son?' He got up and ruffled his son's hair.

'Give over, Dad' said Georgie, but inwardly he was feeling good, he knew his dad was proud of him.

Annie turned to Joey, 'looking forward to starting at the big school in September, Joey?'

'You bet, I can't wait to be wiv, Georgie, Siddy and Bernie. Fings'll be different then.'

'What things is that then, Joey?' asked Mr Powley.

Joey looked across at Georgie, he didn't like admitting that he was bullied by the bigger boys at the primary school where he was a pupil.

'Go on, Joey, you can tell me mum and dad, they won't say anything to your dad'

The last time little Joey had told his dad that he was being picked on at school, had ended up with Dan, getting angry with his son for letting it happen. He then made Joey pretend to be one of the bullies, he told him to 'come at me, like they do to you and try to 'it me' Little Joey was petrified, how could he go and hit his dad? And because Joey just stood rigid with tears in his eyes, his dad smacked him round the face several times and called him a sissy and a cry baby and that he deserved what he got.

'Come on now, Joey' coaxed Annie. 'It can't be that bad.'

So little Joey, told them how, ever since he had been in the juniors, he had been bullied, and made to own up to naughty things some of the other boys had done. He finished by telling them about his dad's reaction and subsequent beating.

'Are any of these boys going to The Avenue?' Asked Mr Powely.

'Four of 'em are'

'Well, not that I hold with fighting you understand, but my Georgie and your other mates, won't let anything bad happen to you over there.'

'You listen to what, Georgie's dad says, Joey. They'll take care of you. Won't you, Son?'

'Yes, Mum, we've already told, Joey that. Ain't we, J.......

'Ain't?'

'Sorry, Dad, haven't we, Joey.'

'Yep, I can't wait to get there. I haven't scared no more!' He smiled, pleased with himself at getting, as he thought, his choice of words right.

Georgie looked over to where his parents sat, he could see they were trying not to laugh at Joey's attempt to correct his speech, they both put their hands over their mouths suppressing a cough.

When George had recovered sufficiently to speak, he suggested that Georgie show little Joey his new toy soldiers that his Uncle Ted had given to him last week. Georgie's uncle Ted was a driver for the fishmongers where his dad worked. He had to be up before dawn each day to drive the lorry down to the coast, where he collected the fresh fish and shell fish to be sold at the shop. One of the fishermen collected the tiny lead soldiers, as did Georgie. Whenever he found he had two the same, he offered one to Ted at a reasonable price, for him to take home to his nephew, whom he had met on the few occasions that young Georgie had accompanied Ted on his run.

Joey always enjoyed himself in Georgie's house, it was like no other in the street. He thought how lucky they were to have this big flat all to themselves. There is the front room that looks enormous in Joey's eyes. Part of the room, has been divided by a big screen. Behind this, is the big double bed that belongs to Annie and George, beside that, are two big old oak wardrobes. Under one, of the two big light and airy windows, the room boasts a dressing table, and on it is a beautiful dressing table set of gleaming glass, consisting of two trinket containers, a rose bowl and two candle holders. In the main part of the room, there is a brown three piece suite, looking a bit worse for wear but still very comfortable. Along the wall stands an oak dresser, this is Annie's pride and Joy, for when she and George married, this was the only piece of furniture that wasn't second hand. Annie, had seen it, in a shop in Peckham High Street and the day that George proposed to her, she went to the shop and put half a crown deposit down. Every week after that until the day they married, she paid off as much as she could. Two day's before their wedding, she had finished the payments and it was installed in this front room. In it, she keeps her best china, her special occasion cutlery, linen table covers and, tucked away in the cupboard, some of Georgie's baby clothes and toys. This Annie referred to, as, her memory cupboard.

The next room is Georgie's bedroom, 'fancy having a bedroom all to yourself' were the thoughts in Joey's mind. He'd give anything to just have a bed to himself, let alone a room. He shared his bed with two of his brothers and his two sisters shared another bed in the same room, the baby slept in her cot, in the front room where his parents slept on a couch bed.

The one thing though, that made Joey think that Georgie's mum and dad must be really rich, was the fact that they had an inside toilet. At his house, they had to go out the back, where, in winter it was freezing, they couldn't even flush the toilet sometimes because the water had frozen in the cistern.

This was a house where hide and seek was great fun, often Annie would come home to find Siddy, Bernie or Joey hiding in the big cupboard that stands in the hallway and houses her clean washing. There is even a separate access to the garden, via a steep staircase situated in the scullery. Oh there are so many places to hide. But most of all Joey liked to go there because Mr and Mrs Powley made him feel happy, Even Georgie's dad liked him. Here he felt safe.

When the boys had gone to play in Georgie's room, Annie turned to her husband.

'George, what would you say, if I said I wanted to take, little Joey away wiv us?'

'Well, Gel, it's like this,' he paused, Annie looked anxious. 'I'd say, that that is a lovely thing for you to say, and that I think we should.' Annie beamed at him. 'Hold your 'orses though, Gel, we got to get round Dan first.'

'Leave that to me, Love, you wait, when we pack up to go in a couple of weeks, little Joey will be sitting up on top of that lorry with the rest of us.'

Chapter Two

'Got a smashing day for it, Annie' called Doll over the fence of the back garden.

'Yeah, makes me wish I was already there, Gel'

'All packed up are yer?'

'Just about, once I get these shirts of our Georgie's in, that's the last of it.'

'How many of his white shirts 'ave you gotta take wiv yer?'

'All of them. You know what my boy's like over his flippin' white shirts, he has to have a clean one on every uvver day. Gawd help us if I haven't got a spare one, just in case he gets the one he's wearing dirty. He won't go out or to school, just sits moping round the house all day, till one's clean and dry.'

'Ow did he get so fussy over shirts?'

'Don't ask me, Doll. I know my George likes his shirts to be white and crisp as new, but he knows we haven't always been able to afford to buy new ones in the past, so he just had to get used to frayed collars and cuffs like anybody else. Not my boy though. No, he saves most of the money we let him keep, from what he earns helping them set up the stalls down the lane. Then, when he needs a new one, he gives me the money. We help him wiv his fares to get to his football matches.'

'You got a good one there, Annie'

'I know, I couldn't ask for a better son.'

'I could' moaned Dolly.

'Oh come on, your Rodney's not that bad.'

'Well no, but it would be nice to see 'im, sometimes.'

'Look, he's got his own family to look after now, he works 'ard and long hours. Why don't you and your Arfur invite them over for their dinner one Sunday?'

'I shouldn't 'ave to invite 'em. He knows he's always welcome.'

'Yeah, he might, but she don't do she? They'd probably think the world of you, it'd make her feel part of the family. Don't forget, she was bought up in an orphanage, she don't know what it's like to be part of a family. Give it a go, Doll. What you got to lose?'

'Maybe I will, I'll 'ave a talk with my Arfur, see what he says.'

They were interrupted by the arrival of Annie's sister- in- law Kath, she and her husband, Annie's brother Jack, occupied the ground floor of the house. They were the main council tenants and it is to them that Annie and George pay their weekly rent.

'Hope you have cleared your larder out, Annie' Kath stood with arms folded across her chest. 'I do not want no horrible smells, coming down stairs, from stale food'

'No, Kate,'

Kath took a sharp intake of breath, knowing that Annie called her Kate to annoy her.

'What do you mean no, and don't call me Kate. How many more times do I have to tell you? My name is Kathleen or Kath if you must.'

'Sorry, Gel, I said no to your not wanting any bad smells under your nose, but in answer to your question, yes, course I've emptied me bleedin larder, taking it all wiv me ain't I?'

'Right well, that's all right then. Don't leave the pegs on the line, they'll get dirty. Anyway, I'll say goodbye now, 'ope, you, enjoy your holiday.'

'Don't you ever fancy goin 'oppin then, Kath?' enquired Dolly, knowing full well what the answer would be.

'Why should me and my Jack go hopping, when we go to Brighton for our holiday's every year. Brighton's such a loverly place, with its clean sea air and us sitting in deck chairs on the pier. No, hopping isn't for the likes of me and Jack.'

With that she turned and went back into her scullery.

Annie and Dolly both push the tips of their noses in the air with their fingers.

'My name is Kathleen' mimicked Dolly.

'Brighton's such a luvverly place for 'hus to go to' Annie exaggerates. The women enjoyed a good laugh at Kath's expense.

'Better go now, Doll. See yer in a fortnight. And eh, think on what I said.'

The Sun shines on the righteous, so the saying goes. Annie, today perhaps, could be the sort of person in mind when that proverb had been invented. There she was, running around the flat making a last check that everything they needed to take with them was downstairs waiting in the hallway. Among those helping to carry the bits and bobs was little Joey, up and down the stairs he ran, all the while wearing the biggest grin on his face that any of them had ever seen before. There wasn't much for young Georgie and his dad to do, it seemed little Joey had found someone else to hero worship. As he followed Annie from room to room, while she checked that the flat was secure, the same words kept going round and round in his head. 'I'm goin' on 'oliday. I'm goin' on 'oliday. Me Joey Smiff, goin' on 'oliday'. He had not been told, how Annie had managed to persuade his dad to let him go, only young Georgie and his dad, knew of the conversation that passed between the Smith's and Annie.

It was two days after Annie and George had discussed the possibility of little Joey going away with them. Annie squared her shoulders as she knocked on the door of Dan and Sally Smith. Sally answered her knock. Hello, Annie, what can I do fer you?'

'Hello, Sal' Annie responded, then thought to herself, 'I won't beat about the bush, I'll jump straight in' She took a deep breath. 'Is your Dan in?'

Sally looked pensive, 'now what?' was her first thought. 'What d'yer wanna see him for?'

'I'd like to have a chat with both of you, don't worry, Sal there's nuffing wrong' she hesitated, as an idea came into her head. 'It's more of a favour really.' Just then, Dan yelled from inside the house. 'Who's that keepin' you yaggin?' I'm still waitin' for that bleedin' cup a char, you was gonna get.'

'It's, Annie Powely, she wants to ask a favour of us, Dan.'

'Well if she want's a loan, tell 'er to come back tomorrer, got a feelin' in me water, my gee gee'll romp 'ome t'day.'

Good sign thought Annie, he hadn't ranted and raved at her turning up on the door step. Sally stood uncertain as to whether Dan was going to come out to them.

'You bringin' 'er in then? The longer you's two stand there yackin' the longer it'll be before I get me tea.' Sally gave Annie a weak smile, she really did not want to invite her in. Annie, would much rather that Dan came to them. Some of the things her boy had told her about the state of Joey's house, made her skin crawl. Well now she was about to see it first hand.

'You'd better come frew' said Sally 'the place is in a bit of a mess at the moment, you caught me just as I was about to start the 'ousework.' Annie inhaled deeply, although the air outside was none to clean, she knew that on the inside of this house it would be much worse.

'What can we do fer you then, Gel?' enquired Dan.

Annie was trying desperately to keep her eyes fixed on him, as he lay sprawled on the most threadbare settee Annie had ever seen. She tried not to look at the baby that sat in a broken, old playpen. Baby Lily, six months old, wearing just a vest and nappy, well that would be fine, as the day was quite warm, but the vest full of holes was a browny yellow colour, with several days worth of food down the front. And her nappy, well, Annie had never seen such a sight as she saw on that innocent little girl. It also was the same colour as the vest, but it was soiled, not only with old excrement but with obvious fresh mess that had escaped from the nappy and was on her lower back and at the top of her legs. Annie wanted to heave.' keep calm gel' she thought, 'live and let live, well for today anyway. Today I'm here for that poor little beggar Joey, plenty of time later to tell them what I think of them.' She found her voice.

'It's like this, Dan' Annie was amazed how natural her voice sounded. 'Me and my George, was wonderin' wevver your Joey could come away with us?'

'What d'yer mean away wiv yer?'

''Oppin' we go every year, down near Yaldin' in Kent.' She continued.

'What!' yelled Dan. 'You expect me to let that lazy little sod go on 'olliday. Why should I let 'im 'ave 'oliday, me and the misses, ain't never bin away since before the little bastard was born.'

'Don't call him that, Dan' Sally pleaded. 'He ain't a bastard, we was married before he was born.'

'Only cause, like a fool I let you trap me into it.'

This wasn't going the way Annie had hoped for. She quickly interrupted their slanging match.

'Give me a minute to explain, Dan' she begged. 'Look, you'd be doin' me and my George a favour,' she carried on as Dan went to stop her. 'Our young Georgie, has got to come with us, whether he likes it or not. Last year he was bored because the mates that he used to meet every year were older than him, they go to work now. We fought that if your Joey came, he'd stop our boy from moanin' all the time.'

'Why can't Georgie stay at 'ome, he ain't as useless as Joey, surely he can look after his self?'

'Your right, Dan, he could,' Well here goes, thought Annie, in for a penny, in for a pound.'

'Fing is though, we wouldn't make as much money would we?'

'What so your boy works does he?' Dan started to show some interest.

'Course he does.' Annie crossed her fingers behind her back. 'He earns about ten bob.'

'Ten bob eh.' Dan was certainly weakening.

'Cor, Dan, we could do wiv a bit extra.' Sally joined in.

'You sayin' I don't giv' yer enuff?' Annie wished that Sally hadn't said anything.

'No, Dan, I didn't mean that' Sally thought quickly, as she was used to having to do.

'I just fought that if Joey had an 'oliday wiv the money he got, maybe the rest of us could 'ave a day out somewhere.'

'Mmm, see what yer mean. 'Ow long is it for then, Annie?'

'A fortnight, Dan'

''Ow long!?'

'We have to make it worthwhile, Dan. Cause while I'm away two of my sisters do my cleanin' job for me, but down 'opping I can earn over the top of what I have to pay them to cover for me.'

''Ere, Dan, I just thought of somethin' else.' said Sally, 'fink of the money we'd save wiv Joey away, one less to buy food for.' Annie smiled, when on the inside she wanted to scream at Sally, 'What food?' Annie knew though, that she had won, as soon as Dan had realised that Joey would be earning money, she knew Joey would be going with them.

'I suppose the kid'll enjoy 'is self away with your Georgie, maybe he can teach him a few fings as well. Alright then Annie, 'e can go.' Capitulated Dan. 'Make sure though that he brings his wages home 'ere, we don't mind if you take three bob out of it though, for his keep. Now that's settled, how about that tea Sal, get Annie one while your about it.'

'Oh no, not for me ta, I've got to get home, me sisters visit today' Annie lied. In truth she couldn't wait to get out of there, away from the smells, the filth but most of all away from the man who treated his children with such cruelty.

When Annie arrived back home, George met her at the top of the stairs.

'How did it go then, Love?' he asked, Annie was blowing her nose as she reached him.

He noticed the tears in her eyes. Georgie was standing behind his open bedroom door, listening to them. Eager to know whether Joey 's dad would let him go hopping with them.

'What's up Gel? He'd better have not upset you.' said an anxious George. 'Come and sit down and tell me all about it.'

As they went, Georgie crept along the passage, starting to feel angry. 'If he's hurt my mum, I'll do 'im' he thought to himself.

'Just give me a minute, George, he hasn't done nothing to 'urt me.'
Both Georgie and his dad let out a sigh on hearing this. Georgie called to his dad.

'Shall I put the kettle on?' He knew that when ever there was a problem to be solved, or if anyone was upset for any reason, the first thing his mum would say was, 'Lets have a cup a tea, things'll not seem 'alf as bad then.' Annie managed a weak smile, as she and her husband realised that their boy had been listening to them.

'Go on then, Son' replied George. Then he turned to his wife and asked quietly 'Do you mind if he comes and listens to what you have to say. Cause I think he'll only worry about you if he don't?'

'No, it won't bovver me. Mind you what I saw weren't none too nice.'
So, when the three of them each sat with a cup of tea, Annie relayed to her husband and son the filthy scene she had just witnessed.

'That poor little blighter, stuck in that old pen, her napkin was soppin' wet. What I don't get is that, although Joey's and the uvver kids clothes are old and tattered and they don't fit them, I've never seen any of them, filthy dirty like that poor baby.' She sighed deeply.
George and his son, felt sorry for this soft hearted wife and mother, who adored children.

'Would you believe he even told Sal to make me a cup a tea! Ugh just thinkin' about it makes me shudder.' Annie stopped as she saw the look that passed between her husband and son. 'Oi, I saw that look, you two can smirk but it weren't funny. I even had to tell a little white lie to get out a there.'

'Annie, how could you, you *never* tell lies.' Annie knew her husband was now taking the mick out of her. He was trying to lighten the situation for her benefit.

She retaliated with 'It was only a white lie I said. Not a proper lie.'
She then picked up two balls of wool from the table and threw one at each of them because they were laughing at her. When one of the balls landed in her husbands cup and the tea spilled over into the saucer. Annie joined in with their laughter.

So, that is how it came about that little Joey, was indeed going on his very first holiday.
Siddy and Bernie's dad Alf Woogitt, arrived with his open back lorry. Alf runs his own little delivery and pick up business. Most of his work came from 'Rag Bags' the rag and bone men, who have one of the yards under the railway arches at the Walworth road end of John Ruskin Street.

'All aboard the 'opping special' Alf called. 'Cor blimey, Annie, you seem to take more and more stuff each year'

'None of your cheek, Alf Woogitt, just you help load everyfing up.'
Alf doffed his hat, 'Yes, your, 'ighness' Joey laughed at him. Alf winked down at Joey, pleased for the boy that Annie and George were taking him with them. His own two son's have often told him about the rough treatment he gets from his dad.

Annie's sisters, Rose and Mary popped round to see them off. They live next door to each other in Olney Road, which is just a couple of streets away. The three sisters were well known in the area mostly because of their other jobs as cleaners of The Avenue School.

'Just came to see that you get away alright.' Said Rose. 'Lookin' forward to it are you, Joey?'

'You betcha. Can't stop and talk now though, got to help Georgie and his dad load up.'

Joey answered with pride. He made a great show of picking up a big box loaded to the brim with various assorted items of clothing and bedding.

'I can see you'll be a big help to our Annie' Mary said, to the excited boy. 'Is his mum gonna come and see him off do you fink Annie?' She asked this quietly of Annie, so that Joey did not overhear.

'Doubt it, Mary, she don't seem none to bothered about him.'

'Hold on, Gel' said George, 'you might have spoken too soon, look'

Sure enough, walking towards them was Sally Smith. In her arms she held baby Lily, and trundling along behind was, two year old Violet, four year old Jonny, holding their hands was big sister, nine year old Rosie. Finally bringing up the rear came Matty, who at seven didn't think much of the fact that his eldest brother Joey, was off on holiday. Much to the on lookers surprise, especially Annie's, all the children were dressed in, if not new, then certainly clean clothes, that actually seemed to fit. They each wore shoes that someone had obviously spent an age with a tin of shoe polish, putting a bit of life back into the well worn leather. Sally carried a large brown paper bag in her hand. She looked from Joey to Annie. Sally smiled, self consciously, all eyes were on her.

Annie moved towards her, knowing that Sally felt uncomfortable, whatever she thought of Sally's treatment of her children, Annie knew it must have taken a lot for her to be there.

'Come to see your, Joey off then, Sal?' Annie asked in a friendly voice.

Sally was grateful to Annie for this gesture. She knew what Annie must be thinking about her, the way most people would think, had they gone into her house, the day that Annie did.

'I couldn't let me first born go off for a fortnight wive out wavin' him off, could I? Anyways, I got a little goodbye present for yer, Joey.' Sally held the brown bag out toward Joey. He hesitated, wondering what was in the bag. 'Present' he thought, 'we don't get fings like that in our 'ouse. Only if our nan and grandad sneak somefing in, or it's Christmas.'

''Ere are, Boy, take it' Sally prompted. 'It won't bite yer or nuffing.'

Joey took the bag from his mum, as soon as he had hold of it, he could feel that it held a pair of shoes. A glimmer of hope ran through him, he opened the bag and pulled out the shoes, his shoes, the ones his mother had taken to the pawn shop all those weeks ago. Sally, as well as the others standing there, could see how pleased little Joey was.

'Me new shoes' he said excitedly, 'You got me shoes back, Mum. How'd yer manage that? Did dad change his mind? Where'd yer get the money for 'em?'

'Joey, what's wiv all these questions to your mum' demanded Georgie 'just give her a kiss and say thanks.'

'Oh, yeah, fanks, Mum.' said a red faced Joey as he went to his mum, who bent down for her son to kiss her cheek. 'Wish she had given 'em to me indoors though,' were his thoughts, 'not in front of all these people.' Joey kept his thoughts to himself though, especially when he noticed the tears in his mums eyes. Joey also noticed how pretty his mum looked today. Her hair had been brushed until it shone, with a pretty little coloured comb thing holding it away from her face. He hadn't seen the dress she was wearing for years, well not since their Violet and Lily were born. Pity she spoilt it by wearing her old cardigan with the holes in though.

Sally turned to Annie, 'I don't want to keep yer, but can I just have a word wiv yer 'fore yer go?'

'Course you can gel, come back upstairs with me, while I get me last bits, leave the kiddies down here.'

Sally gave baby Lily to Rosie to mind, telling the other children to stay there, whilst she followed Annie up to her flat. Sally couldn't help but notice how spotlessly clean and tidy Annie kept her home. Even the carpets, although a bit threadbare here and there, were obviously well looked after and swept regularly. The glass in the windows shone. You could see your face in the highly polished sideboard, with it's pure white, not grey, but white runner that went from one side to the other. Photographs of Annie, George and young Georgie stood in pride of place in the centre. Sally wished now that she had taken Annie to one side, when they had been down in the street, being in her home made everything she had to say twice as embarrassing.

'Well, Gel, spit it out' encouraged a curious Annie.

'I, well, first off, I erm, want ta apologise to you, Annie,' Sally held her hand up as Annie went to say something, 'No, please don't stop me, let me finish. It's taken me all this time, since you came to see me and Dan, to say this to yer. I feel even worse now, after seein' how nice you keep your home. I was disgusted wi' me self that night, but there weren't much I could do about it. Yer see, Dan had been off work for a couple a' days, wiv an 'ead cold. Truth be known, he'd lost the last of 'is wages on an 'orse. Dan's a proud man Annie, if he can't stand his round at the pub, then he don't go down there. He was in a right bad mood. Well, me baby Lily's bin teevin' and so she'd bin crying a lot, any how's, he told me ta leave her in her pen and let her cry, said she'd soon get fed up and stop. But the poor little fing was in pain, so when I fought he was asleep, I picked her up to give 'er a cuddle and 'cos she'd dirtied her nappy, I wanted to change her. Then I did a stupid fing, I laid her down on the bed where he was kippin' she started to cry agen, and woke him up.'

'He didn't hurt her or anything did he?' asked a concerned Annie.

'Well he didn't 'it 'er as such, but he took 'old of 'er and shook her, silly fing is she thought it was funny and laughed. I fink if what 'appened next hadn't 'appened everyfing would a bin alright.'

'What do you mean, what did happen?'

'Well, wiv out being crude, a bit of pooh from her nappy fell on his hand when he was shakin' her. He went berserk, he virtually threw the baby back in the pen and told me that if I touched her he'd do 'er in. said he couldn't take no more.'

'Oh my gawd, surely he didn't mean it?'

'Oh I fink he meant it alright, Annie.'

'So what did you do?'

'What could I do? I had to leave 'er in there. That day you come to ask us if Joey could go wiv yer my little Lily had been stuck lyin' in there for two days.'

'Two days, ah the poor little mite, did he let you give her anything to eat?' Annie asked incredulously, unable to take in what she was hearing.

'Oh yeah but I had to prop 'er up in there, he wouldn't even let me get her out to change her. He said, let 'er find out what it's like to have that muck on 'er.' Sally was becoming upset, as she recalled the sorry sight of her baby.

'The cruel sod' Annie was finding it difficult to hide her anger and disgust. Seeing how upset Sally was becoming, her heart began to melt towards this young woman. She went over to Sally and went to take hold of her arm, in a gesture of understanding. Sally flinched as Annie took hold of her left arm.

'Sorry, Gel, did I hurt yer?'

'Just got a bit of a bruise there that's all, Annie.' For some reason, this made Annie suspicious.

'Show me' she asked.

'It ain't nuffink bad, honest.'

Annie was having none of it, she took hold of Sally's left hand and pushed her sleeve up. What she saw made her recoil in shock. All along Sally's arm were bruises, big purple and black bruises, not only that, but there was also terrible deep angry red scarring.

'Oh you poor cow, what has he been doin' to yer?' She cried.

'Look, Annie, please don't tell anybody about this. All the while he's doin' this ta me, he ain't touchin' my kids.'

'Can't you leave 'im?'

'Where would I go wiv six kids.? Me mum and dad ain't got the room to take us in. Anyway he's told me, that if I ever tried to leave 'im, he'd kill the kids first.'

'He can't mean that, who in their right minds would kill their own children?'

'Well, that's just it, ain't it, I don't fink 'e is in 'is right mind. D'you know, that all the time Lily was crying, it never bovered 'im, 'e just sat and read the comic's that your Georgie giv to little Joey. Look, Annie, I wasn't gonna tell you all this, I'll be alright, I've survived all this time, ain't I.?' Sally gave Annie a weak smile. 'Go and get your fings you need for the 'oliday and don't worry about me.'

'I hate leavin' you knowing all this, but promise me one thing Sal, when I get back if ever you need someone to talk to, you come to me, I mean it now.'

'Fanks, Annie. I promise yer I will. Y'know you and your Georgie are somefing special.'

'What's my boy done that's special, apart from bein' a good mate to Joey?'

'Oh, I fink he should tell yer that in his own time. Lets just say, that fanks to 'im, today I saw smiles on my kids faces that I ain't seen for many a monf.'

Annie and Sally were greeted with shouts and cheers when they came back out. The lorry was loaded and so were it's passengers. George was perched on the old trunk that always went with them, if asked what it contained, Annie remarked, 'Essentials' she said no more. Siddy and Bernie had arrived. Their dad had given in to their continuous pleading to take them with him for the ride. The four boys sat on the wooden base of the lorry, to make it a bit more comfortable they each had a cushion.

Annie quickly made her goodbye's to her sisters Rose and Mary, giving them a rushed peck on the cheek. She then turned to Sally and gave her a little cuddle as she whispered in her ear,

'Take care, Gel' then she called to Sally's youngsters, 'be good for your Mummy, and maybe your Joey will bring a little present back for you all.'

'Will yer, Joey. Can I 'ave a kite then?' asked Matty. Before Joey could answer, the others, all except baby Lily of course, screamed at Joey. 'me want one too Joey' they all shouted.

'Kite, kite' echoed two year old Violet, not having a clue what a kite was, but it must be something nice because Matty and Jonny wanted one. The only one not to say anything was nine year old Rosie.

'What about you, Rosie?' asked Georgie, 'you haven't said what you'd like.'

Rosie lowered her eyes, she could feel her face going red. Joey was not the only member of the Smith family to hero worship Georgie Powley. She brushed the sole of one of her shoes on the pavement, scraping away an invisible mark.

'I think the boys would love a kite' she said in barely more than a whisper. 'They cost lots though, don't they?'

'Yeah, they do. But you'd be surprised what you can find in the country. But that's not what I asked you,' pressed Georgie, 'what would you want for yourself?'

'I know somefing she's always wanted,' said Sally. 'A pretty blue ribbon for her hair.'

'Oh, Mum' blushed Rosie, as she went to hide behind her.

'Come on, Annie' called Alf 'climb on board gel.' Annie was given the 'seat of honour' she got to sit in the passenger seat of the cab. Alf went to crank up the motor, turning the starting handle deftly as the engine sprang into life.

'Wait a minute' came a breathless voice. It was Annie's brother Jack. 'Here you go, Boys, Aunt Kath has made you some fairy cakes for the journey.'

'Ooh ta, Uncle Jack' said Georgie as he got up to take the tin from his out stretched hand.

'They smell great' he enthused.

'Straight out a the oven they are. Fought we'd missed yer.' When his wife wasn't in hearing, Jack let his speech fall below Kath's standards.

Annie leant across Alf in the cab to the open window. 'Tell Kath thanks for me, Jack, they'll go down a treat.' She turned to Alf 'Hard as nails on the outside but our Kath's got a heart of gold underneath.'

At last they were on their way, shouting and waving to those left standing on the pavement.

Alf drove the length of John Ruskin Street towards the Walworth Road, turning right when he reached it, heading first for Camberwell Green, then on through Peckham and New Cross. Annie looked across to Alf. 'You don't normally come this way, Alf, ain't it quicker going Forest Hill way?' 'Yeah, I do as a rule, Annie but I fought little Joey might like to see the kite flyers on Blackheaf, they're normally here every weekend.' 'Ah you old softie.' Annie smiled at him. ' Gerroff. Anyway, makes no odds, Gel, takes about the same time to get there goin' this way.' Annie craned out of the cab window 'seems we're takin' the scenic route, George.' She said laughing. 'Fine by me, Gel. Just tell our driver to miss the potholes in the road, I'd like a nice smooth journey, ta very much. I'm enjoyin' sittin' here watchin' the World go by' George shouted back. 'Oi, I heard that, George Powely.' The boys all laughed along with Georgie's Dad.

Joey was looking around in wonder.

'Is this the country?'

'Sort of but not proper like' informed Siddy.

'What d'yer mean, eiver it is or it ain't.' said a confused Joey. There ain't no 'ouses, so it must be country.'

Bernie thought that he could explain it better to Joey. 'This place is called Blackheaf Joey. It's still part a London but from now on yer don't see many 'ouses, well, not 'ouses like down Camberwell way. Most a the ones we see now'll be where the nobs live.'

'Look over there, Joey' Joey looked to where Mr Powley was pointing.

'Cor, they're flyin' kites. I ain't never seen so many, not even when we've bin to Peckham Rye.'

'Me dad brings me and Bernie up 'ere sometimes to watch 'em fly the kites.'

'Cor really? Peckham Rye's the furvest we've ever bin. They 'ad a fair there once and me dad took us on the carrousel and the helter skelter. I fink that was before our Jonny was born, cause I was only a little kid. But when I'm workin' and I get a load a money, I'm gonna come here and bring all the littluns wi' me.'

'That's a nice thing to say, Joey.' Georgie's dad leant across to ruffle the boys hair. Thinking 'he'll do it as well, he's a gutsy little feller, he'll drag his self out of the gutter his fathers got them all in.' Out loud he said 'I think it's time for a sing song, what say you, Georgie?'

'Yeah, if you say so, Dad.' Then turning to Joey 'This is when you might regret comin'.

'Oi, watch it my lad, ignore him Joey. Just for that Georgie, you can start.'
Joey laughed, Mr Powley was so funny. 'This 'oliday is gonna be the best
time I've ever 'ad. Even if I 'ave to work 'ard as well.'

Georgie started to sing. Joey knew the song, well at least he thought he
did. Then he realised that Georgie had changed the words to one of the
songs that the little kids sang in the school playground, called, 'the farmers
in his den'

An 'oppin' we will go,
an 'oppin' we will go

Ee, I, addio, an 'oppin' we will go.
The farmers got the dough
The farmers got the dough
Ee, I addio, the farmers got the dough.

Joey laughed and joined in when they all sang the song for the second time,
even Annie and Alf, who could hear, if they kept the windows of the cab
open. They sang some more other popular songs, such as;

'Pack up your troubles in your old kit bag and smile, smile, smile.'
'If you were the only girl in the world and I was the only boy'
'Daisy, Daisy, give me your answer do'

Then Annie shouted through the cab window, 'What's your favourite song
then, Joey?'

'Tell yer the trufe, we don't sing much in our 'ouse but once I 'eard me
grandad sing to me mum and after, they was cryin. When I asked me mum
why'd he sing it, if it made 'em all cry, she said they was tears of 'appiness.
Grandad said it made 'im remember 'er when she was a little gel. And he
used ta sit 'er on 'is lap and sing to 'er.'

'Come on then boy, tell us what it's called, then if we know it, we'll sing
it eh, if you want us to that is?'

'Well, it's the same name as me mum, Sally, I'd luv it if yer do know the
words, Aunt Annie'

'Ah, that's a smashin' song young Joey. A lady called Gracie Fields sings
it.' Annie began singing

Sally, Sally, pride of the alley,
You're more than the whole world to me.
Sally, Sally, don't ever wonder,
Away from the alley and me.

Annie's clear voice could be heard by the people enjoying a sunny days
outing on the Heath as the lorry drove by. Joey didn't join in though, he just
wanted to sit and listen and think of the time when his mum had cried, as
her dad sang the song to her. Unlike the many times he heard her crying at
home, that time though, after her tears, he had never seen her look so happy
or so young.

Heading towards the Weald of Kent, Joey stood up in the lorry, he was very excited.

'Look' he called, on that grass over there, cows, loads of 'em'
He couldn't believe his eyes, the only time he had seen a cow was in books at school.

'You'll see hundreds of cows and sheep where we're goin', chickens as well, last year the farmer even had few pigs, right smelly fings they are.' Georgie informed Joey.

As they left the pretty town of Sevenoaks behind, Alf called from the cab. 'Not far ter go now. 'ere, you ain't ate all them cakes back there have yer?'

'Don't worry, Alf, I've made sure they leave some for you and Annie.'

'Pass me in one then would yer, George?'

'D'you fancy one now as well, Annie?' enquired her husband.

'Might just as well, Love, don't trust them boys not to scoff them all.' She laughed.

The lorry passed through the open gate, they had reached their destination. Annie put her head out of the cab window and took a deep breath.

'Smell that, Joey, that's one a the best smells you'll ever come across. Fresh country air and 'ops. Oh it's lovely' to be back.'
Joey was sniffing, trying to see what Annie was talking about. 'Pooh,' he thought, didn't smell too good to him, in fact he thought it was horrible. He wrinkled his nose in disgust.
Georgie looked at Joey, he winked and whispered to him, 'You get used to it after a while.'
Joey soon forgot about the smells as the lorry drove down a dirt track road. On one side he saw rows and rows of trees. Little white and yellow flowers were growing every where. To Joey they were flowers. Annie and George knew better. Over the years they have learnt much about the countryside with its various trees, bushes, flowers *and* the weeds that Joey had just seen. On the other side of the track, Joey saw funny sorts of trees. They were set out in neat rows that seemed to go on forever. Joey had not seen anything like the weird leaves or buds that grew on them, well not in any book he had read.

'What's those, Mr Powley?' he asked.

'Those, Joey, are the hop bines. That's where we'll be working as of Monday.' He supplied.

'Don't worry, Joey, when we get settled, I'll show you round and tell you what goes on.'

'Can me and Bernie come wiv yer, Georgie?'

'Course you can, Mind you, d'you fink your Bernie's up to it?' Smiled Georgie.
Bernie was lying flat out, sound asleep.

They came to a stop outside a row of tin huts. 'Here we are, home from home.' Annie said nostalgically. Just then, a man and woman came out of one of the huts. On seeing them Annie jumped from the cab. 'Tom, Edie, oh it's so good to see you agen, how you been keepin'' She went to each of them and gave them a kiss.

'We've been fine gel' answered Edie. 'Don't seem like a twelvemonth since we were here does it?' Tom went over to George as he climbed down from the back of the lorry.

''Hello me old mate' he said, as the two men shook hands. ''Hello young, Georgie, still playin' football are you?'

'You bet, Uncle Tom, I've got me ball wiv me, so we can 'ave a game tomorrow.'

'I've got the primus on the go, so let's have a cuppa then we'll help you unload.'

'Ta, Edie, a cuppa'll go down a treat.' Annie responded. 'You remember Alf don't you?'

'Course we do, this is what, the third year he's bought you down, is that right, Alf?'

'You got it, Edie.' Alf said, 'nice ta see yer both agen. Got me boys wiv me this time, bin pesterin' me fer ages to let 'em come for the day. Still, it'll be company on the way 'ome.'

Bernie woke up. 'Oh are we there.?' He asked bleary eyed.

'Well one of them'll be company.' Alf laughed.

'I ain't bin asleep' Bernie protested, 'just restin' me eyes.'

The congregation all laughed, heard that one before, was what they were all thinking.

'Well if two of them are your boys, who's the other one?' enquired Tom.

It was Georgie that answered him. 'You've heard me talk about me mates, well the sleepy head is Bernie, the one sittin' next to him is his bruvver Siddy'

''Ello' said Siddy with a wave of his hand.

'And this one here is, Joey, he's gonna be stayin' with us.' Joey smiled shyly at Edie and Tom, then he had a thought. 'If you like, Mrs Powley, I can start the unloadin' while the rest of yer 'ave yer tea.' Joey eager to please, would do anything for Georgie's mum and dad.

'That's good of you son' said George, 'but I'm sure the other lads'll be happy to help.'

So, the grown ups sat, on three legged little stalls, watching the boys carry everything from the lorry and into the small hut that is going to be home for the next two weeks. Joey couldn't keep the surprised look from his face when he first entered the hut. For although Annie had explained to him, that they had been coming hop picking ever since Georgie was a baby and that they used the same hut every year, he was still amazed to see wallpaper on the walls.

Georgie saw the look, 'What's up, Mate, don't you like it?'

'Nah it ain't that, Georgie, it's great, but it's got better wallpaper than we 'ave at 'ome' he marvelled.

'Well it makes it look more comfy and homely' said George as he walked in carrying the big trunk. 'Pity we can't do anyfing about the roof though, can't put wall paper up on corrugated iron.'

'I fink it looks really nice, Mr Powley'

'Thank you, Joey. Look, Son, from now on, what say you call me Uncle George and Mrs Powley, Aunt Annie, eh? Cos you heard Georgie call Tom and Edie Uncle and Aunt didn't you, well they're not his real relatives, it's just, well it's sounds nice.'

Joey thought this a wonderful idea. 'Cor fanks, Mr....' George raised his eyebrows, 'I mean fanks, Uncle George.'

'Right, that's settled then. I'll just go and get our pots and pans and all the other stuff from the cookhouse.

'More stuff!' Said Siddy

'Yeah, mum leaves chairs, a table, cups, washin' up fings, the tilley lamp and primus stove locked in anuvver trunk, in that brick building two huts away.'

'Your dad called it the cookhouse, so why do yer need a primus as well?' asked Bernie.

'Mum takes the primus stove wiv her when she's pickin', so's we can have hot tea any time. The cookhouse is for cookin' in. Sometimes mum cooks egg and bacon out here, on her primus, it don't 'alf taste better.'

Bernie was thinking that it looked like you could have a lot of fun here, especially in the river that Georgie had told them about, where he swam and fished. But he didn't fancy picking the hops. He much preferred going to Leysdown for a week every year with Siddy and his parents and grandparents. 'I fink I'll stick to that he thought.'

Georgie showed them where to put everything. Space was very limited, Georgie mimicked his mum. 'There's a place for everyfing, and everyfing in it's place. Remember that young, Joey.'

'Oi, I heard that, you cheeky beggar. Less of your cheek, and go and get the straw so you can get the palliasses laid down.'

On the floor, against one side of the hut, is a raised area, made of wood, this makes a base for the palliasse, 'It's a cover stuffed wiv straw that the farmer leaves ready in the barn for us pickers to use' explained Georgie, seeing the frown on Joey's face. 'It makes a comfy mattress. Mum and Dad will sleep on the base. Me and you'll sleep on top of the palliasse on the bare floor.'

When, Georgie's dad, arrived back with the trunk, the boys set to work unpacking it. There was an enormous stew pot, two smaller saucepans and a large frying pan. These were hung on hooks hanging beneath a long wooden bench that took up most of the opposite side of the hut from the bed base. Enamel cups, plates, jugs and washing bowl were placed on the flat top.

Joey was amazed at the amount of stuff that came out of 'Annie's trunk' 'Look's more like they were moving house' he thought, instead of spending just two weeks away. Most of the other pickers, were expected to stay at the hop garden until the harvest was finished. Up until young Georgie started at 'the big school' Annie also remained there for the four weeks that it usually took. When it became clear that Georgie was showing how good a scholar he was, Annie and George decided, that four weeks was far too long for him to be away from school. As luck would have it, the farmer, who thought very highly of the work that Annie, and George, when he was there, put in, agreed that two weeks instead of four would be fine, just so long as their rate of picking did not fall off.

Annie came in to check up on them. 'Ah, that's more like it.' She smiled. 'Right, you've all been doin' a good job, so, Georgie, take them off now and go swimmin' or somefing.'

The boys did not need telling twice. Before they left home, Georgie had told his mates to put their swimming trunks on under their trousers.

The grown-ups smiled as they watched the boys run off towards the lake.

Chapter Three

The next day being Sunday, they didn't have to work. It was a time for many of the regular hop pickers, to gather at one of the huts. Today they were all invited over to George and Annie's. Whilst the women prepared dinner and talked ten to the dozen catching up on a whole years gossip. The men strolled down to the pub in the nearby village. The publican and his wife welcomed them, even calling many by name as they recognised them from previous years. They were more than happy to see these 'cockney's' as they referred to them in their bar. For though the Londoners didn't have much money to spare, many of them spent a good chunk of what they earned picking the hops, in the little pub, if not every night, then certainly Saturday nights and Sunday mornings. This time of year was good to country landlords, with the Londoners and passing day trippers, their profits could more than treble. Not every one in the village took the same view, some let it be known to the 'cockney's' that they were not welcome. They didn't pick fights, well only very occasionally, it was more by the looks they gave and their habit of ignoring, pretending they didn't exist, if one of the 'cockney's' dared to speak to them. These people, the Londoner's called 'the snotty brigade'. Of course others in the village were friendly towards them and enjoyed their company, especially when they started up a good old fashioned sing song.

When the men returned from the pub and were rested after enjoying a Sunday dinner of roast beef, Yorkshire Pudding, roast potatoes and the fresh cabbage that the farmer allowed them to pick from his field. The time came for 'fun and games'. Dads, that throughout the rest of the year, were either, too busy, or too tired to play with their children, found that here, with trees, flowers, open spaces and clean fresh air around them, they looked forward to doing the silly things. Like, playing hide and seek with the younger children, or cricket and football with the older ones. Here away from the soot and smog of London, they worked hard during the week but played hard at the weekends.

All this was strange to little Joey. After Siddy and Bernie went home with their dad yesterday, he'd begun to feel a bit lonely for his brothers and sisters. After all, it was the first time he had ever been anywhere, for more than a day, without them. George, noticed that he had been a bit quiet today.

'Right, who's for football now?' He asked. Nearly all the men and bigger boys shouted their positive responses. 'Good. Lets make up two teams then. I want Joey on my side, cause he's a brilliant corner taker.' He put his arm round little Joey's shoulders at the same time. Joey looked up at him. He felt proud to be the first one picked for a team. Just those few words from his Uncle George, made Joey feel ten feet tall. He stretched his little frame to it's full height, happy in the knowledge that he'd always be thought of as a part of this loving family.

'Wiv me and you on the same team, Uncle George, we can't lose.'

Later that day, when everyone had returned to their own hut to have their tea, Annie, suggested to George that, when he had eaten, maybe he could take little Joey down to the lake for an hour or so, to teach him how to fish. The nearest Joey had come to fishing, was with a net at the end of a long pole, when he and the other boys went down to the murky canal, under the old iron bridge just off Albany road in Camberwell.

'I want to 'ave a word with our, Georgie' Annie explained.

'What about, Love?'

'Oh nuffing, serious, it's just somethin' that Sally said to me when we were leavin', about how good he'd been to her'

'All right then, I think Joey would like that, do him good to spend a bit of time with a farver figure. Tell me what it's all about though, won't you?'

'Course I will, if there is anyfing to tell. You go and tell Georgie, that you're doin' it for little Joey.'

George and Joey marched off armed with the two fishing rods that George kept here in the cookhouse. Joey was trying to match strides with those of his uncle, his face upturned listening intently as George was telling him of all the enormous fish, that had 'got away' in the past.

Georgie sat with his mum, outside the hut, his white shirtsleeves rolled up past his elbows, his hands clasped behind his head. Smiling as the two figures passed out of sight.

'That was nice of dad to take Joey off by himself, Mum. Did you see his face, when dad told him?'

'Yeah, bless his cotton socks, you fink a lot of him don't you, Son?'

'He's a good kid, Mum. No one should have to live the way him and bruvvers and sisters do. It's not as if they haven't got no money, his dad's got a job, some families are really poor but they are treated much better than Joey's lot.'

'Didn't Sally and the kids look nice yesterday though?' Annie prompted.

'And, she even managed to get Joey's shoes out of pawn. P'raps Dan did a good turn for once, eh?'

Georgie looked angry. 'What 'im? no chance.'

'Wonder how she got the money then, them dresses the littluns 'ad on looked really nice.'

Georgie started to look a bit uncomfortable, his face was turning red.

'Come on, Son, out wiv it, you had somefing to do with it didn't you?'

'Me? 'ow could I.'

'It was somefing Sally said to me about you, when we was gettin' ready to leave yesterday. Look, if you did help her, I wouldn't be cross or nuffing, in fact after what I saw yesterday, I feel like I wanna do all I can for her as well.'

'What do you mean, after what you saw?'

'I really shouldn't say any of this to you, Georgie and for gawd sake don't you dare tell any one else about this. D'you promise?'

'You got me worried now, Mum, course I won't tell anyone. What is it?'

'Well, I was goin' to give her a little cuddle, because she was upset. I took hold of one of her arms, and she flinched, any way to cut a long story short, I got to 'ave a look at her arm. It was covered in bruises, not only that, but he'd been burning her with 'is cigarettes.'

The more Annie described the scene, she became more agitated, she didn't notice the dropping of her 'aitches. She did how ever notice the shocked look on her son's face. Maybe she had gone too far, after all he wasn't thirteen yet. Did she need to tell him all the details.

'I'm sorry, son, I shouldn't 'ave told you all that. I can see it's upset you.'

'No it's okay, Mum, I'm glad you did. It's just, well I can't imagine a bloke doin' that to a woman. Did she say whevver he hurt the kids bad? cause you know 'ow he went for Joey, that time when he got lost comin' home from Ruskin Park.'

'I don't think he's ever hurt them bad, apart from that time. She said she'll take all his anger on her, so's that he leaves the kids alone. I fink they'll be alright. So come on boy, tell me, what did Sal mean about you.'

'It weren't much, 'honest, Mum. The last couple of weekends down the lane, after I've got the stall's out, I've been lookin' after Peg's second hand stall for her. Her muvver normally has her two kids on Saturday and Sunday but she 'adn't been well, so I offered to look after the stall in the mornin's for 'er.'

'That was good of you, Son.'

'Yeah well, you know she's a widow, well, she couldn't afford to pay me much, so, well, I asked her if I could have some clothes instead.'

'And you got them for the Smiff's, was it you that also gave Sally the money to get Joey's shoes out?'

'You don't mind do you, Mum? I felt so sorry for 'em. And at least Joey don't feel embarrassed bein' here wiv us, cause now he's got more clothes to wear.'

Annie got up from her chair and went over to her son, she took his face in her hands and to his horror, she gave him a great big kiss. Georgie took a quick look round, incase anyone had seen. With tears in her eyes, she said to him. 'Mind, do I mind, oh, Georgie, I'm so proud of you. Your daddy will be too.'

'Don't go tellin' everyone, Mum, if Mr Smiff hears about it, he'll probably hit Mrs Smiff agen.' As it is she had to tell him a lie. She told me she was gonna tell him that she'd got the stuff from the Salvation Army. *And* I don't want me mates finkin I'm a softie.'

His mum laughed. 'I promise you, Son, the only uvver person to know about this, will be your dad. He has a right to know. Look they'll be back soon, what say you and me put the kettle on for a nice cup a' cocoa?'

In the week that followed, Joey learnt all he could about the ways of the hop pickers. He and Georgie and some of the other youngsters, didn't work on the bines all day. Their parents wanted them to go off and have fun. So, Georgie and Joey, were up and dressed by seven in the mornings, ready and willing to go with George and Annie to their allotted run. The boys would stay working until it was time for a dinner break. The afternoons were when their work stopped and their fun began.

Joey was shown how to separate the hops from the bine. When he first saw the size of the canvas hop bins, he thought to himself, that it would take years to fill. Did the farmer really expect them to strip all the rows and rows of bines that stretched out before him. Therefore it came as a great relief to Joey, when Uncle George presented Georgie and Joey, with an old dustbin. 'Here you are boys, you two can use this. Then on payday, you can split the money between you. So no slacking eivver of you. Equal work, equal pay. Fair enough?'

'Fine by me, Dad. We'll work hard, won't we, Joey?'

'Yeah, you bet. Gotta make ten bob alone, ain't I?'

'No problem.' insisted Georgie. Joey didn't share Georgie's optimism.

His Aunt Annie, had told him what she had said to his dad about the money Joey would earn, the day she had asked if Joey could go with them. As Joey looked around him, on his first day at all the tall bines, he thought, 'There's no way, I'm gonna make five bob, let alone the ten aunt Annie told dad I'd get.' But now at the end of his first week, Joey could enjoy the remainder of his holiday, in the knowledge that already, uncle George, had the ten shilling's tucked inside his wallet. For a very proud Joey, had earned that amount in *one* week, not two. Of course, Annie had known that if he worked well, Joey could earn at least double the amount she had told Dan Smith.

Joey enjoyed the camaraderie shared by the Londoners. There was so much laughter all around him. He was very surprised, when he heard some of the ladies, when they didn't realise youngsters were around, tell rude jokes. Not that he understood everything they said, but the bits he did, he found very funny. Then there was the ever popular sing song. Sometimes, locals walking along the lane, close to the hop fields, would stand and listen. A choir of some sixty voices, singing, 'Maybe it's because I'm a Londoner' or 'The Lambeth Walk' in the open countryside, as they worked their way deftly and quickly along the rows of green alley's, was a sound to behold and once heard never forgotten.

When the tallyman came round, and transferred the hops they had picked into his sack, the tallyman, would weigh them, then calculate how much money they had earned. The amount would be written in a book. The farmer used this book, signed by the pickers, to make sure he paid them for the correct amount of hops picked.

'Don't forget to fluff up before the tallyman comes, Georgie.' His mum reminded him.

'What's fluff up then, Georgie?' Asked a confused Joey.

'Well see, it's like this, Joey. Normally me mum does it, she's what we call a fluffer.'

Joey laughed, a fluffer sounded such a silly word, and certainly not one he connected with aunt Annie. 'What, she's fluffy then is she?'

'I'll give you fluffy, young, Joey' said Annie laughing with him. 'A fluffer,' she continued, 'for your information my, lad, is someone who climbs in the canvas bin, and then wiv their hands they, well they sort of fluff all the 'ops up. It lets air get in there, and makes it look like you've got more in the bin.'

'I fink you can be our fluffy, then, Georgie.' Joked Joey. Some of the other pickers had heard the exchange, and one of the other boys called out 'oi Georgie, me mums got a lovely pink scarf, wanna borry it mate?' The crowd all laughed, having enjoyed the banter.

'Now see what you've started' said an indignant Georgie, 'I'll never live it down.' Georgie wasn't really bothered, it was all part of the fun of the close community they shared for a short time once a year.

Much to Joey's delight and amazement, between them, the first week, he and Georgie had made the unbelievable amount of one pound seven shillings and sixpence.

Today, Georgie was going to take Joey into Tonbridge, where there were many shops. The one thing on his mind was, that there be a shop that sold kites. Uncle George, had given the boys some of their wages, Georgie had a whole ten shilling note all to himself. Joey held on tightly to the five shillings that his Uncle George had given to him. Never in his young life had he ever had, more than five pence to spend on something that he wanted.

What a time they had, they went from shop to shop. For the first time in his life, Joey was able to do more than just stand and stare through the big glass shop front windows. He dragged Georgie into toy shops, clothes shops and even furniture shops. The money jangling in his pocket made him feel like no way he had ever felt before. He felt like a somebody, not just a useless thick kid, as he was always being called by his dad, or the target for bullying by boys from his junior school.

'Come on, Joey, we've bin in nearly every shop in Tonbridge, surely you've decided on what you wanna buy.'

'Sorry, Georgie, you getting' fed up are yer?'

'You could say that. Look, lets go and have a drink and somefing to eat, I saw a café back there. Then, I'm only gonna go to the shops where you are gonna buy somfing. Okay?'

'Okay then' sighed Joey. 'S'pose I'm a bit 'ungry as well. But I know exactly the shop I wanna go back to.' The boys found the café, where they ordered a cold orange juice each and a hot buttered scone.

'I'll pay for this' offered Georgie, because he knew the shop Joey wanted to go back to. It sold loads of different types of kites. He noticed that the cheapest one in the window was two shillings that would only leave Joey with three. 'You can pay next time' continued Georgie. Fully refreshed, the boys went off to find the toyshop, Georgie feeling quite grown up, had left the young waitress a whole penny tip.

The assistant in the Toy Shop showed Joey, some of the kites in the price range that Joey had said he could afford. His favourite was the one hanging above his head, suspended from the ceiling, it was bright red, blue and yellow, with a long thin tail. Not for him that one though, when he found out that it cost four shillings.

'This is a nice one.' The assistant pointed out, taking a liking to the young lad, obviously one of the 'London Cockney's she thought, especially when Joey informed her that he wanted the kite for his younger brothers. 'see; it's nearly the same as the one up there.' she pointed above their heads to Joey's favourite. It was to, for it was the same colouring, though the tail was much shorter and it was about half the size, it still looked a really nice kite.

'ow much do it cost then, Lady?' asked Joey.

The assistant thought for a moment, the price written on the box that the kite came from said two shillings and sixpence. 'Ah, you are in luck, Young Sir, this kite is on sale this week' she lied, 'you can buy it for only one and six.'

'She called me sir' he thought, 'wait till I tell me mum that.' To the nice lady assistant he said, 'That means, I've got enough to buy the kite and three a them little rag dolls in your winder' Joey tried to speak the way the assistant spoke, posh, as he calls it. It didn't quite come off, but it sounded a lot better after having spent a week with the Powley's. Joey turned to where Georgie stood looking at the toy planes hanging on wire from the ceiling. 'No' Georgie thought to himself, 'I ain't gonna waste me money on one of them. I'm gonna buy meself anuvver white shirt. Mum won't be too pleased when I get back havin' got butter down this one. She can't say much if I get a new one.' So he looked away from the planes and called 'Joey, I'm just gonna nip to a shop a couple a doors away, gonna buy me self a new shirt while the lady sorts you out. Wait fer me outside here.'

There was something that Georgie had not forgotten, he had been determined from the moment her mum said it, that was to buy the pretty blue ribbon, for Rosie's hair. Georgie felt really sorry for Rosie, more than he did even for his little friend Joey. For Joey had told him many times, that Rosie very often had to look after her two little sisters, and do the cleaning if her mum wasn't up to it. Georgie now realised, what the reason might be. After his mum had told him how Mrs Smith was beaten by her husband,. she probably wasn't able to do much, if she was in pain. So it was to the haberdashery shop that Georgie took himself. On passing earlier, he'd seen all different coloured ribbons on rolls in the window.

'I only hope no one from the farm sees me go in here,' he thought. 'They will call me fluffy from now on. Oh well, here goes.' He pushed his shoulders back and held his head up, as he entered the shop.

Before the boys left the hop garden, they had said goodbye to Georgie's dad. He had to return to his South London home and back to his job at the fishmongers. Annie, thanks to her sisters, was able to take a whole two weeks off from her cleaning jobs. Annie and her two friends, Edie and Tom, accompanied George on the two mile walk to the railway station. The weather was still quite warm, for the ninth day of September, the second Saturday of the month.

'You take care now' George called from the open window of the carriage. 'And make sure them boys don't get into any mischief.'

'Don't you worry, Mate, I'll keep an eye on them for you' Offered Tom. Edie and Tom were going to spend the whole of the four weeks in Paddock Wood,

Both now retired, with their three daughters having long since left home to get married, their time was their own.

'Who's gonna keep an eye on 'im, though eh, George?' laughed Edie.

The steam hissed loudly from the trains engine, signalling that the train was ready to move out of the station. 'We'll be just fine and dandy' called Annie. 'Make sure you eat proper. See you next Sat' day love.'

'Ta ta, Gel. See you next year Tom, Edie'

'Yeah, God willin' George.' replied Edie.

'I hate it when he goes 'ome.'

'Come on, Gel, let's get back and bung the old kettle on eh?' suggested Tom. He knew from previous years, that Annie got a bit tearful after her George left. 'The boys might be there when we get back.'

This cheered Annie, 'Yeah you're right, Tom. I wonder if little Joey has found what he wanted to buy for his bruvvers and sisters.'

''He ain't 'ad much of a life from what you say, Annie. Don't 'alf make you feel sad for the poor little cock.'

'You're tellin' me, Edie, still it's doin' him the world of good bein' here. I've never seen him laugh so much. Come on lets get a move on. Step it out, Tom.'

'Oi yer saucy, Mare' he joked 'these legs ain't as young as yourn you know.'

Still they covered the two mile journey back in no time, and there waiting by the main gate was Georgie and Joey.

'Did dad catch his train okay, Mum?' enquired Georgie.

'Right on time it was, Boy. Well, now then, you two had a good time have you?'

'Cor, Aunt Annie, you should a seen some of the shops in Tonbridge. Some were really posh, we went in nearly all of 'em didn't we, Georgie?'

'Just seein' the little fella's beaming face, has cheered me up' thought Annie. She looked at her son, he caught the look and understood how his mum felt. 'You could say that' Georgie answered his friend. 'he dragged me in an' out, in an' out. We did have a laugh though.'

'Did you manage to get what you wanted, Joey?'

'I sure did, Aunt Annie. You wait and see all the fings I bought, and I still got some money left over.' He announced proudly.

'Well, we're just goin' to go back to the hut to make a cuppa, you can show us then, Love.'

After their tea and Joey had shown, Annie, Edie and Tom, the brand new colourful kite he'd bought for his younger brothers, along with three pretty little rage dolls, he knew Lily and Violet would love the dollies. Even Rosie at nine, would love to have one to call her very own. Annie offered to wrap them back up carefully in the brown paper the shop assistant had put them in, then she said she'd put them in her big trunk, where they would be nice and safe, ready to take home with them next Saturday.

The two brothers from the next hut appeared. 'Watcha, Georgie, Joey' said eleven year old Harry, the eldest. 'fancy a game a football, 'fore it gets too dark'

Georgie, turned to his mum, he didn't like leaving her when his dad had just left. 'That alright, Mum? We won't be long, just have a quick kick about.'

'Cause it is, Georgie, I'm gonna just sit here and have a natter with Edie and Tom. Go on off you go.'

The boys ran off to the open field. All four boys removed their jumpers and laid two at opposite ends to mark out the goalposts. Georgie and Joey, every so often, let the other two get the ball, and even the odd goal. They were not in the same class as Georgie, nor come to that, of the much, improved Joey. The ball went in the direction of seven year old Jim,

'kick it to me now.' Shouted his brother Harry' and kick it Jim did, he surprised all of them. His boot connected with the ball as he kicked it with all his might. The others stared in amazement as it sailed above all their heads and landed about fifty feet on the other side of the barbed wire fence that separated them from the farmers field, where his prize bull grazed.

'That's torn it,' said Harry. 'You'll 'ave to go and get it back now.'

'I ain't goin' in there. That's where the bull is.' answered a terrified Jim

'You bloody well kicked it in there, so you gotta go.'

'Na, I ain't goin', 'Arry, dad said that them Bull's can kill yer dead wi' their 'orns. I'm goin' 'ome.' Was the tearful response from Jim.

'I can't leave it there' said Georgie, me mum and dad paid a lot of money for that ball. Anyway, I can't see the bull in there, maybe it's bin taken to the barn or somefing.'

'You ain't finkin' a goin' in there, are yer, Georgie?' asked a scared Joey.

'I got to, look, you two keep a look out and if you see it, give us a shout, me ball ain't that far.' He didn't sound too convincing.

So, off Georgie went, over the wire fence, he looked round, all seemed clear. Just as he reached the ball, he heard a noise from behind one of trees. 'Please don't let it be the bull' he silently begged. The noise now became louder, it was a noise that he and the others would never forget, a noise they had never heard the likes of before. Not like the gentle mooing of a cow but more like that of a creature in pain. Georgie picked up the ball and as he turned and started to run, Joey saw the bull, it came from behind a tree, nostrils flaring, hooves pounding on the sun baked ground.

'Run, Georgie run' he yelled frantically. The bull kept coming. In his panic Georgie tripped and fell, he was scrambling to his feet, the bull now was no more than sixty feet away, dipping it's head then throwing it back and up. Harry ran off, screaming for his dad.

Joey turned and picked up his jumper that had been one of the goalposts. He ran along the perimeter of the fence, shouting and yelling at the bull, he waved his bright red jumper above his head with his hand. 'Come on, Georgie, you can do it' he screamed to the one person that meant more to him than any other in his young life. 'You can do it' Suddenly the bull slowed, it looked over to where little Joey was running, Joey was still frantically waving his red jumper. To his and Georgie's amazement the bull stopped, threw it's head in the air once more, then headed towards Joey. Georgie ran on, he made it to the fence and climbed through. Joey threw his jumper over the fence, then ran to where Georgie lay panting on the ground.

The two boys watched as the bull, reached Joey's red jumper, he picked it up with his horns and tossed it high in the air, when it landed he went over and did the same again, then stamped on it. After a couple of minutes, while the boys sat speechless and motionless, the giant bull tired of the game and ambled back to where it came from.

Harry arrived on the scene with a few of the remaining men in the hop garden, they were fearful of what they might find. Instead they came across Georgie and Joey, cowering on the grass. 'Fank gawd you managed to get out' one of them said.

Georgie replied in a shaky voice. 'It was, Joey, he saved me'

'It was luck that's all, it saw me and decided it'd prefer to get me.'

'What did you do, Son?' Harry's dad asked, 'cause our Harry said you was a gonna for sure, young Georgie.'

'All I did was wave me jumper in the air, he ain't 'alf made a mess of it, look' Joey pointed in the direction of the now tatters of red wool lying in the field.

'It's red. You clever fing.' Said Harry's dad. bulls always go for anyfing that's red. Didn't yer know that?'

'Somefink in me 'ead told me ta get me red jumper. Me mum always says when we bin naughty, 'don't do that when yer farver gets in cause to 'im that's "like a red rag to a bull." S'pose it stuck in me 'ead somewhere that bulls must like red or somefink. But I just done it, didn't 'ave no time ta fink.'

'Whatever it was young, Joey' Harry's dad continued 'You just saved Georgie's life I reckon. Come on now, let's get yer back to Annie, you alright to walk Georgie?'

'Yeah, I fink so, me legs are still shakin' like jelly though.' He turned to his friend. 'You saved me life, Joey. I ain't never gonna forget this.'

The men helped the two friends back to their hut, relief showing on all their faces. The outcome could have been so different and tragic. But thanks to the quick thinking of a little ten year old boy, the danger had been averted. Annie watched her Georgie and his friend Joey, with the help of a few of the dad's, come towards her as she sat drinking tea outside her tin hut.

Chapter Four

'1936'

Wednesday 9th of September.

Fifteen year old, apprentice electrician for the Metropolitan Police, Georgie Powley, was on his way home from work. He was in a reflective mood. 'Can't believe I've been working for more than a month' he thought. 'I think I'm doin' okay, let's just hope me governor does as well, because I really like it.' Georgie would have been very pleased to know, that, after just one month, that indeed his governor saw great potential in him. He had not hesitated in passing his thoughts on to his senior. 'The, boys good,' he'd said, 'he's a quick learner and far ahead of the others that joined at the same time. I reckon the extra year he did at school done him a lot of good. In my opinion the boy will go a long way.' Oh yes, Georgie would have been over the moon if he had heard this exchange between his bosses. He had been a bit apprehensive on his first day, he had good reason, or so he thought superstitiously, for the date had been Monday the Thirteenth of July. But so far so good, nothing unlucky had occurred at work.

Today was a very special day in the lives of the Powley family. When Georgie gets home, little Joey, should already be there. Even though Joey has reached the height of five foot six, his family and closest friends, still think of him as 'Little Joey'. Annie will have cooked Joey's favourite meal of roast beef with all the trimmings. 'Roast beef on a Wednesday,' some would think it sacrilege 'Roast beef was meant for a Sunday, it's tradition.' Up until three years ago, Annie would have been of the same mind. That all changed the day little Joey saved Georgie's life. Ever since then, on the anniversary of the near tragic day, Annie marks it, by inviting Joey to have tea with them. When she had asked Joey what would he most like to eat if he had the choice, without hesitation, Joey answered, it was the Roast beef dinner they had eaten, that first Sunday down hopping.

'Watcha, Joey, Mum, Dad' Georgie greeted them all. They were enjoying a cup of tea. 'How you doin' wiv my old job down the lane, Mate?' The two friends hadn't seen each other for more than a week. After work, Georgie usually had his nose in one book or another that related to his work as an electrician.

'Ello, Georgie, it's great.' answered Joey 'I can't wait ta leave school and work on Peg's stall full time. How about your job, still goin' well is it?'

'You betcha, I'm really learning a lot, and enjoying it as well.'

'Come and sit down, love, catch up on the two of you's news, while I get you a cuppa and finish the veg off.'

'You don't have to put yourself out like this, Aunt Annie. What I done for Georgie was ages ago now. Any case, he'd a done the same for me. Wouldn't you, Mate?'

Before Georgie had time to answer, Annie jumped in with 'put meself out, what you on about, Little Joey? this isn't puttin' meself out. I'm cookin' a meal for the three people that mean the world to me. How's that puttin' meself out, eh?'

'You know what I mean, you've bin out doin' your two cleanin' jobs. Then to come 'ome and cook a big meal in the middle of the week, that's without the cost of the beef, well it don't seem right. Egg and chips'd do me.'

'Well it won't do for me. You 'ave egg and chips with us on other day's when you come for your tea. This has to be special. And I'll thank you not to mention it again.' She ruffled Joey's hair on her way to the kitchen.

'Give in, Son' said his uncle George. 'You know what you mean to the both of us, and you know it's not just because of what happened three years ago. You've become like another son to us. So do your son-like chores and lay the table.'

They hadn't returned down to the hop garden in Kent since 1933. Annie still had nightmares of a field full of wild bulls chasing her son. Georgie always told her after one of these bad dreams that, 'you've been eatin' to much cheese late at night, Muvver.'

One good thing came out of that near tragedy, apart from little Joey averting the attention of the bull. For after Annie had witnessed the scene of Georgie and Joey being comforted and helped back to her hut by some of the men, and she had cradled the ashen faced and trembling bodies in her arms, Annie came to a momentous decision. When the boys were settled with a nice hot cup of cocoa and she lit a cigarette to have with a strong cup of tea, she decided there and then, that this was to be her very last fag. Her boy was safe and that was the single most important thing in her life. 'fags is bad for yer,' she scolded herself, 'We got just one go at this, and I ain't gonna take no risks that might stop me from seein' my baby grow up. He's bin given anuvver chance, but the good Lord won't give me one if I bring it on meself.' So today was a double anniversary, for sure enough, true to her word. Annie had not smoked another cigarette from that day to this.

'How's your mum, Joey?' enquired Annie, as they were tucking in to their afters of rhubarb pie and custard. 'I haven't seen her for a while.'

'Oh you know, same as normal. Still tryin' to make ends meet. Fing is, me and mum fought it would get better after I took over Georgie's job down the lane.'

'We gather by that it hasn't then, Son?'

'No, Uncle George, trouble is when *he* found out I 'ad the job and was givin' mum most of me wages, he cut down on what he give 'er. Not that that was ever enough as you know. Still fings ain't quite as bad as they used to be, cause I'm able to get a few clothes for the kids. Old Peg's a diamond, she always manages to 'old back some nice frocks for Lily and Vi.'

'Well when you go home don't forget to tell your mum to come in for a cuppa soon. I like to see the kiddies as well.'

'I tell you if they do come, you'd better 'ope that it's while Matt and Jonny are at school. They'll drive yer mad. All they talk about is when you and Uncle George took 'em by charabanc to Soufend in the summer 'olidays.'

'Ah, we wouldn't mind that would we, George?'

'No, we had a smashing time as well. I'll never forget the looks on their faces when they saw the sea. What a picture that was.'

'We had to keep me eye on him all the time we were on the beach. He just wanted to keep runnin' into the water, clothes a'nall.' remembered Georgie. 'And what about your Rosie Joey, she would have sat in that deckchair all day, just watchin' the waves, she'd have had a shock though if we'd let her stay there and the tide had come in' he laughed.

'And that baby sister of yours was a little angel. She loved it when me and your uncle here, held her hands and took her for a paddle. Matty was a good boy, wasn't he,? he was so 'appy to build sandcastle's with Violet all day if she'd wanted. Well up till we mentioned takin' them all to the Kurzel. I fought young Jonny was gonna be sick, the times he went on that carousel. Oh it was a smashin' day out. I will say this to you Joey, although you and your brothers and sisters have had a hard time of it, not one of you is any trouble. Your mum must be proud when she takes you out.'

'Takes us out, that's a laugh. I can only ever remember goin' eivver shoppin' or to me nan and granddads, oh yeah, a couple a times years ago to Peckham Rye. And the reason, they don't cause no trouble, Aunt Annie, is that they're not used to 'avin' fun. At our 'ouse we 'ave to stay in our room when *he's* in, and if he can hear us talkin' or, well, if we dare to laugh, 'he's in our room, before yer can say, Jack Robinson, and 'e goes into a rage, swearing and shoutin' at us. 'E don't arf give a wallop to the back of our legs, sometimes a'nall' Joey finished solemnly.

Annie shook her head, she had heard this sorry tale so many times 'But your mum's all right though isn't she? I mean, he hasn't hurt her or anythin?'

'Yeah, she seems all right, well I fink so, she's bin a lot more quiet lately. Me and mum don't talk much anymore, she don't seem that interested. Don't get me wrong, I don't blame her for the way fings are. I know she tries to keep 'im away from us as best she can. It's why she shouts a lot at the kids as well, it's incase 'e comes 'ome to the noise and starts.'

'Well if ever he starts on any of you, you come here with the littluns until he calms down.' George told Joey in earnest. The people of Walworth and Camberwell knew, that it was 'not the done thing' to come between a husband and his wife or their children. But it is very hard to just sit back and do nothing, when you know that violence is being metered out to women and defenceless children.

The one sad thing about not going hopping anymore, is that Joey hasn't been able to go on holiday with Georgie and his mum and dad. For the last three summers Annie, George and young Georgie have been spending a week at Leysdown, on the Isle of Sheppey in Kent with the Woogitts and rented one of the chalets next door to them. No way was Dan going to let Joey go, for after all, he couldn't earn any money there like he did from picking hops. Georgie felt sad at having to leave little Joey at home. Even so he did have a good time swimming in the sea, eel fishing with his dad and Alf Woogitt, walking for miles along the sea front and best of all, shared in the company of Siddy and Bernie.

Annie had tried to make it up to Joey, by taking him and the other Smith children during the second week of her annual holiday for days out. She and Georgie took them all. That first time back in '34 she took them for a boat trip up the river Thames, even eighteen month old Lily, who Annie pushed round in Georgie's old perambulator, from when he was a baby, enjoyed every minute. Then last year, they took a tram to Regents Park and went to see the animals at the zoo. This again was a first for the Smith children. They ran from cage to cage, calling out to each other all the while. 'Cor, come and look at this Monkey.' 'No come and see the Tigers' What a day that had been. This year, before Georgie started work, they went to Hyde Park, where the two youngest ones, with the help of Rosie fed the ducks with the crusts from the cheese sandwiches Annie made for them all. The four boys, with Georgie and Joey in charge of the oars, hired one of the boats and had a great time rowing on the Serpentine, until the man in charge called out the number of their boat when their time was up.

Annie enjoyed the company of Rosie, 'if I'd been blessed with a daughter' she often thought, 'who turned out like Rosie, I'd have been very happy.' For Rosie at twelve, had blossomed into a very pretty girl, she could never do enough for Annie on these days out. She preferred to stay with her and not go off with the boys. 'Mind you,' wondered Annie, 'could that be something to do with the way she gets all embarrassed when my Georgie talks to her. I know one thing, whenever she comes out wiv us, she always wears that blue ribbon, we know, he bought for her, though he tries to deny it.'

Annie came back to the present, with a start. 'Off day dreamin' again were you, Gel?'

'Sorry, Love, what was you sayin'?'

'Don't worry about it, Aunt Annie. Uncle George was only puttin' his orders in for another cup of tea. You stay where you are. I'll go and make it. My way of sayin' thanks for a lovely tea. Then I'd better get 'ome and give me mum an 'and gettin' the kids to bed.'

'Alright, Joey, love.'

When Joey had gone, Georgie left shortly after to go and find Siddy and Bernie, as all three of them were now working, they tried to catch up with each others as often as they could. They knew where to find each other, sitting on the wall outside the Avenue School.

Bernie had been working with his dad Alf, for just over a year now. He couldn't wait for the day when he was able to drive. Alf, had had a very good year, and had promised Bernie, that as soon as he could drive the lorry with safety and confidence, he was going to extend the business and buy a second vehicle. Siddy left school with Georgie, this past July, he too is working for his dad, but whereas Bernie goes around with Alf all day in the lorry, Siddy, has a tricycle with a trailer attached to the back. He cycles up and down the roads of Walworth, Camberwell and Kennington, all day long, calling out for 'any old rags'. Come rain or shine, his dad expects him to be out there. Alf and Bernie concentrate on the scrap iron side of the business.

As Annie and George were preparing for bed that night, Annie turned to her husband with concern. 'I think after I've done at the surgery tomorrow, I'll go and give Sally a knock'

'You worried about her are you, Gel?'

'Well, it must be nearly a month since I seen her last. Seems a bit funny that's all. Ever since she confided in me about him bashin' her, she's made a habit of comin' in for a cuppa and a chat quite regular like, well most weeks at any rate.'

'Well don't let it keep you awake. If anything bad had happened to her, little Joey would have said.'

'Yeah, course he would. P'raps I'll leave it a while. Was nice tonight weren't it, Love? Mind you, look how quick these past three years have gone, our Georgie at work and little Joey leavin' school in a couple a months?'

'You're right there, Annie Gel, I don't know where the time goes. We'll have to put our heads together and come up with somethin' nice for Joey's fourteenth.'

'Mmm, got Georgie's birfday first, that'll have to be special to. Sixteen eh. Don't seem that long since I was changin' his bum .'

'Oi you sentimental old thing it's far too late at night to start with your trip down memory lane.' They laughed as they cuddled up together.

When Annie was leaving Dr McManus surgery, the following Thursday, much to her delight, she found Rose and Mary, her sisters waiting outside.

'Hello Gels, what you two doin' here so early?' she asked.

Rose, the more outgoing and youngest of all three, answered. 'Mary and me fought it'd be a nice change to go and see our Liz.'

'What, now?' exclaimed Annie.

'No, not right now, yer silly cow. We was gonna do our shoppin' first, then come round for you.'

'What made you decide to go sudden like?'

'My Cliff bumped into Sam down the Rock last night, He said his Liz had had a bit of a fall. It's all right' Mary added, as she noticed the worried look on her sister Annie's face. 'he said she weren't bad or nuffing, but she might need an 'and wiv her shoppin or 'cleanin'.'

'I'm just gonna pop into Sally Smiff's on me way home, what time d'you think you'll be back at my house?'

'She alright is she, Annie.?' asked Rose, 'he ain't up to 'is old tricks agen is he?'

'I'm not sure, but I'll let you know when I see yer. So what time?'

'Me and Rose should be back by 'alf past ten. If you're still with Sally, we'll 'ave a cuppa wiv Kath.'

Annie strode off back along John Ruskin Street. As she reached the Primary School named with the same name as the street. She crossed over, to where there was a little sweet shop.

'I'll just pop in and buy baby Lily some dew dews,' as she called them. They were little sugar covered segments of flavoured oranges and lemons. She knew that Lily liked these sweets, but if Annie were honest, she would admit to them being *her* favourite sweets. If she played her cards right, and with a little bit of persuasion, baby Lily would happily share some with her. 'Mornin', Sal' Annie greeted Sally, when she answered her knock at the Smith's front door. 'Just thought I'd pop me head in to see how you are. Cos I haven't seen you for a couple of weeks' Annie was thinking how white and drawn Sally looked.

''ello, Annie, come on in. Sorry I ain't bin to see yer, but, well, I've bin feelin' a bit off colour lately.'

'I hope it's got nothing to do with his lordship. Cos you said things had been a lot better for a while.'

'Yeah, they was. Now though, 'e's got it in 'is 'ead that there's gonna be a war and that 'e'll get called up.'

'A war! What makes him think that?' Annie quickly turned to baby Lily. 'Here we are Lily, you take these dew dew's to your room and share them with your dolly. Save me one though. There's a good gel.'

Lily's face lit up at the sight of the sweeties. 'Fanku, me save one for, Annann.'

'Now, what was you sayin' about a War, Sal?' Annie continued when Lily was out of earshot.

'Well, when 'im and 'is mates get togevver in the pub, they're always tryin' to put the worlds to right's. Seems one of 'is mates, reckons that that bloke 'Itler is out ta cause trouble and that there'll be anuvver war before long.'

'No, that can't happen, not after the last lot. Me and George have been listenin' to the wireless, and heard all about the man. Some say he's just a jumped up little corporal that's gettin' too big for his boots, others say, that in the three years since he became Chancellor, he's done a lot a good things for the German people. I can't see the powers that be in this Country will want to get involved in another war. Stands to reason don't it, we lost all those poor blighters in the last one. Fank the Lord my George came through it.'

'I pray you're right, Annie. Not for 'is sake though, but me kid's. I'd give anyfing, but that, to get rid of 'im.' Sally trembled as she spoke.

'There's more to it than that, ain't there, Sal, come on tell me what's been goin' on. I thought that things might have got a bit easier, what with your Joey bringin' home a few extra bob a week.'

'That's when fings started to get worse, believe it or not.'

'In what way?'

'Well, he don't give me as much 'ousekeepin' as he did before. Reckons that I don't need it, cause Joey's givin' me money. I tell yer, Annie, we're worser off now. Joey, the poor little bugger, only gets three bob a week, he keeps a shillin' for 'iself, mind you out a that he buy's the kid sweets and fings. Anyway, Dan's got used to bein' able to 'ave more in 'is pocket to spend on beer and the 'orses. But come fursday's it's nearly always all gone.

I tell yer Annie, I 'ate fursday's, I never know what sort a mood 'e'll come 'ome in.'

'Has he been still hittin'' you then?'

'Only on a fursday, if I ain't got no money to give 'im. Daft ain't it, but I pray 'e'll come 'ome drunk, cause then 'e just falls in ter bed.'

'I couldn't live the way you do Sally. This has been goin' on for years now. How much more can you take love?'

'Even I'm gettin' to the point where I don't know Annie. I don't fink I can take much more. The last time 'e 'it me it 'urt so much that I couldn't 'elp but scream out in agony. Jonny came in to see what was wrong, Dan kicked 'im out with 'is steel capped boots on......'

'Oh, Sally, Sally, it just don't bear finkin' about. Was Jonny alright?'

'Apart from a great big bruise on 'is side, yeah. But Dan said that if I ever make a sound like that agen, he'd do more than just kick one of 'em. So I've decided, Annie. The next time 'e touches one a the kid's, I'm off. Don't ask me where, or how, but this time, I mean it.'

'Good for you, Love. And when you do, and I hope that it's soon, don't forget, come to me and George before you go anywhere else. We can give you a little bit of money to help you find somewhere to rent.'

'You and your family 'ave done so much for us already, Annie.'

'I've told you before, Sally, we owe the life of our son, to your son. Look I've got to go now, I'm meeting Rose and Mary. But take very good care of yourself. Do you need any money for tonight, seein' as it's Thursday?'

'No. Ta all the same. I've managed ta keep back enough so's 'e can get a bottle a stout.'

Annie walked to her house, with a sad feeling in her heart.

That evening Annie sat with George and Georgie, mulling over the news that Annie had shared with them earlier. She had first told them about the fall that her sister Liz had had. She had been relieved, when she, and her sisters arrived to find that indeed the fall had not been too severe. She'd apparently tripped over their dog, Scruff. Her knee was badly bruised but other than that she said she was 'fine.' The three sisters though, offered to get her shopping in for a couple of days.

Then Annie had told both her husband and son about her visit to Sally Smith, the outcome of which had not been such good news.

'I feel so helpless' Annie cried. 'But I don't know what I can do to help her.'

'There's not much we can do, Love, but be here if and when she needs us.'

'Dad's right, Mum. You've done a lot for Joey's family. You know as well as I do, even the Police don't like to get involved in a domestic. Look at that family from Kennington. That bloke was beatin' his wife up nearly every day, how many times did it say in the South London Press, that he'd put her in hospital.? Her neighbours had called the cops loads of times. But they said their hands were tied and there wasn't much they could do. It was only after he half killed her, and the Doctor at Kings said he'd testify that her injuries had not been self inflicted, like her old man said, that he was put inside.'

'Listen to your, Son, Annie, he's right in what he say's you know.'

Before Annie could answer, they heard a voice screaming from down in the street.

'Uncle George, Uncle George' the screaming was near hysteria. Then came frantic banging on the front door.

'Oh my gawd, who's that?' Annie startled stood up, looking to her husband.

'It sounds like, Joey' said Georgie as he started to run down the stairs. His dad was close on his heels.

'Please someone 'elp me' the voice begged.

Georgie threw open the door, Joey practically fell into his arms. 'Joey, Joey what's wrong?' implored his mate Georgie. Joey was not alone, standing on the step were all six of the Smith children. Rosie was cuddling a tearful Lily, with Violet hanging on to her skirt. Matty had his arm round Jonny's shoulders, all of them were shaking with fear, with tears streaming down every one of their pathetic little faces.

''e's killin' 'er, Georgie.' He saw his uncle appear. 'Please, Uncle George, you gotta stop 'im.' George, moved his son out of the way, so that he could take hold of Joey's arms.

'Joey, come on boy tell me what's happened?'

'You've got to go over there now,' he implored. '*please*, me dad won't stop 'ittin' me mum.'

George looked at Annie who was standing on the bottom stair, total shock and disbelief on her face. Then he turned to his son   and said 'Georgie, get Arfur, and tell him to follow me.'

Kath and Jack, from the downstairs flat had come out of the sitting room to see what all the commotion was about. 'Jack come with me, there's trouble. Kath see to the kids. Annie when we get there you stay outside till I call yer.'

'I'm comin' wiv yer, she's me, Mum.' pleaded Joey.

Kath came and took him gently by the shoulders and turned him round to face her. 'Come on Joey. Your brothers and sister's need you. If you wait here with me we can calm them all down. But I need you to help me, Joey.' She coaxed him. George and Jack were already half way up the road to the Smith's house. Annie tremulously followed a few paces behind. Doll's husband Arthur from next door, without bothering to change from his carpet slippers into his outdoor boots, ran after George and Jack. He'd heard the shouting and was on his way to his front door when Georgie banged on the door knocker.

Dolly saw that Kath had all the children with her. 'Do you want me to come and stay wiv you and the littluns, Kath?' she called.

'Oh, yes please, Doll. I'm shakin' like a leaf.' She mouthed. Georgie, had slowly walked along the road, to stand with his mother. He put an arm around her shoulders, Annie hardly noticed. Then, Jack came out of the Smith's house. He looked at his sister in law and young nephew, it shocked them both to the core, when they saw the look of sheer horror on Jack's face. It was a look that would haunt them for the rest of their lives.

Jack pulled himself together. He turned to the young man. 'Georgie, run along to Doctor McManus' flat, the doctor lived above his surgery. Get him to come here straight away.'

'Jack' cried Annie. 'What's 'appened to Sally?'

'In a minute, Annie, Oh and, Georgie, when you get there, ask the doctor to telephone for the Police.' Jack finished sombrely.

'Oh, Dear God, he's gone an done it ain't he?' Georgie, wanted to comfort his mum but his uncle told him to. 'go as fast as you can boy.' He turned back to Annie. 'You alright, Gel?'

'Tell me, Jack, is she dead?'

'Well we can't find no pulse. Your George and Arfur are givin' 'er artificial respiration, but none of us 'old out much 'ope.'

'Where's that bastard, as he run off?'

'No, when we got here, he was standin' over her, yellin' at her ta get up.' Annie started to shake uncontrollably. Jack went to her, just as her legs buckled beneath her.

'Steady on, Gel. Come and sit on the wall for a minute. Let's wait until the doc's bin eh.?' He dare not tell Annie any more. He didn't think he could anyway. All he kept seeing, was all the blood surrounding Sally's slight body.

Back in Jack and Kath's flat, the scene was a pitiful sight. Kath and Doll, had made a cup of tea with lot's of sugar in for the six petrified children.

Joey, was pacing the floor 'I should be there' he kept repeating. 'She's me mum, she might need me.' Just below his right eye, which had started to swell, a dark bruise was coming out.

'Joey' Kath asked gently, 'how did you hurt your eye?'

Joey touched the swollen lump and winced. 'I dunno'

Rosie answered for him. 'He tried to stop him from hittin' mum. He jumped on his back, but he pulled Joey off and started to hit him as well.'

Joey started to sob, 'I should've stopped him'

Rosie ran to her big brother and pulled him close to her. 'There wasn't anyfing you could do, Joey love. You tried. But he's too big and strong and, and, *mad.*' she finished.

When the younger ones saw, for the first time in their lives, their Joey, big brother Joey crying his heart out, it started them all off again. Doll and Kath, took two each in their arms and tried to pacify them. The two women looked at each other, shaking their heads. They had no words of wisdom or comfort to offer. They could only imagine what these poor little blighters had witnessed.

It seemed an age before Annie and Jack heard the car belonging to the doctor, come down the road. Georgie was sitting in the passenger seat next to Dr McManus. Georgie wanted to ask his mum if everything was going to be all right. But the look on her face, told him all he wanted to know. Jack went round to the driver's side of the car, so that he could have a few words with the doctor before going into the house.

Georgie went to Annie, still sitting forlornly on the wall. 'Mum,' he said, Annie turned her face slowly towards her son. 'The Doctor's called the Police, they'll be here soon. Where's dad, is he still in there?'

'Yes, Love,' Annie answered. In a voice hardly recognisable to him.

'What about, y'know, 'im?'

'He's still in there as well, wiv yer dad and Arfur.'

The Doctor walked swiftly into the house. 'Georgie, take your mum home boy' Jack called.

'I fink I should stay, Uncle Jack. Just in case, you never know.'

'No, Gel, let Georgie take yer back. We'll come for yer if you're needed.' Jack pressed. Knowing full well, that sadly there was nothing, Annie or any of them could do now, for poor Sally Smith.

Georgie kept his arm around his mum's shoulders, as they mournfully walked back to their house. 'Oh my gawd, Georgie, the kids. What we gonna say to them. What's gonna 'appen to them now?'

'I dunno, Mum, I just don't know.'

'How do we tell them that their farvvers killed their poor mum? I don't know if I can go in there boy.'

'We won't tell them that she's dead yet. Let's say that the doctor is wiv her. I mean we don't know for sure do we?'

'The only way poor Sally's ever comin' out a that 'ouse, will be in a box. But you're right, Son, we won't tell them till the doctor confirms it. For confirm it he will. Of that I ain't got no doubts.'

As Annie and Georgie walked through the front room door of Kath's, all the children ran to them, all except little Joey, he just stood where he was, no words were needed, for he could tell by the grief stricken look in his aunt's and best friends eyes. He turned away to stare out of the window. Not noticing as the Black Mariah Police vehicle passed swiftly by, it's bell clanging loudly.

The five other Smith children crowded round Annie and Georgie. Matty, was the first to speak. 'Is me, Mum, all right?' Jonny then asked through his sobs. 'She will be all right won't she, Aunt Annie.?' The two youngest little girls grabbed hold of Annie's hands, both crying softly. Annie cradled them to her. Rosie looked at Georgie, that look of total devastation tore at his heart. He took her hand and held on to it, she could feel his hand shaking, and she knew, without a shadow of a doubt, her mum had gone from them all forever.

Annie tried as best she could to pacify them. Kath realised at once, that a terrible thing had occurred. She stepped in to aid Annie in her obvious distress.

'Come on now, give Aunt Annie and Georgie room to breathe. Let's all sit down, shall we?' She and Dolly went to the two boys, Matty and Jonny and led them to the settee. Annie picked baby Lily up in her arms, and with Violet clinging to her other hand, she sat in one of the armchairs. Georgie guided Rosie to a chair close to his mum's.

It was Rosie who put the question to them that they were dreading. 'Our mum's dead ain't she?' She asked clearly. 'I knew he'd do it one day' she said it with such finality, it tore threw the women's hearts.

'Shut up, Rosie' cried Jonny, 'she ain't dead. I'm goin' to see 'er now. You see the doctor'll probably 'ave to giv 'er a pill or somefing, but she's alright I tell yer.' He was becoming hysterical. He started to go to the door.

'Come back here, Jonny' words spoken through pain, were forced out of Joey's mouth. As Jonny hesitated, he spoke again. 'I mean it, Jonny, come on, Mate,' he pleaded, 'I need you, Matty and Rosie to be strong for the sake of the littluns.' Still Jonny hesitated, 'Mum would want you to be big and brave, wouldn't she?'

At this, Jonny turned to his big brother. 'I don't wanna be big and brave, Joey. I want me mum.' He finished as he broke down in tears. Joey went to him and put his arms round him.

'Is it alright, Mrs Dawson if I take Matty and Jonny into the garden for a bit?'

'Of course, Love, stay there as long as you need to.' Kath marvelled at the way Joey was taking control of the two younger boys. She knew he wanted to get them alone and talk to them away from the babies.

The time was getting on, it was way past bedtime for the little girls. Lily was already asleep. Within seconds of being cradled in Annie's arms, she had dropped off. Every so often though, her little body shook with sobs. Violet had climbed up on the armchair, so that she could lean against this kind lady that had taken them to so many nice places. She too was falling into a fitful slumber. In the silence the mantle clock ticked on. Broken only when Kath could sit no longer doing nothing.

'I'll go and put the kettle on again.' she said.

Feeling utterly helpless. 'I'll giv you an 'and.' Offered Doll.

When they had left the room, Rosie started to speak, or was it that she was thinking out loud? Annie and Georgie were not certain.

'Who'll tell nan and grandad? I s'pose I will, or Joey might.' She answered her own questions. 'Will they arrange the funeral I wonder?' Mother and son looked at each other. 'What do we do?' Georgie's eyes asked those of his mum. The slight shake of his mum's head, showed that she felt out of her depth. Rosie continued. 'D'you fink they'll put me dad in jail? Bound to aren't they, he's a murderer.'

Georgie couldn't take this any more. 'Rosie' she ignored him, just stared into space. He tried again. 'Rosie.' She turned to look at him, it felt to Georgie that she was looking straight through him. It was very unnerving. 'Rosie,' he persevered, 'do you think we should take the girls upstairs and put them into bed?'

His mum smiled at him and nodded approval at his quick thinking. By getting Rosie to think about the others, will help her to take her mind off her painful thoughts. Rosie sighed, a long drawn out shuddering sigh. After a few seconds she pulled her self together to answer Georgie 'If your mum don't mind, that'd be a big help.' She turned to Annie, who willingly agreed.

'If you can carry Violet up, Georgie, and, Rosie love you'll have to take Lily for me, cos me arms gone...'Annie stopped herself just in time, she had been about to say 'dead' she covered her hesitation well, 'Cor, it certainly 'as, me arms gone numb.'

'Thank you, Aunt Annie, and you, Georgie.'

As Annie heard their steps climbing up the stairs, she wiped the fresh tears from her eyes, saying quietly to Kath and Doll as they rejoined her. 'There goes a lovely girl, who's come of age tonight. Well before her time.'

Back in the Smith's home, George, Jack and Arthur, were going through with the Police, all that had happened since the children's frightening arrival at George and Annie's front door. They took it in turns explaining, how they had arrived at the house to find the front door open wide. How they hadn't bothered knocking. After the terror on the childrens faces they just rushed inside. The scene that met them was an horrific one.

George explained what he'd seen 'Dan Smith was standing over the lifeless body of his wife Sally. He was shouting at her 'get up you bitch, get up.' He stopped unable to go on.

Me and George, er, Mr Powley here well when we saw 'im go to kick 'er, we just ran and grabbed 'im.' continued Arthur.

'Did any of you hit him?' The Sergeant questioned. 'Because my Constable noticed a bruise on his face. I just need to ascertain whether he received it during or after the struggle with his wife.'

'Yes,' admitted George, 'I did, when we grabbed him he tried to get away. He was swearin' at us and tryin' to hit us and tellin' us to get out and mind our own effin' business.'

'Thank you, Mr Powley' he could see that Mr Powley was the most upset by what he had seen, seems he's more close to the family. 'Would you care to continue, Mr Bell?'

'Well, when we got the better of 'im, Jack, that's Jack Dawson there, he found some string on a kite. We used that to tie the bastard up, so we could see to Sally.'

'Did you move her at all?'

'Well, we did turn her over, just to see if she was breavin'.'

George joined in again at this point. 'Look, we knew she was in a bad way. I mean, you can see all the blood.' He turned to where the body of Sally still lay. After the Doctor had examined her and pronounced her to be dead, he had found an old blanket and covered her up 'Me and Arthur know a bit about life saving. Though we fought it was gonna be a waste a time, we still had a go at revivin' her. Didn't work though did it?'

Doctor McManus, who was standing listening to the exchange, tried to reassure George and his friends. 'The three of you did everything you could George. But it's my belief that Sally died when she hit her head as she fell, or was pushed, onto the iron fire surround. Look, I really think I should go and see the children now, if that's alright with you Sergeant?'

'Of course, Doctor, we'll need to speak to you later though.'

'Very well, Sergeant. Are the children at your house, George?'

'Yeah, the poor soul's. They was in a terrible state when they came screamin' at our door.'

'Right, well I'll be off then. I'll probably see you back there.' Dr McManus looked to George, Jack and Arthur as he collected his bag ready to leave.

'Before you go, Doctor, there is just one thing.'

'What's that, Sergeant?'

'We will need to speak to the children, well the older ones at least.'

'Why do you need to speak to them?' asked George, horrified at the thought. 'Surely after what we've told yer, and, well, you've seen for yourself the state of poor Sally. What more can they add?'

'I know it seems a hard thing to do, Mr Powley, but it's obvious from what you've said, that they were here when it started. As cruel as it seems, we have to interview them. So, Doctor, we'd appreciate it if you could remain with them. As soon as we've finished here, we'll come along.'

'What tonight?' asked the incredulous Doctor.

'Sometimes it's better to talk to them as soon after the event as possible, before the shock starts to set in. At the moment they're probably feeling angry as well. That's when youngsters tend to want to get it all off their chests, before they have time to think of the consequences. After all, it is their father we have in the other room.'

'It don't seem right though.' Arthur said.

'Especially if you'd seen their faces.' added Jack.

'I'm sorry, I know how you all feel, I've got kids of me own. But it's got to be done sometime. But we'll leave it up to you Doc. Let us know if you think they can handle it.'

'Very well, Sergeant. I'll see you later.'

The Doctor left the scene of the diabolical crime, leaving the Sergeant trying to find out more about the background of the Smith family. Shortly after Dan had been taken in handcuffs to Carter Street Police station, the Sergeant said that the three men could return home. Luckily they left just before a black van arrived, to remove Sally's battered and broken lifeless body.

Kath opened the front door to find Dr McManus standing there, a grim look on his face.

'Come in, Doctor' she beckoned. 'We're in me front room.' He followed Kath to the room where Annie and Dolly Bell, were sitting both warming their hands on the hot cup of tea they were holding. It wasn't that the room was cold, far from it, for Kath's fire was still roaring and throwing out a lot of heat, the shock of the evening's events were still sending cold shivers down their backs.

'I've just made a fresh pot of tea, Doctor, I bet you could do wiv one.' Kath offered.

'Ooh, yes please, Mrs Dawson.' He smiled weakly at her. 'If you can spare the sugar, I'd appreciate two spoons full. I don't think I'll be getting much sleep tonight some how, so I'll need the energy.'

Annie couldn't wait any longer, she had to hear it from the Doctor, even though she already knew what his answer would be. 'Wasn't there anyfing you could do for her then, Doctor?'

'I'm sorry, Annie, no. Sally was dead, even before your husbands got to her.'

This brought on another bout of tears. 'I've come to see how the children are.' The Doctor said gently. 'Your George said that they arrived here very distraught. Where are they now?'

Doll was the first to recover enough to answer him. 'Joey has taken the boys in to the garden. The youngest one, Jonny, was getting' in a state. I fink he fought it'd be better to get them away from us for a while, cos it ain't much help if we keep cryin.' Just then Georgie with a crestfallen Rosie came back in the room.

The Doctor walked over to Rosie. 'How are you, My Dear?' He asked, thinking as he said it, 'what a silly question, how do you think she is man?'

'I feel like I'm in some sort of dream. Ain't a dream though is it?'

He couldn't give an answer to that, instead he asked 'where are your little sisters, Rosie? I'd like to take a look at them, and then I want to talk to you as well.'

'We've just put them down in Georgie's room. You won't wanna talk to them, will you?'

'No, but if I may I'd like to pop up in a minute, just to see that they're alright?'

'That'd be for the best, Love.' Annie said to Rosie. 'You take, Dr McManus upstairs when he's drunk his tea.' Annie turned to the Doctor, 'Will the men be back soon?'

'They should be, Annie. The er, Police are just having a word with them.' He finished, aware that Rosie was watching him intently. He needed to speak to the ladies without Rosie in the room, things needed to be arranged for the immediate future of the children. Georgie came to his rescue, he realised that there were questions his mum would want to ask the Doctor. To do so in Rosie's hearing would cause even more upset to the young girl.

'Rosie, how's about you and me goin' into the garden for a while wiv the boys, they've bin out there ages, maybe we should go and see if Joey has calmed Jonny down. Eh?'

'Yeah, I could do wiv some fresh air. That's if you wouldn't mind listenin' out for the babies for me?' she looked over at Annie.

'Course not, Darlin' you go wiv Georgie.'

Kate came back in with the Doctors cup of tea and two plates of biscuits on a tray. Having overheard that they were going into the garden she turned to Georgie and Rosie 'Here you are me, Loves, take one a these plates out wiv you, I expect the boys could eat a few a them.'

When they were out of earshot, the Doctor informed the ladies that the Police would be coming later to speak to some of the children. He told them what the Sergeant's thoughts were about 'getting it over with as soon possible' when Annie, Doll and Kath, expressed their feelings on this.

'I'll give them another few minutes together outside, then I will have to go and speak to them, so that I can assess if I think they are up to it tonight. Before I do that, I must ask whether you have given any thought to the problem of where they will sleep tonight. They obviously can't go back to that house.' he finished.

'Course they can't.' agreed Annie. 'Stupid ain't it? but what wiv everyfing goin' on, ain't even fought about that, when those kiddies should be uppermost in our foughts.'

'Come on, Annie, don't punish yerself,' Doll told her friend 'none of us 'ave 'ad time to fink proper. So lets sort it now, before the fella's get back.'

'Seeing as the two little gel's are already in your Georgie's room Annie, be best ta leave them there, maybe we could sort something out so that Rosie could sleep in there wiv them. Kath suggested. 'Good idea, Kath, we could get her some blankets to lie on as a mattress.'

'I've got a spare mattress, we can take it off my Rodney's bed and carry it round, is there enough space in your Georgie's room for it, Annie?'

'Yeah, plenty, Doll. Well that's the girl's settled. I tell yer what we could do for the boys, you've heard me say in the past ain't yer? that since my George came out a the Navy, where he'd got used to sleepin' high up in one a those 'ammock fings, that we now have ta sleep wiv two mattresses. It's all right fer 'im, but me feet don't touch the floor when I sit on it. Feels like climbin' a bleedin' mountain when I go ta bed.' Annie, without realising had just put smiles on the faces of the others in the room.

'Well done, Annie' remarked Dr McManus, 'You've just managed to bring a little bit of light relief to this awful situation'

'Me, what did I do?' she asked in amazement. 'I think the ladies like myself, were visualising you clinging onto the bedcovers and trying to pull yourself up.' 'Go on you cheeky lot' she also found she was able to smile. 'Anyway as I was sayin' before I was rudely interrupted. I'm sure my George can do wiv out one a the mattresses, so we can put it down in our room, on the ovver side of the divider of course, then the three boys can sleep there.'

'That settles that then.' Said Kath, 'just leaves your Georgie. So how about if he slept in my Dora's room. Her beds still in there. Just got to put some clean sheets on.'

'Well done, Ladies' congratulated the Doctor. Now are you sure you have enough bedding. If not I know my wife has plenty to spare. I could pop and get them.'

'Thanks all the same, Doctor. But between us we've got more than enough.' Dolly answered gratefully.

Just then the front door opened, three heavy hearted weary men appeared in the doorway of the front room. 'Where's the kids?' They were the most important people on George's mind.

'It's alright, Love, they've gone in to the garden for a while.' His wife answered him. 'You look all in, the three of yer' she continued sympathetically, come and take the weight off your feet.'

'I could do with a good strong cup a tea, Kath' said her husband as he sat on the nearest chair available.

'I'm on me way, Jack, love.'

'Plenty of sugar, Mrs Dawson' advised the Doctor.

'Here tuck into these biscuits while yer wait.' That was the only thing Doll could think of to say. She'd never seen her husband look so devastated, so helpless.

'The Sergeant said to tell yer Doc, that they'll be comin' in about an 'our.' Supplied Arthur. George stepped forward fully into the room, it was then that Annie noticed what he was holding.

'Found these in the kids bedroom, fought they might bring a bit a comfort to the little gel's' Annie put her hand to her mouth, stifling yet another sob. As her husband walked over to her and put three tiny rag dolls in her lap.

The Doctor coughed, in all his thirty years in practise, he had never been able to come to terms in dealing with youngsters, who through no fault of their own, had had to witness terrible happenings in their own homes. Death of parents through lack of medical care, death of malnourished brothers and sisters, death through violence and of course death through mindless war. He'd seen it all. Being so closely involved in this one, down his street as it were, he was feeling useless, powerless to do anything to help these little lost souls. 'I, er think that I'd better speak to the children now. Before the Police get here.'

'Shall I go and bring them back in here?'

'Yes please, Annie.'

What a pitiful sight they made, Georgie, still holding Rosie's hand. He had his other arm round the shoulders of ten year old Matty, and Joey with his arm round his frightened, and extremely tired, seven year old brother Jonny.

'Is it okay, Aunt Annie if we take Jonny ta bed?' Joey asked .

'Y'know is it, Son. First though, I need you and Georgie to come up and take one a the mattresses off me and yer Uncle Georgie's bed. That's alright ain't it, George?'

'You do anyfing that's needed, Gel.' He answered without hesitation. 'By the way, Rosie love, I saw these and thought you gel's might like to have them wiv you.'

'Oh, I'll take them up to Lily and Violet straight away. They 'ardly ever goes to sleep without them. Fanks ever so much.' It was obvious to all the grownups there, that Lily and Violet would not be the only ones that were thankful to have their Dollies tonight. As she took the rag doll's, a present from their brother Joey's hopping holiday, Rosie's eyes for the first time that night, fleetingly, lost their haunted look. It was easy to see which Dolly belonged to her, it was the one with tiny bright blue ribbons in it's hair.

Chapter Five

The next morning

Annie stood in her tiny kitchen preparing a hot breakfast of porridge that would be followed by toast spread with blackcurrant jam for the extra six youngsters that were sitting in her small back room. No amount of cups of tea, or the old adage that after good nights sleep 'things don't seem quite so bad,' sadly, today did not apply. It had been past midnight before all the children were finally settled in their temporary beds.

The Police had indeed arrived late last night. George and Annie had been allowed to stay in the room whilst the Sergeant asked first Joey then Rosie, to give their recollections as to what had taken place between their mother and father, that led to such a tragic ending.

They told their sorry tale, Joey taking control, taking his first tentative steps into adulthood by comforting his sister on the many occasions when she broke down.

The officers, along with Annie and George, heard the children tell how their dad had arrived home from work earlier than usual. Sally hadn't put the younger childrens few toys back in the bedroom all six shared. As he walked into the front room, his foot connected with baby Lily's spinning top. He'd shouted, 'what's this bloody fing doin' 'ere.?' Before their mum had the chance to pick it up, he'd kicked it across the room with such force, that it crashed through the glass in the door of the small cabinet sitting in the corner of the room.

'He went berserk then' said Joey, through gritted teeth. 'See, he'd made that ugly old cabinet when he'd bin at school.' Joey stifled a sob that was threatening to overcome him.

The sergeant gave Joey time to recover. 'You're doing really well, Joey.' he said gently, 'carry on when you feel up to it, Lad.'

Joey took a few deep breathes before continuing. 'Well me mum could see he was really mad, so she shouted at me to get all the kids into the bedroom. Lily and Violet started to scream, they was scared see. Anyway, he started ta come towards 'em, and before I could get 'em out a the way, he lunged at 'em. He slapped both the babies, then he tried ta get Jonny. He was too quick for 'im though, cause as 'e went to 'it im, Jonny ducked and so 'e missed 'im and 'e whacked his 'and on the door. That made 'im even madder.'

All the while Joey recalled this horror, he avoided looking at the adults. He just stared at the floor. Something that Annie and George were relieved about, they couldn't have borne to see such utter despair in his eyes.

Rosie composed herself, she had to help her brother, he couldn't take all this on his shoulders. He needed her as much as she needed him to get through all these unwanted questions. 'I grabbed hold of Lily then, and Joey carried Violet. We didn't go to our room wiv them though, we took them outside. Matty went after Jonny, he'd gone runnin' out into the street, he fought our dad was goin' to chase after him.'

'And did he?' enquired the Sergeant.

'No, he stayed in the house, that's when he started to go for our mum.' Rosie couldn't go on, she was reliving that moment.

'I went back inside when I 'eard me mum screamin' at 'im to leave 'er alone.' Joey's voice now filled with hatred continued 'I jumped on 'is back, cause 'e was just punchin' and punchin' me mum. But he was too strong for me. I couldn't stop 'im, I couldn't save me own mum. I tried 'honest, I really did try.' He finished on a note of despair.

George went to the tortured boy, he took him into his arms. His eyes pleaded with the Sergeant. When he found his voice he said 'surely you don't need to hear anymore. They've had enough' he begged.

'We've heard plenty. Mr Powley. I am just as sorry as you are that we have had to put them through this. We will go now and leave you all in peace.'

Annie was unaware that little Joey had spent the whole night lying awake, thinking about his mum and the day three years ago when he'd returned from his hopping holiday. He'd sat with Sally and all the other children telling them about all his experiences. He hadn't mentioned the fact that he had saved Georgie's life, Joey couldn't understand what all the fuss had been about. Instead he told them about how each morning, him and Georgie went to the farmhouse and filled the metal jug Annie gave them, with fresh milk that had come from the cows that very morning. And how they collected wood and made it into small bundles.

'They call 'em faggots' he supplied. This made the older children laugh.

'Did yer get the pease puddin' to go wiv 'em?' joked Matty.

'Ha ha, very funny' Joey gave his younger brother a playful clip round the ear. 'The faggots' he continued, 'was for lightin' a fire.' Then Joey went on to tell them about the pole men, and how some of them walked on high stilts, so that they could reach the tallest bines and pull them down for the pickers to reach.. He would never forget how his mum had laughed when he told them how he with Georgie and some of the other boys, had found some wood and made their own stilts. 'Cor, you should a seen us tryin' to walk on 'em' Joey had stood up to show them how they had wobbled all over the place. 'I could take one step but I couldn't get me uvver leg ter move. Anyway after a while Georgie managed ta take five steps. He was sort a leanin' forwards tryin' ter stop 'imself from fallin'.' His bum was stickin' right out, the stilts was goin' in different directions and it was more like he was runnin' Joey stopped and laughed as he visualised the funny sight of his mate that day.

'What 'appened next, Joey?' cried Jonny.

'Well, he fell flat on 'is face right in the middle of some cows dung.'

Sally roared with laughter 'oh I wish I'd bin there ter see it.' she said through tears of laughter.

'Was, Georgie hurt?' asked Rosie. She didn't think it very funny, she wouldn't have wanted Georgie Powley to have been embarrassed or feel he'd made a fool of him self in front of his mates.

'Course he wasn't, the cow pooh was nice and fresh, so it was all soft.' Again this brought fourth more laughter from his mum. 'But that wasn't all' supplied Joey, one a the uvver men who was one a these pole men, saw it 'appen. He comes over and 'elps Georgie up, then 'e says to 'im. "I fink you need just a little bit more practise young Georgie before you go and ask the farmer for promotion."

'Did Georgie see the funny side of it?' Sally asked when she had recovered at the end of Joey's tale.

'Oh yeah, we all 'ad a right good laugh. Trouble was 'e didn't 'alf stink. Aunt Annie wouldn't let 'im come in to the hut until 'e'd gone down to the stream and washed 'imself and 'is clothes.'

The tears had come then. As little Joey lay beside his two younger brothers. He bit into his pillow, to muffle the sound of his sobbing, trying desperately hard not to let his aunt and uncle hear from the other side of the bedroom divider.

Breakfast was a sombre affair. Afterwards Georgie went down to the phone box outside the Standard pub. He telephoned his boss and explained the situation to him. There was no hesitation in telling Georgie not to worry about going in to work that day. Georgie was relieved to hear that, for he'd decided to take the younger children to Kennington Park and let them play on the swings. He felt helpless and didn't have a clue as to best help in a situation like this.

Whilst Georgie along with Joey and Rosie took the littleuns up the park, Annie and George, who also had managed to get the day off work, had a visitor. Their local bobby Constable Bill Shepherd came to see them. He'd thoughtfully changed out of his uniform, so as not to add more upset.

'Any news, Bill?' George asked of his old friend from their school days.

'Well I've just come from the nick now. My Sergeant knows that me and you go back along way, so he asked me to pop in and let you know what's going on.. First off though, mate, are the kid's likely to come in?'

'No, they only left here about half an hour ago to go to Kennington Park. Our Georgie fought it'd take their minds off things for a while.'

'What is it, Bill?' Annie could tell by the look on his face that he was very angry.

'You'll never believe what that so called, man is now saying. He reckons that a couple a days ago, Sally told him during an argument like, that the last three of the kids weren't his.'

'What?' cried Annie in astonishment 'The lyin' bugger. What's made him say that?'

'Gives him a reason for losing his temper. He said that yesterday, he'd got the sack as well. Said his bosses sacked him, cause he had been to the pub in his dinner break and got drunk trying to drown out what Sally had told him. That's not all of it, look this is just between us, off the record like, but, well, he also reckons that little Joey's not his either. Clever sod that he is, bold as brass he was, thing that worries me is, the four kiddies he's denying are his are all blonde, the other two are jet black, like him.'

'Surely they don't believe anyfing he say's, though?' George asked of his friend.

'Well, none of us do down the station do, but it won't be up to us will it? It'll be up to a jury.'

'He won't get away wiv it, he can't. Not after they hear what the kiddies have to say, and all the things Sally told me.'

'I hope you're right, Annie, but whatever Sally told you is classed as hearsay'

'What's that mean then?'

'Well, did you ever see Dan hit Sally, or any of the kids?'

'No, but I saw the bruises and that on her arms. And she told me what he'd done to her.'

'That's what's meant by 'hearsay' You've got to have seen him do it. But I'm sure you'll make a good character witness.'

'Bill, what about the kiddies, what's goin' to happen to *them?*'

'That's the other thing I came round to tell you. We've been onto Welfare and they was going to come round today and take them away.'

'Oh no, I can't let them go just like that, they need to be wiv people that care.'

'I knew you'd feel like that, Annie, so I managed to get them to leave coming here until Monday afternoon, if that's alright with you two that is.'

'Course it is, Bill. It'll give me and Annie time to talk to the poor things.'

'Good. Oh yes, the inquest is set for next Wednesday, so when that is out of the way arrangements can be made to bury Sally. Do you know if her parents are sorting anything out George?'

'Haven't a clue, we've not heard from them yet. Apparently your lot have been to see them. I suppose they might come over today.'

After the visit from their local beat copper and friend Bill Shepherd, Annie and George realised they had some serious thinking and talking to do. So much had happened that they hadn't really thought about where the children go from here.

They agonised over whether they could offer them a home with them. Feeling ashamed, when they knew that for them to do such a thing would bring their level of living standards far below what they striven hard for. Maybe they could take the boys? or perhaps the girls needs were more? Above all, the thought of losing touch with little Joey was the hardest thing to bear. He already was, as far as they were concerned, very much a part of the family.

As it turned out, the decision was taken out of their hands. When the welfare officer called to see them on the following Monday afternoon, it was made plain to them that the future of the Smith children need not concern them. Plans were already afoot.

It was explained to Annie and George that, because Dan Smith had not yet been convicted, he still had some influence on what should happen to *his* children. Therein lies the cruel streak of this so called father, realised Annie and George.

They both sat motionless, shocked to their very core at what the Welfare officer was explaining to them. It seems Dan had said that he would not take any responsibility for four of the children. As far as he was concerned only Rosemary and Matthew were his. He had asked the welfare to get in contact with his parents. Dan's mother and father, after Dan had left home to marry, Sally, had gone to live with his mother's widowed sister in Eynsford, a small Kentish village. He had asked that the situation be explained to them. And that he hoped they could find room in their hearts, 'huh, that's a joke' thought Annie, to have Rosie and Matty go to live with them.

'But I'm sure that they haven't been to see the children for years' put in Annie.

'Well' said the officer, a stout woman of some fifty years in age, all tweed and no heart. No wedding ring on her finger, one of the first things Annie had noticed. 'I am going to see them in the morning. I am hopeful of the outcome, they seemed genuinely concerned for the children when I spoke to them on the telephone.' She finished.

'What about the others. What will happen to them?' enquired George in disbelief.

'I regret to say that they will be taken into care. But I can assure you, our childrens homes are full of contented children.' She continued when she noticed the horror on Annie and George's faces.

'Full are they?' said George sarcastically. 'Contented, who're you trying to kid lady?'

'Look, I appreciate that you are fond of these children, but I can assure you without a shadow of doubt, that the three youngest will find adoptive parents in no time. We have lists of eligible couples just waiting for the right ones to come along.'

'The three youngest you said, what about Joey?'

'Well, it might not be quite so easy in the case of Joey. He is after all, nearly fourteen and soon to be starting work.'

'Let them all come to us' George spoke without hesitation.

'I really don't think that will be possible. I am confident the younger ones will be found good homes.'

'But not Joey? Look we love that boy as if he were our own. We beg you, let the boy stay here.' George pleaded.

'I am not sure that we will be able to allow that, I'm afraid.'

'Why not?' Annie wanted to know. 'It'll be one less mouth for the state to feed' she was becoming very angry with this unfeeling, so called do gooder. 'We've got the room. Joey and our Georgie are closer than any real brothers. As my husband says we love him and he loves us. And we can make sure he don't lose touch wiv the others, if that's *allowed* that is.'

'Look, let me speak to my superior about this. Meanwhile I don't think there would be any harm in Joseph staying with you until a decision has been made.'

'Can't they all stay until you know if this Mr and Mrs Smith are definitely interested in taking *Rosie and Matty*' George emphasized the nick names the children had always been known as. Start calling them by their full names and they won't know where they are

The mourners crowded round the deep hole dug into the soil at the Honor Oak Cemetery. Joey turned to his dear pal Georgie, 'I'm really pleased that mums havin' a good send off. She'd be really chuffed to see all these people here.'

'I bet she can see mate, and feelin' right proud of her kids too.'

'Yeah, we're proud of you, Joey as well.' joined in Bernie. 'and I got to say it mate, but I'm real pleased you're not goin' away.' Joey managed a smile at this, it was unlike Bernie to say things like that, he got embarrassed easily if he, or anyone says to him, 'sloppy things,' as he would say. Siddy just clapped Joey on the shoulder. Thinking of the moment, he and Bernie had run round to Georgie's house after work last Friday. Finding the front door open they had scooted up the stairs calling to Georgie. '

'ave you heard the news?' Siddy blurted, 'someone got murdered in your street last night, do yer know who it.......' he stopped in his tracks as he reached the back room. Bernie, who was a few steps behind, looked at his brother and wondered what had made him stop. He too, then reached the doorway. You didn't need to be a boffin to realise in whose house the murder had taken place. The looks on the faces of everyone in that room, told the story. Siddy thought back, 'funny ain't it how I fought it was excitin' a murder right near us. Then when I found out it was Joey's mum, someone I knew, well, it wasn't excitin' no more. Just so bloody awful sad.'

Most of the women folk in John Ruskin Street had lined the pavement as the cortege made it's way slowly along the road. Some thinking, "there but for the grace of, God" It was a hard life for many families in the area. The promise of work and clearing of the slum houses after the war had not materialized. There were some men folk about, many lowered their heads in shame, in the knowledge that one of their own could go as far as killing his wife. Not bothering that his children were there to see it. They all removed their caps, some wiping away tears that threatened to fall. Everyone to a man, promising that, no matter how bad things got for them, they would never stoop as low as Dan Smith.

The women cried openly as they caught a glimpse of the six kiddies on their way to bury their mum together as a family for the last time. Soon, so very soon, to be separated from each other.

Dan Smith's parents had arrived earlier in the day. They went straight to the home of Annie and George. The atmosphere to begin with was strained. Understandably so, for to all the Smith children they were strangers. The only time Reg and Betty Smith had visited, was for a few short hours when each of the children were born. Even this was done when their son had been at work, for, as they explained to Annie and George, before his marriage to Sally, he had ruled the roost in their household. Both Reg and Betty were quietly spoken, a gentle couple afraid of the little boy that grew into a domineering bully. Betty told them how, even though Sally was expecting their son's baby, she begged her not to marry him. Reg then told them that all she got for her worries was a black eye. They didn't blame the then young Sally. She was infatuated with the big strong good looking Dan, and she told him what his own mother had said, hence the beating. It was plain to see that they felt guilty. Given the choice they said, they would have taken all the children to live with them. Betty's sister Millie, lived in a house with plenty of room to accommodate them all. But no, there again Dan had managed to continue hurting his children, by disowning four of them. At least Annie and George took some comfort in the knowledge that it looked like Rosie and Matty were going to be cared for with love.

Annie had bought new clothes for all the children to wear to the funeral. Not black as was the custom, but navy blue for the girls and grey for the boys. Rosie asked Annie if she thought her mum would mind if she wore her bright blue ribbon in her hair.

'Course she won't mind, Love. Your mum tried her best to keep you kiddies safe. Remember that day you all came to wave goodbye to your Joey when he went hopping wiv us?' Rosie nodded, 'well, she was telling me, how happy she felt, she was so proud of how pretty her gels were and how smart her boys looked. Now that's she's in heaven, she wouldn't want all that to have been for nothing, now would she?'

'I s'pose not. Did you see that I gave the undertaker man a bit of the ribbon I've bin saving for when mine got old. And he put it in me mums hair?'

'Yes I had seen it. I wondered where it'd come from. It looks lovely on her. I bet she's looking down right now thinking how pretty she looks.' Rosie forced a smile at the thought.

'I think you should go back and talk to your nan and grandad, they haven't seen you for such a long time.'

'I don't know what to say to them. They're strangers. Oh, Aunt Annie, I wish we could've stayed wiv you and uncle George like Joey is.' Rosie began to cry softly.

'I wish you could too, Love, but them in authority think they know best. They do seem very nice though, me and your uncle George have had a good long talk wiv them, and I think they could give you both a nice home and make you happy. Look, they're both lookin' at you. They look sad for you. It's not as if we're at the uvver end of the earth is it? We're gonna all keep in touch. Go on, off you go now.'

Annie said a silent prayer to herself. Please don't let me be wrong about them Smiths, and, God, keep an eye on all Sally's other kiddies for us.

'Earth to Earth, Ashes to Ashes,' the vicar's words cutting through the childrens minds, not understanding what they were all about. Only knowing their mummy was with them no more. As people started to leave the graveside, two strangers, a man and a lady came towards Annie and George. Rose and Mary along with Kath and Doll, stood close by the children, as if shielding them from what was to come. The strangers had been standing watching the scene, waiting for the appropriate time to collect Lily, Violet and Jonny to take them to the orphanage.

If the funeral had been an awful thing to go through, the next few minutes would remain in the minds and tear at the hearts of all those in attendance.

Reg and Betty Smith ran to their three youngest grand-children, they cuddled each one, telling them to always remember that they loved them and one day they hoped to come and get them. Then turning to Joey, their first born grandson. 'Joey' his granddad said, 'I promise you, we don't believe a word your dad has said. We know you are all his children and our grandchildren. Your gran and me are so sorry we didn't do more for you and your mum. But one day we hope you will understand. We'll not lose touch with you lad, of that you have my word. We'll love and take care of Rosie and Matty always.' He finished on a sob. It was much later that Joey, when he was able to think clearly, remembered these two people coming to see them. They took all the children to have their dinner at the pie and mash shop, just leaving his mum at home with the baby. Funny though, he'd thought, that for the next couple of weeks after they had visited, their mum seemed much happier, and there was more food in the house.

Reg and Betty then led Rosie and Matty away with tears streaming down their faces.

Sally's mum and dad watched in total despair. 'If only we 'ad more money or a bigger place to live' Sally's mum wailed, 'they could've come to us. We'll never see them agen. I know we won't.' Her husband held her to him, sobs racking his body also. They barely managed to call out their love for the children. 'We love you, Darlin's, don't forget that ever'

Then the three youngest children had to be practically dragged off to the waiting motor car. Their tiny arms reaching out, imploring those who loved them, to let them stay. All the while Joey just stood transfixed to the spot. 'This can't be happening' he said. 'Please let me wake up in a minute and find that it's all a nightmare.'

Annie recognised the Welfare lady coming towards her. 'Such a sad day, Mrs Powley' she said, 'But try to remember they are only young. Children can be so resilient, they will come to terms with all this quite soon, I'm sure.'

'Wish I could be so sure. But then by tomorrow you'll 'ave forgotten all about them won't yer? On to the next lot a poor souls, eh?'

'One cannot become too attached to those who come into our care. I am sure you understand that my, Dear.'

George held on to Annie's arm, he thought she was about to punch this pious woman. Instead she said 'Sometimes, *one,* has to get involved.'

'Yes, well, no doubt we shall be seeing one another again quite soon if you are to become foster parents to Joseph.'

Chapter Six

'Happy birthday to you...happy birthday to you... happy birthday Dear, Joey, happy birthday to you.' Annie sang as she went into the boy's room. Joey wiped the sleep from his eyes, smiling as Annie came to sit on the end of his bed.

'Thanks, Aunt Annie' he leant forward to plant a kiss on her cheek.

'Postman's been' she said handing him the small bundle of white envelopes addressed to him. Georgie was also wide awake now. He leant across the gap of about two feet that separated the boy's beds, and clapped Joey on the shoulder 'Happy Birthday, Mate. Well that's it now, you can leave school whenever you like and become one of the workers like me.'

'Take no notice of him, Joey. You know me and your uncle George have told you, that it's all right by us if you want to stay on at school for another year, like our Georgie did.'

'I know, Aunt Annie, but well, after everyfing that's happened, I reckon I should be out there earnin' as much as I can. I got responsibilities now. If the kids need anyfing or when I'm older and they might let me get them out a that place, I gotta 'ave enough for us all to live on.'

'I understand, Love. Anyways, let's put all that bad stuff behind us for today, come and have your breakfast and show me who all them cards is from.'

No one could have said that the last couple of months had been easy for any of them. The welfare office had allowed Joey to stay with the Powley family until a decision had been reached on what would be the best solution to the dilemma of the future of the young boy. It took more than a month of meetings, discussions and some arguing from George and Annie before the powers that be, gave the go ahead for Annie and George to become, officially, foster parents to little Joey Smith.

Georgie's sixteenth birthday came and went in this unsettling period, although not totally unnoticed, because Annie still went through the same ritual as on the morning of Joey's fourteenth, with presents and cards. It just wasn't celebrated the way Annie had planned. When she found herself apologising to her son on the actual day, for not arranging a party or anything, Georgie made her see that he, truly, was not bothered.

'Mum' he'd said 'I've got everything I need right here, I don't need to have parties and loads a presents to make it a special day. It's special because we're all together. What happened with Joey's mum has made me realise what's important in life. It's people, family, and bein' loved, nuffing else matters.' Georgie's words had overwhelmed Annie, 'when did this son a mine, grow into such a wise and caring young man' she thought.

'Mind you, having said that, Mum' he continued, 'I think it would be good to make Joey's first birthday livin' with us a bit special.' That's when he and Annie started to make plans. Annie's first job had been to write to Mr and Mrs Smith, explaining that she wanted to organise a surprise party for Joey. The icing on the cake as far as Joey would be concerned would be to have his Rosie and Matty there, If it was at all possible. A return letter arrived five days later, they were coming! Next it was time to contact the orphanage where Lily, Violet and Jonny were. This time she wouldn't be fobbed off with any excuses. Since the funeral in September, they had only been allowed to visit on one occasion that was after the children had been there for a couple of weeks. No visits had been allowed prior to this, or since, they said that the children needed time to settle in to their new surroundings.

'We will write to you,' Annie had been told, ' when we think the time is right.' So, Annie took it upon herself to write a short letter, not asking for permission, but informing them when she and Joey would be arriving, and would appreciate the children being ready for her to take them out for a birthday tea with their brother. All Georgie had to do, with the help of his dad, was to get Joey's friends from school. His nan and grandad, all the Woogitts and of course, Doll and Arthur from next door, Kath and Jack downstairs, aunts Rose and Mary with their families, round to the flat where the other half of Joey's family would be waiting, ready for when he and Annie returned.

Annie told Joey, that he could take the afternoon off from school, and that she was taking him shopping. It didn't take him long though to work out where they were heading. Annie was feeling a little apprehensive, until, when they reached the orphanage gates, relief flooded through her, for there they were, Jonny in the middle of his two little sisters holding their hands. It was Violet who saw them first. 'Joey, Joey, Joey' she called, jumping up and down on the spot. Joey ran to them, and flung his arms round all three of them. He turned, there was no need for words, the look on his face told Annie all she needed to know, no presents could mean more to him.

Annie took them on the tram to Charing Cross, where not far from the station there was the Lyons Corner House. There was still quite a few people sitting at the tables. Some enjoying a last cup of tea before catching their trains home. Joey found them all a nice table near one of the windows, it would be fun for the little ones, watching all the hustle and bustle of life in the centre of London.

A Nippy came across to take their order, she smiled as Annie asked for five iced buns, five jam doughnuts and five buttered scones, 'What drinks would you like, Madam?' Annie liked that, madam! 'How about hot chocolate all round?' she asked looking at her small charges. When they all nodded their agreement, the Nippy said to them, 'aven't you got a nice mum, buyin' all them cakes for you?' The children sat still for a short time, suddenly Jonny looked from Joey to Annie, 'she ain't our mum' he said with defiance, 'our mum's deaded, we ain't got no mum no more. But I fink she's our Joey's new mum.' He finished.

The poor waitress didn't know what to say, 'I'm, er, I'm sorry, Madam' she looked around her, hoping her boss hadn't overheard the boy's outburst and blame her.

'Don't you worry yourself, Gel, you weren't ter know.' Annie turned to Jonny, 'Listen, lovey, they couldn't have your Joey livin' wiv you,' she tried to placate the boy.

'Why not?'

'Because he's too old. You know he's goin' to work soon, don't you?' no answer, 'and his job is down The Lane, so he's stayin' wiv us cos it's not far from our house.' Still no response from Jonny, so Joey tried.

'You know that I'll always be your brother, don't you, mate? Wherever I am or whatever I do that can never change, all of us, includin' Rosie and Matty, we'll always be brothers and sisters.'

''Honest, Joey' Jonny pleaded with his big brother.

''Honest, Kid, I'm tellin' you the trufe.'

While this confrontation had been taking place, the nippy disappeared into the kitchen at the back of the tea rooms, returning as quickly as she could with plates of delicious looking cakes, hoping to calm the little boy down before the two little girls started to get upset. She needn't have worried for Lily, and Violet had been more interested in looking at all the people around them, especially, some of the men, with their big hats, shiny shoes and lots of them carrying umbrella's. As soon as the cakes arrived, all other thoughts went out the window. Annie wondered after a while though, if this had been such a good choice, 'cream cakes!' she asked herself, too late now, blobs of sticky cream was spread round the little girls faces, mixed with jam from the doughnuts. When they had drunk the delicious hot chocolate, the Nippy came to Annie's rescue. 'Here we are, Madam, fought you might like ter wipe the kids faces with this damp cloff.' Annie smiled her thanks and cleaned the childrens faces.

The parting had been sad, that was to be expected, but when Joey and Annie promised that they'd be back very soon to see them, this helped.

'I'll come and tell you all about me job' Joey called as the children were led away. Back through big black double doors of the ugly tall grey menacing building, but the woman who met them looked kind and gentle, and it was to her, that Annie and Joey heard the children with excited voices tell of 'the enormous cakes they had eaten.'

The front of the house was in darkness when Annie arrived home with Joey. After she unlocked the front door, Annie told Joey to go up ahead of her. 'Don't look like any ones in up there' she said, 'Just poke your nose in.'

As Joey stepped into the back room, faces appeared from every corner,

'Happy Birthday' they all shouted, and roared with laughter at the look of shock and surprise on Joey's face. He turned back to where his aunt Annie had crept up the stairs behind him. Wagging his finger at her and shaking his head. 'You crafty old, fing you' he said, 'you arranged all this didn't you?'

'Go on in there then.' she gently pushed him into the crowded room. 'Can't start the dancin' till the guest of honour gets his backside in there.'

Joey pulled Annie into his arms, 'Thanks for everyfing, Aunt Annie, I don't know how I'd a got frew all this wiv out you and Uncle George.' He held her close as together they went into the room. The first two faces he saw, were those of his sister Rosie and his brother Matty, grinning from ear to ear.

From that get together, Annie and Betty Smith, decided that they would arrange regular reunions between all the Smith children.

So it was early in December that Annie wrote to her now good friend Betty Smith. Asking if she thought it would be possible, for Betty and Reg to drive Rosie and Matty over to them, on either Christmas day or Boxing day. If they were agreeable she would then contact the orphanage, and arrange a visit for them all with Lily, Violet and Jonny. Annie finished by saying that, although Joey was settling down with them, it was obvious how much he missed his brothers and sisters.

Annie had been over the moon, when she received Betty's swift reply of agreement, and her suggestion that they make it Christmas day, as this would mean more to the children. There remained just the problem of those in charge at the orphanage.

To their delight and surprise though, not only were the orphanage agreeable to the reunion on Christmas day, they made arrangements with the Powley's, for the children to be collected from the home early Christmas morning and allowed them to spend the night. 'No need to bring them back until Boxing Day afternoon' they were told. So now they could spend more time in familiar surroundings and with their separated brothers and sisters.

What a day it was. It started off with the expected tears, not only from the younger ones, but all the adults in attendance. Alf Woogitt had driven George to pick up Lily, Violet and Jonny. They'd left Annie with Joey and Georgie making ready for the onslaught of grown-ups and kids that were going to share a special Christmas day dinner. They moved the sideboard and dining table and chairs, from the back room to the big bedroom come front room. The room was virtually cleared, apart from the big Christmas tree that stood by the window. The winter sun catching the glass of the baubles and making them sparkle like diamonds. Under the tree, they had placed gifts for every child. Jack along with Arthur from next door, went over the road to the Avenue School, where Annie had been given permission to borrow one of their long trestle tables with two bench seats that easily sat seven on either side. The men carried them up the stairs to Annie's flat and arranged them in the back room. Georgie and Joey, under Annie's supervision, laid the table. They set fourteen places, 'fourteen,' Annie quaked, as the sweat rolled down her face even on a crisp December day. 'Please, God I get this right' Cooking for that amount was nothing new to Annie, though. She took her turn at Christmas to have all her family round at her place. The difference this year was that, not was she only having to deal with the feelings of anticipation at seeing all the little ones together again, she was being hostess to people she hardly knew. 'Come on now, Gel' she chided herself, 'you've seen a lot of Sally's mum and dad this past couple of months. Didn't you all get on well and have a lovely time on little Joey's birthday last month. And that Betty and Reg have turned up trumps, you like them. Ah, but what about that sister of Betty's, what's her name, oh yes, Millie, Rosie writes nice things about her, so I guess she must be okay. Trouble is, she sounds a bit posh to me.' Millie had not been able to attend Joey's birthday party as she was recovering from a chest infection. 'Wonder what she'll think about our little house and everyfing.' Annie had no chance to worry any longer, for the sound of a motor car's hooter, made her whip off the flowered pinafore she had been wearing to protect the navy and white new suit she'd bought for this special occasion.

Rosie and Matty came charging up the stairs, after the merest hesitation, Rosie flung herself into her brother Joey's arms. Georgie ruffled Matty's hair and patted his shoulders, before Joey encircled both Rosie and Matty in his arms. They were laughing and crying at the same time. Within minutes of, Reg, Betty and Millie's warm greeting, Annie realised all her fears had been totally unfounded, she and they got on like a house on fire. Millie emptied the big shopping bag full of presents she had brought with her, under the pretty green fur tree, adding to the growing pile of colourful wrappings and bright boxes.

George and Alf arrived home with the little ones. At first, Lily and Violet were overwhelmed, they both stood clutching Jonny's hands. Seven year old Jonny had become their world. He protected them from the other children at the home, who, if he were not there, used to bully the younger girls. These bullies soon found out that, young and little as he was, he could give as good as he got. It was to Jonny that Lily and Violet ran to if one of them had a fall, or when they cried for their mother, or wanted to see Joey, Rosie and Matty. The two little girls felt Jonny's slight withdrawal from the others. They followed his lead. But when Jonny understood that like him and his two little sisters, Rosie and Matty had also been taken to live elsewhere, he didn't feel quite so hard done by. He coaxed Lily and Violet into renewing the closeness and love they had all shared, in spite of the harsh lives they lead under their dad.

Annie had surpassed herself, determined that this Christmas day, still so very close to the day of their mothers funeral, when all the Smith children had last been together, would be a day they would never forget. The trestle table was covered with a crisp white bed sheet, on top of that lay a pretty red tablecloth with green leaves that looked like leaves from a holly tree. Her best cutlery was at each place setting. Her fine china dinner service was at the ready. Only the adults were to eat from these as there was only enough for eight people.

The younger ones would eat their meal from her everyday set. Not that they would notice the difference. The gold and red bon bon's, one for every person sat at the table, added the final touches to the colourful picture.

Georgie had tried to arrange the seating, so that each child sat either next to, or opposite one of their brothers or sisters that they had been separated from, or one of their grand-parents. The three little ones had never seen such a spread. They watched in amazement as 'Uncle George,' carved the enormous turkey he'd just carried in from the kitchen, with Annie following, carrying tureens full to the brim with steaming hot vegetables. When George had piled meat on to the plates, he passed them to Annie, who stacked each one with, crisp roast potatoes, boiled potatoes, sage and onion stuffing, pigs in blankets, carrots, cauliflower and finally Brussel Sprouts. 'I won't pile too much on your plates, you can always help yourself to more but you need to leave room for your Christmas pud' said Annie, and wondered why they all laughed at her.

Three and a half year old Lily, pointed to the bon bon's, 'what's them for?'

'Oops' said Georgie, 'nearly forgot the crackers, Mum. Come on lets all pull them before we eat, cause if we leave it till after, we won't have the strength' he finished on a laugh. Lily, Violet and Jonny, jumped as the bon bon's made their predicted loud crack as they were pulled between two people. But what a joy it was for all the adults to see the childrens faces light up on finding that one half of the cracker contained a coloured paper hat for them to wear, and a little plastic toy to play with. It wasn't just the youngest though that took great pleasure from the crackers, one look at Matty, Rosie and Joey was enough to prove that. Their eyes shone. It did nearly cause an argument between seven year old Jonny and five year old Violet. Inside his cracker, Jonny found a girls ring and he wanted the little blue racing car that Violet had. Calm was restored though by Grandad Bert who also found a racing car as his little surprise. He quickly handed it over to Jonny, who continued to give his sister angry looks, when he thought the others were not looking.

Sticking with tradition, the Christmas pudding was soaked in Brandy, supplied by Millie, before George put a lighted match to it. Annie ran to switch the light off and close the curtains, to get the required effect. The younger children ooed and aared as the purple flames licked the top of the pudding. Then when the flames died, it was served. Annie had placed a new shiny silver thrupenny bit into seven of her every day pudding bowls. The adults had to miss out on this ceremony There came squeals of delight and surprise as each child and that included, Georgie and Joey, minus the squeals, found their shiny coin. Finally, the table was cleared. The washing up being taken on by the men of the gathering and finished in record time, which meant it was time to 'pick the tree'

All throughout the meal, the younger children could not stop their eyes from wandering to where the Christmas tree, stacked with presents stood. They had never seen such a pretty tree, apart from last year, when Annie had taken them see the lights strewn across the roads and round the windows of the big shops along Oxford Street. But the thing they remembered best, was when they went on to Gamages, where they had pressed their tiny noses up against the enormous windows, peering in at all the magical toys and games. The centre piece had been the biggest Christmas tree they had ever seen. Violet had asked Annie if she could have the 'beautiful fairy' standing right at the very top. The wand held in the fairy's hand, had a great big shiny silver star, Violet had see her face in it, just like one of those pretty hand held mirrors she had seen on her aunt Annie's dressing table. Annie had explained to the child that the fairy had to stay on the tree in the window, so that all the other children would be able to come and see it.

As George knelt down on the floor to read the labels on each of the presents, Jonny went and sat on the floor next to him. 'Is them all real?' he asked quietly

'What all these presents do you mean?' queried George,

'Yeah. Is there somefing in all of 'em?'

George looked round the room, a frown on his face, Joey came to his rescue to explain the reason for Jonny's question. 'Our mum used to try ter make our little tree, well it was more of a big twig really,'

Only Annie noticed the look that went between Betty and Reg, a look that spoke volumes to Annie.

'Anyway' continued Joey, 'she'd get lots a boxes and wrap them in coloured paper, big ones to go under the tree, and lots a small ones that she tied to the shoots, she made a real good job of it.'

Reg had to know, 'You did get presents though, didn't you, Joey?'

'Well' he looked at his little sisters, then winked at his grandad, 'Farver Christmas used to leave a toy for all of us.' Joey noticed the look that passed between his fathers mum and dad and it got him wondering if they had sent presents to their grandchildren.

'And he filled our sock up wiv fings, didn't 'e?' continued, Jonny 'Yep, that's right, Jonny he did. And' he smiled at Ida and Bert, 'one of the boxes for each of us and always had a smashin' present in it from nan and grandad Stone.' Then, Joey just knew it, he was right and he felt sad for them and himself and his brothers and sisters. He saw again, his granddad Smith look at his grandmother, as he gently shook his head to his wife, as he knew she was about to ask questions. Milly, Joey saw, reached across the table to pat her sisters hand and mouthed, 'later, Bett.' Ida could have gone over and given Joey a great big kiss for what he had just said. She saw that her Bert had been near to tears. They both felt so helpless, it should be them taking care of their grand-children, not just now but long before the tragedy. Unfortunately, Bert had to give up work more than six years ago, he suffered from angina and was also prone to severe attacks of asthma, being a coalman did nothing for both these diseases. They couldn't give the children much in the way of gifts, but they tried to make up for this with time and love, that is, when Dan allowed visits to take place.

Now though Bert smiled at his youngest grandson, thankful to Annie's suggestion that each of them contribute an amount they could afford towards the buying of a special present for every child. 'Jonny, every single one a those parcels has got a present in it for every one in this room.'

'Cor what even the growed up ones, Granddad?'

'Yeah, Boy, even the growed up ones. honest.' He winked at Joey.

George chose three presents together, he read out the names on the labels tied round them, 'Lily, Violet, Jonny. These are from all your family here, with love.'

Jonny was the quickest to rip all the wrapping paper off. 'it's a racin' car, look Matty, and it's in me bestest colour a red.' Joey proceeded to scrape the car backwards along the floor, then when he let it go, the friction caused it to zoom across the floor, crashing into the feet of any one too slow too move them out of the way. 'Wait till the uvver boys see this back there' enthused Jonny. The grown-ups didn't like that word, 'back there' they all knew where he meant. That awful dingy place that because of their father, was home to the three youngsters.

'Look, Rosie, look what I've got' cried Violet as she held up the big dolly for all to see. 'er eyes open and shut when I move 'er, oh an' look she can move 'er arms an' legs and 'er 'ead turns round.' Violet cuddled the dolly close to her. Her face suddenly taking on a forlorn look, 'she is all mine, ain't she? I ain't gotta put 'er in the toy box 'fore I go ter bed 'ave I?'

Her gran Betty tried to re-assure her 'No darling you don't have to put your new dolly in the toy box, you can take her to bed with you and cuddle her all night. She is all yours.'

'D'yer mean the uvvers can't take 'er?'

'Only if you let them.'

'Well I won't let 'em. She's all mine, you said'

'Careful, Girl, Betty thought to herself' then gently to Violet said 'She is your baby and nobody else's but some of the other little girls may not have been as lucky as you. It might be a nice idea if maybe you could let those that haven't got such a lovely dolly, have just a little cuddle sometimes.'

Violet thought about this for a little while, 'Mmm s'pose so, me mate Liz can anyway.'

All eyes turned to baby Lily, Millie had helped her to unwrap her present. She was just sitting quietly, the little soft and cuddly dolly she had received was held firmly in her grasp. She was rocking the dolly backwards and forwards oblivious to her surroundings. Millie gently touched her arm and whispered to the child, 'Oh, what a pretty dolly, Lily, what are you going to call her?'

Lily rolled her head to one side then the other, as if thinking deeply, then she looked from her dolly to Millie, 'She a ba ba, an me call my ba ba Sue Sue' this brought a smile to the older faces.

'Well, I think that's a pretty name for a pretty baby' finished Millie. Much to Lily's delight. Not to be out done Violet called, so they all would listen, 'My baby's name is Lynn,' then to Millie she said, 'is that a pretty name a well?'

'Oh yes it is, Violet, what clever little girls you are to have chosen such lovely names for your dol... er babies.'

Matty was over the moon with what he received, for Georgie had given him twenty of the lead soldiers he collected. Matty always used to play with them whenever he came to the house. He'd also been given a Meccano set, he couldn't believe his eyes. 'You can make a fort for them to go in' said Reg, 'I'd love to give you a hand makin' one, Son' The women laughed, they knew that would be more for himself than Matty.

Rosie's eyes filled with tears of happiness as she opened the pretty Jewel box, she'd found after removing the wrapping paper. On lifting the lid, she heard the tune of the popular Christmas carol, 'Silent night' she then saw that a tiny ballerina on a little pedestal danced round and round to the music.

'See that drawer on the front' Annie said to her, 'pull it out' Rosie did as she was told, she couldn't believe her eyes, for there inside the drawer was the prettiest silver bracelet she had ever seen. 'Oh thank you, thank you all so much' she cried. Rosie stood up and one by one she kissed them all. Her new found grand parents, auntie Millie, her nan and grandad, George and Annie, she stopped when she got to Georgie, 'Oh what the hell' she thought, and quickly pecked him on the cheek. Even her brothers and sisters were treated to this outward show of affection.

Joey was delighted with the watch, he'd received, he put it on his wrist straight away, fastening the brown leather strap that fitted perfectly. Identical to the watch Georgie had also received, apart from his strap was black. 'Now both of you have got a watch, you've got no excuse for bein' late for your tea on Sunday's.' Annie said to the boys, who looked back at her, more than pleased with their presents. Georgie and Joey still met brothers Siddy and Bernie most weekends over on the school football pitch.

When each of the grown-ups had received their present, to the astonishment of the children, they were each given some more. The girls found new dresses for themselves, even the dollies had different outfits that Lily and Violet could change them into. The boys were given a jumper each. Georgie was more than happy to find, even more of the white shirts he so liked to wear.

'Come on' called George when every last present had gone from under the tree, 'give us a hand to move this table out onto the landing.' This done they lined the benches up against the walls. Annie meanwhile, with the women's help, carried the ready prepared food from the kitchen larder for the buffet they would be eating later, and placed it on the trestle table. Everyone had contributed something, there were sausage rolls, slices of ham, pork and turkey, little chunks of cheese on sticks, some had pickled onions on as well, there was a mound of bread and thanks to, Millie, it was smothered in rich yellow butter. Georgie and Joey carried in the much treasured wind up gramophone, taking care not to drop any of the records that could brake so easily.

'Who's all this other food for?' asked a confused Matty.

'Lots of other people are comin' soon, Boy.'

'Why?' he pressed

'Cos it's Christmas, and we always have a party wiv all our friends and relations, don't worry you'll know all of them. We have a right good ole knees up as well.'

Right on cue, the door knocker banged loudly three times. 'Here comes the first of them.' Finished George. It was no surprise that the first to arrive was young Siddy and Bernie.

What a night they all had, singing and dancing to all the favourite songs, especially knees up mother brown, the kids loved that one. They finished up with George playing his accordion as the others danced the conga and finally the hoke koke. Annie was amazed watching Millie as she did the knees up, catching the skirts of her dress and twirling it side to side, at one point you could even see her long drawers. Millie had noticed Annie watching, she joined her by the trestle table with all the food spread out. 'Phew' she said wiping her brow with a lace edged hankie. 'I haven't enjoyed myself so much for years. I'd forgotten how energetic you had to be to do all those dances' she laughed.

'To be honest, Millie, I was a bit worried that this wasn't your sort of thing.' Annie remarked.

'What! a good ole fashioned Kennington gel like me?'

'What d'yer mean, Kennington gel?' queried Annie in disbelief.

'Don't forget, Annie, that I am Betty's sister. Born and bred in Kennington Park Road. It wasn't until I went into service, when I was fourteen that I moved away and joined the landed gentry.' she laughed 'That's where I met my Stuart, I'll tell you all about it one day if you like.'

Annie most definitely would like. She was even more curious now about this nicely spoken but very likeable lady.

Chapter Seven

Johnny, Violet and Lily

'1937'

In February, a childless couple visited the orphanage where the three youngest Smith children were in care. Mr and Mrs Wilson had come to see whether here they just might find the answer to their years of prayers. After eight years of marriage and failing to have children of their own, they decided to take the first tentative steps in to the unknown world of adoption. The dreary façade of the building only added to the nervous tension they were feeling. Yet when the big double doors were opened by a motherly looking elderly lady, in answer to their knock, with such a friendly smile on her face, they felt more at ease.

Matron and proprietor, Marion Piper-Jones, took them to her office. Over a cup of tea, she quizzed the Wilsons about their home, family, work, income, likes and dislikes, the questions seemed endless. Yet the Wilsons understood the importance of them all. They in return, asked many of the questions that had been going round and round in their heads.

'For instance' Mr Wilson asked, 'do we have total control of the children? or are the welfare people involved throughout?'

Marion Piper-Jones, explained that, in the case of fostering, each child remains in the overall charge of the state. On the other hand, in the case of adoption, the adoptive parents have full control. The child becomes theirs. That is why the process takes far longer than fostering. The authorities need to know that any new family genuinely have a love for children and are prepared to take a child on for life.

The matron had been impressed with the Wilsons, they seemed to be a very caring and gentle couple. 'What say I take you on a guided tour. The children are all at play at the moment. I warn you, it may get a little noisy, but after what some of them have seen in their short lives, letting off a bit of steam at the weekend, can only benefit and start to heal their tortured souls.'

Mr Wilson looked at his wife with raised eyebrows, 'tortured souls' the look said. His wife leaned close to whisper in his ear, 'a bit dramatic' she said, then to herself 'I hope'.

It was Mrs Wilson that first caught sight of the pretty little girl sitting on one end of the see saw. Her long blonde curls were bouncing as she went up and down. She had such an infectious laugh. 'Look at that adorable little girl over there dear' she pointed in the direction of five year old Violet Smith. Matron Piper-Jones, looked to where Mrs Wilson pointed. 'Ah, yes, Our Violet, such a pretty child. Quite well adjusted, considering' she finished.

Mrs Wilson became concerned, 'Considering what? she asked.

'Did you read in the newspapers, the story of a poor family that lived in Camberwell? anyway, the father is in prison awaiting trial for the murder of his wife. Apparently, he beat her to death in front of the children.' She waited for the sharp intake of breath that always followed when she recounted this story to prospective fosterers and adopters.

This time though, the response was not what she was used to. Others would mumble some sort of insincere words of sadness, while moving quickly on to the next child.

'Oh the poor things. You said children, the little girl, Violet you say? she is one of how many?'

'Violet's story is quite involved. Shall we go and sit in the conservatory, out of the cold, and I will try to explain.'

They made their way back into the building, with the sounds of happy laughter of a certain little girl ringing in their ears.

Half an hour later, Matron left the couple to think over what she had told them about the Smith children.

They threw many questions at each other 'Were the three here in care, really the children of the man accused of murder? If so, would he try to get them back if he was found not guilty?' Mrs Wilson voiced her fears.

'Should we first get to know them before we worry about such things. After all, a pretty face is not the most important factor in adoption, is it my dear?'

His wife nodded her agreement. She was staring at the youngsters still on the see-saw. 'I don't know why I didn't see the likeness in the three of them,' she smiled. 'Just look at the youngest, she has such a cheeky face.'

'See how the boy cares for them?' observed Mr Wilson. 'That probably stems from his older brother. From what the Matron says, they were a very close family, and the eldest feels responsible for all of them. That young fellow is trying to be a man well before his time.' Mr Wilson spoke with a growing feeling of compassion for Jonny Smith.

'Before we do anything, Dear, we must seriously think about this. We made a firm decision that if it were at all possible, we would love to adopt a little girl and boy. The boy looks to be about seven and Violet as we know from Matron is five. The ideal ages for us. Could we be the ones to break all their hearts by splitting them up again! Taking two and leaving one.?'

'She is cute, that little one, isn't she?'

Mrs Wilson smiled secretly to herself. Her husband seemed smitten with the baby of this little family. If she had her way she would scoop all three up and run away with them to the car right here and now. 'Look, let us just ask Matron if we can spend some time with them all, they might turn out to hate us on sight.' she finished with a laugh.

Mr and Mrs Wilson turned down Matron's suggestion that she bring the children in to the conservatory to meet them. They preferred to brave the cold February morning and see the children in a relaxed environment.

'I say, Young Man' Mr Wilson in a friendly voice and smiling as he approached Jonny who was pushing the see-saw up and down. 'I've been watching you for ages. How about if you sit up behind one of these young ladies,' Violet giggled at being called a young lady.

'I'm not a young lady, Mister, 'e's me bruvver not a young man'

'Oh right, well then, er, perhaps if you tell me your names that would be better.' Violet went to speak again but before she did, Jonny jumped in with 'Oi, Violet, I'm the oldest 'ere, so I do the talkin'. Me names Jonny mister, and these is me two sisters, you just 'eard me say that ones name.' he poked his tongue out at Violet. 'and this one 'ere' he put a protective arm around his little sister, 'she's the baby of our family, baby Lily.'

'Well how do you do, Jonny.' Mr Wilson spoke formerly to the young boy and held his hand out to shake his hand. Jonny thought this so grown up, he turned to look at both his sisters as he took the outstretched man's hand. 'Now as I was saying, Jonny, you've been doing all the hard work, how about if you jump up behind, er, Lily, I'll give you all a go?'
He could see Jonny wanted to say yes, the boy's face lit up momentarily. But it disappeared as quickly as it came to be replaced with a serious look.

'Are you 'ere to pick a kid to go and live wiv yer?'
Mrs Wilson, who had taken over pushing the see-saw whilst Jonny had been talking to her husband, stopped the movement as she tuned to look at the little boy. 'We are here for that reason, Jonny. We don't have any children of our own, but we dearly would love to. Matron was telling us that your big brother now lives with a new family, is he happy there?'

'Yeah, Joey's lucky, 'e went ta live wiv aunt Annie and uncle George *and* 'is bestest mate Georgie. Them posh people wouldn't let us go wiv 'im though.'

'I bet your Joey would want you three to find a nice family like him.'

'Course 'e do, Lady. But uvver times when people 'ave come 'ere, they only wanna take one of us. The last ones wanted our Lily, but I made sure they didn't. I ain't gonna let 'em split us up.' Jonny finished fiercely.
Intrigued Mr Wilson asked Jonny how he managed that.

'I told Lily to wet 'er drawers. They soon went away.' he said proudly. Instead of shocking the Wilson's, Jonny's outburst just endeared him to them even more.

'Good for you, Jonny.' Mr Wilson patted him on the shoulder.

'Push push,' said Lily, bored with all this talking.

'Oops, I think someone is getting fed up' laughed Mr Wilson. 'Come on, Jonny jump on, all I'm offering at the moment is to give you all a ride. okay?'
They went from the see-saw, to the slide to the swings, by now Jonny was beginning to feel comfortable with these two nice people. He allowed Mr Wilson to push him on the swing.'igher, 'igher' he called. For a while all thoughts of being big brother to Violet and Lily forgotten, as he reverted back to being a normal eight year old boy. When the time came for the Wilson's to go home, it was to three woebegone faces they said goodbye.

'Will yer come and see us agen?' Violet asked

'Shut-up Vi, wot's the use a them comin' agen, it ain't no good getting' ter like 'em, they can't take all of us ta live wiv 'em.' finished Jonny solemnly.

'Can't we just come and get to know you all better, maybe take you out somewhere?' Mrs Wilson spoke with feeling.

'If yer promise that yer ain't doin' it, just so's yer can get round me, and after a while try ter split us up.'

'We give you our word, Jonny. We will never split the three of you up.'

Just then Lily took Mrs Wilson's hand. 'I like you, Lady' she said smiling up into her face.

Jonny knew just what his baby sister meant. They did seem nice. 'Okay then, if yer promise, I s'pose it'd be okay fer yer ter come agen.' he capitulated.

And so that is how it came about that two months later, at Easter, Georgie along with the six Smith children were heading for Kennington Park. They were all in good spirits and still had the taste of the smashing dinner of pie and mash that Georgie and Joey had run to the Walworth Road for earlier. Georgie carried Lily most of the way, that was until she saw the paddling pool, she wriggled out of his arms and ran to the edge. It was a lovely spring afternoon, many families were sitting round the pool in deckchairs they had carried from home, watching their children. The little girls tucked their dresses into the elastic round the legs of their knickers as they splashed about. The boys, with some dads taking control, were sailing their little toy boats. Every so often there would be screams and tears when a boat capsized and sunk.

Rosie carried an old towel that Annie had given her. She knew that there was no way the younger ones could walk straight past the pool. 'Just in case gel' she'd said to Rosie. For the next two hours *all* of them had a really good time. The older ones using the little ones as an excuse, to do all the silly things they did. They went from the paddling pool to the playground, they took turns in pushing each other on the swings, the boys trying to see who could get nearest to going over the top. They went on the slide and on the big umbrella, Lily didn't like the umbrella, a couple of boys pushed it too high for her, but Joey made sure she was safe, he held on to her tightly. It was a very tired two little girls that returned to Annie and George's home that day. Whilst the youngsters had been out, the adults had taken the opportunity to discuss the future with the Wilsons. Both sets of grandparents were there, along with Millie and Annie and George. Mr and Mrs Wilson realised that 'these were good people' as he and his wife tried to reassure them all that they had fallen in love with Jonny, Violet and Lily, and they wanted to become mummy and daddy to all three. It was quite clear that the children were becoming very fond of them. Especially as Jonny now knew that he and his little sisters would not be parted.

'We couldn't have asked for a nicer couple to adopt the little ones' said grandad Bert, wiping a stray tear from his eye. As they all stood on the pavement waving as the Wilsons drove Jonny, Vi and Lily back to the care home. Understandably there had been many tears from the three youngsters. However nice and caring the Wilsons were, nothing could replace their own flesh and blood.

'Are we really gonna live wiv you for *ever*?' Jonny asked Mr Wilson incredulously.

'Well, I'd say until you are at least twenty, when by then you might be fed up with us as fussy old parents and decide to move out.'

'I ain't never gonna leave yer'

'That sounds good to me, but can we try saying it this way, Jonny?' persuaded Mr Wilson. 'try it like this, *I am never going to leave you.* don't you think it sounds better?'

'S'pose so, our Rosie talks all posh now. She might like it if I do to. Right ready, 'ere I go, *I am never gonna leave you*, how's that?'

'Very good, my, but aren't you a quick learner.' he praised the boy. Jonny beamed from ear to ear.

'Are you all packed?' he hesitated slightly before adding that little word that can mean the world, 'Son?'

'Yep, Matrons lookin' after me stuff. D'yer know just now, when you called me son, did yer mean it proper like, cos me Uncle George calls me that sometimes, but I ain't, or s'pose I mean I'm not 'is son am I?'

'When I said it, Jonny, I meant it in the true sense of the word.'

'What d'yer mean, true sense?'

'Well, I meant that when I used the word son, I meant it as just that, *my* son. I hope it doesn't upset you, for we are still getting to know each other.'

'No, I liked it. Will Vi and Lily be your daughters?'

'You bet they will. Now come on my son and lets go and see if those daughters of mine and your mummy have finished getting all the girls bits and bobs together.' He took hold of his sons hand and went in search of the rest of their family. Jonny was looking round, hoping that some of the others in the home could see him now. Many of the older boys had not been very nice to the Smith children, they used to call them silly names, all because of the terrible thing that their dad did. 'Huh' Jonny thought, 'I've got a new dad now, one that even 'olds me 'and, me real dad never ever done that.'

They met Mrs Wilson, who was holding tightly onto Lily and Violets hands, in the Matrons office. Each of the children's belongings was neatly packed in brown carrier bags. They wore the new clothes that their new mummy and daddy had given to them the day before.

'Well, I must say, all three of you look very smart.' commented Matron Piper-Jones. 'Now you be good children for Mr and Mrs Wilson.'

Jonny looked pensive, 'How will people know that you're our new mum and dad, cos your names Wilson and ours is Smiff?'

'Would you like to be called, Jonny Wilson?' asked his new daddy.

'I don't mind, but I fink I'd keep forgetting. Can't you two be called Mr and Mrs Smiff?'

The three grown-ups smiled at each other, 'bright boy I've got here' thought Mr Wilson, before thinking of answer. 'Thing is, Son, because we are a lot older than you, and we know lots of people, and things like our bank, work, and oh all manner of things. It would be difficult for us to change our name now.' Jonny thought about this for a while, then he turned to his sisters and said 'from now on, your names is Violet and Lily Wilson, got that?' Both girls nodded, neither of them having a clue as to what their brother was on about.

'We have to wait a while longer Jonny before we legally become your parents, but it won't hurt for you all to start practising your new name.'

'You are gonna be our mummy and daddy though ain't yer?' he asked in a scared voice. He liked it when he said mummy and daddy. Some of his old friends from John Ruskin School called their mum and dad that, and they were the ones who had really nice dads who didn't hit them or their mums.

'You bet we are' answered Mrs Wilson. 'that's why the welfare people are letting you come to live with us now instead of waiting until next month, when all the legal bits and pieces have been finalised.

In fact it was a situation that suited all the departments involved. The authorities didn't expect to find any couple willing to adopt three children, let alone a couple so obviously suited to the sometime trials and tribulations of adoption.

So, after saying their goodbyes to the Matron, the three children piled into the back of the Wilsons motor car. Lily and Violet clutched a dolly in each of their arms. In one they held the tiny rag dolls that their brother Joey had bought for them, such a long time ago. In the other arm they cuddled the 'babies' that had been under the Christmas tree at aunt Annie's and uncle George's. Jonny kept his bright red friction racing car in the pocket of his new trousers.

It was fitting that the sun was shining as the new family unit arrived at their home to begin such a big adventure for them all. Although the children had visited the house before, they couldn't control the excitement that was welling up. As soon as they stepped inside they made their way to the back door. Keen to go and play in the lovely back garden. The first thing Violet saw was a swing at the back and standing next to it a slide. Mr Wilson was quite proud as he watched all three take turns in coming down the slide, pleased to see that all his efforts in making it were going to be worthwhile.

The Wilson's were not hiding their heads in the sand, they realised that there would be some stormy times ahead. He and his wife hadn't had much practise at this parenting game. And from all they'd learnt about the childrens backgrounds, they didn't have much experience of living in a normal family. He laid his arm across the shoulders of his wife, 'Well mum, this is it, no turning back now. Any regrets?'

'*Regrets*? I've never felt so happy in all my life. Whatever comes along, we'll work it out together, as a family, *dad*'

Shortly after the children moved in with them, the Wilsons, after a lot of soul searching decided that the children were still young enough to forget all about their lives before going to the orphanage, even Jonny who turned eight in February. Jonny and Violet sometimes asked about Joey, Rosie and Matty, but they accepted the answers their mummy and daddy gave them, that Joey was very busy at work and Rosie and Matty were helping their gran and grandad in the big garden they had, that took so much time up.

So, it was with this in mind, that Mrs Wilson wrote to the Matron of the home. Asking that if Mrs Powley should be in contact, would the matron be so kind as to pass on the enclosed letter. For she and her husband would prefer if their address were not given to anyone.

Mrs Wilson wrote,

Dear Mrs Powley   I will be in touch after the children have settled down in their new home. Both me and my husband think it best not to take the children to Eynsford in July, as they were very upset at Easter, when they had to say goodbye to their brothers and sister. So we think it best to wait until we will possibly bring them to the Christmas get together at your home.

Yours faithfully Mrs E Wilson.

As Annie did not have an address for the Wilson's, she went to see the Matron. Annie wanted to make sure that the children could still go down to Eynsford next month to enjoy a holiday with all the family. But to her amazement she was three weeks too late. Matron explained that the adoption was being speedily finalised, and how fortunate the Smith children were to have found such a wonderful couple willing to take all three of them on. Annie asked if Matron could give her the address so that she could get in touch with the Wilsons telling them of the exact date they were going.

'When Mr and Mrs Wilson came to us with the children at Easter,' Annie explained, in her 'airs and graces' voice as she put it,   'they said they thought it was a good idea for them all to keep in touch as much as possible. So I'm quite sure they'll be coming.

Mind you it's been a bit of a shock to find out they left here weeks ago. Mrs Wilson never said a word about the adoption might go frew so fast. I thought she would have wrote me a letter, just so we know the kiddies are alright.' Annie finished.

'I do understand how you feel, Mrs Powley, but unfortunately I have given my word that I will not give the address of the Wilson family to anyone. I think that they have a fear of the father changing his mind about their parentage and if he were acquitted, he might wish to find them. I tried my best to re-assure them that this could not happen, that he relinquished all parental rights. But possibly all is not as bad as it appears my dear.' Matron opened a drawer of her desk and extracted an un-opened envelope, 'you see, Mrs Wilson asked me to pass this on to you at your next visit.' she finished with a smile as she handed Annie the note.

Two days after Annie had been given that note, she along with Rose and Mary decided that they would do a bit of Police work. Annie remembered Mrs Wilson telling her that her Mother-in-law lived in Freemantle Street, that lay between the Lane and the Old Kent Road, as did her husband up until the day they got married. So, between them the three sisters were prepared to knock on every door in the road until they found a Mrs Wilson. Rose and Mary, met Annie after she'd finished cleaning the Doctors surgery. The ladies walked with determination down virtually the whole length of East Street Market, luckily still being quite early, the lane wasn't too busy. They turned right into Exon Street just before East Street met Old Kent road, this led directly into Freemantle Street. They could see that most of the houses were well cared for, they had neat little front gardens, with pebbles marking out the front paths that had little triangular tiles of red and green, giving an impression that the inhabitants were comfortably off. This made their task easier, if they had knocked on doors in some of the roads in Camberwell and Walworth and asked the occupier if they knew so and so, they would have more than likely received an earful of abuse. Always suspicious of any one they didn't know knocking at the door. For all they knew they might be from the landlord, or been sent by the loan shark trying to recover monies lent. But in this nice tree lined quiet road, no curtains twitched in response to Annie and the others knocks. It only took them fifteen minutes before Rose called over to her sisters, 'Annie, Mary,' she beckoned to them with a wave of her hand.

'This nice lady says that Mrs Wilson lives next door, but she reckons that Mrs Wilson is away at the moment. Isn't that right love?' Rose turned to the elderly lady standing in her doorway, with a duster in her hand.

'That's right' she answered, 'her son and his wife have gone to live in the country with a cousin of Evie, she's my neighbour Mrs Wilsons daughter-in-law.'

'Has Mrs Wilson got more than one son then?' asked Annie, an uncomfortable feeling setting in.

'Oh no Dear just her Michael, mind you, she's near ready to pop with happiness at the moment'

'Why's that?' Mary wanted to know.

'Well,' she leant towards the ladies and spoke just above a whisper, 'her Michael and Evie, couldn't have kiddies of their own.' Annie felt as if her heart was stopping. 'Shame, because they loved children so much, anyway, bless their hearts, they've gone and adopted *three,* a boy and two little girls. What pretty children too, lots of blonde hair and bright blue eyes. Ah, they make such a lovely sight. My neighbour, Mrs Wilson, is over the moon, that's where she is at the moment, helping the new family to settle in.'

'Do you have their new address?' Annie asked hopefully,

'No sorry, Love. Why don't you call again in a few weeks, she should be back by then.'

Annie wrote her address down on a piece of paper, and handed it to the helpful woman.

'When Mrs Wilson comes back would you mind givin' her this, it's my address, maybe she'd be good enough to either write to me or pass it on to her son and daughter-in-law, they might have lost it.' The woman took it from Annie and told her she would pass it on as soon as Mrs Wilson came back home. They thanked the woman for her help. Annie had a sinking feeling that they might not be able to find out where the children had moved to. If Mrs Evie Wilson had wanted them to know, she would have written.

When by November Annie had not received a letter from any of the Wilson's, she paid a return visit to Freemantle street. On getting no reply at Mrs Wilson's house, she once again knocked on the next door neighbours house. The neighbour remembered her at once. She remarked how surprised she was to see her again. 'Didn't she write to you then, Dear?, only I passed on your address to her. But soon after Mrs Wilson returned from the visit to her family, a removal lorry turned up one day 'and I've not see hide nor hair of her since' the old lady finished.

Chapter Eight

Rosie and Matty

'1938'

'Oh I am so excited, Auntie Millie' said thirteen year old Rosie, to the elderly woman who had become very special to her. 'It seems years instead of just seven months since I saw Joey and Georgie. Just think, for a whole week, we're all going to be together. See how the sun shines.' She continued as she pulled the curtain back from the window.

'Yes, Child' Millie smiled at her sisters grand-daughter. Thinking back to the day two years ago, this Saturday just passed. What a sad and sorry sight they made as she had gone to welcome them, on hearing her brother-in-laws car pull up on the gravel on the driveway. Their tear stained little faces staring out through the window at the back of the car. Young Rosie gripping Matty by the hand. Millie smiled to herself, 'I'll never forget the way she put me in my place when I bent to give them a welcome kiss, and I made that terrible mistake of calling them, Rosemary and Matthew. Well if looks could kill, I'd not be here today. "My name is Rosie and my bruvvers name is Matty. Please remember that." And she stormed into the house dragging poor confused Matty with her. Look at her now, she thought, she's clever, articulate, very generous and oh so pretty.'

Rosie interrupted Millie's memories 'You've got a silly look on your face, what were you thinking about?'

'Oh just remembering a certain little girl when she first arrived here with her little brother in tow, showing such spunk and courage and I might add, just a touch stubborn.' she smiled over the last remark.

'Well I didn't know you then did I? Nor gran and gramps really. You were all wicked people to me, taking us away from Joey and the others.' Rosie went across to the older woman and she put her arms round her and kissed her cheek. 'I know better now though,' continued Rosie. 'you have all given us nothing but your time and your love.'

Millie held her close and returned the kiss. 'You know, My Dear, when my beloved Stuart passed on, he left a huge gap in my life who would have thought that it would be filled by a couple of young scallywags. You and Matty have given me a new lease of life, something very precious to live for. Oh my, aren't we getting all sentimental?' she laughed. 'Come on let's go and wait for them outside.' Arm in arm, they made their way to the front door. Just as they reached it, Matty came tearing through the garden gate. 'whats the time now?' he called.

'Five minutes later than the last time you asked young, Man. Your aunt Annie said in her letter to expect them about two thirty, I repeat *about* two thirty, it's only a couple of minutes past, they'll be here soon.' Millie smiled at Matty, thinking how he'd also changed in the two years. Not just in looks but character. He'd turned from a introverted, shy skinny little thing, into this sturdy, confident, cheeky and against all the odds, extremely intelligent eleven year old who'd settled, without any fears, at the local boys grammar school a few weeks ago.

Matty had been running up and down the road for the last half an hour, Impatient, for their special visitors to arrive. 'They will come, won't they?' he questioned his aunt Millie. For how ever happy he and Rosie were living here, their other family, and that includes the Powley's, are of equal importance to them. 'Of course they will, Mat, you know what they say, "a watched pot never boils"

'Hang on' said Matty, as he strained his ears, 'I can hear a car engine.' With that he belted off up the road again, leaving his sister and aunt smiling after him. Rosie automatically put her fingers to the bright blue ribbon in her hair and pushed a loose strand behind her ears, she straightened the blue skirt she was wearing, and brushed her hands over the crisp white blouse. This did not miss the attention of Millie, who just gave a discreet smile of knowing.

Reg and Betty Smith were just finishing making up the spare beds. The extra bedding had been washed and aired ready for the arrival of their week long quests. They were giggling like young school children instead of Betty being in her sixtieth year and Reg already having reached sixty one. They moved this bed here and that bed there. 'To me' Reg would say, in manoeuvring one of the mattresses, 'no, to me a bit' laughed Betty. They too were looking forward to the time when George turned his new Morris Minor motor car onto the drive.

'I can't believe how well things have worked out with the children. Do you know, Reg? I find it hard to remember what it was like before they came to live with us. How all three of us sat and talked things over. How our lives would change with two youngsters in the house. Things you and me would have to give up, how your wages would have to stretch to the needs of growing kids.' Reg joined in as Betty laughed. 'Oh my, and how our lives have changed' she finished.

'You could say that, Love. I feel like a kid agen meself. I can't wait to get home from work in case I might be missing something.' Reg worked at Eynsford railway station. He'd been lucky, in that shortly after applying for a transfer from the busy London Bridge station, a vacancy had arisen at Millie's local station, no more than a ten minute walk away from this beautiful house that Reg and Betty now shared with her.

'And what a change in Millie, she said she doesn't have the time now to sit on all those committees, and there's no more evenings of bridge and boring coffee mornings. Thank goodness for that, I never could get used to all those snooty women coming here most days in the week. That's why I always offered to make the refreshments, so's that I could keep out of the way most of the time in the kitchen.'

'And I don't have to do all the fetching and carrying for every Tom, Dick or Harry or should I say Harriet! They only use jumble sales and the like to get rid of all their rubbish they couldn't be bothered to chuck away. Cor blimey, call themselves *ladies*, you saw some of the dirty old cloves they just chucked in them sacks. I reckon they used to let their dogs use them to lie on. Not fit for anyone however bad their situation notice how none of them ever asked why their stuff wasn't on the stalls to sell. All show a lot of them are. Glad your Millie don't have much to do wiv the likes of them no more.'

'It's funny how Rosie sorted the good eggs from the bad though. She's more than happy to muck in for a good cause if it's one of the genuine ones in the village that needs Millie's help. I still can't get over how much Rosie reminds me of Millie when she was the same age, not just in looks, although, when you look at that picture of Millie before she left home, they could be mistaken for twins. Our Rosie's got her head screwed on, just like my Millie did. She's gentle and caring, yet not afraid to stand up for herself. And woe betide anyone who upsets any of her family and friends. I can't believe how lucky we were that they both settled down so quickly with us three old codgers.' laughed Betty.

'Yeah me neither. I suppose with them being that bit older, they was just happy to be with people that cared about them. And the fact that they knew we'd never keep them from Joey and the littluns. They trust us gel, and they learnt in no time to love us as much as we love all our grand-kiddies. Mind you, Bett, it still makes you wonder how, wiv her years of living with that man, Rosie's turning into such a young lady, and clever wiv it.'

'She's definitely a throw back to our Millie. Look what *she's* done wiv her life. Our dad were nothing like *Dan*, but we was really poor, yet to hear Millie talk you'd think she had always come from a well to do background.'

'Yeah you're right there.....hold on, Gel, listen....thought so, that's our Matty shouting, they must be here.'

As the car was coming to a halt, Matty was already reaching for the door handle. 'About time too. I've been waitin' ages.' he called. Then he noticed that Joey and Georgie were not in there. His grandad was sitting with his uncle George in the front and his nan was with aunt Annie in the back seats. When he got the door open he asked confused 'where's Joey and Georgie?'

'Don't panic, Son' replied his grandad Bert, 'they'll be here in a tic'

Rosie had joined them along with Millie. When Annie saw the look of horror on Rosie's face, she quickly began to explain. 'Georgie's got a surprise for you all, so he told us to get here first. Now do you mind movin' out of the way, so's that me and your nan here can get out?' Betty called from the upstairs window 'kettle won't be long, smashin' to see you all agen.'

As they were all hugging and kissing hello on the drive, there came the roar of a motorbike engine, they all looked to the road just as Georgie with pillion rider Joey turned into the drive.

Immediately Matty left the welcoming celebrations and ran over to Georgie. 'Cor, when did you get this?' Totally ignoring the brother he hadn't seen for five months.

'Oi, what about me?'

'Oh, sorry, Joey, 'ello, 'ow are yer?'

'Excuse me, Young Man' interrupted Millie 'did you or did you not ask me to help you with your diction? 'ello 'ow 'are yer' she mimicked. Everyone laughed.

'Oh yeah sorry, Auntie Mill but look at this bike, it's smashin''

'Glad you like it, Matty. I might just take you for a little ride on it later.'

'Cor honest, Georgie? What make is it?'

'It's a Triumph, one a the best.'

'Come on now, Boys. We haven't come all this way to talk about bikes as soon as we get here. There'll be plenty of time for all that later.'

'Here here, well said, George.' congratulated Millie.

The hugs and kisses started again as soon as they walked into the house to the waiting Betty and Reg. Rosie had somehow ended up in between Joey and Georgie, who both took hold of one of her hands, swinging them as they walked. 'It's so good to see you, Joey' she said to her brother.

'What about me then' said Georgie, 'are you pleased to see me as well?' he looked straight into her eyes.

'Course I am' Rosie could feel herself blushing and lowered her head 'You didn't give me a chance to say so' she finished bravely.

'Well that's okay then. You look different somehow.' Georgie said as he scrutinised the top of her head.

'She's growing up' intervened Annie, 'make yourself useful, come and pull these new boots off me feet, they're pinchin' me' Rosie gave Annie a smile, 'thank you' it said.

'Two vehicle family now then eh, George?'

'Got to let them do their own thing sometime Reg. Mind you,' he leant forward so that only Reg could hear him, 'Annie was none too pleased the day our Georgie rode it home. She don't rest at night till she hears him ride the bike to the back of the house.'

Everyone had been looking forward to this week together for months. George, Reg, Georgie and Joey, were lucky enough to book their annual weeks holiday for the same time. Millie and Betty had been busy discussing which places to visit. For the rest of today though and tomorrow, would be a time for the men to relax, either down the pub or just idling away the hours in the garden. The women, however, had geared themselves up for a mammoth gossip. What the younger ones would choose to do would be left entirely up to them.

They ate a light salad for tea sitting in the garden, taking advantage of the still warm, early July evening. 'Listen to that' remarked George.

'Listen to what?' asked his wife

'Silence, nothing but a few birds singing. I could get used to this way of life.' he finished on a long sigh.

'Go on you daft old bugger, we'd have to get up at four in the mornin' to get to work' They all laughed at Annie's tongue in cheek answer.

Annie wanted this evening to be one where they all just enjoyed each others company. Renewing the friendships and the family ties. They certainly did that, with games of cards and Monopoly, they listened to the wireless and finished the evening off with Georgie showing them how well he could now play the accordion. Taught by his dad of course, which George made sure they were aware of. Tomorrow would be time enough for them to discuss the more serious matters.

Annie confided in Millie, that she and George had some news that might affect Rosie and Matty. She explained that Joey felt he should speak to his brother and sister without the grown-ups there. So, after breakfast, the four youngsters took themselves off for the morning down to the ford, armed with fishing nets, cricket bat and ball and Georgie's old football that held memories of another field another year. Matty carried *the* most important thing, a picnic hamper containing enough food and pop to last them for days.

Joey let Matty walk on ahead with Georgie, he could hear them discussing the ins and outs of Georgie's motorbike. He was grateful to Georgie for making it possible for him to talk to Rosie by herself.

'Tell me, Rosie' he started, 'are you and Matty *really* happy living here?'

'Why, Joey, is there something wrong?'

'*No*, nothing wrong, it's just that you're me kid brother and sister and I can't help but feel I should be doin' more for you.'

'Look, Joey, none of us could've stopped what happened to our mum. We were all too young. But in answer to your question, well, more than anything, I wish we could all be together, but that's all down to *him*. I wish he was the one that was dead' Rosie spoke with all the hurt and anger that was always bubbling away just below the surface.

'We all wish that, Kid.' responded Joey as he put his arm round his sisters shoulders 'If it wasn't for him disowning me, Jonny. Vi, and baby Lily, we wouldn't have all bin split up.'

'I wonder where they are now. At least Matty and me get to spend Christmas and holidays with you. And we write to each other all the time. We don't even know if they're safe and well.' Rosie began to cry softly.

Georgie turned to look back and saw how upset she was. He wondered if Joey had told her his news, and she hadn't liked what she'd heard. Whatever the reason, he turned to Matty, who was unaware of the scene behind him. 'Hey, Matt, what say you and me run on ahead and get a quick kick about in. Cos your Rosie don't mind cricket but she's not so keen on football is she?' Matty thought that a great idea, Georgie still played for the 'Hamlet,' and he was the best footballer Matty had ever seen.

Rosie composed herself, 'Joey' she began hesitantly, 'would it be bad of me if I said that I was happy, would I be letting you and the others down, being selfish like?'

'Course you wouldn't. Does that mean then that you are, come on be honest.'

'Well, yes I am happy. Gran and Gramps couldn't do more for us. They really love us, they're not doin' this because they thought it was the right thing to do. I've heard them talkin' when they thought I was in bed asleep. D'you know, they used to send mum money?'

'I thought that was the case. From just some of the looks they gave each other, when ever we talked about how bad things used to be. I think *he* managed to get his hands on most of that as well. Poor ole mum. But that was then, this is now, this is our future. Does Matty think the same as you?'

'Are you kidding. Sometimes I think he doesn't even remember what it was like before. No, that's not quite true, but Joey, you should see him, he's a changed boy. He laughs a lot, he's made so many new friends, *and* he can bring them back to the house, Millie's always saying 'the more the merrier.' If I'm honest I'd say that we've all changed, and for the better. Us three really are so very lucky. Aunt Annie and Uncle George think the world of you, mind you, they always have. And me and Matty have got three wonderful people spoiling us rotten.'

'You don't know what it means to me, to hear you say that. But I promise you, Rosie, one day we'll all be together agen.'

They continued on their way until they reached the field where Matty was trying to get the ball away from Georgie, who could dribble a ball as good as Stanley Matthews, or so, Matty thought, and when Joey told him his news he started jumping up and down and whooping with glee, the others looked on in astonishment. It was Rosie who asked the question 'Good to know that you think it's a good idea, Matty, and you're not upset' 'Course it's good. If Joey is my, bruvver, and he's Georgie's, bruvver, then that means that Georgie is my bruvver as well. When he's a First Division player, I'll get to meet all me hero's.'

Back at the house, when they were all enjoying a cool drink, George, with Annie's approval, decided the time was right to tell those gathered of their news. When there was a lull in the conversation, he coughed to clear his throat. 'Me and Annie have got a bit of good news to tell you. Well it's good news for us, and we hope that you think the same. Before I tell you it though, I just want to say a few things. We've come to think of you five as more than just friends, we think of you as family. Same as we do with all the kiddies. You was wiv me in court for Dan's trial, Reg, Bert, and I know like me you'll never forget or forgive him for what he said that day.' Betty reached across and took her husbands hand in hers as George continued. 'He knows and we know it was a pack of filfy lies. All of them kids are his, not just Rosie and Matty, clever bastard, oh sorry....' he looked at Dan's parents

'Don't apologise, George' said Reg, 'we've called him far worse than that, I can tell you. Don't worry about hurting our feelin's, we disowned him a long time ago.' He turned to Betty who nodded her head slowly. 'It's a terrible thing to say, George, but he's no son of ours. Carry on with what you were saying.'

'I was gonna say, how clever he was and how quickly he came up wiv it. He still had poor Sally's blood on his hands when he told the police that he'd done it cos, he'd found out that four of kids weren't his. I suppose you'd call it lucky that Rosie and Matty are dark haired like him, whereas Joey and the younger ones are fair headed. And we all know who the jury believed don't we, even after they'd listened to little Joey give his evidence.'

'That was because they were all men' interrupted Millie. 'If that jury had been made up of wives and mothers he would have swung. But no, they found him not guilty of first degree murder, instead the judge gives him a sentence of fifteen years, a crime of passion indeed. Oh I'm sorry George, it just makes me so mad, the thought that he could turn up here one day and claim rights to his children.'

'Don't worry on that score, Gel, the kiddies'll be grown up themselves, they'll never want anyfing to do wiv him. Not after what they all saw that night, they won't forget that. Anyway what you said just then Millie, brings me to what me and Annie have been trying to get the courage up to tell you. Last April, we got notice that our application to legally adopt young Joey was accepted and as of two weeks ago we got a new son and our Georgie the brother he's always wanted.'

The room became silent each thinking their own thoughts. Betty was the first to recover, she let go her husbands hand and stood up, she then held her arms out towards Annie and George.

'We all knew it was on the cards, come here both of you, congratulations' she said as she embraced them. 'Do you really mean it?' asked a concerned Annie, 'You know we loved him like he was our own before all this happened.'

'The way I look at it is that we've not lost a grand-son, we have gained one along with an adopted son and daughter.' At Betty's words, Annie looked at Ida and Bert, what about them?

'I couldn't agree more, Bet'. At last Bert spoke up, 'One big 'appy family that's what we are. I don't mind sayin' that a ways back me and Ida was worried that we'd lose *all* our grand-kiddies. But you've never left us out of their lives. You include us in evry'fing, for that we fank you with all our 'earts.'

'I think this calls for something a bit stronger than orange juice.' suggested Millie, 'Lets all take a stroll down to the Plough, it should be opening about now.'

'When we get there, I have something to show you' said Annie, 'Do you think we'll bump into the youngsters, Millie?'

'I would think so, they are probably just about ready to tuck into the picnic. Talking about picnic's, is that why Joey along with Georgie has gone off with Rosie and Matty, is he going to tell them the news him self?'

'Yes' answered George, 'Joey thought it best that way. He wanted to make sure they understood that it makes no difference to their relationship.'

It didn't take long to find the three boys and one girl, sitting on the riverbank. Rosie had laid a check tablecloth on the grass and arranged the sausage rolls, sandwiches and chicken drumsticks on a plate for each of them.

'When we've had a drink in the pub' called Reg, we'll come and join you for a while before we go back to have something to eat.'

'We could save you some of this if you like' Rosie called back 'we've far too much'

'You speak for yourself' chimed in Matty.

'Don't worry, Matt, ours is all ready and waiting for us back home.' laughed Reg.

In the background Joey gave a thumbs up sign to George, signalling that he had told Rosie and Matty his news and that they had taken it well.

When they were all gathered together sitting on the rivers edge at Eynsford ford, Annie took an envelope out of her handbag. 'I thought I'd wait until we'd all had time to enjoy being together again before I showed you these.' She produced from the envelope half a dozen photographs. She handed two over to Reg, Betty and Millie, two to Ida and Bert and the last two she gave to Rosie for her and Matty to look at. There were gasps as they all stared in wonder at the three figures staring back at them. Ida was the first to find her voice, 'I don't believe it' she said, 'look at them, look 'ow much they've grown.'

'They look so happy' came the view of a proud yet sad grand-father 'When did you get these photo's, Annie?'

'They arrived on Monday, Reg. And before you ask, no, I still haven't got a clue where they are.'

'Did the envelope have the same London postmark on it?' enquired Millie.

'Yep, so they're still using this friend of theirs to send letters and that on to us.'

'I still don't see why though, what good did it do by takin' them away from us? said Joey, 'look at us, we don't live togevver no more, but it ain't affecting us is it?' he couldn't help, nor care about reverting to his old way of speaking, 'we're all doin' okay.'

'We know how you feel, Joey lad' said his new dad, 'but Mr and Mrs Wilson, thought at the time it was the right thing to do. They reckoned the littluns got too upset after the get together last year when they had to go home wivout you three.'

'I know this sounds a bit daft, but are there any clues in the photo's, that maybe we could work out which part of the country they're in. Let me take a closer look? Millie studied the picture of Lily, Violet and Jonny, but all she could see in the background were flowers and trees, and what looked like a rope swing hanging from one of the trees. 'No, I think these were taken in a garden.'

'Jonny looks ever so much like you now, Joey' observed Bert.

'And our Violet is nearly as tall as him.' added Betty.

'Do you think they'll have forgotten us, Gran'

'Of course not, Rosie Love, I didn't see my Millie here for four years when she went into service, but we never stopped thinking about each other.' She smiled at her sister.

'The main thing we have to think about, is that they all look happy and well cared for. Them smiles on their faces are real enough. That Mrs Wilson also wrote a note'

'What does she 'ave to say, Gel' asked Bert

Annie unfolded the piece of paper that had been wrapped around the photographs and started to read the contents out loud.

'Dear Mrs Powley,
Lily, Violet and Jonny are well and very happy.
They've settled in at school and made lots of friends.
They have brought a ray of sunshine into our lives.

Please forgive us for moving away, we thought it was for the best. They are young enough to put the terrible thing that happened behind them given time. We hope that their sister Rosie and brothers Joey and Matty are well and settled in their new homes. If you are still in contact please pass these pictures on to them. I will send more next year, via my friend in London, so that you can see how well they are.

Kind Regards Mrs Wilson.'

No one spoke for what seemed an age. Annie took the initiative, 'Come on now. At least we all know that they are alright and it's obvious that Mr and Mrs Wilson think the world of them. Don't forget, there's not many would take on three kiddies. So let's have no more of these long faces, Matty show me how to catch fishes with this net of yourn.'

There was just one thing that worried Rosie about what Joey had told her today. He'd said that he'd changed his name. He was going to be called Joseph Smith-Powley. 'Did that mean that Georgie would be her brother now?' she was confused. 'Can you marry an adopted brother?'

The week passed too quickly for them all. Today was their last full day together. By eight in the morning the two cars were loaded with deck chairs, a foldaway table, bottles of water, tea, sugar, milk and the primus stove, on which they would be able to boil the water to make plenty of cups of tea. The best part though, would be when the breakfast was being cooked. The smell of frying bacon, eggs and sausages in the open air was nearly as good as when the time came for eating it. Last night they had all, without exception, chosen the place they most wanted to visit for a second time this week, to spend the last day. 'Dymchurch,' came the unanimous shouts when the vote was taken. Georgie left the motorbike at the house. So they all piled in the cars. Reg's car was able to sit six comfortably, as the front seat was a bench seat. That left four to travel with George. Both drivers were proud of their cars, for en route they passed many others whose engines had over heated in the hot July sun.

They drove through the High Street at Dymchurch passing the small fairground that later they would all walk back to. Matty rubbed his hands together in anticipation. When they were here the other day, he'd managed to spend most of his pocket money. It was riding on the ghost train again that he was looking forward to best of all. They travelled on for no more than half a mile to where they preferred to park the cars. The sign read, 'St. Mary's Bay' here for a small fee you could drive the car along the dirt track with grass areas for parking either side. Reg and George chose the left side where the ground was flat and there was plenty of room. The other side was banked and if you weren't careful, you could easily tip out of your deck chair. It did have the advantage though of being right on top of the sea wall, from where you could watch those making sand castles or just playing games on the sand. When the tide was out, it left an enormous area of pebble free golden sand. St. Mary's Bay beach is re-knowned for safety when swimming, making it a popular seaside resort for people of all ages.

'Mind how you go, you lot' called Annie, as the youngsters immediately upon getting out of the parked cars, began striping off their outer clothes, to reveal the swim wear they'd put on underneath before leaving home.

'As soon as you've had your swim, cover your shoulders up especially you, Joey. Your backs already burnt from the other day.'

'Yes, Ma' he called over his shoulder as he ran with the other three.

George looked across at Annie. He knew what that one word 'ma' meant to her. She had a silly satisfied look on her face. Being 'ma and pop' to Joey, was still so new to them all. He thought back to the day, not so long ago, when those adoption papers had arrived. They worried that maybe this was something they wanted more than Joey. But the look on his face when they told him that, as of that day he was their son, made them so very happy, he wanted and needed them as much as they did him. It was Joey that a couple of days later, walked in the back room after work and greeted them with those two little words that spoke volumes. Joey had confided in his new brother Georgie, that he wasn't sure what to call Annie and George. 'Do I still call them aunt and uncle?' he asked of him. 'Cos that don't seem right somehow.'

'That's a tough one, Mate. Don't you feel you can call them mum and dad then?'

'Not really, cos me mum, me real mum that is, well I'd sort a feel I was lettin' her down. And the word *dad*, well, It'd always make me think of *him*, when ever I said it.'

'Yeah, I can well understand that. What then? you can't shout out oy you, when you want them.' he laughed.

'I've got it' Joey said as it suddenly came to him 'How's about ma and pa, what do you think of that, eh, Bruvv?' he finished, nudging Georgie's arm, pleased with the idea.

Hearing Joey call him bruvv, brought a smile to Georgie's face. It hadn't really sunk in until that moment. 'Yeah, that'll please them, *Kid*. And while we're on the subject, *Bruvv*, just remember who's the oldest. So what I say's goes, okay.'

'No change there then, when you was just me mate, you was a big old bossy boots.' Joey ducked as Georgie went to grab him. 'Come on then, dear *old*, Bruvver a mine, see if you can catch me.' Georgie chased his brother until, when he caught up with him, they both fell to the floor in fits of laughter.

'Comin' on wiv me, Rosie?' Georgie said, as they stood in the queue to ride on the ghost train.

Matty not too keen on that idea said 'hey, Georgie you said I could sit with you this time. What d'you want to go and sit next to a gel for? They only scream all the time.'

'I'll have you know, Matty, I am not a silly little girl, *I do not scream,*' she emphasised each word to make her point. 'Just for that' she turned to Georgie, 'I'd love to go on it with you, Georgie. That is if you're paying.'

For years he'd had a soft spot for. He thought about her on many occasions, 'Only in a brotherly way of course.' he would tell himself. 'Tell you what, Matty, me and you'll have two goes after to make up for it.'

'That certainly would make up for it' Matty thought. 'Come on then, Joey, guess for now that leaves you and me.'

'Charmin,' for that, I'm gonna go and get nanny Stone to come on wiv me.'

There followed a lot of teasing as Matty and Joey persuaded both grans to go on the scary ride. The only other noise heard in the darkness apart from the squeals of the older ladies, was that of Rosie, she screamed throughout the whole ride. Georgie had to bite his lip to stop himself screaming, but that wasn't in fright, it was due to the fact that Rosie was digging her fingernails into his arm so hard that she drew blood. 'Oh come back, Matty' he pleaded. 'all is forgiven.'

That evening the women drinking a well earned gin and tonic, after the hectic day out, sat with the youngsters in the garden. At nearly eighteen, Georgie decided to stay in the house with the men, where, if he was lucky, his dad would let him have a glass of beer along with them.

'What d' you fink of this Nazi bloke 'Itler then, George?'

'To be honest, Bert, he scares the life out of me.'

'Do you think we will get dragged into another war then? cos, I hate to say it, but I think we will.' joined in Reg.

'I think you're right, Reg. He's been trouble since the day he became chancellor back in fifty free. I don't understand the German people though. If all the things we hear over here about him are true, how can they all follow him, he seems to have them under a spell. You'd think after the last lot, none of them would want to go frew it agen. Huh, war to end all wars, my foot.'

'Yeah I know what you mean, Bert. He's a bloody dictator out ter rule not only Germany but the World I reckon. I tell you what, this 'oliday 'as done my Ida the world a good, she's been getting' herself in a right old paddy lately. She can't stop finkin' about war and what'll 'appen.'

'I doubt whether there's a person in this Country that hasn't been thinking the same thing. I'm fed up with hearin' the government say that there won't be a war. What a load of old cobblers eh. If they really believed the rubbish they're spoutin,' how comes gas mask are bein' distributed and air raid shelters goin' up all over the place. *And*, why the 'eck have men like me signed up to be air raid wardens. You tell me that?' George turned to look at his son who was listening with interest at what was being said.

'He hasn't got a clue what might happen' George thought to himself, 'Just like us lot here when we had to fight in the last one. We thought we were brave, goin' off to fight for our Country. People with flags wavin' us off, if them muvvers had known what they were sendin' their boys off to, there'd a been no flag flyin' just millions of tears. I don't know if I could bear it if my boy's have to go through what we did.'

Georgie was going to join in the conversation, until he saw the frightened look in his dad's eyes. 'Hey, You lot' he said instead, 'this is our last night together, and from the way you're all talkin' it could be our last time together for a while. So lets go outside and join the others, and forget all the bad things for tonight.'

'Got good sense this boy of yours, George, come on, he's right lets not spoil this special time.' remarked Reg as he stood up, ready to go into the garden.

Chapter Nine

'1939'

Sunday September 3rd

'Annie' George called to his wife who was in the kitchen preparing the Sunday dinner. 'it's nearly quarter past eleven, you going to come in here and listen?'
Annie sighed, before answering him. 'I don't fink I want to hear what he's got to say.' but never the less, she found herself walking into the backroom to join her husband and her two sons. Georgie was tuning in the wireless. At exactly eleven fifteen, the announcer told the millions of people listening in, 'that they were now going over to Downing Street.' The next voice they heard was that of the Prime Minister, Neville Chamberlain.

'I am speaking to you from the Cabinet Room at 10 Downing Street.
This morning the British Ambassador in Berlin handed the German government a final note. Stating that unless we heard from them by eleven o'clock that they were prepared at once to withdraw their troops from Poland, a state of war would exist between us. I have to tell you now, that no such undertaking has been received, and that consequently this country is at war with Germany.'

For a time, there was not a sound to be heard. No children playing in the street, no cars driving by, no sound of horses hooves clipping along the road just the gentle tick tock of the mantle clock. George was the first to break the tension. 'We knew it was comin' but deep down I can't believe we're goin' to war agen.'
Annie searched for her handkerchief in the pocket of her pinney. Her two boys looked at her, sixteen year old Joey, and Georgie at nearly nineteen, didn't know how to comfort her. Annie blew her nose, squared her shoulders and turned to walk back into the kitchen, saying as she went, 'Well standin' here won't get the baby barfed will it?' falling back easily into her tough cockney manner.
'Get that bottle of whiskey out of the sideboard, Joey. I think we could all do wiv a stiff drink.'
'George, Annie, did you hear it?' came the shout from Jack downstairs.
George went to the top of the stairs, 'Yeah we heard it all right mate. Do you and Kath fancy poppin' up, we're just about to open up a bottle, and have a stiff one?'
'Be right with you, Mate.'

When all six of them sat clutching their glasses, George stood up. 'I fink we should all raise our glasses, and wish God speed to all, Our Boys.' He looked across to his boy Georgie before going on, 'that are goin' off to fight, God bless and take care of them all and their families,' he finished on a sombre note. '

'And here's to a quick end to it all.' added Jack.

No sooner had they made the toast and drained their glasses, when an eerie wail screamed in their ears.

'Oh my gawd' cried Kath, 'surely they can't 'ave got 'ere this fast?'

'I doubt it, Aunt Kath,' reasoned Georgie, 'but just in case lets get down the Anderson.'

'What about me dinner?' wailed Annie, 'I'd just turned the oven on to warm.'

'Don't worry about it, Ma, I'll just turn it out, I don't suppose we'll be down their long anyway.' Joey tried to re-assure his ma understanding that Annie was confused and frightened. We all are he thought, with that terrible noise all around.

George and Jack shepherded their wives down the winding stairwell that led from Annie's kitchen into the backyard. Jack slipped into his kitchen to switch their oven off. He grabbed a packet of Rich Tea biscuits on his way through, after having remembered to collect his and Kath's gas masks. Georgie picked up the half full whiskey bottle and a couple of the glasses they had just been drinking from.

'Joey don't forget them bleedin' gas masks' called his dad.

'Ugh, it smells damp down 'ere' exclaimed Kath, 'it's so dark and dingy,'

'Come on old, Gel' Jack tried to re-assure his wife, 'now we know it's really goin' to happen, me George and the boys will try to make it as comfortable as we can. We'll get another tilley lamp in here, so you can do a bit of knittin' if we 'ave to stay down here for a while that is.'

'Yeah, Jack's right gel. Look we made a good job wiv the bunks didn't we?' George said as he looked around the shelter. 'Tell you what, you gel's make up a box a fings that'd make it better. Come on Annie, you and Kath tell us what fings we'd need.' So for the next ten minutes or so the men were able to keep the minds of their wives occupied with thoughts other than what was going on outside.

It was the turn of Georgie and Joey then. When both women decided they couldn't think straight and had run out of ideas, Georgie started to remind them of the day the Anderson shelter had arrived. 'Do you remember, Mum? You said when you got home from work that mornin' and there it was, just dumped out the front. Oh you should've seen your face when I came home and you told me that you'd phoned up the Council to complain that someone had dumped a load of old rubbish outside your front door.' he laughed, jabbing Annie in the ribs with his elbow.

'Ow was I ter know, that that heap of tin was an air raid shelter?'

'Cor, I'd've loved to have been a fly on the wall when that bloke from the Council office got here.' joined in Joey.

'Oh, you can laugh, My Boy, but what about you four blokes then, what a laugh me and Kath had watchin' you tryin' to put it togevver. Eh, Kath?'

'Yeah, it was funny. All I kept hearin' Jack say was, 'where's the flippin instructions?' 'I don't know what he was on about, it came with instructions.' Annie and Kath were now having a laugh.

'You couldn't call them instructions, they was double Dutch, weren't they, George?'

'Yeah, but despite them, we did a bloody good job of it.'

'You did, Pa?' interrupted Joey, 'me and Georgie did all the hard work. Diggin' an hole four foot deep and about five foot wide by six foot long, or whatever it was, anyway, it was a bloomin' lot of earf to move, especially in the hot wevver.' Joey finished with a grimace.

'Who piled all that earth back on then eh? me and your uncle Jack, not far short of two foot fick it was when we'd finished.'

'I fink, if I remember rightly, Dad, Joey and me did most a that a'nall.'

'Gertcha yer cheeky buggers the pair of yer. At least me and Jack can take the credit for how homely we've made it. These bunk beds look well comfy' George was about to continue with this playful act of arguing, when another long wailing sound interrupted him. Annie sitting next to him, jumped, 'what's that?' she said.

George patted her hand, 'it's all right gel, that's the all clear. Weren't too bad was it. Come on lets get out of here and go back indoors. At least you still got plenty of time to get the dinner cooked.' He put his hands on Annie's backside and pushed her up the steps of the shelter.

'Oi, you watch where you're puttin' your 'ands.'

When they were all standing in the garden, every one of them first looked skywards, then looked along the rows of back gardens, nothing had changed. All they saw were their neighbours coming out of their shelters, doing exactly as they did. Voices could now be heard in the street on the other side of their garden wall.

Doll and Arthur from next door emerged through the opening of the Anderson, followed by their son Rodney carrying his four year old daughter, he turned at the top and held his hand out to help his heavily pregnant wife climb the last step. It pleased Annie to see them united, as a family should be. Doll and her daughter-in-law Vera, had become the best of friends. Doll replacing the mother that Vera never knew. It all came about, after the part Doll played in caring for the Smith children the night their mum was murdered. As she said to Annie many times since, 'Poor old, Sally, can't be with her kids through no fault of her own. I was a silly old cow ta let jealousy, and that's all it was Annie, I was jealous of Vera takin' my boy from me. But that night taught me a lot. Those poor little buggers, I'll never ferget their faces. It made me fink, I tell yer. So now I've got a second chance, and nuffing is gonna come between me and my family agen.'

Annie thought of those words now. 'Would this war come between families, split them up, some never to return to their mothers?' She called out to her friend, 'Alright are you, Doll?'

'Yes fanks, Annie. Frightened the bleedin' life out of us though.'

'Don't forget what I said to yer about comin' round to us if ever there's a raid'

'I don't wanna be a nuisance to you and Kath though.'

'Who said you'd be a nuisance' Kath said, trying her best to let Doll know that they would be happy to have her company in the 'dungeon' as she now thought of it. 'You're worse at playing cards than Annie is, so I can take you both to the cleaners.' she laughed.

'I need ta bring me pennies wiv me then do I, Kath?'

'You better do. Well I'm off inside now, it'll be tea time before I get this joint a beef cooked.'

George and Jack decided that they would take a walk down to the local ARP station, just to make sure everything was okay. Both of them earlier in the year had signed up for duty, but they were told at that time that the response had been unbelievable. The head warden said at the moment they would not be needed, but he would keep them on standby, to call on, if and when required. The scene as they arrived was one of utter chaos. People were shouting at the wardens. Jack managed to get one man to stop yelling long enough to tell him what the problem was. 'We didn't know where we was meant ter go' he said angrily to Jack. 'I dragged my lot to two bloody shelters, not one bugger inside would let us in.'

'Maybe they were full up' offered Jack,

'I betcha they weren't, bloody cowards down there, that's what they are. I got eight kids, and the bastards wouldn't let 'em in. An' if these so called air raid wardens don't do somefing about it, I bloody well will.'

'Come on now, Mate,' George had a go at trying to pacify the man. 'Give them time to get everyfing sorted out. None of us expected this to 'appen today. Everyone should be allotted to their own area shelter, the wardens'll soon get fings sorted. Look give us yer address an I'll look into it for yer, 'ow's that?'

'You one of these wardens then? cos if you are where's yer badge?'

'Me and me bruvver-in-law Jack here, we're only on stand-by.'

'Well I reckon they need blokes like you ter sort 'em out. Anyway I live in Bethwin road.'

'Go 'ome now and see if yer families okay, Mate' said Jack giving the man a friendly pat on the shoulder. 'Promise yer we'll do what we can.' Jack smiled at George after the man walked away, much calmer now. 'I'm glad my Kath can't hear me.'

'Why's that then, Jack?'

'She'd start telling all her la-de- da friends that I'm turning into a loud mouthed slob.'

'I think it's much safer to revert back to our roots. Not that me and you are posh, not by any chalk, but we have tried to drag ourselves out of the gutter.' He stopped talking because the shouting in the small hut was becoming louder.

The next day as Georgie rode his motorbike home from work, he was rehearsing in his head how he would break his news to his mum. After the scare yesterday, he didn't want to add to her worries. 'Don't beat about the bush,' he told himself, 'just come right out with it.'

His dad and Joey were already home from their work. He could hear them talking to his mum in the backroom. He decided to wait on the stairs for a while, give them time to finish what they're saying. They were each regaling the various tales of Peoples reactions to yesterdays declaration and subsequent dashes for shelter. Both of them telling Annie how they'd never seen so many people in one go in their individual shops.

'Must have done a good trade then,' remarked Annie.

'Not really, Gel, I said people not customers.' George laughed. 'I think most of them just wanted to be with other people. Talkin' about it seemed to help.'

When Joey returned to work after the family holiday at Millie's in July. His boss Peg had greeted him with some very good news. While he'd been away, his lady boss, Peg, had taken a lease out on a small shop when one became vacant right behind her stall.

Peg greeted Joey that first morning back with, 'you'll need to get yourself some more good white shirts, and a dark suit would look smart.'

'What you on about, Peg?' Joey asked confused,

'See that?' she pointed to the shop behind. Joey looked at the window, 'no you daft sod, look at wot's wrote above it'

Joey looked up, to his astonishment the sign above the shop read

'Clothes - Pegs. High quality. Low cost ' then in smaller letters underneath

'Manager Joey S –Powley'

As Joey's mouth fell open, Peg said 'I didn't fink it a good idea to put Smith-Powley, some might fink you was some posh bloke. Wot d'yer fink then?' she asked standing with her hands on her hips, a silly grin on her face.

'I can't believe it, are you serious about his, Peg?'

'Serious! d'yer fink I'd a gone to all the expense of 'aving that sign done if I wasn't serious?' She felt she had a lot to thank young Joey Powley for. He had a knack of making all her customers feel special. He'd never forgotten how good he felt that day when Georgie took him shopping into Tonbridge. The lady behind the shop counter in the toyshop had called him *sir.* So, no matter how poor some of the women looked when sifting through the second hand garments, he referred to them all as madam. He became a popular figure down the lane, and for being fair. He would put clothes 'by' until the customer had enough money to pay for them. Word spread, and now, since opening the shop where the clothes were of good quality, but still the best value to be found for miles around, they had people coming to them from, places like Streatham, Forest Hill, Bromley and even one travels by train from Eltham. Peg still ran the stall outside with the help of a young boy just left school, and she found a reliable young girl, just a few months younger than Joey, to be his assistant.

Joey continued telling his ma of the days events. 'It was the same for us, Ma, loads a people but not much money changin' hands. Mind you some of the stallholders didn't turn up. That got them all wonderin' if maybe a bomb had landed somewhere yesterday. Getting' in a right old stew some old dear was, luckily your copper mate, Bill Shepherd turned up, he put them right.

Told them that no bombs had dropped, it had been a false alarm. You watch, bet all the pitches'll be full agen tomorrow.'

Georgie heard his mum interrupt Joey 'Could a sworn I heard Georgie's bike.' so he silently went back down a few of the stairs, then made a point of climbing back up noisily.

'Thought I did' his mum said. 'Hello, Son, sit yourself down, I was just about to go and dish up.' she walked out of the room. Georgie said hello to Joey and his dad, then instead of sitting down he walked over to the window.

'Had a good day, Boy?' asked George, to his sons back. Georgie didn't hear him, he was still trying to work out how to tell them.

'Oi, daydreamer' repeated George.

Georgie turned to look at him, 'Sorry, Dad did you say something?'

'I only asked if you had had a good day, Son that's all.'

'Oh, right, same as usual you know.'

George looked closely at his son. 'Something going on there,' he thought. 'Got something on his mind.'

Usually when they ate their tea, it was a time when they all chatted about their days work, not today though. Each had their own private thoughts. Annie was worried that the sirens might go off again, and this time it could be for real. George, was trying to work out why Georgie was so quiet. All that kept coming into Joey's head was a picture of his new assistant at the shop. Linda, 'cor, what a looker.' As for Georgie, he couldn't wait to get tea over with, so that he could tell them what he'd really been doing today.

'Spit it out, Son' George could stand it no more. Annie and Joey looked from him to Georgie. With a cough to clear his throat Georgie began.

'Look I don't want you to get upset, but, well in me dinner break today, I signed up.' he finished in a rush.

'I knew it,' said his dad. 'The moment you walked through that door, I knew it.'

Georgie turned to his mum, she was just staring at him. 'I'm sorry, Mum,' he said. 'but some of the older blokes at work said that if you join up before you get called up, you stand a better chance of goin' into a branch of the army that can use your skills.'

Annie found her voice, 'The older blokes at work! It ain't gonna be them that's gotta go and fight, is it?'

'Calm down, Annie, love. Georgie's right in what he says.' Georgie smiled his thanks to his dad for understanding.

'But lots of the teachers over at the school today, was sayin' that it ain't gonna be like last time, they reckon this war'll be over be Christmas.'

'I don't think so, Mum,'

'But what if it is. If you join up now, you could be sent where the fightin' is. You might end up in some uvver country fightin' their battles against 'Itler and it might not come to anyfing over here.'

'Look, Love, Hitler's already invaded Poland, he's not goin' to stop there. I know it hurts, but we've got to give Georgie our support.'

Annie turned to Joey, 'I s'pose you'll be tellin' me next that they want sixteen year olds to join up and you'll be off. Georgie,' she pleaded, 'you're not nineteen yet, surely it ain't too late to tell them you've decided to wait a while.'

'It is too late, Mum, I know it's hard for you, but I've made me mind up. I'll be goin' to have a medical and after that I'll get notification of where I have to report to.'

Annie got up, 'I need ta be by meself for a bit. I'm gonna go for a walk.'

'Don't go too far, Gel will you.'

'No don't worry, George. I might take meself round to my Rose and Mare's.'

Georgie went to follow his mum, he didn't like being the cause of her anguish. His dad shook his head at him and waved him to stay where he was. When they heard the slam of the front door, he said to his son, 'Give her time, Son. She'll come round.'

Joey who had sat silent throughout the exchange asked his brother what branch of the armed forces he'd applied for.

'I don't know one from the other. I told the Sergeant that I was a sparks and he's made a note of that on me form.'

When Annie came home much later that night, she walked in the room and asked the three of them if they'd like a cup of hot chocolate. Then matter of factly said, 'No more sirens tonight then. Rosie's finkin' of sendin' the kids away. Evacuatin' them to the country. Can't say I blame the gel. Oh, one fing, Georgie, you know you won't be able to wear your white shirts in the army. You'll be wearin' khaki from now on.' And with that, before anyone had the chance to comment on anything she said, she went to the kitchen to make the drinks.

George smiled at the boys. 'She's goin' to be just fine.'

Before Georgie went to sleep that night, he sat and wrote a letter to Rosie. He thought she would want to know that he soon was going to be a soldier. They had spent a lot of time alone together in July. Just enjoying walks along the river. They said to Joey, that it would be nice for Matty if he spent more time with his big brother. He smiled to himself as he remembered taking her hand to help her across a stile, wearing a bright blue ribbon in her hair.

Before George went to bed, he told Annie he was just going to make sure the shelter was dry. Once alone, sitting on one of the lower bunk beds, he put his head in his hands, and wept.

Annie arrived at the Avenue school on the Wednesday at the normal time of quarter to four. Mary was already there, ready with the keys in her hand to unlock the cupboard where they kept all the cleaning paraphernalia. There was no sign of Rose.

'Where's, Rose?' Annie asked of her sister. 'Nothing wrong is there?'

'Depends on what way you look at it.'

'Why what's happened?'

'She's down her Edna's school. Her Ronnie came 'ome yesterday wiv another letter from 'is teacher here, about evacuatin' him. So she's 'ad to go and see what the uvver school are doin'

'Has she made her mind up wevver her and Ted are goin' to send them away then?'

'Yeah. You know our Rose don't want them to go, but Ted's persuaded her it'd be for the best. That's why she's gorn to speak to the teachers. In Ronnie's letter it said that if they 'ave any younger bruvvers and sisters that are goin' as well, they 'ave to fill in these forms, so the authorities know exactly 'ow many kiddies will be goin.' Mind you, loads of them 'ave already gone from the two schools and our Rose is frightened that her two'll get split up like some of the early evacuees 'ave done. She wants to make sure Ronnie and Edna go together, else, she reckons they ain't goin''

'Can't blame the poor gel for that. Does she know when it'll be?'

'Well Ronnie's letter said Sunday. I tell yer Ann, it's gonna right break her heart.' 'What this Sunday? Surely not!' 'It's the troof, Annie. I don't know, what wiv your Georgie signin' up and now the kids bein' sent to God knows where. I wonder what's becomin' a this world. And that's a fact.'
Just then as the bell clanged to mark the end of the lessons, a crowd of eleven year olds, still in their first month at the big school, charged down the passage, making their way to 'freedom' as the older boys called the end of each school day. Where would they all be in a few weeks. Would the school remain open? Only time will tell what this war has in store for them all. They were soon to find out about their jobs though. As they were just finishing off the second classroom, the headmaster caught up with them.

'Ah there you are, Ladies' he greeted them with a smile. 'Is Mrs Trotter in another part of the school?' Annie explained her sister, Rose's absence.

'It's not good news I'm afraid. Most of the parents of the remaining pupils from this school, have taken the decision to evacuate their children. We only received notification yesterday. That meant we had to inform all families the same day. I'm afraid it doesn't give them much time to prepare their children. It seems they will be leaving from the school by charabanc on Sunday.'

'My sister's just told me about the letter our, Rose, Mrs Trotter's boy got. Do you have any idea where the poor little mites will end up, Sir?'

'Please don't let this go any further, until we know for definite, but we believe that it will be somewhere in Dorset. The last four of our younger unmarried teachers will accompany them and I believe teachers from other local schools will do the same. Tell Mrs Trotter to try not to worry too much, as I'm confident that our teachers will not let any harm come to any of them.'

'So, where does that leave us, If you don't mind me askin,' Sir? It's just that if we are gonna be out of a job, I'd like to know, cos Mr Macdonnal can only do a bit of part time work. He caught a packet in the last lot. I'm the only one who earns enough to pay the bills. My Cliff and Terry ain't bin left school long, so they don't bring much 'ome.'

'The way I see it at the moment, Mrs Macdonnal, is that if we stay open, only a couple of classrooms will be in use. We might amalgamate with other schools, but then we may have to use their premises. As yet nothing has been finalised. I am so sorry, but for the moment that is all I can tell you.'

'Don't worry, Mary, we'll sort something out, when the time comes. Thanks for comin' to see us though Sir. We'd appreciate it if you could let us know what's to happen as soon as you know.'

'Of course, Mrs Powley, Annie. Well I won't keep you away from your work any longer. I'll have your husbands to answer to if I make you late home, to cook their evening meal.'

'You still going to cook our special meal tonight, Gel?'

'It's the ninth of September isn't it? So, Course I am, George. I've been doing it for the last five years and I'm not going to let no bleedin little war mongerin' mad man stop me.'

'Good for you, Love.'

'Anyway, it might have to be the last one we all share together, wiv our Georgie goin' off to war.' Annie finished on a sad note.

'You mustn't think like that, Annie. Today is the sixth anniversary of our Joey saving Georgie's life. 'im up there wouldn't of made that happen, for anyfing bad to go wrong now.'

'I pray you're right, George.'

'What time do I need to get the car ready for in the mornin?' George changed the subject.

'Well, Rose says that the charabanc should be leavin' here about half past eight. Her and Ted want to see them safely on board first. If we leave straight after that, we should be well in front of them, that way we can find somewhere at the station to see them arrive.'

'I can't see why they couldn't have left from Waterloo or somefing. Why make them go all that way by chara first?'

'The government reckon there's still goin' to be 'undreds of fousands of the poor little perishers, and it'd take too long to get them all away safely wivout losin' 'alf of them, so they fought it best to use some out of town Stations. Mind you, I can't help but wonder if it's all a waste of time. We've not had any raids or anyfing. I wouldn't mind bettin' you, that they'll all be back in a couple a weeks. Some muvvers I know who's kiddies went off with the first lot are talkin' about bringin' them home already.'

'Well, let's hope you're right, Gel and they'll soon be back where they belong.'

When the boys came in, they all sat down to eat the celebratory tea of the usual roast beef Joey's favourite meal, aside from pie and mash that is. As always the main topic of conversation on these occasions was remembering the fun of hopping, they never dwelt on the memories of the fearsome bull. The tensions of the last few days forgotten for a few short hours.

For most of the older children, the evacuation was a big adventure. Although some of their teachers were going with them, they believed that there weren't enough of them to teach them all. Annie heard one boy say to his mates, 'I bet them teachers is comin' just to look after the littluns.' one of his friends asked him 'what makes you fink that?'

'Stands ter reason don't it, they need a lot more teachin' than us. We know everyfing already. And they need a grown-up to wipe there eyes and their bums.' he laughed at his own joke.

Looking around at some of the younger ones, Annie thought, 'maybe he's right in a way. Some of these are barely more than babies. They shouldn't be goin' off and leavin' their muvvers.'

At exactly eight thirty when all eight charabancs were full, the convoy made it's way to Camberwell New road. Little faces were pressed up against the windows. It was the start of a long tiring days journey for them all. First they were to be driven to a railway station at Reigate in Surrey. From there, a train would carry them through the Surrey and Hampshire countryside. Their final destination was a place called Fordingbridge. That was the latest information given to the headmaster.

George made good time. He'd planned the route the previous night. Rose and Ted sat holding hands, quietly in the back of the car throughout the journey. Apart from the times when Rose checked with George that they were going the right way. He parked the car in a convenient spot from where they could see the road and watch for the arrival of the convoy. A couple of the other parents lucky enough to have use of a car parked behind them. They made quite a big welcoming party. Rose who although she was in conversation with one of the other mothers, kept one eye on the road. 'Here they come,' she suddenly called.

As the charabancs came to a stop, the driver opened the door and one of the teachers climbed down and stood on the pavement. As each child emerged the teacher told them to make an orderly line in pairs. '*Do not wander off*' she ordered sternly to the assembled line.

George and Annie followed Rose and Ted to where twelve year old Ronnie and his ten year old sister Edna stood next to each other in the ever-growing line.

'Now don't forget to write to us as soon as you know where you're goin' to be stayin.' Rose said to her son. 'I've put ten envelopes wiv our address already written on it and they've already got a stamp, so it won't cost you no money. There's plenty of paper in each one, so you've got no excuse not to write every coupla weeks. When you send the last one, let me know in your letter and I'll send some more paper and stamps. Promise me now, Ronnie.'

'Yeah, okay, Mum. You've already told me all this.'

'Well I just wanna make sure you both don't forget to write.' she then turned to Edna, 'put your letter in wiv your bruvvers, don't go wastin' the stamps.' Edna just nodded, she was beginning to feel scared.

'And don't let them split you up, Ron, me and yer mum are relyin' on you to look after your sister. You're gonna be takin' my place as far as Edna's concerned. It's down to you to make sure no harm comes to her.'

'Okay, Dad, but you teller she's gotta do what I say.'

Edna was now very close to tears. The thought of her bossy brother giving her orders all the time made her throw her arms round her mum. 'I don't wanna go,' she cried 'he'll be 'orrible to me all the time.'

'Oh no he won't,' Ted gave his son a warning look. 'Once you get settled wiv a family, then you both become their responsibility.'

The charabancs they'd arrived in started to make their way back to Southwark and the Avenue school to pick up the next set of evacuees. As soon as they had departed another assortment of school buses and chara's took their vacated parking slots.

'Look at them all,' Annie said amazed. 'Surely they can't all be goin' to the same place?'

'I doubt it, some are more than likely goin' to be dropped off at towns on the way.'

'I hope you're right, George.' said Rose as she watched hundreds of pairs of little legs clamber out to stand on the overcrowded pavement.

The teacher in charge of the group from the four schools in Camberwell and Walworth blew her whistle. All the children had been told, that when she blew on it three times, that that was the signal to all follow the leading group into the station. It meant a train was approaching. A guard had said that with so many little ones, it would be safer for them to wait outside. The last thing any of them wanted was a child to fall onto the railway lines into the path of an oncoming train.

The sound and sight of more than four hundred children shuffling slowly one behind the other, was one that nobody, if they had been there to witness it, would ever forget. Even some of the 'tough' boys, had that lost expression on their young faces, they pulled their caps down   to cover the tell tale signs in their eyes as they headed into the unknown. They all carried brown bags or one of mums shopping bags, the luckier children carried small suitcases. Ronnie and Edna were among these. Georgie and Joey thought it would be easier to carry, and they could sit on them if they found that there was a lot of standing around, so the young men had gone out and bought one for each of them. They all wore identity labels round their necks on string and carried small brown paper bags, where on the journey, they would find the packed lunches their mothers had lovingly prepared for them sandwiches fruit and for some of the luckier ones, some sweets. Gas masks were thrown over their shoulders.

Annie and George kissed their niece and nephew goodbye, George telling them, that he would try his best to drive their mum and dad down to see them as soon as he could. Then they walked to a spot where they would be able to wave to the children on the train, leaving Rose and Ted to say a private farewell to their young children.

At the entrance to the platform, the pair turned for a final glance at their mum and dad, and as Rose and Ted craned their necks to see them, they saw something that they would never forget. Their son Ron put his arm round his little sisters shoulders and pulled her close. He didn't know that his parents could see him as he planted a loving kiss on her cheek and whispered in her ear. Whatever he said, worked, for they saw Edna look up at her brother and smile. 'I think that they are goin' to be just fine.' said a very proud father to his equally proud wife.

Two weeks after waving the children off, both Annie and her sister had news to exchange. They sat with their other sister Mary in Annie's back room, where over a cup of tea, Annie began with her sorry news. 'My Georgie had his medical yesterday. Passed it A1 he said.'

'Does that mean he'll be leavin' soon then?' asked Mary

'Who knows, but I hope not. I wish he could stay here until after Christmas at least.'

'Yeah I hope so to, Gel.'

'Me a'nall,' added Rose.

'Well, there's not much I can do about it, so until it 'appens I'm goin' to try and put it to the back of me mind.' Annie said resolutely. 'Come on, Rose, tell us what the kiddies 'ave to say.'

Rose pulled the crumpled sheets of paper out of the envelope. I tell yer this before I start, some of it, if you read between the lines, it breaks your heart. My two seem all right now though. She began to read the first and amazingly long letter from Ronnie.

Dear mum and dad

Well we're here. It took us ages to get here. The train went ever so slow and it was jam packed. Edna cried a bit cos she was getting tired but I give her me apple and that cheered her up. We got off the train at a place called Ford something or other then we had to go on another bus to this place with not many houses. The houses are not like back home they are all by themselves with big front gardens. The lady that took us said her house is called a cottage it's really big inside oh her names mrs Tickner but she said we can call her auntie Bea shes okay. On the first night me and Ed had a room each but none of us like it. it was ever so dark and real early in the morning all you could hear was loads a birds making a racket. This lady picked me and Ed out straight away we was one of the first, we went to what is called the village hall and they give us a glass of milk and some biscuits when we got there it was dark out. Me and Ed are now going to share our bedrooms with some kids that nobody picked. The first night, they had to sleep in the hall. I don't fink they was wanted cos there was 3 of them, and they said they'd go home if they couldn't be together. Some others looked really poor, they had really old cloves on and I heard one toffee nosed lady say that they needed a good scrub and they was a long time when it was there turn to see niity nora. I don't know if they've got anywhere to live yet. Anyway anutie Bea said she fought it right that brothers and sisters should be together. So we went back with her this morning and now they are going to come and live with us. I don't mind though cos even though too of them is girls the other one is a boy called Bob, and hes only a coupla months yunger than me. We get loads to eat and stuff. I think we are lucky cos when I was talking to some of me mates from school they are not happy. On his first day Pete Andrews was smacked by the bloke where he is cos he didn't wash his hands before his tea. Next week we have got to go to school, only in the afternoon though cos the kids that already live here have to go in the mornings we have to share the school. Think we mite have trubble with the local kids shood be a larf. Love Ron

Dear mummy and daddy

I fink Ronnie had told you evryfing. Sept that I had to sit on Ronnies lap all the time on the train it was hot and I was scwoshed. I am all rite now the lady is nice. My bedroom is pritty and now Ive got too new frends Terreasa is the oldest cos shes 14 and Pats not much older than me. The ladys brother is cuming to make bunk beds in our bedroom for them to sleep on I have my own bed all reddy. we have got a big back garden wiv lots and lots of pritty flowers and a swing hanging from a big tree. I miss you and daddy love from Edna xxxxxxxxxxxxxxx
Oh I forgot auntie Bee said she will rite to you next week. By By

'I can't tell you gels how relieved me and Ted was when we got these letters. I was beginnin' to fink we'd never see our two kiddies agen.'
Rose wiped away a tear. She wasn't alone in doing so

Chapter Ten

'1940'

Saturday September 7ᵗʰ

The new Head Warden George Powley of ARP post fifteen, hurried home after his mornings work. He had received word that tonight could be the beginning of intense bombing raids. Putting an end to what many Londoners still called 'the phoney war.' George could never understand how they could call it 'phoney.' With Georgie now recovering at home from leg wounds he'd received during his and the many thousand other service men's frantic and in some cases miraculous escape from the French beaches of Dunkirk back in May. A hero Georgie might be but in a short year he'd changed from a happy go lucky teenager into a man that, when he closed his eyes each night could not stop the scenes of his friends and comrades being blown to pieces in front of him. Of course George was very proud of his boy, even before it came to light that Georgie was to receive a bravery award. Although severely wounded himself he managed to drag his Commanding Officer and a Private, both with chest wounds into the sea where he could see one of the small boats in the flotilla heading in his direction. He had to shout at the men, ordering them in no uncertain terms to 'kick yer bloody legs. I ain't leavin' you 'ere, but I ain't gonna die 'ere eivver, so less you wanna kill me a'nall, do as I bloody well tell yer an' kick yer, Bastards.'

The officer in question when he had recovered sufficiently, visited Georgie at his home. He had no compunctions in giving Annie and George the full story of their son's bravery. He finished by adding that ' if it were not for your son, Private Jenkins and myself most definitely would be among the thousands left on that beach to die.'

George was now hurrying to the homes of wardens that assisted him in covering the houses that were in the St. Pauls Ward. Tonight he wanted them all on their guard. Every householder must strictly obey "the blackout ruling." He found Jack, who was now the chief shelter warden, digging up the last area of the tiny back garden that still had flowers growing. The remainder of the garden had already been re-planted with lettuce, onions, potatoes, carrots and various other vegetables. Everywhere flowers in gardens were replaced with vegetables. With so many of the ships carrying food to Britain being sunk by the day, the new Prime Minister Winston Churchill had introduced food rationing, every month something new was added to the ever-growing lists of foods on ration.

'Jack' George called over the back wall. 'We're to go on full alert, Mate.' Jack stopped his digging to lean on his garden fork. 'Do you think this time it's the real thing?'

'Yep, I reckon up until now, they've bin playin' with us. I'm off to make sure all the other ARP 's are ready.'

'Right you are, George. I'll go and check on all my shelters.'

'Good. Can I leave you to speak to all your shelter wardens?'

'Yeah course. I'll do that first. What time do you think it best for us to get to the ARP station?'

'If we say we'll all meet at four, between us we can make sure they are all aware of what to do, if, or I think I should say *when* the balloon goes up.'

Just as they were about to go their separate ways Joey cycled up. One look at the two men's faces told him something was afoot. 'Hello, Pa, Uncle Jack. What's up then?'

'Tonight could be a bad one, Son.'

Joey nodded his head, nothing more to say. 'What can I do then?'

'I tell you what would be a help,' his dad suddenly thought, 'can you shoot over to post twelve in Amelia Street? They've been havin' problems with their phone lately. Go and just make sure they've heard. Old Billy Jackson's always there on a Sat'day afternoon.'

Georgie was helping his mum lay the table in the back room for their usual Saturday dinner of pie and mash, he heard their voices. He opened the window just as he heard his dad ask Joey to go over to post twelve. 'Dad,' he called, 'something up?'

'Yeah, Son, we're on alert.'

'Right, I'll be right with you. Tell me what I can do to help.'

'There's not a lot to be done at the moment.' Georgie knew his dad worried constantly about the injury to his knee. But Georgie was determined to prove the doctors wrong, that said he'd probably never walk without the aid of crutches, or in the very least, never walk without a severe limp. Already he only used one crutch, and it certainly didn't stop him from riding his beloved, Triumph. So now Georgie ignored his dad, turning to Joey instead.

'Did I hear that you're goin' over to post twelve, Mate?'

'Yep, to make sure they've got word.'

'Right , well in that case, how's about I shoot over on me bike. I'll be there and back before you get into the Walworth road.' he ribbed his brother.

'Ha de ha, you big head.' countered Joey, 'go on then, hoppy.' he smiled at Georgie, knowing of his determination to overcome his wounds.

Their dad capitulated. 'Okay, Georgie, you do that then maybe Joey can give you a hand Jack.'

'Suits me, George. Tell you what Joey, it'd be a big help if you could alert the Warden in Grosvenor Terrace, he mans it all day. Then go to Bethwin road and Farmers road. If the Wardens not there, give their shelters the once over for me, Lad.'

The men went their separate ways, both thinking of what might lie ahead tonight, and of their duties. So far in the few raids over, London, their territory had come through virtually unscathed. George went off in the direction of Olney Road, seeking out his brother-in-law, Ted Trotter, his knock was answered by Rose who welcomed him with the words, 'Guess what, George? my Ted reckons if nuffing 'appens soon, we can bring the kids...' she stopped when she saw the expression on her brother-in-laws face. 'What's up then, come on tell us?' Ted got up to greet George as he followed his wife into the parlour. He looked from one to the other. 'I gavver from my Rose's question then, that you don't fink it a good idea to bring them home yet?'

'Sorry, Rose,' George looked from Rose to Ted. 'We've had word mate, it could be startin' and there's a good bet that it's gonna start tonight.'

'But I miss them so much, it ain't fair. Why now?'

'Cos I think we gave 'Itler such a pastin' in the sky, that he wants to teach us a lesson. He's bound to step up the raids now, he's been losin' so many aircraft. I bet there'll be an all out bid to bomb the docks and railways to stop essentials getting' frew and he thinks we'll give in.' George answered.

'I miss them too, gel but I'd rarver they stay where they are, if, there's gonna be raids.' Rose nodded, sadly, she knew her husband was right. 'Right, George,' Ted continued, 'I suppose we now put inta action what we've bin practising all this time eh?'

'You got it, Ted. Tell each warden to pass on that we meet at four.' All the ARP Wardens under George knew exactly what they had to do. It worked like this, George informed Ted, who covered the next closest roads to him, in turn Ted would go to the next closest Warden to him, this carried on until every Warden in post fifteen was aware of the situation. Likewise, Jack did the same with his team of shelter Wardens. Added to this the shelter Wardens had to check all the shelters under their control for damage, kids had habits of breaking into them and using them as dens, sadly others thought it fun to remove essentials that were stored inside. Although shelters were checked on a fairly regular basis, after such a period of relative calm, some may have been over looked, and time was not on their side at the moment.

Jack set off for the Walworth road. Post fifteen covered a very large area. On his way he called at the homes of other shelter Wardens passing on the information. He decided to leave the shelters in John Ruskin Street until last. Arthur should be home by then and he could do with the help.

Before Georgie left to go to post Twelve, he went into the kitchen where his mum was just finishing dishing up the pie and mash. She was singing along to the haunting words of Vera Lynn singing, We'll Meet Again that was playing on the wireless at the same time dabbing at her eyes with her hankie.

'Hello, Boy,' she smiled, 'I don't know why I listen to this song, it always makes me cry. Do you know they was playing it on this wireless the day we got back from seeing you off after your embarkation leave? Daft old fing, that's your, muvver.'

'Mum,'

'What, hungry are you? I'm nearly done.'

'No it's not that. Sorry but you're goin' to have to keep the dinner warm in the oven.'

'Why, your, dads home isn't he? Cos I could've sworn I heard his voice a while ago.'

'Yeah he's home, but he's got Warden fings to sort out.'

'What right now, can't he eat his dinner first? Don't taste the same warmed up. Where is he? I'll have a talk with him.'

'Too late, he's gone already. Joey's helping uncle Ted, and I said I'd nip over to Amelia Street and give a message to Billy Jackson.'

'What's goin' on, Georgie?'

'I'm not sure, Mum. Wait till dad gets back eh? Look I got to go now. Won't be long.' he gave his mum a quick peck on the cheek and hurried to the stairs as quick as he could with his crutch.

'Don't rush, you'll end up fallin' down the stairs, then where will you be?'

'At the bottom' Georgie called back laughing.

He left his mum shaking her head with a smile on her face. It hurt her to see her once athletic son unable to go more than a couple of steps without the aid of a crutch. She prayed that his hopes for a full return to fitness came true, but at the same time, she didn't want it to happen too soon, for then he would have to rejoin his regiment.

That day South London escaped the deluge of bombs that fell over the river in East London. The newspapers reported the next day that hundreds of women, children and elderly folk lost their lives or were injured. Bombs rained down on the docks and devastation came to the houses close by, the poorer sector taking the worst of it. From Post fifteen the men could see the sky glowing red in the East End of London, from their side of the fated River Thames.

They all did their jobs that had been rehearsed daily since George and Jack took over nearly a year ago. People still ran round in circles not knowing which way to go, the fear they felt wiping all memory of which shelter was allotted to them. Jack, Arthur, Alf Woogitt with the help of Joey did all they could to calm people down. George and his team kept an eye for incendiary bombs and any fires starting up. Georgie stayed in the Warden hut, each hut had to be manned in case they were needed elsewhere. Before they had time to regroup the second wave had attacked, they heard the German planes coming back well before they came into view the, searchlights picking them out, the sound of ack ack. The ARP's doing their best to keep spirits up down in those 'dungeons' where babies cried and mothers held them so close, as if it would be the last time they did so.

Annie sat with Kath and Doll in their Anderson. They could hear the roar of the planes engines. That night they only heard distant thuds as bombs fell far away.

The next night the sirens sounded again. 'Oh me gawd,' Annie said to herself. Then shouted down the stairs to her sister in law 'Kath, you there?'

'Come on, Annie, don't stand up there talkin' get down 'ere quick. I'll just bang on the wall to Doll.' When they arrived at the entrance to the shelter, Doll was already there. At the sound of the sirens starting up, she had just grabbed her coat and run out to go through the gap in the fence especially made by George and Jack for her use. Tonight, the bombs seemed closer.

The three women sat huddled together on one of the lower make shift bunk beds. Clutching each other's hands as the shelter vibrated to the sounds of the bombs going about their destructive business. Annie tried to think of something to say. Apart from the odd prayer and fright induced cursing, no one uttered a word.

'Come on, Gels,' her voice sounded several pitches higher, 'we can't just sit 'ere like frightened rabbits every night, we'll go bleedin' mad. Did I tell you that they need more women at the factory?' After the schools evacuations Annie and her sister Rose had gone to work where forces uniforms were made. Mary had remained as the sole cleaning lady at the Avenue, she also had taken over Annie's long time job at the Doctors Surgery.

'Busy is it then?' Doll asked, realising that what Annie said was true. Who knows how long they'll keep this bombing up for.

'Busy's not the word, Doll. We can't keep up wiv demand. Our Lizzie's goin' to apply tomorrer. She wants to work afternoons only.'

'Can yer do that then?'

'That's what they're tryin' to set up. If they get enough people apply, they're gonna make free shifts. The mornin' shift'll be from seven till one, then the afternoon shift'll start at eleven and finish at five and the early evenin' one will start at free and finish at nine. That way instead of the eight hours we do at the moment every day, there'll be free lots of six hours. The bosses have told all of us that we can do as much overtime as we want, so that we won't be out of pocket wiv the shorter shifts.'

'So you won't lose out then, if this comes about?'

'That's right, Doll. Mind you it'd suit me better, cos doin' eight hours every day when you haven't been used to it, don't 'alf come as a shock.'

'So what shift will you choose?' Doll wanted to know.

'I think the afternoon shift of eleven till five would do me just right.'

'What if there's a raid?' Kath asked

'Oh that's not a problem. We've got a basement been specially made stronger. It's a lot safer than any shelter I've seen. It's got proper beds, water ta make tea, I tell you this, they certainly know how to look after their workers.'

'Do you think I'd like it there, Annie?' Kath who hadn't been to work since her Doris was born questioned.

Annie thought about this, taken aback somewhat. It was the last thing she'd expected Kath to ask. To be honest, she wasn't at all sure it was the place for her sister-in-law to work. Some of the girls working in the factory were loud and their jokes went past the mark, let alone near it.

Kath noticed Annie's hesitation. 'Don't you think I could do it then?'

'It's not that I don't think you can do it Kath, but well I'm not sure if you'd feel out a place. Some a them gels can be very coarse y'know.'

'So can I, Annie, when it's required. You should've seen me where I worked before I married Jack. My language would have shocked you.' she finished smiling at the recollection.

Doll and Annie laughed at the thought of it. 'Tell you what then, Kath, 'ow's about me and you applyin' I've bin meanin' to do me bit for the war effort. I'm fed up wiv workin' at the laundrette.'

'If you're game then so am I, Doll.'

Annie couldn't believe her ears, Kath wantin' to go back to work. 'Well there you go,' she thought to herself, 'just shows you shouldn't judge people.' Then she turned to Kath and said,

'Good on yer, Kath, I bet your Jack'll be real proud of you.'

Kath felt good, silly how a little bit of praise could do so much. She never felt more closer to Annie than at this very moment.

'Will you let us know then, Annie if this comes about?'

'You bet I will, Doll. And if you two come on the same shift as me and our Rose, if she changes over, then I promise you this, you'll 'ave a bleedin' good laugh.'

They went on to discuss the problems of food rationing. It was beginning to make the life of wife and mother extremely difficult.

'What I don't get,' said Doll angrily, 'is 'ow quick after rationin' came about, the food seemed to just disappear out a the shops. Surely we make enuff food in this country to get by. We still got farms and flour mills, I tell yer I don't get it.'

'Think yourself lucky now a days if you can find any decent meat in the shops.' Kath added.

'And look how much you're allowed when you do find it. I tell you what we should do....'Annie was interrupted by yet another loud explosion, they could feel the ground shake.

'Carry on, Gel wiv what you was sayin'. Doll said bravely.

'Well what I thought was this, if we are goin' to be spendin' a lot of time down here, lets make good use of it.'

'In what way, Annie?'

'Well, Kath, I know there's some fings you and Jack don't like, sugar for instance, neivver of you take that in your tea do yer?'

'Yuck, no we don't. What you getting at?'

'There must be fings that you like but me and George and the boys, or Doll and Arfur don't. So next time we come down here, and I pray it's not for a long long time, but if we write down all the things on ration that we don't like we can maybe swap wiv one of the other of us for something that we do. Get it?'

'Oh I see what you're on about. 'Ere that's a good idea. What say you, Kaff?'

'I can't see any harm in giving it a go.'

So it was decided that they would each bring a pencil and some paper with them the next time the sirens blasted through the calm. Little did they know, that for more than fifty days and nights, they would have plenty of opportunity to write their swap lists.

For their men, those nights sent them to scenes of such horror of which their wives would never fully know of the whole sad story. Georgie thought that nothing could be worse than his nightmares and memories of the beaches in Dunkirk. That was until the first time he helped to dig in the ruins of a house where a young mother lived with her four small children. It was in the early hours of the morning after bombs had rained down incessantly. The first of which fell shortly after the warning sirens, there had been little time to make way to the public shelters. The panic spread like wild fire, people running all over the place. Mums dragging half dressed children behind them, those not so quick on their feet were being knocked to the ground by the hurrying mass. It tried all the patience and training of the ARP Wardens to bring the chaos under control. Neighbours of a young family told of how, the mother had previously said, that she wanted to make sure she dressed her children in the warm clothing they would surely need if the raid was to be prolonged, perhaps this was why she and they didn't make it to the shelter in time. It was that first bomb to fall in post fifteen area that night. Every Warden along with the emergency services tried desperately to locate the family. Every so often the fire chief would call for silence, hoping that they might hear a shout or just any noise that would give them hope that somewhere in the darkness they might find life. It was Georgie, crutch thrown onto the glass and debris covered pavement, that saw something first. He called for quiet, as he bent and touched what looked to be the hand of a dolly. Others came across to him, and gently they moved the rubble surrounding it. Georgie bent to take hold of the hand, he recoiled in shock as the realisation hit him. 'It's a, Baby,' he said, bile rising in his throat. 'It ain't a, doll, it's a, Baby.'

The men worked faster, using their hands to scrape all the rubbish away from the tiny human hand. All the while Georgie held on, his fingers gently rubbing the cold little fingers. Then as the men worked and more of the arm was revealed, it became obvious to the fireman by Georgie's side. 'You can let go now, Son.' he said gently to Georgie.

'No I can't. They might still be alive and they'll know someone's wiv 'em.' he carried on caressing the hand.

The fireman looked round at the other rescue workers. Georgie's dad saw the look, he stepped forward and took hold of his son by the shoulders. 'Come away now, Georgie, there's nothing more you can do for the poor little mite.'

'No, Dad, not yet, let's get 'em out first, you never know.'

George looked at the fireman who shook his head and indicated with his eyes that he get his son away.

'Listen to me, Georgie,' George tried again, 'This lot know what they're doin'. If they say it's no good, then believe me it's no good. Come on we've got more work to do elsewhere.' He prised his son's fingers away from the still, chubby fingers and helped him to hobble back to where his discarded crutch lay.

Later that morning four tiny bodies, one with only one arm, followed that of their mothers as they were removed from the collapsed ruin that once was a happy family home, a scene that was to be repeated again and again throughout the whole of the Capital.

George took his boys over to one of the many hundreds of mobile canteens set up by the WVS and the WI throughout the bomb damaged areas. He made them drink tea with plenty of sugar in. The night was far from over. They had to get the less injured to specially adapted classrooms that became first aid centres back at the Avenue, where medically trained teams awaited them. Then it was consoling those whose homes had not survived the onslaught and again getting them back to the school, where other classrooms had been turned into temporary rest centres. Here families could get something to eat and drink, again with the services of women volunteers until the local authority rehoused them. Some families after being bombed out, were lucky enough to have relatives they could stay with, away from the nightly terrors of London.

That September and October, news of many terrible disasters found their way to Post fifteen. Two shelters in the neighbouring ward took direct hits, some crawled out alive, most didn't. George heard of an ARP post where fourteen people lost their lives, among them were six wardens. Even the King and Queens home didn't escape, one night a lone bomber found his target, the Palace received quite a bit of damage. It was hard to find one street in the capital that escaped the carnage. People started to feel frightened of being buried alive down the public shelters. Thousands that lived in the city near Underground Stations started to use them as shelters. The authorities, at first tried to put a stop to it, but they soon realised this was pointless. Joey had first hand knowledge of sheltering down the Underground. He had taken Linda up West to the pictures to see The Wizard of Oz, starring the American favourite, Judy Garland. On their way home the alert sounded, they just followed the hoards of people down into Piccadilly Circus Tube Station. When he eventually got home in the early hours, he told his family who'd been waiting up for him to get home, of the sights he'd witnessed.

'You should've seen it.' he recalled, 'there must have been well over three thousand down there. There was all these buckets every where that they used as toilets, cor the stink. Anyway, we didn't fancy staying there, so we thought we'd find somewhere else before the bombing started.'

'Not the sensible thing to do, Joey.' admonished his dad.

'You weren't there, Pa. I can't begin to tell you how horrible it was. Anyway, as it turned out we had no choice but to stay there. When we tried to get back up top, there was all these people with their kids sleeping on the whole length of the escalator.'

'What while they was still movin?' The men couldn't help but smile at Annie's face when she asked that.

'Course not. Them and the lift had been switched off. So me and Lin found a space on the stairs and waited for the all clear.'

Since then the government had relented and word had it that they were going to install basic essentials in all Underground Stations. The incident at Balham in October brought more fears with it for the underground shelterers. Balham station received a direct hit, amazingly most of the six hundred down there were rescued. Sixty four people were not so lucky they were buried alive.

When Annie read or heard about such tragedies she wondered how her husband and men like him coped with the hell of their ARP rescues.

Another bomb landed in Royal road, the road that Annie and her family's back garden lay. Thankfully the two families from the homes that were destroyed were safely in a shelter. The windows in nearly every house within a hundred yards blew out. But as George said to Annie the next morning, as Annie was cursing as she swept up the splinters of glass.

'What's a few panes of glass. Compared to what others are suffering?' He knew as soon as he said it that he shouldn't have. This was his wife's way of dealing with the fact that, had the bomb fallen just a mere forty foot closer, it may have landed on the shelter that she, Kath and Doll sat in. He went over to Annie and just held his arms out to her. She fell into them and sobbed her heart out.

Annie's firm had indeed been able to put into action the three shift system. Perhaps, the response to their advertising for more workers had been overwhelming due to the fact of the shorter working day. For many busy mothers and wives wanted to do their bit for the War effort, but up until then, didn't think they could manage. The hours were long working in a factory, that was bad enough but to then have to go back home where they had to cook, clean and look after their family, well many thought it seemed impossible. That was no longer the case. Doll and Kath applied for and were taken on as afternoon workers along with the already transferred Annie and Rose. This meant they often had time to help out over the road at the Avenue School rest centre. They tried to amuse some of little children thereby giving their parents, or in most cases the mother, time to come to terms with what had happened to their home. On one of these occasions, Annie was talking with an elderly lady who was explaining that most of her kitchen had collapsed.

'Me old man's round there now, trying to shore up the back wall. I don't know if it'll be safe enough to go back to.' she finished on a resigned note.

'Where do you live, Luv?' Annie tried to keep the woman talking, talking always helps, she thought to herself.

'Hillingdon Street, the bomb must have 'it the 'ouses behind us. We ain't got a winder left.'

Annie didn't hear the last of what the woman was saying. Her heart started to thump. 'What side of the street you on. I mean which street do you back onto?'

'Olney Road.' came the answer that Annie dreaded.

'Sorry, Luv, I gotta go.' the woman watched in amazement as Annie ran to one other lady helper. It wasn't until she heard Annie nearly scream the words 'Kath, Olney Road got it last night.' that she realised that the kind lady that had taken the time to talk to her, obviously knew someone from that road.

Neither Annie or Kath had seen their husbands since the first alert the previous night. Both men, even though they were exhausted had gone straight to work. A happening becoming so very common for them. Georgie went with his dad and between them they ran the fishmongers. They took it in turns to go out the back where George had installed a camp bed to get forty winks. The shop no longer the thriving business it had once been. They sold what fish Ted was able to get from the fishermen, most of the time all he came back with was shellfish. George counted himself lucky though, because the owner of the shop retired to Surrey soon after the outbreak of war, he told George that as long as the takings covered his wages he could manage the shop and make any changes he thought necessary during hostilities.

So as Annie and Kath ran all the way round to Olney Road, they didn't know whether they would find their husbands there. 'Surely' Annie told herself. 'if it had come down near Rose and Mary's houses either George or Jack would have got word to us.' But then her imagination took over, 'they wouldn't 'ave done if fings was really bad. They wouldn't want us there till they'd got 'em out.' She ran faster still, Kath bravely trying to keep pace with her. As soon as they reached Herion Street, they could see virtually down the whole length of Olney Road stretched out before them. Rose along with Ted and Mary next door with Macky and their two boys, Cliff and Terry lived right at the opposite end. It was hard to see from where they were exactly where the bomb had landed. So they set off again, this time at a brisk walk. As they got past the Church they could see people standing around down the road a bit further. Then with relief flooding through them both, they saw that it had fallen close to the scrap yard. Annie stopped and sat down on the front wall of one of the houses, Kath joined her.

'Phew.' Kath spluttered between sharp intakes of breath. 'For someone with short legs, you can't 'alf run, Ann.'

'And for someone as old as you you're none too slow neither' relief tinged with humour made Annie's voice shake. They sat on the wall for a minute or so, catching their breath and controlling their churned up feelings.

'Come on,' said Kath, now that we're here we might as well go and see the gels. They must be shook up.' As they walked past the site of the bomb blast, it sickened them to see all the personal belongings of who ever lived in the houses now lying broken and twisted scattered over the pavement and the road.

They found the two sisters drinking tea in Mary's dust covered kitchen. Both looked shocked and distressed. It was Mary that told Annie and Kath that an elderly couple who refused to go down the public shelters had been killed. Mary said she and Rose had known and been friends with them ever since she and Rose moved into the road many years before.

Chapter Eleven

Joey's eighteenth birthday in November was celebrated in the dark dank dungeon in the back garden. Just as his brother, Georgie's twentieth had been the previous month. On that occasion though, spirits had not been as high as there was just, Annie, Joey, Kath and Doll to raise a cup of tea to Georgie to celebrate his special day. Every night without fail the sirens blasted through the air. Annie had insisted that for just this one night, Georgie and Joey stay with her in the shelter. Normally the boys would be off helping their dad out at the wardens hut. But just for once, she wanted to see them the following morning without that total look of shock and despair on their young faces. Tonight after getting them to sing a few songs with her Kath and Doll she wanted to see smiles in the morning as they remembered a night of fun and laughter, Just as it used to be, as it should be. She understood of course their need to be 'out there doing their bit' to give help where it was most needed. She worried how much more of this carnage they and her husband could take. They, and all other ARP wardens worked non-stop, helping people to shelters, then keeping a sense of calm amongst them all, digging buried people out from under the rubble that once was their home. Then dealing with the bereaved. No-one should have to deal with such sadness and madness on this continuous scale.

Annie did make Joey's day special. Thankfully, it had been fairly quiet in post fifteen that night, so even George had been able to take an hour off to spend with his adopted son.

So, on Joey's birthday, everyone grabbed the bottles of drink, glasses and plates of sandwiches filled with nothing more exciting than cheese and pickle. Cakes made with dried egg, and as Annie insisted on calling them, sausage rolls, unfortunately they were sausage free, filled with vegetables instead. They quickly made their way down to the shelter on the first wail of the siren. It was quite a squeeze, trying to fit all eleven people in there. Not that Joey minded, as he found himself squashed between Linda, his assistant from the second hand clothes shop, on one side, and his ma on the other. Kath sat next to Annie with Doll opposite, alongside side her, sat Arthur, then Jack. George climbed up on to the bunk above them with Georgie by his side. Opposite them on the other upper bunk sat Siddy and Bernie, who for the first time since they had joined the air force, as ground crew, had been given leave that coincided. Unfortunately, for their family and friends the boys were stationed in Yorkshire and the only time they could get home was when they had at least a seventy two hour pass. Even then the journey home took up a big chunk of their time. The only thing that helped them through special family celebrations was the fact that both boys were stationed at the same base. And today, as luck would have it, they were back with their two closest friends celebrating Joey's birthday, falling easily back to the time when they were just four young boys happy in each others company. Sadly no one from Joey's other family were there to share his birthday. His nan and grandad Stone, Bert and Ida, had on the insistence of Millie, gone to live in her house in Eynsford. Millie had also pleaded with Annie, George and the boys to go there, but they had refused. George had too much responsibility in his local ARP unit and Annie's family all lived close by. Joey had the shop and of course there was Linda. Georgie knew it would not be a good idea to stay in the same house as Rosie. It had been Joey who thought it for the best that they not come to his makeshift party. He had spoken to Rosie, Matty, both sets of grand parents and Millie on the telephone.

As head Warden George had been able to jump the queue in having a phone installed at home. The parcel that held birthday presents from Joey's family in Eynsford arrived a couple of days before. Everyone in the shelter drank to Joey's health and happiness, as the war raged on somewhere, outside. Tonight though, they were all in high spirits, relaxed due to the fact that for the last few nights they had had the luxury of sleeping uninterrupted in their own comfortable beds. No sirens, no bombs and no endless hours of sitting in that 'dungeon' listening to the constant drone of enemy aircraft on their killing missions, gone for now, the sounds and the earth shaking around them, as the bombers found their targets. Jack stayed for a short time only. He and George were tonight, at long last, going to take a well earned rest from their ARP duties. Jack knew that if he didn't go and make sure the others were coping with whatever was being thrown at them tonight, then George would feel it his duty to do so. But tonight was Joey's night and his pa should spend it with him.

Annie and George joined in with the fun and banter of the occasion, all the while knowing that at the first opportunity, their Joey would be off to the Navy recruiting centre.

''Ere, Georgie, I forgot to say congratulations, Mate. Mum wrote and told us about you gettin' the DCM. Made me feel real proud, knowin' one a me best mates was an 'ero.' Bernie leant across the gap between the bunks to shake Georgie's hand.

'Yeah me a'nall, well done, Mate.' said Siddy who followed his brothers lead.

'Ta. But what I did was nothing compared to them men, boys and women that sailed their little boats over there. Without them, well, it don't bare thinking about. They loaded their boats with men until they all but sunk, then took them back to where the bigger boats were, dropped off one lot then sailed back into hell to do it over again.' Georgie fell silent, mentally visualising the horror yet again. Then to his two friends he spoke more harshly than he meant.

'Wouldn't have been so bad if you'd have got your fly boys up there in time.' Georgie made the remark but tried smiled as he did so, to take away any offence that they might have read into it. Back then the thousands of Soldiers on the beaches, were cursing the lack of air cover they received.

'The Air Force was there, Georgie, but it was no good. We just didn't 'ave enough planes. It wouldn't 'appen now, Mate. We got new planes comin' in daily. Next time we'll show 'em what for.' Siddy told his mate, understanding his reasons for feeling so strongly about that time. He had heard so many terrible stories from the men lucky to have survived. Anger was the strongest feelings they all shared for something that should never have happened.

'I reckon you might be right, Sid. Anyway what's past is past.' Georgie smiled at his mates, it wasn't their faults and tonight was certainly not the time to go into the rights and wrongs of the doomed operation. 'Linda's not come here to listen to war stuff, she's come to have a good night. Ain't that right, Love?'

'You bet it's right, Georgie.' Linda answered him smiling.

Joey understood his brothers reasons for not wanting to pursue the days of Dunkirk. He was the one who had comforted Georgie on the many nights when he screamed out in his sleep. It was only with Joey that Georgie had shared the horrors of those nightmares. Joey knows all about nightmares. The two young men often sat whispering in the darkness of their bedroom. Unlocking for a short time all the fears and sadness that they hold firmly under lock and key to the rest of the world at all other times. Georgie is the one person that has seen Joey wake in the morning in a cold sweat. Knowing that again his brother has just witnessed his dad beating his mother to death, and he tries each time in his sleep to stop the beating, but it always ends up with the same result.

Linda was fast becoming a regular visitor to the house. She and Joey had been seeing each other outside of work on and off for the last year. Joey insisted that they keep it casual, saying many times that they were both too young to get serious. In truth, Joey was scared of what the future might bring. He knew that as soon as he reached eighteen that he'd be applying to serve in the Navy. It wouldn't be fare to expect Linda to sit at home, waiting and wondering if she would see him again. She was young, she could easily find someone else while he was away. He knew he was in love with her and he was pretty sure Linda felt the same way about him, but he pushed that to one side. So they both kept up the pretence of being just good mates who enjoyed each others company and the odd stolen kisses.

Georgie saw right through this act. Anyone just looking at them together could tell how they felt about each other. He watched them now sitting on the bunk bed, Joey's arm thrown loosely round Linda's shoulders, his fist clenching and unclenching as he tried not to pull her even closer. The look in, Linda's eyes as she took in every word he muttered had, love screaming out of them.

'Silly, Sod,' thought Georgie, 'He don't know how lucky he is. She's a lovely girl, we all think the world of her. Still who am I to say what's right and what's wrong. They are still young but sometimes I wonder if what others say about take your happiness now, while you still can, ain't a bad thing.' Suddenly the face of Rosie came to him. 'Now there's young for you,' he told himself. 'She's not even seventeen yet and I'm twenty.' The pair had corresponded up to the point where Georgie embarked for France. The letters were friendly and impersonal, more like brother and sister keeping the other updated with news from home. Since Georgie's return from Dunkirk he had seen Rosie a couple of times. The first being when Annie had telephoned and told them all at Eynsford, that he was back in this Country and safe, although badly wounded in the leg. Rosie had begged her grandpa to drive her to see Georgie in hospital. The whole family came again when he was discharged to recuperate at home.

'Why did I have to go and fall for a girl no more than a baby.' he thought feeling sorry for himself. Then a saucy smile appeared, 'mind you, what a beautiful baby she's turned into.'

'What you got that silly look on your face for?' said Siddy from opposite.

'Who me?' questioned Georgie, 'I didn't know I had a silly look. I was just thinkin' about havin' anuvver glass of beer before you and Bernie guzzle it all.' he lied.

'Yeah pull the uvver one, Georgie. I know that look when I see it. It's one I see all the time at the base. You was finkin' about a skirt.'

'Oi, d'you mind, Siddy. If you're talkin' about a girl, say girl, we ain't a bit a skirt are we, Gels.'

'I didn't mean, You and Mrs Bell and Mrs Dawson were a bit a skirt, I meant someone like Linda 'ere, she's a nice bit a skirt. You uvver free are more like a bit a granny bloomers.'

Everyone laughed, but Annie had the last laugh, she grabbed Siddy's foot that was swinging just above her head, and before he had time to pull it away, she whipped his shoe off and tickled his foot. 'I'll give you granny bloomers.' she said to the shrieking of a ticklish Siddy.

Chapter Twelve

'1941'

'I still can't get used to this bloomin' blackout, George. It's so creepy walkin' home from work in the dark.' said Annie, not long home from work and preparing the evening meal.

'I know what you mean gel. I bumped into, oops, pardon the pun, but last night on me blackout rounds, I came across, shall I say, old Harry Burns, he was comin' along the road ever so slow. I knew someone was there but I couldn't make out who. Anyway I calls out 'evenin' mate' course Harry recognised me voice, and he says ''Ello, George it's me Harry Burns'

'Well I could just about understand what he was sayin'. To be honest I fought he was drunk.'

'Harry's not a big drinker is he?'

'No, well that's what I was thinkin'. Anyhow by now we were standin' close together, so I asks him if he's all right. He shines his torch into his face, Cor blimey, Annie, you should've seen the state of it. Seems the night before, on his way home from work, remember it was real foggy night before last, anyway, all of a sudden, smack, he's walked bang into a lamppost.'

'Ooh' sympathised Annie, sucking in her breath. 'Poor bugger, in pain is he?'

'He certainly looked it last night. He's got two black eyes, his cheeks all swollen and he's cut his lip bad. It's all very well bein' told to shine the tiny shaft of light from your torch on the ground, but by the time it catches something in the beam, more often than not your heads found it first.'

'That's why I hate it comin' home from work in winter. It's not so bad when you're in the main road, cos the edges of the pavements have been painted white, so's you at least know when you're goin' to step into the road. It's when you get in the road that I get scared. The cars seem to be on top of you before you've had time to see them comin'. It's an 'orrible feelin' when you can hear its engine, you know one's comin' from somewhere, but you can't see anyfing, well not until it's right on top of you that is. You can hardly see its lights.

'Worse in the country lanes though, Annie, what wiv no pavements, quite a lot of the deaths and injuries frew the blackout have been there. Anyway no more talk of that. What magic have you come up wiv tonight for our tea?'

'Sorry, Love, no magic tonight. I stood in one queue down the lane on me way home cos someone said they had some nice fresh Ham and Tongue in.'

'And?'

'Typical, when I got to the front, all they had was *pot luck* sausages.'

'Is that what we've got then?'

'Yuk, you must be jokin'. They looked more of a greeny colour, worse than the rubbishy greyish ones. So I'm afraid it's good old Woolton Pie tonight. With a little extra though.'

'Somefing nice eh?'

'I've put a nice little bit a lean bacon in it, that I swapped for an egg wiv Kath.'

'That was a good idea of yourn.'

'Well all of us get somefing out of it.'

Georgie had taken to giving Joey a lift to work on the back of his motorbike. Annie and George heard the roar of the engine as it pulled up at the back gate.

Joey was the first to appear with Georgie not far behind, leaning only slightly on a walking stick that aided him when climbing up the stairs. Joey pulled a brown envelope out of his coat pocket. 'Met the postman on me way out this mornin'' he said after greeting his parents who saw what he held in his hand.

'When?' was all his pa asked.

'Sat'day week the 11ᵗʰ Pa.' Last November, as soon as he was eighteen, Joey had, as expected by his family, been to the Navy recruiting centre. Not long after that he had to report to Hither Green where he had undergone a medical and a short intelligence test, of which he passed in both. He had applied to be in signals. Thanks to his pa, who over the last year or so had been teaching him all his knowledge of Morse code and semaphore, gained during his time in the Royal Navy in the First World War, Joey had got what he applied for. He now continued quietly yet firmly. 'I know you don't want this, Ma, but this is how it's got to be. I was goin' sometime. At least I've got what I wanted. It says that I'll be goin' first to receive further training in the signals.'

'I'm pleased for you, Son.' George went over and put his arm round him.

'Well pleased ain't exactly the word I'd use.' said Annie, but I will say that it's good that at least you're gonna go and do what you want.'

'Are you allowed to tell us where you'll be sent to first, Son?'

'Yeah, I don't see why not, Pa. I'm to report to, of all places Butlins at Skegness.'

'Butlins! ain't that one a them 'oliday camps?' asked Annie in surprise.

'Yep, mind you don't s'pose there's much of an holiday feel to the place now.' added Joey.

Georgie had some news of his own, but he thought it better to wait until tomorrow. No need to add further to his parents anguish. Earlier today, when both his mum and dad had been at work, he had telephoned the Commanding Officer who's life he had saved. His knee was getting better by the day. The officer had said to Georgie that if he had got to the point in his recovery that he felt himself capable of returning to the OME, he would try to get him transferred to a static unit. He now worked himself at one, desk bound, due the severity of his wounds, overseeing the training of new recruits into the Mechanical Engineers. The officer told Georgie that he would gain automatic promotion from his present corporal status to that of Sergeant.

All too soon Annie and George stood with Georgie at Waterloo railway station with the hundreds of other mums, dads, sweethearts, brothers and sisters, waiting for the trains that were soon to carry their loved ones off to a place they may never return from.

'Don't worry, Ma, they said that I'll get leave after me initial training. I'll be back here before you know I've gone.'

'I pray you're right, Joey, Son.'

'Tell you what, as soon as they tell us we can come home, I'll ring you, but you got to promise me one thing.'

'What's that then?'

'Have some pie and mash waitin' for me when I get there.'

Trust Joey to make a joke of it, George was thinking. These two boys of ours always put others feelin's before their own. Annie and George had every reason to feel very proud. Here they were, waiting to send eighteen year old adopted son Joey off to fight in the war. He had given them the chance to see Georgie grow into a fine young man, by turning the attentions of a raging bull away from Georgie onto himself. In turn, that meant that later in life, Georgie was there to drag two men off the blood stained French beach. Both boys had, in their own ways, been to hell and back, yet somehow remained the most generous, caring and loving sons anyone would be proud of.

As the train approached, Georgie was the first to take hold of his brothers hand to shake it, then as they looked into each others eyes. 'Bugger that' said Georgie, and let go his hand and they embraced. 'Take care, you hear me, Bruv?' said an emotional Georgie.

'I will. Don't go bein' too hard on them trainees when you get to Woolwich. Just remember your bruvvers one a them as well.' The young men smiled at each other. Brothers they may be, but they will always think of each other as the closest of best friends, a bond never to be broken.

George and Annie lingered over their goodbyes. Both without knowing, that the other was remembering the same thing. The night a frightened young boy came banging at their front door.

Joey was one of the lucky ones. He managed to find a seat before the train became full of service personnel from all the armed forces. He caught a final glimpse of his family standing on the platform. Even on this cold January morning, he started to feel a comforting warmth, generated by so many people pressed into a confined space. He let his mind wander back over the last few weeks. Starting with the annual letter and photograph sent from Mrs Wilson. Soon it would be four years since he last saw his little brother Jonny and two baby sisters, Violet and Lily. Every year that she wrote, Mrs Wilson apologised for the separation, but she still maintained it had been for the best. She assured them that all three were very happy and contented. Judging by the smiles on their faces in the photograph Joey could well believe it. 'One day,' he told himself, 'one day me Rosie and Matty will find them.' Then he turned his thoughts to Christmas. At least he had been able to spend a couple of hours with his other family. Thanks to his pa, who got them all out of bed at eight in the morning on Christmas day and to everyone's surprise drove them down to Eynsford. The only other person involved in the subterfuge was Millie. Her lot wondered why she was so intent on them going to early mass, she virtually pushed them all out the door. It had been worth it though, for her to see the looks of disbelief on their faces when they turned into the driveway to find George's Morris parked there. Joey smiled to himself, no one else in the train took any notice, many of them were also reliving good times.

'Crafty old sod that pa of mine' he thought, 'I wondered why he kept tellin' us not to send our presents through the post. He must have been planning it for a while.' Joey let out a long drawn out sigh. He'd tried to keep his mind off one person, he had no chance though. He'd lain awake most of the previous night, his thoughts in turmoil. Glad that this morning she couldn't come to the station to wave him off, she had to look after the shop. He knew his reserve would probably have crumpled and more than likely he would have proposed there and then in the freezing cold on a crowded railway platform. He remembered now how they had sat in the tiny alcove, partially obscured from other diners, in the restaurant that had candle lit tables that were covered with crisp white linen. Throughout the meal they glanced at each other, when they thought the other wasn't looking. Linda struggled to eat the delicious food that had been put in front of her. She had to get something off her chest first.

'Look, Joey' her voice had come out louder than she expected through her nervousness. Joey looked up surprised at her tone. She lowered her voice to no more than a whisper, 'It's no good, I can't go on like this. For goodness sake you're going into the Navy tomorrow.' she took a deep breath, 'are we a proper couple or are we just friends?' There she'd said it at last, it had only taken her nearly a year. Joey put his knife and fork down and stared at his plate for what seemed like an age to Linda. 'Well?' she prompted, beginning to think that she had read the signs wrong, doubt began to set in. Maybe he didn't love her the way she loved him. It could be just an excuse saying that he didn't think it right for them to get serious because he was joining up. 'What do you want me to say?' Joey looked so very sad at that moment, Linda's heart went out to him. 'Joey, surely after all this time we can be honest with one another. I've got to tell you before you go exactly how I feel.' She took a deep breath, 'Joey Smith-Powley you old fashioned fool, I love you, and I want to be with you, for how ever long that is. There! I've said it.' she finished in a rush.

Joey reached out and grabbed Linda's hand his was shaking. 'Oh what the hell,' Joey said a smile coming to his face, 'Course, I love you, I feel the same as you, but....'

'Oh, Joey, why do there have to be but's'

'Because I don't want you to be left alone if something happened to me. You're far too young.'

'I understand what you're saying, but *I* could get killed in a raid tomorrow or anytime, we can't live like that. In these times we have to grab happiness while we can.'

Joey thought long and hard about what Linda was saying. He asked himself, 'did he want to risk losing her.' he knew the answer to that.

'Look, I'm goin' to be away for six months. If we still feel the same for each other after that, well, before I get posted to a ship, I'll ask you to marry me.'

'Oh, Joey, ask me now.' she begged, 'Why wait six months?'

'Please, Love, let me do it this way. My mother married young, and boy did she regret it.'

Linda knew the story of Joey's parents. 'But that was because of who she married. You're not your dad and I'm not your mum.'

'I just want us both to have more time, I need to be sure that what we feel is the real thing. Neither of us have been out with many other people.'

'I don't need time to know that I love you more than any thing else on this earth, Joey. But if that's what you really want, then I'll go along with it.'

Joey leant across the table to kiss her. 'Thank you for understanding. I love you so very much.'

Now as Joey sat on the train taking him away from Linda for such a long time, Joey wondered if he had made the right decision.

George, Annie and Georgie caught a bus back to Walworth road. Many ambulances passed them enroute. When George enquired of the conductor if he'd heard of any major incidents in the area, he was shocked at the reply. 'ain't you 'eard, Mate? the Bank Tube took a direct 'it last night. The last I 'eard they'd dug out over 'undred bodies. That's what most a these ambulances are toin' an' frowin' to.' A sad day for the Powley family just turned into an even sadder one.

Georgie only had two days left at home before donning his army uniform that now had the added extra stripe on the arms of the tunic. His OME badge shone from the polishing it received. When he stood in front of the long hall mirror to inspect himself, a good feeling spread through him, for the image staring back, was one he thought he'd never see again. Okay so he wouldn't be rejoining his old unit, going to the front or wherever their skills were needed. From now on he was to train the new recruits that would be in the thick of things, repairing and servicing all combat vehicles, so vital a part in this cruel war.

He collected all the electrical and mechanical reference books he had acquired during his apprentice years with the Metropolitan Police. He packed these along with a few of his personal belongings in to the small case that would fit easily on the pannier of his motorbike. Finally he tied his walking stick to the case, he only needed to use it, when his leg became tired.

'I've made you a cup of tea, Love.' his mum called from the kitchen.

'Thanks, Mum.'

'Have you got room for these cakes I made and just a few sandwiches to go with them?'

'We have got a canteen there you know.' he laughed. 'I'm only going to, Woolwich.'

'Be that as it may, but it don't hurt to have a bit extra.'

'No, Mum. I reckon I can find space to put them in. Anyway shouldn't you be getting' ready to go to work?'

Just as he said that, Kath called up the stairs, 'You ready, Annie?'

'Give me two minutes, Gel.' She quickly grabbed a comb and pulled it through her hair. 'Now you be careful, Georgie, keep off that leg as much as you can. And make sure you get to their shelters.'

'Yes, Mum. Go on with you woman. I'll more than likely be home for a weekend in a couple of weeks.'

Annie kissed her boy affectionately, as he followed her to the top of the stairs. Kath called out her goodbyes to him. Last night most of the family and a few friends had come round to wish this young hero of theirs all the best in his new position. Just as they had done, before Joey took Linda out for the meal on his last night.

Georgie took his time over the cup of tea. Wondering whether he should give Rosie one last call before he left. 'No' he told himself. It was just last week when he'd last spoken to her on the telephone. That time it had been to wish her a happy seventeenth birthday. He recalled her words now, when he asked if she was going to do anything special to celebrate.

'Well, one of Millie's friends sons has asked to take me to the pictures.'

'Oh, who's that then, have I met him?' Georgie knew his tone had lost its friendly note.

'No. He was away at university before applying to join the air force. He doesn't leave till next month.' Rosie knew Georgie wasn't happy about this.

'Over eighteen is he then?'

'Of course, I don't go out with kids you know.' she was enjoying this.

'Go out with a lot of blokes then do you? You've never mentioned it before.'

'You never asked.' Then Rosie thought she had gone far enough. She was only doing it to see how he would react. When they were together, she felt that there was something special between them. The brother and sister relationship they'd shared seemed to be turning into something more. Something she had wanted for years. It was just a feeling she had, but the way she caught him looking at her sometimes, when he thought she wasn't watching. So now she changed tac, 'Come on, Georgie, I'm only having a laugh, course I haven't been out with lots of blokes. And to be honest, this son of Millie's friend is so up himself, thinks he's Gods gift. I think he's been out with nearly every girl that lives in the village.'

'So you're not going to go out with him then?'

'I didn't say that. I haven't made up my mind yet. I do want to see the film though.'

'Look, Rosie, I don't like the sound of this bloke. He might... '

'Might what, Georgie?'

'Well, he might try something.' Georgie couldn't believe he was having this conversation with Rosie.

'I can look after myself. But if you really don't want me to go, then I won't.'

'I think it'd be for the best. Look if you like I'll come down and take you on me next twenty four hour.' Georgie realised what he had just said. 'that is if you really want to see this film, if it's still showing, I wouldn't want you to miss it, just because of what I said.'

'That would be smashing. Do you still want me to write to you like before?'

'Only if you've got the time. I reckon to get home a bit more now. So it's up to you really.'

He knew as he said it, that he may have talked her out of writing with his couldn't care less attitude. If only he knew that Rosie knew him better than he knew himself.

'Well you let me know the address and we'll see. But I'm holding you to taking me to the pictures.' There the conversation came to an end as the others wanted to wish Rosie happy birthday. It did leave Georgie with an awful lot of thinking to do. Rosie was now a young woman. A young woman with men after her it seemed. He didn't think he liked that one little bit.

When Georgie arrived at the Woolwich Barracks, the first person he met was, Private Jenkins. Jenkins saluted his new Sergeant smartly. It took Georgie a while to place the face. When it dawned on him he smiled and extended his hand.

'Good to see you again, Jenkins. I must say you look much better than the last time we met.'

Their last meeting had been on the day Georgie had been discharged from hospital. He had gone round to where the more serious cases were. Private Jenkins had received the more serious wounds of the three men. Yet he had been able to extend his hand to the then, Corporal whose shouting, swearing and ordering him to kick his legs, penetrated his semi conscious and pain riddled head and that made him obey with an instinct that consequently saved his life.

'Good to see you too, Sergeant.' he replied whilst still standing to attention.

'At ease Private.' Georgie commanded. 'Is this your new posting as well?'

'Yes, Sergeant, arrived yesterday.'

'Fully recovered I hope.'

'Well apart from losing one of me kidneys, I feel on top of the world, Sergeant. Thanks to you. Could I shake yer 'and agen though, Sarg, just to say thank you proper like. From me and me missus and me two kids?' he finished. Georgie took the Privates outstretched hand.

'Anyone would have done the same.' Georgie found all this hero stuff a bit embarrassing, so he continued speaking to Jenkins. 'Sorry to hear about the kidney. Thought you might have been invalided out though.'

'They tried. But the CO put a word in here for me, we got quite close during our stay in 'ospital. Somefin' in common I s'pose.'

'Good sort that one. I've also got him to thank for this posting. Do you know where I should park my bike?'

'Yes, Sergeant. I'll take you there. Then I'll show you where to report to. You'll find fings a bit more relaxed here, if you don't mind me sayin,' Sarg.

They all work long hours but wivout the worry that the whole lot'll be blown up as soon as we've repaired them, unless a bomb lands here of course. So far nearly ev'ry bloke I've met was at Dunkirk and they're all determined to get as many vehicles back where they're needed. It was 'ard when we 'ad to destroy so many tanks an' that before clearin' out a there. So it must be a good feelin' ev'ry one of them pullin' togevver to get the repairs done in double quick time.'

Georgie was given a day to acclimatise to his new role in the army. He met the others in charge of training and spent the good part of the day watching the more experienced men pass on their knowledge to the trainees.

Life for the remainder of that year back in Camberwell went on as usual. People getting on with their lives as best they could in these dreadful times. The one thing on most peoples minds was wondering if the next bomb to fall would have their name on it. Whilst elsewhere, Hitler's armies continued on with their invasions that were leading to more and more Countries having to surrender. Europe was fast becoming under the detested control of the Nazi regime.

Without the boys ration books, Annie didn't have very many things to swap with Kath and Doll. Up until then she had done very well out of the arrangement. Each new week brought with it more items of food being put on ration. Shortage of tea was one of the hardest things for Annie and many like her to come to terms with. No longer could she enjoy the many cups of tea and a jaw with her sisters or neighbours. In the mornings at breakfast she would make a pot of tea with one small scoop of tea leaves, with just enough hot water to allow her and George one full cup each. This was the best cup of the day. Throughout the remainder of the day, after Annie got home from work, she would top up the pot using the same leaves with boiling water. When George came in from work, Annie would add a further half scoop of leaves, even then there was no resemblance to the golden liquid in their cups that morning. Nearly every day, Annie found herself in one queue or another. Word would go round that the butchers up the Walworth Road had fresh chickens or pork in. So the queue would grow and grow, stretching sometimes half the length of Walworth Road. *If*, the story was true and that he did indeed have these in stock, you had to be at the very front to get lucky. Even though every single person, even those right at the back of the queue knew this, they stayed put. Always with the hope that today could be your lucky day. Rarely was there any bad feelings, sometimes tempers inevitably would flare up, especially if they thought one person had been sold more than their rations allowed, or the most likely cause of aggravation was when someone tried to push in. Annie had witnessed a couple of fights between women. There would be the one who was queuing in the accepted and unwritten rule way, minding her own business, only to have another walk up plain as you like, who would edge her way in the line to stand in front of her. The air would turn blue, before one or the other made the first point of attack. Punches would be exchanged, hair nearly yanked out from its roots, biting, kicking, you name it, these ladies would go at it hammer and tongs until someone stepped in to pull them apart. This usually fell to a passing man. Annie was no coward but it didn't do to get involved in such incidents. She often wondered afterwards, what chance Hitler would have if left alone in a room with these women. On the whole, most women used queuing as an opportunity to have a good old gossip and there was plenty of banter going on. The usual answer to the question, 'what you queuin' for, Gel?' would most likely be, 'ain't got a clue but wiv a queue this long it must be somefing good.'

On a bright Saturday in late march, Rose popped round to show Annie her latest letter from her children. It had been seven months since she and her husband Ted had last seen them. True to his word George had driven them, along with Annie, on the long drive to the small village on the Hampshire and Dorset boarders. Georgie, who had recently left hospital, offered to mind the shop. So they were able to leave early on the Saturday morning, then return late on the Sunday. It was an emotional reunion as was to be expected. The only bit of comfort Rose and Ted could take, was that at least their children had been so very lucky in the fact that, Bea Tickner, was the most caring, kind and gentle person who adored children, especially the five that were now in her care. This was no 'show' put on for the benefit of the evacuees family, it was obvious that all the children had come to love and respect Bea in return. Rose couldn't help but feel slightly jealous, of someone other than her looking after her two. She knew she should feel only gratitude, and even though she took an instant liking to Bea, she still felt it wrong that through no fault of her own, someone else was standing in her rightful place as their mum. It was now eighteen months since young Ronnie and Edna had been evacuated. Many evacuees had returned early in 1940, when Londoners thought that the expected bombing raids were not going to happen. Rose desperately wanted her two to come home, but she was persuaded to wait. At the time she had felt so heartbroken she dearly wanted them back with her. How glad she was though, when later in the year and the bombs fell, she counted her blessings that her children were not among those frighteningly high numbers that had been killed.

George arrived just as she was about to read the letter.

'Hello, Gels,' George greeted them both with a peck on the cheek. 'What's that you've got, Rose, kids are keepin' up writin' to you then?'

'Yeah. This one's from our Ronnie. Flippin' amazin' ain't it. Turned into proper little letter writers ain't they? They don't write ev'ry week now though, still some muvvers I know are lucky if they get a letter in a six munf. At least my two take it in turns to write a coupla times a munf.'

'You haven't read it yet have you?'

'No, you're just in time, George.' Rose unfolded the piece of paper.

Dear Mum and Dad

First, thanks for me birthday presents and money. You shouldn't have sent me that much. I paid for all of us to go into Fordingbridge where we had a smashing fish and chip tea Auntie Bea. Wow what a treat that was. First time we've had that since we've been here. Tell the others I will be writing to them next week to say thanks. Glad to hear that Georgie's better, you should have seen the faces of my mates at school when I told them my cousin was going to get the Distinguished Conduct Medal for bravery, they was dead jealous. It was our Pat's thirteenth birthday two days ago, and I hope you don't mind but I saved some of my money to take her to the pictures in Fordingbridge. Her dad can't afford much, I told you she hasn't got a mum didn't I? Then when we got home Auntie Bea had invited some of our friends round and we had a bit of a party, it was for both of us. Pat was ever so happy it made her cry. Teresa's starting work soon. She's got a job helping to cook our school dinners. Pat likes the idea of that. Me and Bob are going to look for some work. Well I am fifteen now. My teacher said she'll give me a good recommendation because I've done so well at my maths and English. Bobs good as well so it would be great if we could get a job together. I help Pat out sometimes with her homework. I don't have to tell you about Ed, cause she's going to write next week. Be great if you could get Uncle George to bring you to see us again. Auntie Bea sends her best wishes and says she'll write soon. Lots of love from Ron.xxx

'He talks about Pat a lot, don't he, Gel. Do you fink it's the first flush of love?' Smiled Annie.

'That's what me and Ted fought, Annie. I hope that Bea is keepin' an eye on them.'

'Don't be daft you two, he's a growing lad, and by the sounds of it, is growin' into a generous one. Pat's still just a kid, If there was anyfing in it, do you think he'd be telling his mum and dad that he used his birthday money to take her to the flicks?'

'I s'pose when you look at it like that, George, you're right. And yeah, he is turnin' into a good boy ain't he?' Rose finished with a smug look on her face.

'If things quieten down, Gel, maybe we could go down and see them again maybe in the Summer, eh?'

'Oh, George, that'd be smashin' if we could.'

Chapter Thirteen

March went on and April turned into May. A month that brought with it one of the heaviest and long lasting raids. The magnificent building of the House of Commons was hit and there was a lot of damage.

The death toll from the raids continued to rise, the number of civilians killed broke the hearts of the Londoners. Break their hearts as it did, it didn't break down their guts and determination that they would never surrender. There were many times when they felt downhearted, sickened, fed up to the teeth with rationing and the dreary blackout. The daily task of making sure not even a speck of light was visible to the outside of the house. Woe betide anyone who left chinks of light showing. The one mistake many made at the outset of the blackout, was when opening their front door and forgetting to turn the passage light out before doing so. Those that were caught out by the ARP wardens, who would shout at the top of their voices for all to hear, '*get that light out*' were always amazed as there seemed to be a Warden right by their house when they had their lapse in concentration. George made Annie laugh, when he told her about one family down the road from his wardens hut that were always leaving the passage light on, they had four teenage boys that were in and out all evening.

'The husband comes out the other day, just after I'd had to shout out again, and accuses me of spying on them.'

'Why'd he think that, George?'

'Well he couldn't work out how I could see what was going on from me hut that's a fair way off from his house. Anyway, I was fed up with this lot not doing their duty, so I made him come and sit in the doorway of the hut.'

'Why?'

'You'll see in a bit. He hadn't been there for more than ten minutes when a big chunk of the pavement and road lights up. "what's that?" he asks, scared like. That mate is your passage light, shining like a full moon on the street.'

'Does it really shine as bright as that, George?'

'You believe it, Annie. When the moons behind clouds and there's no street lamps and no cars, I tell you that it's like the black hole of Calcutta out there. And any light on shines really bright.'

'What did he say?'

'He couldn't apologise enough. I think it scared the living daylights out of him. He shot off back to his house looking up at the sky all the time. Reckon he fought the Germans might have pin pointed his place or somefing. And d'you know what?'

'No, what tell me?'

'The next night, he comes to see me in the hut just after the sirens had gone off, and he says he wants to volunteer to join us in the ARP. Anyway, I said I'd contact him when all was quiet. As he walks off to join his family in the shelter, he calls out, ''by the way, Mr Powley, soon as I got in last night, I took that flamin' bulb out. You won't need to be shoutin' at us no more.'' Made me chuckle that did.'

Georgie hadn't been able to keep to the arrangement of taking Rosie to the pictures. The twenty four hour passes he thought would come regularly didn't materialise. Back in February he made a quick call to break the news. 'As soon as I do get leave, I promise I'll make it up to you.'

'Any idea when that's likely to be?'

'Well the way things are going here, I doubt whether it'll be for weeks yet.'

'Oh well, can't be helped can it?'

'I'll either put it in a letter or give you a call when I know for sure.' Georgie should have left it there but instead, he heard himself go on to ask, Did you go out with that fly boy on your birthday?' he quickly added, 'Cos I wouldn't like to think you were stuck at home.'

'Actually I did go out. Not to the pictures though, went out and had a nice meal.'

'Behave himself did he?' Georgie could have kicked himself, why didn't he just keep his big mouth shut.

'I wouldn't know. You see I went out with a couple of girls from the college.'

'Why do I feel so relieved' Georgie thought. Out loud he continued, 'That's nice. Good crowd are they?'

'Oh yes. I've made some real good friends there.'

'How's the shorthand coming along? In your last letter you said that it was hard going?'

'It's beginning to sink at last. At least I know I wasn't the only one struggling.'

'Oh good, good.' Georgie was now starting to struggle to find things to say. It was always like this lately. 'Oh well, I'spose I'd better get back to it.'

'Is it really that busy there, Georgie?' Rosie needed to know that he wasn't just putting her off. She could tell he didn't know what to say next. After all, he would be twenty one later in the year. She wouldn't believe that someone as good looking as him, didn't go out with loads of girls. She found herself getting hot and bothered when she thought of another girl running her fingers through that natural quiff in his hair. It made him look so sexy.

'Honest, Rosie. from Monday to Saturday afternoon, we are training, some nights we don't stop till gone nine. Then, Sundays, me and the other trained sparks help out with the more difficult repairs, the ones we daren't let the trainees get their hands on. Damaged and broken down vehicles are arriving in big numbers every day.'

'I believe you, thousands wouldn't.' Rosie finished with a laugh. I'll wait to hear from you then, Georgie.'

By mid June the air raids had become sporadic, and no where near as devastating. Some families that had moved out of London slowly but surely began returning to their homes, if they still were standing that was. It meant that Annie no longer went over the road to the school where bomb victims were cared for in the immediate aftermath. She looked forward to going to work these days. They were allowed to have the wireless on and listen to 'Music While You Work.' Last year, the two favourite songs, where all the women joined in singing at the top of their voices, was one by Gracie Fields. 'Wish me luck as you wave me goodbye.' Then with even more gusto and pride the day after a bad raid, they'd join in with, 'There'll always be an England.' Trouble was some of them got carried away they would start to dance round the factory whenever they heard Glenn Millers band play, 'In the mood' If they are not stopped quick enough the whole production comes to a halt. The bosses are good, but not that good. They need production to be at its full potential at all times. This year the girls like to sing the latest songs such as, 'Bless 'em all' and especially their Vera's, 'White cliffs of Dover.' Next Wednesday, workers from all shifts had been told that they were in for a treat. 'Workers Playtime' was coming to the factory to entertain them for an hour. So even if you were on the early or late shift, you were invited to come along.

After the boss had announced this piece of exciting news, there was a lot of laughing and joking amongst the workers.

'You going to get up and give us a song then, Annie' Kath called above the roar of the machines.

'Get away wiv you. Not bleedin' likely.' Annie shouted back.

'Come on, Annie, you got a good voice.'

'You can shut up a'nall, Doll. I ain't gonna make a laughin' stock a meself.'

'Don't worry, Doll.' Kath mouthed, as she gave a conspirital wink. 'We'll get her up there.'

A few of the others noticed and gave a thumbs up sign to Kath and Doll. They all knew Annie was not only good for a laugh, but good for a song too.

Two weeks later, Germany invaded Russia but not even this startling news could dent the feelings of excitement amongst the girls on the assembly line. The production team from Workers Playtime had, kept their promise to come to the factory and given the women a day to remember.

Two days later and Annie was in her element, as she laughed and pretended that she was back on the make shift stage at the factory with the performers from 'Workers Playtime.' She insisted that her co-workers had practically pushed her up there to sing.

'What else could I do once I was on the stage? I'd have looked daft just standing there, so I obliged them.' But today this was the only audience that made her life complete, an audience of three. Her husband and her two boys, who had arrived within a day of each other, home on leave. Joey had been given two weeks, and Georgie a seventy two hour pass. Joey had finished his preliminary training, 'come through the exams with flying colours,' he'd proudly told Georgie and his ma and pa.

'Should get a stripe up pretty soon. It won't be long before I catch up with you, Georgie.' he laughed.

'Not so fast, Kid. There's a whisper going round that we might be getting a new Division.'

'What do you mean?' Joey asked with interest.

'Well it seems that one of the big wigs wants to join all sparks and Mechs in one unit. If it does gets the go ahead, I can't see it happening for ages though.'

'You in favour are you, Boy?'

'I reckon so, Dad. P'raps then I can do more on the electrical side, after all that's what I applied for in the beginning.'

'You've learnt an awful lot more about mechanics though haven't you.'

'Oh yeah, don't get me wrong, Dad, it's just that *when* all this is over and I go back to me civvy job I want to make sure I'm up to the mark. I'll be lookin' for a quick promotion.'

'Why did you say to, Joey "not so fast" when he said he was catchin' you up though?'

'Well, Mother Dear, My CO told me that if this comes about, I could be in the runnin' for another step up.'

'What my, Boy an Officer?' wailed Annie.

'You never know, but keep it under your hat for now.'

Georgie arrived home the previous afternoon. He had planned on going down to Eynsford after spending an hour or so at home. That was until his mum told him that Joey would be arriving in the morning. He telephoned Rosie to tell her that he would pick her up the following day at about five o-clock. 'Put your glad rags on.' he told an excited Rosie. And no matter how much she pleaded with him he wouldn't tell her where they were going. He was feeling chuffed with himself for getting hold of two tickets, that were like gold dust, to see Gracie Fields sing at a show in London.

The plan was that Rosie would spend the night at his house, then the next day George would drive them all back to Eynsford so that Joey could see the rest of his family. Joey also had plans for the evening, first though, he needed to find something he'd wrapped in tissue paper and put in Annie's memory cupboard along time ago. Then he asked his ma, what was the best thing to clean gold with. Of course Annie wanted to know what he was up to.

'Look, I've got something to tell you all.' His mum, dad and brother knew it must be important, because whenever Joey was nervous or upset over something, he always ran his fingers over the tiny scar beneath his right eye, caused by the ring his father wore, on *that* night, so the three of them gave him their full attention.

He coughed to clear his throat. 'It's about me and Linda,' he paused, not quite sure how to put it.

His dad helped him, 'well we know how close the two of you are, Son. Come on spit it out whatever it is.'

'I know neither of us is even nineteen yet, but, well, tonight I'm going to ask her to get engaged.' the words rushed out of his mouth.

Georgie was the first to react, he went forward to shake Joey's hand. 'Good on you, Joey, congratulations. Thought you was going to wait until after the War?'

'That was the plan, Georgie, but well, I got to thinking about something Linda said, it made sense that's all.'

'When are you plannin' to get married, Son?'

'Don't worry, Ma, we're not going to rush into anything. But I want to show her that I'm as serious about her, as she is about me.'

'Then me and your ma wish you all the happiness, Son. Isn't that right, Gel?'

'Course it is. It's as plain as the nose on me face that you love each other. Now come here and let me give you a big kiss.'

'You do like, Linda, don't you?' said Joey to his ma.

'Like her? She's spent more time in this house than she has in her own this past six months. If you didn't end up marryin' her, our Georgie would've had to.'

'Do what?' said a shocked Georgie. 'What you on about, Mum?'

'Well, she's already like a daughter, so someone would've had to make sure we didn't lose her.' she finished with a smile.

'Show us the ring then. I gather you've got one?'

'I've got one, Georgie, but I didn't have to buy it.'

Then the penny dropped with Annie and George. They remembered that the Undertaker had given two rings to Joey, as far as he was concerned, regardless of what, Dan Smith, said, Joey was the eldest child, Joey's, mum Sally had worn the rings. One, was an engagement ring the other a Wedding ring. Joey would have wanted nothing to do with them if his gran and grandad Smith hadn't told him at the funeral, that they had bought the rings for his mum. Their son, Dan had left them in no doubt that no way was he going to throw good money away on rings for the silly young girl that trapped him. These had been their Wedding gift to Sally. The rings had been to the Pawnbrokers many times so that Dan could put the money on a horse, in the end, Sally had sent them to her mother in law for safe keeping. And it was she who passed them onto the Undertaker for when Sally was laid out in his parlour. So, Joey took the three diamond encrusted engagement ring from it's tissue paper and after giving his family a quick glimpse, transferred it to a tiny black velvet lined ring box. The other ring, a gold band, Joey had given to Rosie as the eldest daughter. So it seems this evening was going to be pretty special all round.

'Oh, Georgie, that was great. Did you see those beautiful dresses she wore. and wasn't she funny. What song did you like best.'

'Hold on, give me time to get a word in edgeways. Yes, didn't notice, very and Sally.'

'eh! What you on about?'

'Answering your questions. One: Yes it was great Two: I didn't really notice what she was wearing. Three: She was very funny and four: I liked her singing, Sally best.'

'Oh you idiot' Rosie playfully punched him. But tell me now, how did you manage to get such good seats? let alone the tickets. They must have cost a fortune.'

'Nothing to it really.' He sniffed and blew on his nails then pretended to shine them on his army tunic.

'Big, Head. Come on tell me, or else?'

'Or else what?'

'Erm, or else, when we get back to your house, I'll tell Aunt Annie and Uncle George that you took me in the back row.' she laughed.

'You wouldn't?'

'Try me, Buster.'

'Okay, you win. Not much to it really, there's this Private Jenkins back at the depot, his brother works at the theatre. Sent him four tickets.'

'What and this Private Jenkins gave two to you. Are you good buddies then?'

'Well sort of. We've got a lot in common and yeah of late me and him have become mates.'

That was the truth, he didn't have to go into any more detail than that.

Georgie had left his motorbike at Rosie's house and the pair of them had caught the train to London. So that night, they caught the bus home to Camberwell.

'Can we go up top. It's years since I've been on a double decker bus?'

They climbed the stairs and Rosie made her way to the back seats. They both sat quietly for a few minutes as the bus made its slow progress round Trafalgar Square, heading towards Waterloo Bridge, then on through the Elephant and Castle before reaching their destination of the Walworth Road. The night was clear, the light from the moon shining down on to the ruins dotted frequently along the route.

Through gaps in the taped up windows of the bus, they could just make out many of the famous London Landmarks that tourists visited in the pre War days. Buildings that had stood for hundreds of years, were either now reduced to rubble or looking derelict with gaping holes where windows had once been. Georgie was aware that the scenes they were passing were upsetting Rosie. He put his arm across her shoulders and pulled her to him. 'One day' he said, 'all this'll look like nothing happened. It'll be rebuilt and the shops'll be crowded out again. You'll see.'

'I hope so, Georgie. But we're not doing too well in the War are we? I know that that Lord Haw Haw bloke tries to frighten us into surrender by spouting off all about how the Germans are beating us, but I can't help but think that what he says might be true and what our people say isn't.'

'I know what you mean. But that's what that traitors good at. He does put fear into people. Maybe our government don't always tell us the whole truth but I reckon it's best we don't hear about everything in too much detail. If the BBC broadcast exactly how many planes we've lost and the extent of bomb damage, the Germans'll hear and that will only fuel their determination.'

'Yeah,, I s'pose you're right. But how much longer can we go on like this? In a few months I'll be eighteen and although I don't mind admitting that I'm scared out of my wits, I'm going to join the WAAFS.'

This was something Georgie had never contemplated. Rosie joining up? No, that was not what he'd expected to hear. 'You don't have to do that, Rosie. You could do war work in a factory or become a land girl, but goin' into the WAAFS, why d'you want to do that?'

'I don't *want* to, Georgie. No more I suppose than you or any young person wanted to join up. But we are at War and if we want to live and bring kids into a free world not run by Hitler or the likes of him, then like you men, it's the duty of us girls to do our bit.'

'You've changed so much, Rosie.' This was the first time that the two of them had really sat and talked seriously. He was seeing another side of the girl he had looked on as a sister for so long now.

'Not really changed, Georgie, just growing up.' As she said that, Rosie turned her face so that it was within inches of Georgies. Their eyes locked. What Rosie saw in his made her feel that there was maybe a chance that he was seeing her as a young woman, a young woman who had loved him since she was a little girl who was given a length of bright blue ribbon. Georgie was battling against the feelings that were welling up inside him. Suddenly it hit him like a bolt of thunder. Here, sitting so close to him was the answer to the question that had plagued him over the last couple of years. He'd been out with lots of girls but every time they wanted to take things a step further, he'd backed off and lost interest. Always at the back of his mind was this feeling that this wasn't the one for him, he was waiting, searching for something or someone. And as he stared into Rosies eyes he knew he'd found it.

'Rosie.' he spoke gently, nervously, 'what would you say, if I said I wanted to kiss you?'

Rosie eyes lit up, her lips trembled, she felt like she should pinch herself to find out whether she was dreaming. She tried to keep her voice light-hearted, just in case, 'What a peck on the cheek like brother and sister?'

'No, what I feel at the moment is most definitely not brotherly.' he smiled as he said it, not wanting to frighten her off.

'Well in that case, yes please, Georgie, kiss me.'

After what seemed like an age they came up for air. Georgie stroked Rosie's cheek.

'Do you believe in love at first sight?' At the look of confusion on Rosie's face, Georgie smiled. 'I think I do, cos I think I saw you properly for the first time tonight, not as me little sister but a very beautiful and sexy young woman. Even though I'm sure you've been in my subconscious for years.'

'Are you saying that you love me, Georgie?' Rosie asked breathless.

'I think I am. Does that worry you? I mean, what do you feel about it?' He felt like a little boy, wanting something so much but not sure whether he really deserved it.

'Oh, Georgie, don't you know. I thought everybody could see how I felt about you. I loved you from the day you bought me my pretty blue ribbons.

It sounds daft I know, a nine year old, but from that day my love for you just kept on growing. I can't say when it turned from loving you to being *in love* with you, my feelings just matured over the years.'

'If I'm honest, deep down, I knew my feelings towards you were changing. But I tried to push them to the back of my mind. You were and still are so much younger than me.'

'Georgie, I am nearly eighteen! and three years is nothing. Maybe when I was thirteen and you were coming up to seventeen it seemed like it, but not anymore.'

'What do you think the others will say?'

'I don't know and I don't really care. I don't mean to sound harsh. But I don't want anyone or anything to come between us.'

'Please don't take this the wrong way, My Love,' he liked the sound of those words rolling off his tongue and so did Rosie, 'but, look, do you think we should keep this from the family until after your birthday. It won't stop us meeting or anything, but I don't want to think of your grand parents and Millie getting at you. If we wait, I think they'll take the news better.'

'Just as long as it doesn't come between us, then I will. After all what's another couple of months, when already I've waited eight years.' She finished smiling up at the man who had just made all her wishes and dreams come true.

Joey and Linda found themselves a quiet corner in the Standard pub. Both of them were tense. Joey was feeling nervous, he kept playing with the tiny black box in his pocket. His ma had found the box for him, 'to give the ring a nice setting.' she'd said to him. Next to him, Linda sat on the edge of her seat. Remembering the last conversation they'd had before he went away to do his training. Neither of them had referred to it in their letters to each other. Linda worried that maybe she had been pushing him into something he wasn't ready for. It was Joey that broke the awkward tension. 'Still fancy me then do yer?'

'Well so far nothing better has come along.' Linda matched his light-hearted banter.

'Should hope not. If they had of done, I'll just put what I've got in me pocket back where it came from.'

Still they were toying with each other, playing games, uncertain.

'Ooh, what you got in your pocket then, Joey?'

'Oi you saucy, fing. Not what you're finkin'.'

He took out the box. 'Here we go' he thought to himself, 'this is it' His face became serious as he took hold of her hand. 'Linda, I've done a lot of finkin' while I've been away. I've known that I fell in love with you soon after you came to work in the shop. And I want to prove to you how much I love you and no matter what might lay in store for us, I now realise that, no one knows what's round the corner, if we did then we'd always be scared to commit to anyfing. But I want to commit to you. Linda will you do me the greatest honour and make me the happiest man alive by agreein' to become my wife?' he lifted the lid to the box.

All through Joey's beautiful speech her eyes were misted over with tears. 'Oh, Joey. Of course I'll marry you. I love you so much too.' Joey took the ring out of its box and placed it on the third finger of Linda's left hand.

'Do you like it?' he needed to know.

'It's *the* most beautiful ring I've ever seen.'

'It belonged to my mum.' Joey then told her the story of the rings. 'I hope you don't mind that it's not new.'

'Joey, that makes it even more special. I'll treasure it always.'

Georgie was glad that he and Rosie had decided to keep their secret to themselves for a while. He knew that Joey was going to propose to Linda that night and he didn't want to steal any of the limelight. Joey deserved all the happiness he could get. Annie and George waited impatiently for the two young couples to get home. Even if it did mean that they would have to stay up far later than usual. Georgie and Rosie were the first to arrive just after ten thirty. Joey and Linda had picked up a fish supper to take back with them as a celebration, having already telephoned George to ask if they fancied some. So when they got in it was to find the table laid with plates, knives and forks and six glasses. When everyone was settled around the table George stood up.

'I know it would've been a lot nicer if this was Champagne' he said pointing to the port in the glasses, 'but hopefully we can get some of that for your Wedding.' he smiled at Joey and Linda. 'So for now this'll have to do. Joey and Linda, we'd like to wish you both our sincere congratulations and hope that when the day of your marriage does come, it'll be celebrated in a time of peace.'

In the morning all six of them squeezed into George's car. He was usually against overloading it but today was a special occasion. When they arrived at Millie's home the good wishes and hugs and kisses started all over again. Except for fifteen year old Matty, he thought Joey was in his words, 'bananas' to want to start thinking of getting tied down at his age.

Millie was the only one that noticed a change in Rosie. She saw the glow that radiated happiness shining from within.

As promised, George and Annie made another visit to Ronnie and Edna, with an excited mum and dad for company in the car.

What a difference they found when they arrived at the pretty little cottage. Edna had been looking out of the window for the last hour or so eager for her parents arrival. No longer was she the pigtailed eleven year old they had waved to on that sad day. It was a confident tall thirteen year old young lady that threw herself into the arms of her mum and dad. Her pale complexion had been replaced with rosy cheeks and a healthy look. How she had changed in the time since they had last visited.

'I shan't need to fill my kettle from the tap, at this rate' Bea had appeared at the doorway, 'I can fill it with all these tears,' she smiled as first Annie then George went over to her to give her a kiss. Eventually Rose and Ted followed suit when they had their emotions under control. 'Sorry about that, Bea,' said Ted, 'Who'd a fought I'd miss this little minx as much as I 'ave.' He cuddled his daughter to him.

'What time will our Ronnie be home from work, Edna?' Ronnie now worked in one of the banks in Fordingbridge along with his friend Bob.

'He'll be back in about an hour, Mum.' Edna noticed Pat had come out to greet her parents. 'You remember Pat don't you everyone?'

'Course we do' answered Rose, 'How are yer love?' she went over to kiss her on the cheek.

'Very well thanks, Mrs Trotter. Did you have a good journey?'

'Very nice, thanks. We stopped and had a nice welcome cup of tea and a cheese roll on the way down.' Rose was thinking how grown up Pat looked, she seemed much older than having just turned fourteen. What good manners she had now, quite the young lady. 'Mind you to be fair to the gel Rose,' she scolded herself, 'she was no more than a little kiddie the last time they saw her. Amazin' what a year can do.'

An hour later all the hugging and kissing started all over again, not quite so much enthusiasm this time though. It embarrassed Ronnie, after all as he told his mum and aunt as they fussed over him, 'give over, I'm not a kid anymore, I go to work now you know.' All the while he kept looking to see Pats reactions to their mothering ways. Annie wasn't the only one to notice the looks. Rose decided she'd have a quiet word with Bea as soon as she could. But for now she was just going to enjoy being with her babies again, even if they cringed when she called them that.

Rose followed Bea into the kitchen under the pretence of helping to make the tea.

'Bea, I need to ask you somefing. Don't take offence at this, but well, I can't help but notice how close my Ronnie is to Pat, he talks about her all the time in 'is letters. What I mean is, he's a growin' boy but she's barely forteen.' Rose was taken back when Bea started to laugh.

'I don't fink it's funny, Bea.'

'Oh I'm sorry Rose but you just wait I can hear Pat coming downstairs now after changing her clothes. When you see her you'll know why I find it so funny.' Just then Pat came into the kitchen. Rose's jaw nearly reached the floor, if it hadn't been for the fact that the voice now speaking was indeed that of the young girl, Rose would have sworn that it was a boy standing in front of her.

'Cor, that's much better.'

'Feel more comfortable do you now, Dear?'

'Too right I do, Auntie Bea.' Gone was the pretty girl that welcomed them not more than an hour ago who had worn a smart lemon blouse and blue skirt. In her place stood this person unrecognisable to Rose, wearing a boys shirt, long trousers, boots on her feet and to finish the look, she wore one of Ronnies old caps on her head.

'Need a hand with anything?' Pat asked, standing with her hands in her trouser pockets.

'Not at the moment, Dear. I'll give you a shout if I do.'

When Pat had left the kitchen Bea turned to Rose. 'Close your mouth, Rose or the flies'll get in there.' she was enjoying this.

'I fought it was a boy comin' in. Is that how she dresses all the time. I mean all right is she?'

'Course she is. Our Pat is just a tom boy. She doesn't go to school dressed like that nor if she's out with me. But at the weekends and sometimes after school I give in to her. She loves nothing better than going round with the boys in the village. Mind you they were none too keen in the beginning, especially her brother Bob, hated the thought of his kid sister tagging along all the time.'

'I fought her and my Edna was best friends. Don't they play together then?'

'Not quite as much as they did. See those two have become just like sisters, they tell each other all their little secrets and things like that, but as with most sisters they have their own sets of friends. Your Edna has just started to help look after children after school whose mums work in the factories, Our Terreasa put a word in for her at the school.'

'My Ed, lookin' after kids?'

'Yes, she and two of her school friends. I hear that the young ones think the world of them.'

'Well I never. Wait till I tell my Ted. So what does Pat do when Edna's doin' that?'

'Pat helps out the local farmer. She mucks out the horses stables, cleans the chicken coops, does anything the farmer asks her to do. Then Saturday mornings when Edna is still with some of the children, you'll find Pat up on the village green, either playing football or cricket with the boys. She's better at it than most of them. So now they just treat her as one of them. You should hear the way they talk to her sometimes, I'm always having to remind them that she is a girl.'

'I feel a right Charlie now. Fancy me finkin' somefin' was goin' on.'

'Don't feel like that, Rose. I know how hard it must be for you to be separated from your two and a virtual stranger telling you about the things that they get up to. It must get harder as time passes.'

'It does, Bea. But I'm hopin' that they might be able to come home to us soon. Things are quietenin' down back in London now.'

'It'll be sad for me when that time comes, but at the same time wonderful for you. You should be proud of those two kiddies. I can't believe how lucky I was when I picked them to come and live with me. I can tell you, there's many a family in this village and the surrounding ones that weren't as lucky as me. Some of the stories I've heard, make your hair curl they would. Still at least I know I won't be losing all five of them'

'What do you mean?'

'It seems the others dad has remarried and to a woman much younger than him. Terreasa knows her well and can't stand the sight of her. Anyway their dad wrote to say that even if the raids stop he'd prefer it if they stopped where they was until after the war, reckons his wife needs plenty of time to adjust to the idea. More like she don't want them.'

'But that's terrible. She must be a right cow. Do they know about this?

'Oh yes, they don't seem in the least bothered. They only worry about the time when Edna and Ronnie go back home. Understandable that.'

'How do you feel about it?'

'Over the moon. As far as I'm concerned they have a home here for as long as they like. My boy'll never come back here to live. He's decided that after the war, God willing, he's going to emigrate to America.'

'That'll be hard for you won't it, Gel?'

'It will, Rose. But if that's what he wants.... Come on that's enough of talk like that, lets get back with the others, you've come a long way to spend a couple of days with those kiddies of yours. So let's make the most of it.'

Arm in arm they went in search of their shared families.

Chapter Fourteen

'1942'

'Hope you're steering well clear of those, Yanks.' Georgie joked with Rosie over the telephone.

'Who, Me? Of course I am. What do I want with a yank when I've got me very own Captain in the British Army for.'

'Oh it's me rank that attracts you is it?'

'What else could it possibly be. Apart from that cute quiff of yours.' Private Rosie Smith of the Womens Auxiliary Air Force joked.

'How's my best girl settling in then?'

'Excuse me! Best girl? Only girl if you don't mind.'

'Whoops, slip of the tongue, my one and only.'

'That's better. Well, it's not quite as bad as I expected. The CO's not a bad old stick. Trouble is the men don't think much of us being here.'

'They'll come round soon enough. If I'm honest I know that I'll more than likely feel the same way when our intake arrive. Don't forget all we've ever known is, "you Jane, me Tarzan, me bring home the bacon, you cook it." Bound to take a while to adjust, Sweetheart.'

'You'd better think yourself lucky that you're in Berkshire while I'm in Kent. You just might find out that some of us *women* have a good left hook, *My Darling.*'

Georgie was now based at Arborfield centre in Berkshire. He was part of an advance team that were preparing the way for turning the once Army Remount depot into a base that would co-ordinate units of the newly formed Royal Mechanical Electrical Engineers training establishment. Georgie wore his Captains uniform with the new REME emblem with pride. To be involved from the outset in this merger of units was a great privilege in itself. To go up the rank as an officer was beyond words. 'Right place right time' was his answer to others that felt they had been overlooked. For indeed he knew that many OME officers got no further than Captain. It was felt that although their electrical and mechanical experiences were beyond reproach, their combat experiences in some cases were limited.

In contrast, Rosie was at the beginning of her WAAF duty. After her initial training, of which she herself claims to have "got through by the skin of her teeth" is now fortunately based at Biggin Hill airfield in Kent, within easy reach of her home and family in Eynsford. Georgie had not wanted her to join the forces. He had tried to persuade her to become one of the Land Army girls. 'They do an important job,' he'd argued. All to no avail though, Rosie had long ago made her decision.

'That would be a waste of all the secretarial skills I've learnt at college. I'm not off to fly bombers Georgie. Most of my time will be spent stuck behind a desk' Rosie strongly put her point across to him. The airfield in the first year or so of the war had suffered many bombing raids, craters could still be seen around the perimeters. Great gaping holes in the runways had been hurriedly repaired using all the skill and know how of those on the ground, so that their boys could take off to chase the bandits from the skies and then return to land safely on the makeshift runways.

Now they put all their differences of Rosies choice of work to the back of their minds. Both happy that unlike many others parted in the war, they were able to chat to each other on the phone once a week, keeping the other up to date with news from home.

Georgie told Rosie that his cousin Edna had returned from the Dorset village in May, but her brother Ronnie had decided with his Parents permission to stay on for another year. He was doing very well at the Bank and didn't think it fair to leave them as soon as they had trained him. Edna missed her friend Pat, who along with Terreasa and Bob, as previously thought had stayed there. His Aunt Rose and Uncle Ted promising that Edna could go and stay at Bea's cottage during the school summer holidays.

In March petrol for private use had been banned. This made life more difficult. It meant that Georgie could no longer make quick visits home or to meet Rosie when he had a few hours off. The only way he could get home was to travel on the overcrowded trains. That was apart from the couple of times he'd had to go back to the Woolwich depot on army business, when he would use his own motorbike, taking a quick detour over to Camberwell. On just such an unplanned visit early one evening in April, Georgie had not received the familiar loving welcome when he bounded up the stairs. His mum and dad were sitting together on the settee, his dad holding his mum who had been crying in his arms. Fear shot through Georgie, 'Who is it?' he wondered, he knew something had happened to someone close to them all. On his mum's lap was the old photo album, open at the page of their last holiday down hopping. The faces smiling out from the page were of himself and his mates, Joey, Siddy and Bernie with Annie sitting in the middle. His dad looked at his mum, such sadness radiated from his eyes. When his mum saw him standing in the doorway fresh tears spilled over from her eyes.

'What's happened, Dad?' he forced the words out.

'I'm so sorry, Son. We've just heard, young Bernie Woogitt was killed yesterday.'

Georgie sat down heavily on the nearest chair. 'No. Not Bernie,' images of his old mate flashing before him. 'What happened?' Did he really care, did he really want to know. Wasn't it bad enough to know that Bernie had gone from them for good.

'It was his first flight since he'd qualified as a navigator.' His dad started to tell him. Georgie remembered Bernie's last home leave when he had bored them all silly with his non stop chatter about the course he was on. He finished by telling them that he'd dreamed of flying since he had been given a toy airplane one Christmas years before. So as soon as the chance came his way to follow his dream he grasped it with both hands. Never had he been content like his brother Siddy to remain as ground crew, vital as their work was, he wanted to be 'up there, amongst it,' as he put it. He was over the moon when he was accepted for the navigational training school. 'Seems they got hit over Germany just as they were about to head for home. Went up in a ball of flames.'

'Did any of the other crews see any parachutes?'

'No, Son, apparently there wouldn't have been time for any of them to get out. But it would have been over quick for him, he wouldn't have known much about it.'

Georgie put his head in his hands and wept, he wept for Bernie, for Siddy and his parents, he wept for all the Bernies and their families and finally he wept for himself for his loss of a good friend from his boyhood days. There could be no funeral, for Bernie was somewhere in the waters of Germany. One day when this madness was over maybe Georgie, Joey and Siddy would go and be close to the spot of the final resting place of Bernie.

Before Georgie returned to Arborfield, his dad took him over to the Avenue School, where on a wall just inside the assembly hall was a large wooden plaque. Engraved in gold were lists of names. The first time Georgie had seen it was on the day that the headmaster had erected it. It bore the names of two young men that had attended the school. Now as Georgie looked on it for a second time, the list had grown to nearly twenty. Some of them had been in the same class as him. Their remembered faces swimming before his eyes. And soon, one more name would be added.

Georgie spoke the words he was thinking, 'At least Bernie got his dream, Dad.'

'You know me and your mum pray every night that we never get to see the name of anyone we know on this board. We pray for the ones who do get on it and their families but most of all, selfishly I s'pose, we pray especially hard that we never read you or Joey's name on it. It frightens me now though, cos after all our prayers we are still goin' to see young Bernie's name added.' Georgie didn't have any words of wisdom for the man that had guided him throughout his life. What could he say? He could only hope and pray along with his parents that no other loved names including his and Joey's would be there for them to read.

In July George drove his beloved Morris to Alf Woogitts yard covered it in a tarpaulin and patted the bonnet. 'Oh well back to shankseys pony'

He'd hoped that the ban earlier in the year might have been short lived, so had waited in the vain hope that he once more would be able to enjoy the freedom that it afforded him and his family. From now on though, It meant no more visits to and from their great friends in Eynsford, friends that if their Georgie and Rosie continue on the path they have chosen, will one day become related by marriage, a further bond to seal the closeness they already have. On Rosie's eighteenth birthday back in January, where all the Powley's, Smith's and Stones had gathered in Millie's home for a small party, Georgie and Rosie had announced to the gathering that they were together and very much in love and hoped to marry one day. The anticipated looks and words of disapproval failed to appear. Instead it was Millie who summed up their families feelings.

'Bout time you went public.' Georgie and Rosie had just stared in amazement at each other. They thought that they had hidden their feelings well. Rosie was the first of the couple to speak. 'What do you mean you knew?'

'Of course we did. It's been obvious to us all since the day young Joey got engaged to Linda.'

Georgie looked at his dad, trying to judge his reaction to the news. 'What about you, Dad, what do you think.' He so wanted his Fathers approval.

'Me, I think it's the best news we've had since Joey and Linda's.'

'Mum?'

Annie was dabbing at her eyes with her hankie. George couldn't work out if they were tears of sorrow or happiness.

'I couldn't have wished for anything better than this.' She walked across to Rosie, 'I've always thought of you as a daughter and wished years ago that if I'd have been blessed with one, then I'd have wanted her to be just like you. Now it looks like me dreams are goin' to come true.' Rosie went and hugged her.

Georgie turned to Rosie's two sets of Grand-parents. 'You don't think I'm too old for her do you?'

Reg answered for them all. 'When we noticed that your feelings for each other were changing, I can't say we didn't all sit down and talk it over lad, but we could see you weren't goin' to rush our Rosie into anyfing that she wasn't ready for. And now that she's a young woman of eighteen and I might add with her head screwed on, I know I speak for all of us when I say that we couldn't be more happy and proud of the man she's chosen.'

There followed congratulations all round, the only sad note was that Georgies best friend and brother to both him and Rosie had not been able to get leave. There was one other thing that marred the celebrations, that was that the long awaited and overdue letter with news and photo's of Lily, Violet and Jonny, usually sent to Annie before Christmas, had not arrived. No one said as much, but they all held secret fears for the safety and whereabouts of the three youngest Smith children.

Joey, who was now based at Chatham Royal dockyard in Kent, had been undergoing even more training. Something big was in the pipeline all ratings were aware of this. As he'd first been led to believe after his initial signals training, Joey did infact get his first stripes up. He'd palled up with a bloke from Streatham called Ernie Pipe. They met during their days at Butlins. The pair hit it off straight away. Ernie was a great hulk of a man, over six foot six tall with bulging muscles. But you'd be hard pushed to meet a more gentle and caring man. He had suffered the terrible loss of his wife and daughter during a raid at the outset of the war. Most men in his position would be fired by anger and wanting revenge. Not Ernie, the love of his departed wife and the knowledge that she would want him to learn to live without hate and thoughts of revenge, kept him whole. He'd once confided in Joey that he'd live his life to the full, take everything that it cared to send his way, store all the memories up in his heart and mind and when he is reunited with his wife and daughter, share every experience with them. To Joey, this was the most beautiful thing he had ever heard another man say.

August arrived amid frantic movement at Chatham. Kitbags were being filled with personal belongings, hasty letters had to be written and sent home. Joey had more notes to write than his fellow Sailors, he scribbled hurried words to everyone of his extended family, telling them he was off on an adventure and would see them soon. The organising and preparation finalised, Joey and his fellow signal operators were on the move. No destination had been given, secrecy was of the utmost importance. They were not privy to their destination. Joey and Ernie had so far been lucky enough to stay together, they hoped that this would continue.

Pleased that they were once more destined to remain in the same unit, they boarded a train at Chatham Dockyard station on the very first day in August, and it was many hours later that they found themselves being deposited in the Scottish port town of Greenock. When all naval personnel were assembled, about thirty in all, two or three of them, all in signals, made up of signalmen, telegraphists, and coding operators, were assigned to their posts.

The ships awaiting them were fourteen merchant vessels. All picked for this secret operation, because they had the added advantage of some, in that they could travel up to speeds of fifteen knots. Luck stayed with Joey and Ernie as they were both appointed to an American ship named the 'SS Santa Elisa.'

'So much for all this cloak and dagger stuff' Joey remarked, pointing out to Ernie the crates being loaded from the quayside. 'I reckon we can take it from them that we are off to Malta.' Ernie shook his head as he read the writing on the big crates. *'HM Dockyard Malta'*

'Looks like this could be the big one for us, Corp.'

The next day, Sunday the 2nd of August the convoy set sail. The sea was calm the sun shone brightly,

'Just the sort of fine summer day for a cruise' some of the men joked.

It was becoming vital to the allies that at all cost they must do all in their power to stop Malta from being taken. The tiny island had so far withstood constant bombardment. Much of its land being bombed to devastating effects. The people were running short of all basic essentials. It was uncertain how long the Maltese people could bare the onslaught. Food was scarce, medicines limited and the much needed fuels and ammunition was becoming virtually non existent. It was now imperative that somehow these essentials be got threw to them. The tide of fortune was not going the way of the British and allied forces. The past year had seen them retreating more than advancing. This convoy to Malta had untold responsibility and hope pinned on its success. It became clear just how important a task these merchant seamen and the naval and army personnel were involved in, as, when they were a few miles out to sea, the enormity of it was there before them. Joey and Ernie stood up on deck, they couldn't believe their eyes, between them they counted the different class of ships. It was as they were going about their signalling duties that they came to know the exact count. The fourteen merchant vessels were being escorted by no less than, two battleships, four aircraft carriers, eight cruisers and forty destroyers. The enormous American oil tanker *'The OHIO'* was also in the convoy. Each of the merchant ships carried the same cargo of, flour, food, medical supplies, coal, petrol and ammunition. Later their Captain informed them that there was a well thought out reason to this and that was, if just one of the ships made it through to Malta, the whole operation would be classed as a success. Supplies from one ship alone would alleviate immediate problems for the Island.

The warm sunny days continued as the convoy made its snaking way towards the straights of Gibraltar, which they reached by midnight on the 9th day of the same month. They hoped to sail through the straits undetected. All the crew knew of the dangers that they faced. Two days later as Joey stood on deck taking his turn on watch duty, those dangers stared him in the face. He watched in shock, then horror as the aircraft carrier 'Eagle' started to spew smoke, he raised his binoculars and the enormity of the situation struck him. The 'Eagle' had been hit by a Torpedo from an Italian U-boat. Men were jumping over the side, within what seemed just seconds she was listing heavily, then she was gone. From then on they came under fierce air attack. Hundreds of Italian aircraft tried to halt the convoy. Valiantly they fought back. Their anti aircraft guns hitting their intended targets and reducing the planes numbers considerably. Every merchant seaman, navy personnel and soldier had been told of what lay in store for them. Still they steamed on. Ahead lay even more danger, for they came within one hundred and fifty miles of enemy controlled airfields. On one side lay Tunisia, on the other Sicily. Each new attack lessening the size of the convoy. Then it was the turn of the German and Italian E-boats. One by one ships were being sunk, men either being blown or throwing themselves overboard on their Captains command 'to abandon ship.' On Thursday the 13th of August the 'SS Santa Elisa' became one of the casualty's.

Joey was standing on the deck with Ernie along with most of the crew, they were preparing to abandon the burning and listing ship on the orders of their American Captain. One side of the sea around them was a red flaming blanket of burning oil. The ship listed dangerously with water pouring in through the gaping hole, put there by a purple haze of fast moving light fired from one of the E-boats. Joey and Ernie embraced.

'See you in the nearest pub in Malta, Nob.' Joey joked .

'The first rounds on you, Pal.' answered Ernie in the same vain.

Then came another explosion from her bows. The final straw for the, 'Elisa'. The last Ernie saw of Joey Smith-Powley that day was of him being blown off his feet and hurtling towards the black merciless waters below.

Ernie, along with many others from the 'Elisa', was picked up by the lifeboats sent out by the 'Penn'. He scoured the faces of every man he saw once aboard the rescue ship. He didn't see his pal Joey.

The 'Penn' was now heaving under the weight of its extra 'passengers'. In the distance the 'OHIO' lay stricken, her engines silenced. As part of her extra weight she carried two fighter planes, shot down by the men aboard, then landing in the lap of their enemy. The 'Pen' made its laborious way to where 'OHIO' sat motionless. From here on in, Ernie pushed his grief for his friend to one side. He took in everything that went on around him. All the men knew they were so close now to Malta. The remaining merchant ships made haste. The 'Penn' remained alongside the 'OHIO' that, with her help the valuable cargo of oil on board the disabled ship, was slowly pushed, pulled and guided to a docks where the sight that greeted them was something to behold. Ernie stood on the crowded decks making a memory to share with his Pal Joey, either in this world, if they found each other, or in the next. As far as the eye could see the people of Malta lined the quayside, they waved banners, flags, hankies, scarves, the noise of their cheers rang on in the ears of the men long after they had left the ships.

Regret to inform you......feared dead

The words swam before Annie's eyes. She sat down heavily on the settee. It was Kath who stopped midway of pouring herself out a much needed cup of tea on returning from her shift at the factory, that heard the piercing scream. '*No*' She banged the teapot down on to the table and ran to the stairs. 'Annie, you all right?' there was no response. She called again as she took the stairs two at a time. 'Annie, what's wrong?' She found her sister-in-law sitting rocking backwards and forwards, muttering over and over, 'Joey, Joey, Joey.' Then Kath saw the piece of official looking paper lying at Annie's feet. She knew then without reading it, what it said. She took hold of Annie and cradled her in her arms. Annie's cries of anguish turned into wracking sobs. It was to this scene that George arrived home from work. Kath left the two of them in their shared grief. Later she took them both up a cup of sweet precious tea with Jack by her side. The four of them sat for a few minutes in silence, until Jack offered to let the rest of Joey's Family know. George said that he'd be grateful if Jack phoned the Eynsford side of the family. He himself would get in touch with Georgie. 'What about Linda?' cried Annie, 'how do we tell the poor gel?' Her tears came once more.

'I'll ring Georgie first, Love. Then I'll go round to Linda's house.'
George gripped the phone, his knuckles white as he waited for someone at the other end to fetch his son.

'Hello, Dad,' came the cheerful response from Georgie, on being told that his father was on the line.

'Georgie?' he couldn't go on.

'What is it, Dad. Mum's all right isn't she?' came his worried question.

'It's not your mum, Son, it's our....' he got no further,

'Not, Joey, Dad. Please say it's not Joey?'

'I'm sorry, Son, but a telegram came this afternoon.'

'When? How? Where did it happen?'

'All we know is that it happened somewhere at sea.'

'Does it say that he's, he's actually dead?' the word was such a hard one to say. He had to force it out.

'It say's presumed and that a letter will follow later.'

'There's a chance then that he could have been picked up or something?'

'I don't know, Georgie.'

'Then until someone says otherwise, I ain't gonna give up on 'im. Did they say what day it was?'

'On the thirteenth.'

'There you go then. That's my special date. If it had happened I'd 'ave felt somefing, I know I would. He's out there somewhere, I tell yer, Dad.' George knew his son was clutching at straws but if this was the only way he could deal with his loss, then so be it. Meanwhile though, he needed to know whether Georgie wanted to tell Rosie or did he want him to.

'Leave it to me, Dad. I'm goin' to speak to me CO right away. I'm sure under the circumstances he'll let me take the bike. If he does then I'll go straight to Biggin Hill tonight.'

'Will you be able to get home as well?'

'Yeah, I'm pretty sure I will. So I'll more than likely see you sometime late tonight. Tell mum I love her.'

Georgie's CO was indeed sympathetic and granted Georgie immediate compassionate leave, as did Rosie's Senior Officer on being informed of the reason why a REME Captain had turned up at the base demanding to see Private Smith.

Rosie's surprise had turned to shock when she went to confront the man she loved. She had been about to tell him off for getting her into trouble with her CO. But deep down thrilled that he had turned up out of the blue. One look at his face and a fear gripped hold of her so tightly that she thought that her very breath was being squeezed out of her. Georgie took her into his arms and gently whispered, 'I'm sorry, Love, it's our Joey.'

The next day, both sets of Joey's family descended on the home of Annie and George, or ma and pa as Joey lovingly called them. The women thought until that moment that they were all cried out, not so, for as soon as they held each other in their shared grief, the tears fell unchecked once more. The men tried to hide their grief, telling themselves that, men shouldn't cry in public, but after Georgie, a hero, and a tall strong brave army Captain could hold them back no more, each man there, found a quiet corner, glad of the large white handkerchiefs they carried.

Some four weeks later, the promised letter arrived. There was nothing in it that gave them hope. Just brief details of how Joey's name was not amongst those of the men who were listed as being rescued by other ships. It went on to say how brave he and all the men involved were and that they should feel very proud of him.

Still Georgie refused to believe that he'd never see Joey again. Now though, he kept his thoughts to himself. He understood that the others needed to come to terms with their believed loss. To not give up hope for them, meant living each day on a dream. To him, it meant living each day with a means to an end.

Chapter Fifteen

'1943'

Reg used his final precious gallon of petrol that had been stored in his garage for nearly two years, to drive the family to Camberwell so that they could all spend Christmas together. The intention was for them to leave home early on the Christmas Eve morning. For a while Reg didn't think they were going to make it. His car had been parked in the garage for so long, with him only occasionally remembering to go and 'start her up'. He turned the ignition time and again, only to be given a sickly whirring sound for his efforts. The freezing December weather did not help matters. 'Don't panic, *yet,*' he told himself, then blowing into his cold hands to warm them. 'Check the battery Reg, it's probably gone flat, or needs a top up.' He continued telling himself. The rest of the family had gathered inside the hallway, wrapped up well for the wintry temperatures awaiting them on the other side of the front door. Scarves, gloves and thick warm winter coats were in abundance.

Impatient to be on her way, Millie opened the front door, 'You there, Reg?' she called

'I'm in the garage.'

'Not a problem is there?' Millie crossed her fingers, 'oh I do hope not.' she thought.

'She won't start.' Reg's voice sounded exasperated.

That was not the answer Millie wanted to hear. Today of all days. She had been hoping for more than a year now, that something wonderful might happen. Today the reality hit her, she would have to go through with the task that had been asked of her. For the umpteenth time already this morning she opened her handbag to make sure *it* was there. 'Is there anything I can do to help?' 'Silly woman,' she thought. 'What do you know about cars.'

Reg poked his head round the garage door, 'feeling fit are you?'

'I don't like the sound of that.'

'Well I can't get it to start, so, I reckon we're going to have to try bump starting it.'

'Good thing we live on a slight incline in that case then. I'll go and tell the others.'

Millie went back into the house to break the news. The unlikely band of pushers filed out after her one by one. Bert and Ivy, now past seventy, Betty in her early sixties and finally, Matty, a fine tall strapping seventeen year old.

'Bert, you get behind the wheel, Mate.' Over their years of living together, the two men had become good friends. They often, before petrol rationing, took themselves off for a drive. Bert had been so grateful to Reg for teaching him to drive. Quite an achievement for someone of his tender years. That was one of the things about rationing that upset them both, for it came into being just about the same time that Reg retired from the railway, when the two had been looking forward to more happy times of motoring. Mind you, the other members of the household took great delight on teasing Reg and Bert about the day they left home soon after having eaten their Sunday dinner. The plan was for them to do a 'dummy run' to find the best way to get to Canterbury, where Millie's widowed sister-in-law lived, Reg and Betty thought it would be a nice birthday treat for Millie. Everything was fine for the first few miles, the surrounding countryside being familiar to Reg, or so he thought. 'There's a nice little café a few miles ahead,' he confidently assured Bert. 'If I remember rightly it's called the 'Rose of Tralea.'

'Good, I could do wiv a cuppa.'

Half an hour later and Bert turned to his mate, 'How much further to this café, Reg?'

'Can't be far now, Bert.' not sounding quite as confident now.

'Where abouts are we?'

'Well I don't know the name of the place, but don't worry it looks familiar to me.'

'That's what's worryin' me, this road looks familiar to me a'nall, an' I ain't never bin this way in me life before today. You sure we ain't goin' round in circles?'

Reg slowed the car as they approached a crossroads.

'Did you hear me, Reg, are we lost?'

'I heard you, I was just trying to get me bearin's.' He looked at the three roads ahead. 'is it left, right or straight on?' he thought to himself, before finally turning to Bert with a sheepish look on his face.

'We're lost ain't we?' Bert had read the look on Reg's face, no need for words.

'Sorry, Bert, but I think we are. Trouble is every road looks the same. I know it's years since I last went to Canterbury but I thought it'd be easy enough to find agen.'

'But when you went before, you was able to follow the signs weren't yer?'

'True. Bloody stupid idea takin' down all the sign posts anyway, how are people expected to get about. We've been goin' round and round for ages now and not seen any sign of life. A body could die of thirst or starvation out here.'

'Steady, on Reg, we ain't in the dessert, just somewhere in the Kent countryside.'

Eventually they came to a petrol garage, good thing they did, as the fuel supply indicator was bouncing in and out of the red. The owner at the garage, who was used nowadays to motorists getting lost, told them exactly where they were, to Reg's disbelief they were just a mile away from the Isle of Sheppey Bridge. Bert scribbled down the owners hastily given directions back to Eynsford. 'You should be 'ome in less than forty minutes' were his words. Two and a half hours later, a very tired and fed up pair had walked stiffly through the front door in Eynsford.

Bert eased his enlarged frame into the drivers seat, something else Bert had learnt since living in the country with these kind folk, was, how good it felt to have a full belly. In London they lived from day to day, no looking forward, no dreams, just hoping to get enough money to put a plate on the table with enough food on it to give them a chance of surviving another week. His health had improved enormously, as had his waistline. Reg had found part time work for him at Eynsford station, it might have been only three mornings each week, but it gave Bert that much needed push to his ego and self confidence. Even Ida looked forward to each new day, she found lunchtime work at the local infants school. Added to this, Ida insisted on cooking the tea, or dinner as Millie called it. She and Bert had never taken handouts or accepted charity. They were eternally grateful to Millie for asking them to come and share her home, to escape the horrors of the bombs, it also meant they would be close to Rosie and Matty, but it had been on the understanding that they 'do their bit'

'Let the hand brake off, Bert, and I'll just roll it back out of the garage first.'

'Right you are, Reg.'

The car rolled backwards down the drive. No need for Bert to steer clear of the gates, for no longer did the ornate iron gates divide the drive from the pavement, they had long since gone, along with every bit of spare iron to be melted down and re-cycled into much needed fighting components. When Millie was first notified of this, she had a little moan to her family.

'What will be the next thing to go?' she'd said. Later though she took great comfort in the knowledge that even the King and Queen's railings had been removed. 'Oh well, at least we're in good company.' she'd laughed with Betty.

Bert turned the wheels so that he was facing down the hill. Matty took hold of his Nan Stone's arm. 'Hey, what do you think you are doing, Lady?'

'Helping to push the car, what do you fink?'

'No sorry, I don't think so, Nan.' he smiled and gave Ida a cheeky wink. 'Leave it to the young ones.' Matty knew that would get them going.

'Oi you cheeky bugger, you sayin' I'm old?'

'Actually' joined in his gran, 'I feel flattered. Thank you, Dear.' she curtseyed to Matty.

Matty ducked as Ida tried to give him a gentle clip round the ear.

'When you've finished you lot' called Reg.

So Reg, Millie, Betty and Matty started to push with Ida trotting alongside. At the second attempt, when Bert engaged the clutch the engine sparked into life and the car shot forward, nearly depositing Betty to an undignified fall onto the road. It was Ida, who following close at hand had managed to grab hold of her by the arm at the vital moment. Matty clapped his Nan Ida who bowed to the applause. 'Fink on, Boy, next time I'll show you just what this old lady can do.' They all laughed as they piled into the car. Millie gave a huge sigh of relief, or was it resignation?

Georgie and Rosie had managed to swing it so that they both had leave to spend Christmas eve at home. Unfortunately, Rosie had to return to base by

6pm. on Christmas day. Georgie's leave ran until midnight on Boxing Day. One of the perks for Georgie as an officer was that he had been given permission to use his motorbike, on the proviso that he deliver some notes over to Woolwich Barracks. This suited Georgie, as he planned to pick Rosie up at Biggin Hill on his way home, making life much easier for her, as finding transport on Christmas Eve was not a simple task.

As he waited outside the perimeter gates, Georgie thought back to the last time he and Rosie had spent time together. It had been in August, the third time that they had been able to get together since the day of *that* telegram. It was also the first time that they had both had more than two days together since Rosie joining up. They had four glorious days in each others company. Two were spent in Camberwell with the remaining two down in Eynsford. It was during this time that they had decided on a date for their wedding. Georgie had always maintained that they wait until after Rosie had turned twenty. No amount of arguing from Rosie could sway his resolve. Not even when she pleaded. 'look at poor, Linda, if she had had her way she would have at least been Joey's wife. She says she feels cheated out of something very special.'

'*Special*, why, does she want to be called a widow?' Georgie knew he was being harsh. He loved Linda like a sister, but he still found it difficult to talk about Joey with her. 'He thought they were too young. He wanted to wait, not rush into it because of the War. He needed to know that what they felt for each other was going to last them a lifetime.'

'That's not fair, Georgie and you know it. She just wanted to belong to him in every way. She wanted his name, and maybe you never know, she might have had his baby.'

'That's the last thing Joey would have wanted. I know that for a fact, that's one of the things me and him used to talk about. After the life you lot had, the last thing he wanted was a kid of his growing up without a proper loving mother *and* father, he wanted his kids to have everything he didn't, and to do that it needs both parents. You of all people should understand that.' Rosie knew she was beaten then. But deep down she knew what Georgie was saying made sense. Didn't she also want the very best possible life for any children she and Georgie might have. Still, she couldn't help feeling in some way that Linda also had a point.

Rosie comforted herself in the knowledge that at least Georgie hadn't said that they had to wait until the War ended. For who in this World knew when that was likely to be. So the date had been set for Wednesday the 3rd of March 1944.

Now though, the young couple were met by Annie and George who had been eagerly listening for the sound of the bikes engine, and the rest of the family that had beaten them there by half an hour or so. The enormous turkey that Reg had carried up from the car was roasting slowly in Annie's oven. They all laughed as Matty gave his impression of the 'oldies' pushing the car, glad to have something to lighten the tension they were all feeling. Linda arrived half way through his story, so for her benefit he started all over again. This was the second Christmas without their beloved, Joey. None of them could remember last year. They had not celebrated it, their loss to close, to hard to come to terms with. Today though, they would remember and get through it together. They were determined to enjoy it. Joey loved Christmas, the last thing he would have wanted was for his family to go into permanent mourning. It wasn't going to be easy, they all realised that, but even Linda said 'they'd give it a darn good try.'

Ida asked Annie about the one other thing that was always on their minds, 'Anything special in the post this year?'

All eyes turned Annie's way, 'no.' she answered sadly. 'This is the second Christmas since we last heard anything.'

'They don't even know that their big brother's gone.' said Rosie, 'that's if they remember any of us.'

'Course they'll remember us,' insisted Matty, 'Jonny won't have forgotten, he'll tell Violet and Lily about us.'

Millie coughed to clear her throat. 'Whilst we are on the subject of the little ones,' she had started now, she knew there was no turning back. 'There's something that I have got to tell you all.'

Millie opened her handbag and extracted two envelopes. The room became still and quiet, all inquisitive eyes turned on Millie. One envelope, she placed carefully on her lap, the other she lifted the flap and took out the piece of paper and unfolded it. 'Before I read this, let me put you in the picture. As you know we all received letters from dear Joey written on the day he left Chatham for his embarkation.' she waited for the sudden intakes of breath she heard from those around her. 'Well I am going to read the one he sent to me, to you now. I promise you will begin to understand what this is all about as I read to you.'

'I don't get this' said Annie, echoing all their thoughts. 'it's sixteen months since.....' she was unable to go on.

'Please, I know how hard and strange this must seem to you, but I beg you, for Joey's sake, bare with me.'

'Go on, Millie,' Georgie encouraged, 'if this is something Joey wanted, then I for one want to know about it.' He looked across to Linda, she smiled at him and nodded her approval.

'Right, well my letter,' it begins with the usual, and bless him he thanked me for being part of this wonderful family.' she smiled at them all, 'I should be thanking you. Anyway to continue. It was during his last spot of leave, that Joey gave me this other envelope. He knew something was in the pipeline, but nothing more than that.' she held this now in her other hand for the others to see. 'Joey asked me at the time to hold on to it until a later date. It was not until I received his final letter that he gave me further instructions. Joey asked me to still hold onto the other one and leave it unopened. He said that he prayed the time would not come for it to be opened and that one day he hoped to come to me and take it back unread. But then, if luck were not on his side and he didn't make it through the war, then, well, he wanted me to read his letter to you.'

'Why have you waited so long, Aunt Millie?' Linda was feeling very confused, 'and why you. I'm sorry, that sounded rude, I didn't mean it like that. I just wondered why he didn't send it to me.'

'He had his reasons, of that I am sure, My Dear. You see, in my letter, he asked that I wait at least a year before reading this to you. He said just in case his ship had gone down but he might have been picked up by the enemy and it could take that long before word got back that, he was indeed alive but a prisoner. And why did he pick me to do this, well, I think that he knew how hard this would be, even for me, for I loved that boy very much, but it would be even harder for any of you.' They were becoming fidgety, wanting to get on with it. Millie carefully opened the sealed envelope that held two sheets of paper,, full on both sides with Joey's handwriting. Millie took another deep breath as she began her onerous task.

Somewhere in England 1942

Greetings my, Dearest Family,

Hey come on chin up. I know this must be weird for you all but think how weird it is for me as I write it. It's all a bit strange, because this is one letter that I hope nobody gets to read. If you do though, well, what can I say. I guess to start with sorry won't be too bad, cos I hate to think of putting you through any more heartbreak, as this letter might open up wounds that had begun to heal slightly. (Big 'ead ain't I. Cos I'd like ta fink you didn't ferget me that quick.)'

This caused his family to smile.

'Sorry Aunt Mill, couldn't miss an opportunity of making you speak cockney. Anyway back to it. I know I don't have to tell you how much you all mean to me but I'm going to anyway. I just hope that when you get to hear this, that the people that mean so much to me are still there together.
First I'll start with Nan and Grand-dad Stone. (Well I've got to start somewhere, there's not any favouritism intended.) It makes me happy to see you settled and that life at last is treating you good. I know that you felt guilty over what happened to our mum, your daughter Sally, but we knew you tried to get her to leave him. I'll never forget you singing to Mum, Grand-dad, or the way she laughed, that's the way I always remember her. You two did all you could for us kids, I don't mean financially, that wasn't important, you gave us love, that meant more than money, cos we didn't get a lot of it. Mum tried her best, but well, he wore her down and we were a bit much for her sometimes. Anyway thank you, and I love you both.'

Millie paused, and closed her eyes for a few seconds, unable to see the sadness in the room. On a deep breath, she went on....

Next, Gran and Gramps Smith. Just because our father was your son, I hope that you understand that I never once wanted to put the blame on you. I will say that I was a bit concerned when you came forward and took Rosie and Matty back to your home. Having already seen the little ones being dragged off, I did wonder if I was going to lose contact with all my brothers and sisters. We didn't really know you, did we? But gradually I came to realise that had it not been for you two, life would have been much harder. It wasn't that you didn't love us. I now know it was that your own son locked you out of our lives. I want to say thank you to you and also that I love you both. You've made Rosie and Matty's life more happy than any of us could have wished for, and you've never let me forget that I mean just as much to you as they do. Whoops getting a bit emotional now aren't I? Pass the hankies round ma.'

Right on cue, Annie had just risen to get her own hanky from her handbag. Her tears adding to the already silent ones of nearly every woman and man in the cosy back room.'Who's next then? Let's stay in Eynsford shall we?' You thought wouldn't get another mention didn't you, Milly? Well you're wrong so there' Millie smiled.

You know, without you, none of what has taken place over the last few years might have happened. You opened up your home and your heart. You are one very special lady. I'll always remember you doing 'knees up mother brown' and the look on ma's face was a picture as she and us got to see your bloomers.'

Millie stopped reading for a moment as sniggers replaced sobs, she shook her head, smiling, then as she read, '

I love you very much Thank you'

She was unable to go on for a while, she too needed her handkerchief, she blew her nose trying to calm her trembling hands. Before going on.

Matty, what can I say to you oh brother of mine. Not a kid anymore are you, mate? (Don't worry, I'm not going to embarrass you) I just want to say one thing. Please don't rush into joining up, if the wars still on that is, It's not a barrel of laughs, nor is it brave. It's a hard life for most of us, and I can tell you, right at this minute I am scared. Yep, I don't mind admitting it. I don't know what's lying in wait for me out there. Matt, let them call you, but whatever happens, always remember, never volunteer, never push yourself up front. And take great care of yourself and have a happy and long life. See that wasn't too bad was it?'

'Is it alright if I pour meself a beer, Uncle George?' Matty stood up, his face red. His grandparents looked at him, George saw the look, 'Come on, it's Christmas, and well I reckon our Joey'd think it a good idea. Lets all take a break and have a glass of something. What say you, Millie?'
'I think that's a wonderful idea, George, I knew this was going to be hard, but really I didn't realise how hard.'   'I'll just pop in the kitchen and put the spuds on.' Annie was glad of the time alone.
When they were all settled once more, Millie carried on from where she had left off.

'My dear, Rosie, well, Sis, all I want to say to you is, don't go doing anything rash. I know just what an independent thing you are. I couldn't have been happier when you and Georgie got together. Mind you I know that you had planned it from when you were a little girl.'

Georgie took Rosie's hand and squeezed it tight. Her eyes mirrored his with tears so very close.

'You used to drive me bonkers every time I came in from playing with him. "was Georgie there? did Georgie get all the goals? What did Georgie talk about? Did Georgie mention me?"

Rosie covered her face with her hands. Laughter rang out in the room.

'I bet that's got you blushing, Sis. But seriously, take great care of each other and maybe if you've got any of that blue ribbon left, how's about wearing it one day a year just for me. Maybe on Ma's special day. You can imagine I'm there. And if some of the roast beef goes missing!!!.
I love you very much never forget.

'My ma and pa my very special mum and dad

Annie and George grasped for the others hand. Mum and Dad, he'd said.

'What can I say to you two? Even before I came to live with you I loved you. It was just because you used to treat me in the same way that you did Georgie. There was always something special about you. Maybe it was simply that you liked me. I have been proud to have you as my, Parents. Life with you has been full of fun and love. You don't know how good it felt when I was younger and if I had any problems, for once there was someone there for me ready to listen and help. What would all of us Smith kids had done that night and the following days of our nightmare without you two. God bless you, Mum and Dad, I couldn't have loved you more if I had been born to you. Phew, even I'm starting to upset meself, I need one of your hankies, Mum.'

Millie put the letter aside for a moment. 'Linda the next part is for you, Joey's put a little note here, to the effect that, well, he didn't know at the time of writing this, whether a year down the line you would, er, still be with the family.' Millie was unsure if she had put it in the best way.

'In other words the daft beggar thought I might have found someone else.'

'You can't blame him, Lin. I understand where he was coming from. He always worried that you were both too young.' Georgie tried to put Joey's thoughts into words.

'Oh, I know, I know, Georgie. What does he have to say, Aunt Millie?'

'As Millie is reading this out, then that must mean my, Darling that you are there with the rest of my family. This is very hard for me, just as it will be when you hear what I have to say. I hope you don't mind it being read out in front of the others. You know how I feel about you. At the time of writing this I still think I did the right thing in making us wait to get married. But if Millie is reading this to you then it proves how much you care. So when I think of it like that maybe you were right and I was wrong. Listen to that carefully Georgie. Anyway my love, in time I want you to go out there and find happiness with someone else, I'm definitely not such a good catch that

no-one can live up to me!! Just keep a corner of your heart reserved in my name. You were my first, and last true love.

Linda got up and walked out of the room, Annie went to follow her but George put a restraining hand on her arm. 'Give her a few minutes, love. Millie was relieved to have a break for a little while, she, like everyone else was finding it so hard to cope with. Linda walked slowly back into the room, she gave Millie a little smile and slowly nodded her head. 'please go on, Millie.' I'm fine'
Millie picked the sheet of paper up and once more began to read.

Well, Georgie me old, Mate, me, Brother, the one person who knows me as well as I know myself. I know how you would have reacted when I went missing, the same way as I would if it had been you. I don't have to spell it out for you do I? But I will say this, thank you, for being the best friend any bloke could ever hope to have. And thanks for being my brother. Take care of this wonderful family for me mate, and in that, I include, Linda, whether she's there or not, even though we didn't make it to the church, I think of her as my wife, so she's a big part of the family.
Georgie, there is a big, big favour I need to ask of you....'

Suddenly Georgie interrupted Millie mid-sentence. 'I know what he wants me to do.' The others all looked in his direction.
   'He wants me to try and find the kids. Am I right, Millie?'
   'Yes, Love you are.' Millie carried on reading.

I know this won't be easy mate, but I need you to do something that I promised myself, Rosie and Matty I'd do. Try to find Jonny, Violet and Lily for me. But please don't blame yourself if you can't find them. It's been made clear to us that the Wilsons don't want to be found. If by some miracle you do find them though, please tell them that their big brother never forgot them nor stopped loving them. Cheers bruv and no more heroics eh? Take great care. I love you.

Georgie stood up. 'I promise every one of you here today, that I will do every thing in my power to find them.
Does Joey have anything else to say?'
   'He just finishes with,

'Remember me with laughter, not tears. With memories of good times and not bad. And to keep a corner of your hearts just for me, then I'll always be no more than a whisper away.
My love to you all, my Dear, Dear Family, Now stop blubberin' and enjoy yourselves!! from your, Joey.'

'Now I think we can understand why Joey wanted me to wait all this time before reading the letter to you. Look at us all? This was the last thing he wanted.' Millie scolded them. 'We owe it to him to get on with this Christmas and enjoy it. Who knows what tomorrow might bring.'

'You're right there, Millie. I'm goin' to make sure each and every one of us enjoy today, or else.' 'George finished with a smile. 'How's that dinner comin' on, Annie?'

'Just fine, Love. Just fine.'

'Come on, Georgie, why don't you and your dad give us a song.' Linda was determined to make her Joey's wish come true. If he'd been there he would have been one of the first telling jokes and making them all laugh. 'This is for you my love' she whispered under her breath.

Chapter Sixteen

'1944'

What wondered the people caught up in this never ending War, would a new year have in store for them. Six months previously, Georgie had had a new Sergeant transferred to his unit. As soon as the two men met they clicked, maybe, Georgie often wondered, could it be because the new man reminded him of Joey? Not in looks, apart from they both had light blonde hair, but in their attitude to life and many of shared mannerisms. Whatever the reason, Georgie and Morris Weller spent all their off duty time together. Whether it was off to the local for a well earned pint or just a quiet stroll along the country lanes surrounding the camp. Morris was yet another survivor of Dunkirk, he had applied to be transferred over to the REME where he thought his knowledge of all things electrical would be of some use. In his civvy days he loved nothing better than taking old wirelesses to bits and building a new one from scratch. Their homes back in Southwark, were within a few miles of each other. Morris came from the Old Kent Road. On a couple of occasions when their leave coincided, they each had visited the others home. Although Morris was a couple of years younger than Georgie, he was infact recently married. He'd married his childhood sweetheart, Joyce. Rosie had met the couple and found that in Joyce she possibly could have a close friend. The two girls started to write to each other. Joyce was training to be a nurse at Guys hospital.

Preparations for Georgie and Rosie's wedding were well under way. It had been a joint decision on both their parts for it to be a quiet affair, with only immediate family and a few close friends and neighbours. The ceremony was booked to take place in St. Paul's church in Lorrimore Road. Although Rosie's home was in Eynsford, it was she that decided she wanted to be married in the Church of her childhood years. It also certainly made the arrangements of getting guests to the wedding much easier. All the grandparents along with Annie and George had been putting a little bit aside over the preceding weeks. A small 'do' it might be, but there was no way they were going to let this day pass without giving the young couple a day to remember.

Georgie and Morris were sitting in the canteen enjoying a much needed breakfast of bacon and eggs. More and more broken vehicles were arriving every day. They and the trainees were working longer hours trying to repair and replace damaged parts before arranging for them to be shipped out to wherever their fighting armies desperately needed them. Both men were tired having had just a couple of hours sleep the previous night. Georgie lit a cigarette, a habit he had picked up on his return from Dunkirk, the Captain of the small fishing boat that had been his and others saviour, had stuck one in his mouth after relieving Georgie of his double burden. He never smoked in front of his parents, he remembered the struggle his mum had had over the years of trying to 'kick the habit'. Not that he smoked too many, just on the occasions when he needed a lift and thought smoking would help. He turned to his friend, making sure he blew the smoke in the opposite direction, Morris was not a smoker.

'There's something I've been meaning to ask you, Wellsey.' Georgie used his nickname for Morris. 'I'm short of a best man, nothing would please me more if you would stand up for me.'

'I thought you'd never ask, Powley, Captain Sir.'

'You'll do it then?'

'Course I will, Georgie, I'd be honoured.'

'Good on you. That's that then.' He leant across the table and shook Morris's hand. The sad look that came into Georgie's eyes went not un-noticed to Morris, he knew what his friend was thinking about. He knew that he was second best, that Georgie would give anything for it to be Joey standing by his side on his wedding day. Georgie talked constantly and lovingly of his brother. Morris knew, that with the wedding a mere four weeks away, with no mention until today about a best man, that secretly, Georgie still was hanging on and hoping, although the thread of hope was fraying, he clung to a miracle happening and that Joey would turn up one day.

'Georgie, I know I'm not Joey, but I'll do me best to make it a happy day for you and Rosie, just like your Joey would have done. From everything you've told me about him, I'll be proud to stand in his place by your side.'

Georgie couldn't answer his friend, he smiled and nodded his head.

Rosie was also having regrets, not about marrying Georgie, but about the fact that somewhere out there she had two sisters that should have been walking up the isle behind her. In her minds eye she could picture Violet and Lily wearing apple green bridesmaids dresses, carrying a posy of pink and white rose buds, their blonde curls held in place by a band of tiny daises. Inside the Church she saw Matty and Jonny, wearing red carnations in their buttonholes, ushering guests to their seats. Then she walked towards the man she loved more than life itself, beside whom she pictured her brother Joey. 'Please God and Joey, if you can hear me,' pleaded Rosie as she sat in the makeshift Chapel on the airbase, 'help us in our search for our babies, lead us to the right place, the three of them are out there just waiting for us to come to them. I know it.'

A couple of weeks earlier, in one of her letters to Joyce, she had asked her to be her matron of honour. Joyce having been put in the picture of how the Smith's had suffered, replied that she would love to stand by Rosie's side and share the day with her. Linda was more than happy when asked, to be a bridesmaid to the sister of her lost love. Siddy Woogitt would be at Matty's side. The numbers added up, even though most of the faces were not as in her thoughts.

Then on a clear crisp morning in March, Rosie walked up the aisle, either side of her Reg and Bert heads held high proudly matched her steps as she linked arms with both of her grandfathers. They left her standing beside the boy and man of her dreams and when the Vicar asked 'who gives this woman to this man?' in unison they answered, 'we do'. As Reg and Bert made their way to take their seats between the already tearful, Betty, Ida and Millie, Rosie turned to Joyce handing her posy of red Roses, then turning to Linda she gave her a little rag doll that wore bright blue ribbons in its hair. Georgie's shaking hands became still the moment he looked at his beautiful bride. He could see the pretty blue ribbon entwined in Rosie's hair beneath her veil. As the ceremony was coming to an end, through her tears, Annie saw her son gently take hold of Rosie's hand and place Sally Smith's gold wedding band on her finger. Her thoughts and heart went out to Sally. A sadness tinged with anger settled on her, so unfair that this wonderful moment had been cruelly denied to her. She looked round the congregation searching for that other face that was missing. Many tears of happiness and regret were cried that day. But above all else, love was in abundance.

As Georgie and Rosie left the church, they where overwhelmed at the sight that greeted them. Between them, Morris and Joyce had spoken to friends of the couple that were in their regiments, who willingly agreed to form a guard of honour for the happy couple to go through.

'So much for our idea of a quiet Wedding' Georgie whispered to his new wife. He obviously didn't say it quiet enough for suddenly he felt a tap on his shoulder.

'You didn't think your families would let you get away with that do you.' laughed Georgie's dad.

'Thanks, Dad.' said Rosie smiling at the pleased look on her brand new father-in-laws face.

The next sight that greeted them made everybody laugh for there parked in the road outside was Alf Woogitt standing by the side of his open lorry, the same one that used to transport the Powley family with all Annie's wares, down to their temporary home of the Hop Fields in Paddock Wood. The old lorry looked much different today though, for Alf and Siddy had draped ribbons and balloons from all four sides. Tied to the back were old tin cans that rattled and clanged all the way back to Annie and George's house, where the reception was being held. The big front room had been emptied of every stick of furniture except for Annie's pride and Joy the oak dresser, everything was piled up, including the double bed in the small back room. On the wide landing, trestle tables, borrowed from the school again, were piled high with all manner of food. To some the sight of plates of carved chicken seemed like and illusion. 'One of the perks from living in the Countryside', said Millie, as she winked at those eager to get their hands on the delicious looking buffet.

The beautifully iced, three-tier wedding cake held pride of place in the centre of one of the tables.

'Don't dare try to cut the top two,' warned Betty quietly in Rosie's ear, 'they're made of iced cardboard, only the bottom tier is real cake.'

Alf Wooggitt, true to his word, drank very little throughout the celebrations, as he had offered to drive the couple back to Rosie's home in Eynsford, where they were going to spend the next three days as their honeymoon. Annie, Kath and Doll between them were going to put the rest of the family up for that period. Just the way they did all those years ago for the Smith children. So as usual, this whole close unit was pulling together.

In June a new deadly menace was seen in the skies across the Kent Countryside, making its pilot less flight towards London where it's people thought that they had long since seen an end to such destructive forces. The V1's, quickly nicknamed by the British as 'Doodlebugs' claimed its first victims on the 16th. Word spread quickly throughout the Capital that flying machines without pilots were landing and blowing up on impact all across London seemingly non-stop. Once more many of its people were afraid to venture out. Some families, if the stories were to be believed, packed the essentials and virtually lived in their Anderson shelters for days on end. This being a time when silence could be your killer. Londoners watched and listened in fear for the sound of a V1. Eyes scanned the skies, praying that the engine noise would continue on until selfishly it passed over them. If the engine cut out people ran for shelter knowing this was when the monster fell to reap its havoc on those unluckily enough to be in its path.

Joyce was the first one to witness at close hand, a rocket plummeting down. As she later told her story, sitting in Annie's back room shaken and drinking one of Annie's famous cups of sweet tea. She had been waiting at a bus stop, on her way to start the two o-clock shift at Guys.

'All of a sudden, I heard this strange noise, it was loud but not the same as an aircraft, anyway, I looked up and just as I did, the noise stopped. I knew it was one of them 'Doodlebug' things straightaway, anyway, it sort of twisted its way down, like when you see a plane shot down at the pictures, everything seemed to be happening in slow motion. I couldn't move. It felt like my legs were made of lead too heavy to lift. Then bang, suddenly there was bits of bricks and glass flying all over the place. For a while after there was complete silence, then all I could hear was kids screaming. I realised it must have come down on the school.'

'Oh gawd luv us,'

'No, it's okay, Annie it didn't. It hit the bombed out clothes factory next door.'

'Thank, The Lord, for that.'.

'Trouble was, it was during the kid's dinnertime, so there were lots of them in the playground.'

'Were any of them hurt?'

'Most of them had nasty cuts, but four of them were in a bad way. I did all I could for them until the ambulances arrived. Two had head injuries, one's arm had been nearly severed by flying glass. Another little girl was trapped under part of the factory wall that had collapsed.'

'Oh, Joycie, was she alive?'

'Yes, and conscious. After I'd done what I could for the others, I sat and held her hand, she told me her name was Susan and that she was going to be eight next week.' Joyce started to cry, the shock starting to set in. Annie comforted her as best she could until her sobs subsided.

'I couldn't face the hospital wards. I just started walking, next thing I knew I was outside your front door. Don't know why though, cause shouldn't you be at work at this time?'

'Normally I am, but one of the girls that does the early shift wanted this mornin' off. So I swapped with her.'

'I'm glad that you did.'

'Do you want me to ring the hospital for you? They must be wonderin' where you've got to.'

'Oh, yes please, Annie.' Joyce told Annie the number to dial and who to ask for when she got through. Whilst, Annie made the phone call, Joyce went to wash her face and hands, blood was still splattered on them.

'Thanks for phoning the Ward Sister for me. I bet she's wasn't impressed with me. After all, I see worse than that come onto the ward every day of the week.'

'Yeah, but it's different when you see it happen, then to find out that it's kiddies that's been hurt. Anyhow, she was understanding and sympathetic but said she'll expect you back on duty tomorrow. Now get that tea down you before it get's cold there's a good girl. Then you stop and have your tea with us before my George sees you home.' As Joyce went to protest at Annie's generosity, Annie quietened her, by tutting and shaking her head.

The terror of the V1's in September were replaced by the even bigger terror of the V2 Rockets. Unlike their prototype, the V2's were enormous rockets that carried far more explosives, therefore the devastation they created was on a much bigger scale. On the 25th November, a Saturday, where shoppers young and old, crowded the shops hoping to find a rare bargain as yet another War torn Christmas was fast approaching. A V2 found it's heaving target of a packed Woolworth's store in New Cross. The papers reported over one hundred and fifty innocent lives were lost with a further two hundred or so injured. The big store had been raised to the ground. Two of Annie, Kath and Doll's co-workers had taken their children out to look for Christmas presents for their daddies serving in the forces. They became statistics, part of the ever increasing numbers of the dead.

Once again, Annie, Kath and Doll found themselves entombed in the 'dungeon' as the dreaded wailing of the air raid sirens screamed their warning. They tried to think up new ways to beat the monotony and push away, the thoughts that were always in their heads of what was happening outside, were their men safe? Or were they dealing with terrible scenes once more. The women were bored with knitting and playing cards.

'I've got an idea to pass the time' offered Kath.

'Come on then, Kath, tell me and Doll what it is.'

'Oh you'll probably think it daft.'

'Look, Kaff anything is better than sittin' 'ere lookin' at each other.'

'All right then, Doll. But promise you that you two won't laugh cos it's a bit childish.'

'We promise' cried Doll and Annie, getting impatient.

'Well, I thought we could see who can come up with the most slogans.'

'What write them down you mean?'

'No, Annie. It'd be more fun if one of us started, then the next person says one, then the next, and so on until one of us can't think of anymore. That persons then out, leaving the other two to go on until one of them gets stuck..'

'Oh I get it. Sounds like it could be a bit of fun, what say you, Doll?'

'Yeah, come on lets give it a go. Who's gonna start?'

'You go first, Kath, seein' as it was your idea. How long do we get to think of one before we're out?'

'Ooh eck, I hadn't thought about that. I know how about if the one who's just got one counts to twenty?'

'Okay. Right, ready when you are, Kath. Then you go next Doll and I'll follow you.'

'Dig for Victory. Grow your own food.'

'Don't waste food. Better pot luck with Churchill today than 'umble pie under 'Itler tomorrow.'

'Turn raw material into war material.'

'Make do and mend......Go on Doll your go.'

'I know, I know. Erm... Careless talk costs lives.'

The longer it went on, the harder it got. But it caused them all to have a good laugh as they tried to rush each other into quick answers and they became totally tongue tied.

If anyone could have heard what was coming from the shelter, they would have been forgiven in thinking that, down there three more women had not been able to handle life in war. 'Lost their marbles' would have been how neighbours described their ramblings.

Chapter Seventeen

'May 1945'

Finally, the World was at peace. Hitler, was dead, the coward had committed suicide. Japan surrendered after the United States had dropped their atomic bombs that reeked devastation on the Japanese people. Prisoners of War, returned home to the bosom of their loved ones. Many young men, on returning from their own private hell, were to find that their once loving wives had found solace in another's arms. Young women left holding the babies, as their GI lovers sailed or flew back across *'the pond'*. Many girls that married their GI following on later, leaving the shores of their homeland and loved ones behind. The atrocities witnessed by the allied forces as they walked amongst the skeletal frames of the Jewish people. They had come to liberate those held in the German POW camps. Staring dead like eyes with gaunt faces that were to never forget the abominable scenes they witnessed. Loved ones, young and old, being marched into gas chambers, only for those left standing to then live through the total horror of having to bury their lifeless bodies.

It was May the sixth; the War in Europe had ended. The people of Britain celebrated like they had never done before. Roads up and down the country were lined with tables, chairs and piano's that had been wheeled outside. Home made bunting stretched from house to house, children wearing an assortment of party hats, waving the Union flag and balloons, if they could be found in the shops. There was dancing and singing that lasted all through the night. They sang with pride, they sang with relief, after nearly six years of life becoming almost unbearable, they knew that they had made it. For some though, they still had to wait until those bombs were dropped, for the rest of the World to find the same peace. Children that had stayed in their evacuation billets slowly drifted back home.

Georgie and Rosie spent their first Christmas together as husband and wife. In the New Year of February 1946, Georgie became a civilian once more. Having been demobbed on of all days the thirteenth of January, he was returning to the job, he'd left more than six years ago. This time though, his years of experience in the REME had led to his automatic promotion to a fully skilled electrician. His friend, Morris was joining him. Georgie had been to see his old boss, who had spent his War years as a member of the Local Defence Volunteers (LDV) or 'Dad's Army' as it became known, due to most of its members being over the age of call up. He had no problem putting into action the request Georgie had made to him that day. If Captain Georgie Powley DCM asked that if there be any vacancies for his Sergeant to work for the Met. as a well qualified sparks, then he, Georgie, would be obliged if his name be put forward. As Morris's pre war work was not that of an electrician, he was taken on as Georgie's Mate. 'That means you will start off as my assistant.' Georgie explained to a grateful Morris.

Rosie's demob date came through as the second week in March, much to her annoyance. She wanted to be with Georgie as soon as possible. They were going to buy a little house in Olney Road. Both of them had been saving hard to make this possible.

That left Georgie a couple of weeks to start the one thing that had been on his mind since the Christmas before last. He had his motorbike, he had petrol in the tank, even though rationing continued, and now he had the time. With the help of Morris he was going to start the task of trying to find Jonny, Violet and Lily.

The first place they went to was the old home of Mr Wilson's mother in Freemantle street. His mum had told him about her visits there all those years ago. Georgie knew it was a long shot. 'But you never know' he told his mum and Morris, 'she might have only moved away temporarily and come back. If not, well, we might get lucky with the new people, they could have her new address. Whatever, we've got to start somewhere.'

'If you don't get any joy at her house, try the next door neighbour.' she advised Georgie.

There came no response to their knock on Mrs Wilsons house. In answer to their knock next door a young woman carrying a screaming baby in her arms opened it.

'What can I do for yer?'

'Sorry to bother you,' Georgie called above the noise from the baby, 'I'm looking for a Mrs Wilson, I believe she used to live next door.'

'Wouldn't know, mate, 'Ubby and me only moved in 'ere last week. I ain't seen 'ide nor 'air of me neighbours up ters yet. Owe yer money do she?'

'No nothing like that.' Georgie assured her. Not wanting her to start spreading rumours about whoever lived in that house now. 'She's probably getting on a bit now. It's her son, we're looking for, used to know him way back. He moved and I lost his address.' lied Georgie.

'Oh well, like I said, ain't seen 'em. I can tell yer though, that her next door can't be that old, cause I've seen a young gel in their back garden.' She lost interest when she found out that no scandal was involved. 'You'll 'ave ta come back anuvver time.' with that she closed the door with a bang, shouting at the baby to 'shut yer bleedin' noise up.'

'I doubt whether she was the nice friendly neighbour me mum was talking about.' laughed, Georgie. 'Sounds like a new family have moved in at Mrs Wilsons.'

'Where to next then, Powely?'

'I think we should go and give the matron at the orphanage where they were, a visit.' They walked back to John Ruskin Street to collect Georgie's motorbike. They made their way through streets that still showed the scars of war. Teams of workmen could be seen everywhere, clearing sites ready for the new promised properties that would take their place. In some areas, high rise blocks were appearing in the skyline, offering spacious clean bug free flats. Families were queuing to be among the first to be offered one. In Royal

Road, just behind his house in John Ruskin Street, where a bomb had landed in the early days of the war, prefabricated homes were built, as a temporary measure the government said, Prefabs, as the locals called them, were also quite popular. Annie frowned on them, 'You wouldn't catch me livin' in no box like them things.' Her husband, had disagreed with her.

'I tell you this much, Annie, they're a darn sight better than what many of the people living in them came from. Fancy having a bathroom? and do you know that they've even got a refrigerator? And the kitchen's got all fitted cupboards and that.'

'Have they? Still, give me this lovely home of ours any day.'

At last having taken in all the sights, Georgie and Morris arrived at the big depressing building of the childrens home. He parked his motorbike on the gravel drive at the front.

'Cor, bit morbid isn't it, Georgie?'

'You could say that. I wonder what sort of people decide to build a place like this, then bung scared little kids inside.' Georgie shivered as he knocked on the big doors.

It took a while but eventually they were opened by a large red faced woman.

'Yes? Can I help you?' She asked in a not unfriendly manner.

'We were wondering whether Matron Piper-Jones still runs the home.' Georgie asked with the air of a Captain of the British army.

'I am, Matron Piper-Jones, how may I help?'

'Our visit is in connection with a family of three children that were once housed here.'

'Might I ask the names of these children?'

'Their names were Jonny, Violet and Lily Smith.'

Matron raised her eyebrows but kept her voice level 'And who might you be?'

'Captain Powley and this is Sergeant Weller.'

Matron looked impressed, and just a little concerned. 'Would I be right in thinking that you are related to Mrs Annie Powley.'

'You would, I am her son. My wife is also the sister of the three children. May we step inside?'

'Of course. Follow me, and we can continue this in my office. When they were all seated the Matron cleared her throat, 'What is it that brings you here after all this time?'

'We are trying to trace the whereabouts of the children. Obviously the War stopped us from doing so any earlier.' replied Georgie.

'I really don't think that I can help you, Captain.'

'Didn't the Wilsons give you any idea of where they moved to?'

'Even if they did. The law forbids me to give out information regarding adopted children. That is unless the adoptive parents wish to keep in contact.'

'Mrs Wilson used to write to my mother, enclosing photographs of the children. For some reason she stopped doing so in 1942.'

'Yes I know....' The matron had slipped up, she tried to cover her mistake, 'What I mean is, Mrs Wilson kept in touch with the home for the first few years.'

'Surely then, you must have known where she was writing from?'

'Look, I truly am sorry. But as I have already told you, I cannot give any details out. Anyhow, I also had no contact after 1942. I really must ask you to leave now as it is nearing the childrens lunch time.'

'Just one more thing before we leave, Matron. Was it you that forwarded Mrs Wilsons letters on to my mother?' The Matron wrung her hands together nervously, Georgie knew he had hit the nail on the head. 'Please, Matron. Their eldest brother's ship went down en route to Malta, he left a letter for us, just in case you understand, his last wish was that somehow we find them, just to make sure that they are safe and well cared for.' He and Morris waited, they could tell the matron was a caring woman, she was battling with her conscience.

'I admit that I did pass on the letters. I will say no more than they were posted to me somewhere in Somerset. Now please, I beg you, go now.'
Georgie held out his hand to her, she took his in a firm grip, 'I wish you luck.'
Morris threw his arm round Georgie's shoulders, 'well, that's a start, Mate. Better than a brick wall eh?'

'More than I hoped for, I can tell you that. Come on lets get home and tell me mum.'
When they walked in to Annie's back room, Joyce was there waiting to meet Morris. She was looking at the last set of photographs of the children that had been sent. After the men told them what they had found out from the matron, Joyce said 'at least it looked like the children were well cared for, if the school uniform that Jonny was wearing was anything to go by.' Georgie jumped up and snatched the photos out of Joyce's hands.

'Say that again, Joycie.'
'I said that they are wearing good school uniforms, why?'
'Mum, can you get me dad's magnifying glass?'
Annie sensed the urgency in her sons voice. She found what he needed and handed it to him.

'What is it, Son?'
'It was staring us in the face all the time.'
'What was?'
'Look, Mum.' He lowered the magnifying glass for her to look. 'What am I s'posed to be lookin' at?'
'The badge on Jonny's school blazer, see, it's got the name of the school. And now we know what part of the country they're in.We're getting' there, Mum, we're getting' there.'
That night, Georgie rang Rosie at the base, she was as excited as he was, tears of joy spilling over. 'What do we do now?' she asked of him.

'Well, tomorrow I'm going to see if I can get an address for the school.'
'And?'
'Then me and Morris are going to catch the first train there.'
'Oh I wish I could come with you. I want to be there when you find them.'
'Let's not get too carried away, Love. They might not be there any more. This could all be a wild goose chase.'

'Oh I hope not. Will you ring Matty and the others for me? I'm already getting funny looks for tying up the phone. And hey, I love you so much, my Dearest Husband. You clever old thing.'

Georgie and Morris alighted from their long slow train journey at the small sleepy Somerset village of Watchet. They waited until the guard had carried out his duties before approaching him. 'Good afternoon, I wonder could you direct us to the village school.' Georgie raised his hat in politeness.

'I can that, Sir, I can that. You takes a right turn out of station, you carry's on walking till you comes to the High Street, then you comes to the Church and the school be next door.'

'Oh good, not too far to walk then?' Morris smiled at the guard. 'Any café's in the High Street, I'm gasping for a cup of tea?'

'There be 'Molly's Tea Rooms' Makes a lovely pot of tea she do, and if they takes yer fancy, she'll do yer a nice plate of fresh Devon cream cakes.'

'Now that I like the sound of' Georgie said rubbing his empty belly.

'From down South is it, Gents?'

'That's right.' both answered in unison.

'Well, seein' as there be no more trains back there today, have you got a place to stay this night?'

'No. that's something else we were going to ask you.' That made Georgie realise how foolish he and Morris had been. They were so intent on just getting here as soon as possible that they hadn't given a thought to where they would spend the night.

'That be no problem, Sirs. 'Molly's Tea Rooms' be a guest house as well.'

Georgie thanked the friendly station guard and they started to make their way towards the High Street. In 'Molly's' they drank the hot strong tea thirstily and managed to gorge three cakes that oozed with the fresh cream each. After booking a room for the night, the men went in search of the school. All the while they walked, Georgie looked at the passing faces. Would he remember the Wilsons if he were to see them. Come to that, would he recognise the children. The last time he had seen them was the Easter of 1937. Nearly nine years ago. In his minds eye he pictured them still at the ages they were then, but in reality Jonny was seventeen, Violet fifteen and baby Lily, no longer a baby at thirteen.

As they walked he took out the last photo of them and studied the faces closely. The end of the school day was fast approaching, mothers were gathering outside the gates to meet the younger children. Georgie and Morris walked past them and into the playground towards the main entrance door. They soon found their way to the Headmasters office and were greeted by his secretary. Georgie explained, in brief, the reason for their visit, without actually mentioning the name Smith or Wilson as they became known. His tummy felt like it was doing cartwheels, he didn't think that it was all down to the cream cakes. His hands started to shake and he rubbed them together trying to dry the sweat that seemed to be spreading all over. He sent a silent message to Joey. 'Wherever you are, Mate, look, I'm getting real close to findin' them.' He was excited yet apprehensive at the same time.

'Jonny would no longer be at the school, he'd probably left more than a year ago. Even Violet might have left. At least he knew Lily had not yet reached school-leaving age.' The Secretary interrupted his thoughts, she ushered them in to the Heads office. After introductions had been made, Georgie nervously began his explanation to the Headmaster of the events that eventually led him and his friend to his school. The Head listened with interest, leaning forward and resting his arms with his hands clasped, on his paper filled desk.

'You see, Sir, this family were parted, all because of the lies of a murderer. We are not here to cause trouble for Mr and Mrs Wilson, on the contrary. It's just that we need to know that the three of them are safe and well.' He took the photograph out of his wallet and showed it to the Head. 'They looked happy when Mrs Wilson sent this to my mother, surely it could do no harm for them to know that their other family have never forgotten them and love them very much. We are not here to drag them away.' Georgie finished his tale, trying to gauge the thoughts of the man sitting opposite him who was studying the photo.

'I remember the family when they first came to live here.' Morris nudged Georgie on the arm and gave him a thumbs sign. Georgie was holding his breath. 'What a little tough nut Jonny was. Mind you he did have to put up with a lot of the older boys taking the mick out of his cockney accent.' He smiled up at Georgie who slowly let his breath out realising that he was so close. He found his voice 'Yes, that sounds like young Jonny.'

'He soon put a stop to that, though. He decided to pick a fight with the leader of these boys, I know I shouldn't laugh, I'm meant to condemn violence, but, well this other boy was nearly twice the size of Jonny. Anyway, it took just one punch on the nose from Jonny and the boy went howling home to his mother. From that day on Jonny became a bit of a hero, with lots of the other children trying to learn to speak like him. It was quite funny I must say. He never ever raised his fist in anger to anyone in this school from that day in the junior school, to the day he left the senior. I'm sorry, that's not what you've come here for is it. You want to know if I can help in your search.'

'That's okay, if nothing else I can take back some of your memories with me. Is Lily still a pupil at your school, Sir?'

'Sadly, no.' Georgie's heart sank.

'Nothing happened to her did it?'

'Oh no, not to her, or any of the children. It was to their parents. Such a sad time, we had hopes of Jonny going on to University, a very bright lad, you can be proud of him. Violet, or Lettie as she was known, seemed to be following in her Brothers footsteps. Then there was young, Lily, so full of mischief.' He smiled as

pictures of the family came to him. 'She had only been in the senior school a short time when the accident happened.'

Georgie, who had been enjoying hearing what the Headmaster recollected of the children, shot forward in his chair, fear gripping him.

'What accident?'

'Mr and Mrs Wilson had been visiting friends a few miles away. They hadn't planned on staying out long as Mr Wilson hated driving in the blackout. Apparently, they were having such an enjoyable day, that before they knew it, it was quite late. Driving along the narrow dark lanes home, he couldn't have seen the bend in the road until it was too late, we don't know for sure, anyway the tyre marks found by the Police in the road pointed to the fact that he braked too late, went off the road and crashed in to a tree. They were both killed instantly.'

'Oh, My God.' Georgie and Morris sat motionless, they had never thought of anything like this happening.

It was Morris that spoke first. 'And the children, where were they when this happened?'

'Safe and sound at home with their grandmother. Thankfully.'

'When was this?' Georgie thought he already knew in which year it happened.

'In the winter of 1943.'

'That's why mum didn't hear from Mrs Wilson after that. Where are they now, do they still live in the area?'

'I'm afraid not. You see, Mr Wilson's mother took the news badly, as one would expect, but she felt that she no longer wanted to stay here, much against the wishes of the children. They were happy and settled here. They missed their parents very much and to be uprooted so soon after, well, lets just say it was a sad day for the whole village when they boarded the train.'

'Do you know where she took them?'

'I can't see any harm in telling you, after all, I doubt whether the grandmother would stop you seeing them, she might be pleased to share her burden.'

'Burden?' queried Morris. 'Surely her grandchildren, adopted or not, are not a burden.'

'You have to remember, Mr Weller, when she lived here she must have been into her seventies. Three teenagers to cope with is not the easiest for any of us. I should know, I have over thirty of them every day, right outside this door.' He gave a faint smile. 'So in answer to your question, Captain Powely, Mrs Wilson Snr. took them back to South London. I believe that is where the family came from.'

'I don't suppose you know the address, Sir?'

'No, only that she said, she was going back to where everything was familiar.' As Georgie and Morris prepared to leave, the Headmaster stopped Georgie at the door. 'If you do find them, and I hope that you do, tell young Jon to write to me. I'd very much like to know what he has done with that clever brain of his.'

Chapter Eighteen

It was a forlorn pair that Annie found sitting on her settee when she arrived home from work the next day. She knew by their faces that all had not gone to plan. She sat, as they put her in the picture. She shook her head in sadness on hearing that the Wilsons were dead. Feeling guilty as she thought back to the silent bad things she had called the couple after contact had been severed. Later, Georgie had the unenviable task of getting in contact with the rest of the family. Matty said he'd get leave as soon as he could, he wanted to be their with them. After serving in the air force for the last year of the war, he decided to stay on, against the wishes of all his family. He took to flying like a duck to water, he loved every minute spent above the clouds free as a bird. The only consolation to them all, was the fact that the Headmaster had only good things to say about the children. It seemed that at least up until 1942 they had been loved and well cared for. When Rosie said to Georgie 'where else is there to go? you've done all you can.'
He answered, 'no, no I haven't. I'm not giving up just yet. We're getting closer, I know we are.'

The next day, something happened to put the childrens whereabouts to the back of their minds for a day or two. Annie, George and Georgie had just finished their usual Saturday dinner of pie and mash, when they heard the bang of their doorknocker. Georgie went down to open the front door, he was met by a giant of a man, twisting his cap between his fingers nervously.

'Yes, Mate, how can I help?' Georgie asked in a friendly voice.

'I don't know if I've got the right house or not, but I'm lookin' for the Powley family.'

'You sure have got the right place, I'm Georgie Powley, what can I do for you?'

'I'm sorry to come wivvout lettin' you know first, but, well, my names Ernie Pipe, I don't know if that name means anyfing to you.' he waited while Georgie racked his brains, the name rang a bell, but where from.

'I'm trying to place where I've heard the name before, look sorry, Mate, why don't you come up and then you can tell us what's on your mind.' Georgie stepped back allowing Ernie to climb the stairs ahead of him.

'Mum, Dad, we've got a visitor, I'm bringing him up.'
The first thing Ernie saw when he walked into the room, was an enlarged photograph of Joey in uniform, it had pride of place in the centre of the sideboard. Georgie saw the sad look come into his eyes.

'This man has come to see us about something, sorry let me introduce you, this is Annie and George Powley. Mum, Dad this is Ernie.....' suddenly it dawned on Georgie where he had heard the name before. 'Ernie Pipe, weren't you our Joey's mate?'

'Yeah, I was wiv 'im that last day.'
Annie sank back down on to the chair, her legs had turned to jelly. The colour from their faces drained. George, was the first to make a move, he took hold

of Ernie's hand and shook it firmly and warmly. 'Let me take your hat and coat, Son. Sit yourself down. How about a cup of tea?'

'Fanks, Mr Powley, maybe in a minute a cup a tea would go down a treat.'

'So you were with our Joey. Can you tell us what happened exactly?' Georgie needed to know, but did he really *want* to know?

For the next hour or so, broken only by Annie excusing herself to go and make the tea, when really she had to have time alone, if she was to go back in there and listen to her boys last hours. Ernie told his mate, Joey's family about everything that had happened to the pair of them. From their days of training, to the time they realised they were to be part of the biggest convoy to set sail. Later known as 'Operation Pedestal.' They were to carry the much needed supplies to the tiny Island of Malta, such a vital voyage in the effort to hold onto the Island. Ernie finished at the point where he and Joey had arranged to meet in the nearest pub, rather than say goodbye.

'I'm sorry it took all these years before I come to see you. But it was months before most of us got back home, then I was put on another ship and off I went agen. Then you know what it's like, the more time that passes the 'arder it gets. But lately I've been finkin' about Joey a lot. I'm workin' as a plumber, civvie side of the Police. I remembered Joey sayin' somefing about his bruvver workin' for them before the war.' he looked at Georgie for confirmation.

'That's right, I'm going back there soon.'

'Anyway, I'm sorry I left it this long.'

They all made this hulk of a man welcome. Remembering now, how much Joey had thought of him as a friend. The longer he sat with them, the more at home he felt. He started to tell them about some of the fun he and Joey had, and some of the escapades the pair of them got up to.

'Mind you once he got his stripes up, he had to be a bit more cagey.'

When it was time for Ernie to go, Annie and George stood at the window and waved to him until he went out of sight. He took with him the knowledge that today he had been made to feel part of this special family unit that Joey had talked constantly of. They had made him promise to come back Sunday week and have dinner with them Then Linda and Rosie, who was able to get leave most weekends, leading up to her demob, would also be able to get to know Joey's sailor pal.

The following Saturday, after Georgie had ridden to Biggin Hill to collect his wife Rosie, they and Annie, on a whim of Georgies, took another walk to Freemantle street.

'Won't do any harm will it?'

'Cause it won't, Boy, after all we only spoke to one of the neighbours. Maybe she had friends that still live there somewhere.'

Rosie was telling Georgie and Annie how boring life was on the base now. Not that she would ever in her life, want to go back to the days of waving to the crews and counting them as they took off in their mighty flying War machines, then repeat the practise on their return, but more often than not, never reaching the same number that took off.

Suddenly, Annie, who was walking between them, arms linked with theirs, stopped walking, she was staring ahead of her.

'What's up, Mum?' Georgie watched the blood run from her face concerned.

'Look over there, that young feller kicking the ball to them little kids.' her voice was strained as she pointed.

Rosie and George looked to where she pointed. They too froze on the spot.

'It can't be' Georgie could barely say the words.

Rosie moved forward, her heart was beating fit to burst. Suddenly, as if he could feel eyes on him, the young man turned her way.

'Jonny?' she whispered, he looked hard at her, he knew she had said something but it had been no more than a whisper.

'Jonny?' this time she spoke louder, the blood was rushing in her ears.

He started to walk towards her, a frown on his handsome face, a face so like his big brothers, it was uncanny.

'Do I know you?' before Rosie could speak he looked at her closer,

'I do, don't I? You seem so familiar to me, but I can't place.....' then it hit him, the face of a young girl came into his head, holding his hand, letting him cuddle her rag doll. 'Rosie?'

They ran the last couple of yards falling into each others arms. Tears from both of them running unchecked down their faces. Annie and Georgie gave them this time alone to cherish. Georgie cuddled his mum to him, through his tears he whispered, 'we've done it, Joey, Mate, we've found them, we've found them.' then his tears fell unashamedly along with those of Annie.

Jonny lifted his head, wiping his eyes with the back of his hand. Then he noticed the other two.

'You're, Georgie, I remember you,' then he smiled at Annie, 'Aunt Annie?'

'Yes, Love, it's me and Georgie and Rosie. At last we've found you.'

Holding tightly on to his Sisters hand, Jonny took them inside his house, the house that Mrs Wilson lived in before going to live with her son and his new family. Once inside the tears fell again, Violet, or Letty as her adoptive parents called her, could just about, when prompted by Jonny, remember these faces from many years ago, when she had been no more than six years old. Lily was the one who found it all very strange. Until Georgie mentioned the rag dolls that Joey had given his sisters. Although she had been a tiny baby at the time, on hearing that, Lily went to her room, she returned carrying the rag doll in one arm and in the other she held the 'baby' that she had received that last Christmas they had spent together. It seems that over the years, Jonny had not let either of his sisters forget that out there somewhere they had two more brothers and a sister. Rosie went over to Lily taking the 'baby doll' into her arms.

'Hello, Susan' she said.

'You remembered what I called her!' Surprise sounding in Lily's voice.

'How could I forget anything about our last Christmas together?' Rosie turned to Violet. 'Did you keep your baby doll, Violet?'

'You bet I did. She sits on my bed with Raggy. I still can't believe this is really happening.' Violet spoke the same thoughts that every one of them was thinking.

Although the overwhelmed three had greeted Mrs Wilson as soon as they had entered the house, she had stayed sitting in her armchair staring at the interlopers. The reunited family had so much to tell each other. The worst thing was when Jonny wanted to know where Joey was. When Rosie gently explained what had happened, fresh tears, this time of despair and sadness, came from the three youngest Smith children.

Mrs Wilson remained silent, seemingly oblivious to what was taking place around her. Annie tried to get her to talk, but Violet told her not to bother. 'She's been like this for a while now. She just sits in that chair all day. She don't speak to us, I don't think she knows who we are any more.'

'How long exactly, has she been like this?' Georgie asked Jonny.

'For nearly a year now.'

'Who looks after you then?' Annie couldn't believe what she was hearing.

'We do. We all muck in and do the cooking, the housework and the washing.' Violet told them in a tone that spoke volumes. They were not happy living like this, that was plain to see.

'Gran took care of us when we lost mum and dad,' said Lily, 'even though none of us wanted to leave Watchet. But, well she did her best, now it's our turn to look after her.' She finished on a resigned note.

They sat and talked for hours, until Annie noticed the time, and knew that George would wonder where they had all got to.

'Do you ever leave her on her own, I mean, is it safe to?'

'Yeah, she's safe, we just give her, her meals and switch the wireless on. I just have to let Mrs Chard two doors away know where we are going and what time we should be back, and then she pops in to check on her for us. When we get back she's exactly where we left her.'

'Do you think you could leave her for a while now, Jonny? Because I know your uncle George,' she turned to the girls, 'that's Georgie's dad in case you don't remember,' well I know he wouldn't believe it if we took you all back with us now.'

'Where do you live now then, Aunt Annie? Only our mum and dad told me years ago that you'd moved'

'What did they say that for? We still live in John Ruskin Street like always, Son.'

A look of disbelief crossed Jonny's face.

'Look,' Georgie could see that something was very wrong here, 'how's about we shoot off now, then we can get to the nitty gritty stuff later. For now lets all enjoy being together.'

What a night it was, everyone trying to talk at the same time. All with stories to tell. The next day was even more special. The Eynsford side of the family had sat up for most of the night, unable to sleep after, Rosie had telephoned to tell them the wonderful news.

By eight o-clock the next morning, both sets of grandparents, Millie and unexpectedly Matty, who had been granted immediate compassionate leave by his Group Captain, were knocking on the door of Annie and George's house. Impatient for when Jonny, Violet, and baby Lily, came back to continue where they had left off last night.

It was to an emotional scene that Georgie led Ernie Pipe into that Sunday. When he suggested that he come back another day, he was told quietly yet firmly by Annie, 'not to talk such nonsense.' She felt that having him there on this day was like having Joey that much closer to them. So Ernie sat and listened as the three youngest Smith children told their long lost family of their lives, since they had been together last. In turn, they answered all the questions coming at them from all directions. There was so much the others needed to know. Jonny explained the one thing that, Annie, Georgie and Rosie had not understood when Jonny first mentioned it the previous day.

'Mum and dad told us years ago that you had moved, Aunt Annie, they said they came here to tell where we was moving to but you didn't live here anymore. And all the time we've been back here, you were just a twenty-minute walk away. I don't understand why they said it.'
Annie not wanting to spoil the memory of their adoptive parents too much, had to be careful in her answer.

'I don't think they meant to hurt you, Love. From what I know, they was always worried that your real dad would one day try to find you. See, we never ever did have an address for you. For the first few years, at Christmas time, your mum used to send us a letter telling us how you all were and she sent photos as well. Then they stopped, course we know why now.' 'But we've been back here for nearly three years. If you hadn't gone back again to where granny Wilson used to live, we might never have found each other.'
Letty fought back tears.

'Don't you believe it.' said Georgie going over to comfort her. 'We would never have given up. We'd have found you one day.'
Then it was the turn of Ernie, all those that hadn't met him until today, were intent on him telling them all about Joey and his days in the navy. Finishing with Ernie assuring them that he searched the hospitals and first aid centres of Malta in the hope that he'd be able to trace Joey.
The day was bittersweet. Two extreme emotions were displayed of untold happiness against the despair of loss, found them smiling and laughing one minute, then sighing and holding back tears the next. There was one more thing that had to be discussed, that was, where they went from here. The ideal solution for all concerned would be for the young Smiths to go and live in Eynsford. Millie yet again showing her love and compassion.

'We have lots of room. Now that Rosie's married and Matt is in the air force.'
'What about, Granny Wilson?'
'If her doctor thinks she is up to the move, Jonny,' answered Millie, 'I don't see any reason for her not coming as well. Who knows, when she's in different company, she might improve. Can she walk?'
'Oh yes' answered Letty. 'She isn't ill as such, infact she's very strong.'
'Would you like to come and live with us?' asked Betty.
The three couldn't disguise the happy looks they gave each other.
'We'd take care of you. It might be a bit late in the day, but we'd give anyfing to be part of your lives.' Ida gripped Bert's hand.
'But what about my job?' asked Jonny, 'I couldn't travel that far every day, and I've got to earn money.'

'You don't have to worry about things like that, Son. Between us lot, money is the least of your worries.' George said determined to do all he could to bring this family together again.

'Hey, Jonny, maybe you could get a place at College or University, seeing as your old headmaster reckons you're a bit of a boffin.' Georgie laughed across to Jonny.

'That was the plan before the accident.' He looked at his two sisters he couldn't keep the excitement out of his voice. 'Well, Letty, Lily, what do you want to do?'

'I can't think of anything I'd like better. To be back with our real family again, well it's like a dream come true.' Letty's face was glowing with happiness.

'Me too' said Lily. 'I've got more lost time to make up. I had the least time as a Smith but little things keep coming into my head as we sit here. I can see a pretty Christmas tree with lots of lights and ever so many presents around it. I feel like I'm coming home.'

None of them could have put it in such a wonderful way and with such true feelings.

Part Two

Chapter Nineteen

'Sam Teel'

'1946'

'Morning, Sam' called Sam's friend, and Sister of the convalescent home, a halfway house for men of the armed forces that were either using this time to adjust to their new artificial limbs, or waiting for their next round of 'rebuilding' surgery.

'Morning, Louise, what a nice one is it too.' he replied, cleaning the windows in the main hall.

'Just what the boys need, after the rain we've had over the last week.'

'Exactly what I thought when I woke up. When they're ready, I'll take them into the gardens.'

'Sounds good to me, Sam and if it stays as warm as this, maybe cook could organise a picnic lunch. Pity James can't join us, he's got a full list this morning.'

James was Louise's husband and permanent in-house Doctor. 'The home' is situated in part of James's family home In Richmond. When his parents retired to live in Switzerland, they left the eight bed roomed property in his charge, to do with as he so wished. It had taken Sam, Louise and James nearly a year to convert the downstairs of the house into individual bedrooms, small they may be but they gave the occupants a sense of privacy. All of them would have spent months if not years, in a general ward of a hospital. In total there were now eight of these rooms decorated in bright shades of blues and greens. The bedding matched the curtains, no flowers here though, the rooms were typically fashioned with ideas gathered from some of the men waiting to be transferred there. They each had two small but comfy armchairs, ready for much appreciated visits from friends and relations. In the corner of the rooms, tiny hand basins had been plumbed in. On the opposite side of the hallway there were two bathrooms and the communal lounge. Next door is a small library with books on lots of subjects that hopefully covered all tastes. 'Guests' often use this room to relax and entertain visitors. The upstairs of the house needed very little work. Louise and James use three of the rooms, one as their bedroom, another as a sitting room and the third doubled up as a study and dining room, not that they had much time for socialising. Sam had one room as his bedroom and another as his own private sitting room. One of the smaller bedrooms had been turned into a bathroom for him. Louise and James used the original one that his parents had had installed just before the onset of the last war. The two remaining rooms they made into self contained bedrooms, each with a shower and toilet installed, plus facilities for making hot drinks, these rooms were for the use of any quests relatives that travelled a long way to get there. If any emergency arose that needed surgery, the patient was transferred to the local hospital. James dealt with minor Surgery cases on site, using the old garage, converted into a treatment room and doubling up as a consulting room for his private patients.

The project had used up most of the money James's parents had left him and Louise, but how proud they were when their doors opened in May to admit the first of their 'guests'. They thought of the men as 'quests'. Their aim was to give the home a feeling of being in a hotel

As a registered convalescent home for ex-servicemen, they did receive some financial help, nowhere near enough to cover their outgoings though. To supplement this, James held a private clinic, trained as a surgeon and greatly respected in his field, meant that rich elderly ladies sought his opinion on all manner of ailments, mostly, to his annoyance very minor. Still he couldn't afford to 'look a gift horse in the mouth,' as Louise frequently reminded him. All in all the three friends were quite content with their lot. Only Sam, sometimes, was seen to be 'somewhere else.'

The sun did indeed continue to shine, the day was getting warmer as it wore on. Sam wheeled those that were unable to transport themselves out into the beautiful grounds. The lawns were surrounded by all manor of species of flowers. There is a path that leads from the house down through a wooded area of trees to the waters edge. It was to this place that Sam invariably could be found during his off duty hours. He loved to hear the water slosh up against the bank and watch as the long boats glided by with men pulling hard on the oars.

'Why can't I just let the past be the past and live for the now, for what I've got here and not what I might have had elsewhere.' These thoughts, often found their way into his head. Louise and James knew when their friend needed them most. They were always there for him during these difficult periods. Not today though, today as he sat amongst the men of the army, navy and air force with the wireless playing popular tunes of the day. It was a day for light-hearted banter, with maybe a hand or two of cards. No doubt, Geoff, who came and cared for the gardens, among many other things, would be there to join them and help with those that couldn't hold the hand of cards. Geoff, himself a veteran of the first war, lived in the poorer area of Richmond until their house took a direct hit from a V2 back in '44. Now he classed himself, his wife, Alice their daughter, Janice along with Janice's two year old son, Tim, to have struck it lucky when they answered the advert that Louise had placed in the local newspaper, for live in help. Alice and Geoff, were able to share their time between caring for their grandson and the hours spent working in the home. Alice 'did for them' as she called it. This genuine and sometimes very funny, couple had turned out to be Godsends. Janice, a staff nurse at the local hospital, split her precious free time between playing with her son, Tim and helping out wherever she could in the home. The wages Geoff and Alice received were quite low, although they lived rent-free in the old barn that had been converted in to a small cottage, Louise and James sometimes felt guilty that *they* were the winners in the arrangement and had voiced this opinion to Alice and Geoff. Geoff, would hear none of it. 'We got more than most people we know. We got a decent roof over our heads. We got food to fill our belly's. We got more than a few coppers in our pockets but most of all we get to be wiv them that we love and them that appreciate us.' Even the sad sights of some of the 'guests' did not put Alice off. Instead she mothered or bullied them, depending which frame of mind the men were in.

James found his way into the garden, the last of his wealthy ladies, gone home satisfied with the mild headache pills James had prescribed for her. He came and sat in the spare garden chair next to Sam. 'You lucky, beggar, been out here all day have you?'

'Who me? You should think yourself lucky James that you've got me to come out here in this hot sun and then sit and play cards listening to some old duck on the wireless.'

'Oh my heart bleeds for you, Mate. I couldn't even get away for the picnic.' The pair laughed. 'I understand that you, Old Chap will try to pacify me by doing wondrous things in the kitchen and tonight and we get to sample it?'

'Watch it, *Old Chap*, or you might just end up with a bowl of tinned soup.' Sam thought the world of Louise and James, he often wondered if it hadn't been for them, he daren't think what might have become of him. Louise and James had many times said that, no way would they have achieved their dream for this house, if Sam hadn't been with them and they meant it.

When all the men were settled in the dining room, Sam went through to the kitchen. Cook, had already dished up the men's dinner and was ready to take it to them. Tom, one of the flyboys, came to help her. Everyman did his bit, well as much as his disablement allowed.

'I'll wash up for you, Cooky.' offered Sam. 'Then I'll get on with cooking our dinner.'

'You saucy sod, Sam Teel, how do you always get away with it?'

'What?' he answered cheekily

'You know what. I prepare everything for you then you make out to Louise and Doc. James that it was all done by you.

'I won't tell them if you don't.' he laughed as Cooky swished a teacloth in his direction.

'You'd better tell me now, exactly, what delicious meal I'm doing?'

'The butcher gave me a lovely cut of meat today, I only went in for minced beef for the boys. So I thought you all deserved a treat, I know it's in the week but it won't last till Sunday.'

'You still haven't told me what it is?'

'Oh silly me. Well fink yerself lucky, cause you're goin' to serve up roast beef with all the trimmings, how 'bout that in the middle of the week?.....'

Sam didn't hear her last words. He was seeing that tiny ray of light shining behind that door again. But every time he went to open the door, the light went out.

Cooky Took Sam by the arm and led him to a chair. 'There you go, Sam, sit yourself down, Lad.'

They were all used to these moments of Sam being 'somewhere else,' as had become the habit of calling these episodes. Sam sat in the chair, a frown creasing his brow as if he was trying desperately to remember something that was on the tip of his tongue, but there it stayed. He fingered the nearly invisible scar near his right eye, gently rubbing it as he always did when he was in this state of mind. Gradually, as usual, his eyes lost their glazed look and with two deep breaths he was back in the kitchen. 'Sorry, Cooky, what were you saying?'

'Just that the meats in the oven, the spuds are all peeled ready for you to put on and the vegetable are all prepared and ready to go.'

'You're an, Angel, Cooky, thanks.' His voice sounded resigned and with a tinge of sadness.

'Alright are you now, Sam?'

'Me? yeah I'm fine. What made you ask that?'

'Well you went off 'somewhere else' just now.'

'Did I? What was you saying when I went?' he had a hint of cheekiness in the question. He couldn't help but smile at what they called his, *affliction?* or whatever it was.

'I was saying how lucky you were to be able to have a roast in the week.'

'Yeah, I remember now. Thanks, Cooky.'

When all the men were settled in their rooms for the night, either reading or listening to the wireless, Louise and James were enjoying a pre-dinner glass of sherry in Sam's sitting room.

'Fanfare please' Sam entered the room holding a tray above his shoulder. 'Look at that.' he boasted, 'just like a professional.' The others laughed as he nearly dropped the whole lot as he bent to put it down on the table. He had already carved the joint downstairs, now it lay nestled among crisp browned roast potatoes with carrots and peas fresh from their garden, with a huge jug of gravy by the side. 'No Yorkshire pud. Sorry but it tastes awful using dried eggs. I could've nicked one of the men's morning fresh eggs, but I thought, nah, I better not.'

'Cooky would have had your guts for garters if you'd pinched her 'boys' treasured eggs. Talking about, Cooky,' Louise continued as she piled her plate with roast potato's. 'She told me that you went 'off somewhere' this afternoon.'

'I don't know, can't a man have any privacy when he goes off.' Sam tried to make light of the situation.

'What brought this one on, do you remember, Sam?'

'Always, The Doctor eh, James?'

'Good job one of us is, look at the way you've hacked this delicious roast beef to pieces.'

'The knife was blunt.'

'Anyhow back to business. Can you remember what it was?'

'Funnily enough, it was something to do with the beef, James.'

'It's been happening far more lately, Sam. Maybe at last that door of yours is beginning to open up more.'

'I hope so, Lou.'

'Are you happy here, Sam?'

'You know I love being with you guys, but, lately, Louise, the feeling that it's somewhere out there that I should be, want to be even, is getting stronger.'

'It's that time of year again isn't it?'

'What, September you mean?'

'Uh huh, every year these memory flashes become more frequent.' Louise turned to her husband, 'but over this last week, well it's been happening a lot. Why do you think that now, after all this time that it's happening love?'

'Well think about it. This is probably the first September since Sam came to us that things have become more settled. You're far more relaxed now Sam, true?'

'You could be right. But I'll be honest with you both. It's beginning to get me down again. Because little things happen and whoosh the light comes on, but it's getting to the point where I feel like I did at the beginning. On bad days, I tell myself that the guys here are far worse off than me, then that gets me through the day. I just can't get to that light before it goes out.'

'I hadn't realised things were getting that bad. I'm sorry, I should have, not because I'm a Doctor but because you're my, dear friend.'

'Don't worry you two, soon as October comes, I'll be back to normal.' They all laughed at the choice of word.

After having made great pigs of themselves, Louise offered to make a hot drink, coffee for her and James and as usual tea for Sam. As she handed him his tea, Louise patted her tummy smiling, 'wow I'm full fit to burst. That was a lovely meal, Sam. How naughty though.'

'What do you mean naughty?' laughed Sam as he took the cup and saucer from her.

'Well, roast beef and all the trimmings in the middle of the week.' She jumped as Sam's cup and saucer crashed to the floor.

'Sam, you okay?' James, the Doctor now, was in attendance.

'That's it, that's it.'

'What's it, Sam?'

'Roast beef, James, roast beef in the middle of the week. That's what Cooky said as well.'

'Do you know what it means?' Louise was becoming excited.

'No, I can't work it out, but, someone else used to say that to me. I just know it. I can feel it.'

'Sam, I think now is as good a time as any to go over everything that has happened from the first time Louise saw you in hospital in Valletta.'

The three talked until the early hours going over events that started way back in 1942.

'What a sorry sight you were, Sam, when I saw you on that first morning after you'd been admitted to my ward.' Louise started to go over the events of that time. 'All you had on was an old blanket wrapped around you. No one seemed to know what happened, I spoke to the men that carried you in on the stretcher. All they knew was that you had been taken off one of the ships that made it through to us in Malta. The Sailors from the 'Penn' said they picked you up out of the sea when your ship, went down. They assumed you was an

American, and so unfortunately did we, as nearly every other chap that they brought to us, was.'

'And that's why none of the Americans that came searching for their pals recognised me?'

'That's right, Sam. Mind you, even your own mother would have had a job to. You were swathed in bandages. Added to that, you were in that coma, it wasn't until months later that you began making mutterings. It was only then that it was obvious you were English. You were covered in oil and at some point you must have been close to where the sea was aflame with burning oil, that accounted for the burns to your back.'

This was not the first time that Sam had been told of his apparent rescue.

'And you said before that I wasn't wearing a Royal Navy identity tag, so that meant that I was probably in the Merchant navy?'

'That's right.'

'But why when you say that, do I think that I *was* in the Royal Navy. Don't ask me why, but I get a picture of me in the uniform.'

'Perhaps your dog tag came off in the explosion, like your clothes.' James suggested.

'Maybe, anyway, go on, Lou.'

'You'd received a nasty bang on the head, and apparently these men that carried you in had been told to tell us that you had not regained consciousness since being picked up.'

'That's where I came in, Sam.' said James, 'you had fractured your scull and only time would tell us how severe your head injuries were. You had us worried there for a while I can tell you. You and many hundreds more. You were out of it all the time the island was still taking a hammering, but what a difference it soon made to the islanders and to us Brits out there after your convoy got through with the so much needed supplies. Anyway, back to you. You remained unconscious for over two months, then you were in and out of it for the next three.'

'That's when I came round fully and this nightmare began.'

'You were such a favourite with my nurses, especially Pauline, do you remember how she used to sit reading to you during her off duty hours?'
A smile appeared on Sam's face. 'Oh yeah, pretty little thing she was.'

'It was her that gave you your name. I laughed when she told me how she'd come up with, Sam Teel, clever though.'

'I'm glad that she was good with anagrams, otherwise you might have just settled for the word she got it from, *Maltese or maltesa*, can you imagine being called that. She came back to England before us, didn't she?'

'Yes, that's because she was suffering from unrequited love.' Louise laughed. 'No, she returned home because a 'Doodlebug' had destroyed her elderly parents house and she was needed here. She was falling in love with you though. I've never told you this bit, but, she said sometimes, when you looked at her, she thought she could see love in your eyes, but it went as soon as it came, she said she could tell that the look wasn't meant for her, but someone else.'

'So she thought that somewhere out there, was a girl that I was in love with?'

'That's what she thought, Sam.' Louise looked at her husband, 'imagine if that had happened to me.' she thought, 'would James still be waiting for me to come back to him, after four years.' She prayed that if, someday, Sam's memory came back, that he would find his love and she had waited for him. As if reading her thoughts Sam spoke with such sadness.

'If there is a girl, she probably after all this time, thinks I'm dead.'

'Come on, Sam' James spoke sternly, he had to shake the negative feelings off Sam. 'You've got to think positive thoughts only. You know once you start to wallow in self-pity that door closes up for a long time. Today it has opened more than once, lets try to get you to reach that light.'

'Thanks, James, you're right. Carry on, Lou.'

'Well, as you know, by the time you had recovered sufficiently to be discharged, the three of us had struck up a friendship. You came to live with us in our tiny apartment. When you had fully recovered, you became a valuable asset at the hospital. That reminds me, you know you must have worked in electronics or something, because you were a wiz repairing and rewiring the damaged electricity cables.'

'I didn't, but my brother did. He taught me all about electricity.' Louise and James sat in shocked silence. Sam looked from one to the other. 'What's wrong with you two?'

'Sam, do you realise what you just said?'

'What you on about, James. What did I say that made you two speechless?'

'You just said and I quote, "my brother did, he taught me all about electricity."'

'Did I?' Sam thought back, 'Bloody 'ell, I did, didn't I?' His hands trembled. 'Do you think it's right what I said. Do you reckon that I've got a brother?' His eyes bore into those of James.

'I'm sure of it, Sam. That's how these things happen after a head injury. Few cases never get their memory back, but in most cases part or full recovery occurs, it can take days, weeks, months or as with you, years.'

'Do you think mine will come back completely?'

'That I can't say, but hey, cheer up, this has been a start, a good start. I think you should get some rest now though. You look done in.' It was true suddenly Sam looked drained.

'Okay if you say so, doc.'

'We'll talk some more tomorrow, Mate.'

Louise helped Sam to his feet, all his energy seemed to have left him. 'Goodnight, Love. Sleep well.' Sam expected to lie awake, thinking all night. Not so, for as soon as his head touched the pillow he was asleep.

Sam was feeling excited and refreshed the next morning. The first thing that came into his head on waking, was, 'I do belong to someone, I have a brother somewhere.' He was whistling 'We'll meet again' as he walked into the kitchen. Cooky was pleased to see him in this mood, for she had worried about him last night. 'Dinner go alright did it, Sam?'

'Perfect, Dear Cooky, just perfect. Any bacon going spare, I could just go a nice fried bacon sandwich.'

'I can spare one rasher that's all. Seein' as it's Sat'day.'

Louise and James joined them in the kitchen.

'Don't tell me you two want a bacon sarnie as well.'

'Cor, that would go down a treat, Cooky.'

'I'll say the same to you, Doctor that I just said to Sam here, I can let you have one rasher and that's all. What about you Sister Lou?' Cooky had her standards, and respect for the doctor and sister came high on her list.

'No. it's alright, Cooky, a bowl of porridge will set me up nicely, thanks.'

Cooky, otherwise known as Maggie Coule, started to prepare the breakfasts. Sam made himself busy by pouring out four cups of tea from the big enamel teapot.

'Did I tell you that me brother and his wife are comin' to spend the weekend wiv me, Sister Lou?'

'No you didn't. Which one is this?'

'My George.'

'Got far to come has he?'

'No, he lives South of the river.'

'Oh whereabouts?' Louise was interested as her family lived in Lambeth.

'Amelia Street, just off the Walworth Road.'

'Tell Georgie to pop into Arments and get us some pie and mash.' laughed Sam.

James, who had been glancing through the newspaper that Cooky had bought on her way to work, stopped mid-way through turning over to the next page.

'Say that again, Sam.'

'What? about the pie and mash, you'll love it, James, specially with loads of liquor.'

'Sam!'

'What?' he couldn't make out why they were all staring at him like that.

'Sam, who's Georgie?' James spoke quietly,

'Georgie, he's me brother.....' the penny dropped. *'My brother.'* His knees nearly buckled under him. James came to his side and made him sit down, before he fell down. Cooky was wiping her eyes with the bottom of her pinney. Louise crouched by Sam's side. 'Oh Sam, Sam, can you remember anything else?'

'I don't think so. I can't even put a face to the name. But I know it's true, I *do* have a brother and his name *is* Georgie.'

'What do we do next, James?' Louise's bright eyes looked up at her husband, where she saw the same watery brightness reflecting.

'I think we should go to... where did you say, Cooky?'

'The Walworth Road, and Sam's right, there is a pie and mash shop there called Arments.'

'We can't both go can we, James?'

'No, sorry, Love, you'll have to stay here.'

'Oh, Sam, I wish I could come but you understand don't you?'

'Don't be daft, Lou, course I do. Bloomin' 'eck, I can't stop shaking.'

'Well you drink this nice cup of tea, I'll just put another little bit of sugar in.'

'Good for a shock eh, Cooky?' smiled Sam.

When Sam and James were ready to leave, word had spread round the home. All the men called out their best wishes to Sam and that they were keeping their fingers crossed for him.

'Find a telephone and ring me straight away if anything happens.' Louise ordered her husband.

The two men drove off in James's dad's old Riley, heading towards the river Thames, where hopefully, something wonderful was waiting on the other side for Sam Teel.

'What's the date today, James?'

'Erm, it's Sunday the 8th.'

'One day early.'

'What's that, Sam?'

'I don't really know, but there's something special about the ninth of September. I can feel it.'

They drove on until they reached the Elephant and Castle. 'Slow down, James.'

'Do you recognise something then?'

'Not exactly recognise, but deep down I know that I've been here before.'

Walworth Road stretched before them. 'Tell you what might be a good idea, Sam, I'll find a quiet road and park the car, and then I think it would be best if we were to walk along the road. Perhaps we'll find this pie and mash shop of yours.'

James turned down a road on his right, it was called Manor Place. He secured the car and hoped that the street kids wouldn't get too inquisitive. They started to walk, staying on the right hand side. Not too far along, Sam stopped to look across the road to where the local market was, there were throngs of people pushing and shoving trying to get to the stall they wanted.

'Seem familiar, Sam?'

'Yeah, there's a shop down a bit on the right, but I can't remember what it's called or what it sells, but I know it's important to me.'

On they walked. There it was, the sign above the shop read, 'Arments Pie and Eel shop'

'Do you want to go in?' James asked Sam after watching him stand and stare at the shop for a couple of minutes.

'No, I think we should go on a bit further.' his voice sounded distant, in another place.

They stopped and read the street name. A slight smile appeared on Sam's face. He nodded his head slowly. 'John Ruskin Street. Down here, James.' He didn't know or understand what was going on, he just knew in his heart this is where he had to go. His steps became quicker, James matched them and walked silently by his friends side. It seemed they had walked for ages along this very long road. James was hoping that they would be able to find the way back to the car. He was being led by Sam, to where, who knows? At one point, Sam stopped outside a house that looked derelict. He shivered and automatically his hand went to the scar on his face. Then with a gentle shake of his head, he continued on.

'This is it.' Sam stopped at one of the houses that stood on a corner.

'What? is this where you lived, Sam?'

'I'm sure it is.'

'What about the one back there, you seemed to take an interest in that one as well?'

'No, I didn't get the same warm feeling that I'm getting now. This is home, it must be.'

They walked forward and were standing in the small neat front garden. Sam walked slowly up to the front door, he had his back to the pavement. Footsteps approached, and then he heard a voice that made the hairs on the back of his neck, stand on end.

'Excuse me gents, can I help you?'

Slowly, Sam turned, one whispered word left his lips, 'Georgie?'

Georgie swayed, James went to support him.

'Joey?' the brothers looked in disbelief at each other. Then Georgie fought the giddiness that was making his head spin. He walked tremulously towards Joey, tears starting to stream down his face.

'Joey, it is you.' Then they were locked together in an embrace, their bodies shaking with the force of the emotion they were feeling. James stood watching them, his own tears rolling down his cheeks unchecked but at the same time he was smiling at this wonderful reunion he was privileged to witness. Finally, the two men broke apart, holding each other by the arms, afraid that if they let go, the other would disappear.

Georgie was the first to break the spell. 'I don't know where, why, how or what, that can come later. All I know is that you've come back to us.' He turned suddenly, remembering that Joey had not been alone. 'I'm sorry, I forgot you were there.'

'Don't worry about me, Georgie is it?' he wiped his face with the back of his hand.

Georgie took a step closer to James, still keeping one hand on Joey's arm, he held his other hand out to James. 'That's right, Georgie Powley.'

'Pleased to meet you, Georgie, you'll never know how pleased. I'm James by the way. So, Sam, sorry, Joey,' he smiled at his friend,. 'You have finally come home.'

Georgie looked puzzled. 'It's a long, long story, Georgie. I'll just say that until hearing your voice just now, I couldn't remember who I was. Are you going to let us in then, Bruv.' Oh how good it was for him to be able to say that word and how good it made Georgie feel to hear it once more.

'I don't live here any more, Joey. I live in Olney Road with my wife, Rosie.'

'So you went and did it.' Joey let out a long happy sigh. ' Now not only are you me brother but you're me brother-in-law as well. He saw the look of confusion on James's face, 'another long story, James. I'll tell you all about it, now I can remember it, that is.'

Georgie used his set of keys that he'd always kept. He went up the stairs ahead of Joey and James. His mum and dad were sitting in their usual places at the dining table drinking tea.

'Hello, Son.' Annie greeted Georgie. 'You been running? you look all flushed.'

'Mum, Dad, you ain't gonna believe this. I don't fink I do meself. But I've got the best surprise waiting out here for you, well more of a shock really, but prepare yourselves for something not much short of a miracle.' He couldn't keep the excitement out of his voice, he sounded like a little boy, the fresh tears falling.

'What is it, Georgie?' his dad sensing that his sons tears were not due to anything bad and his long since departed cockney accent coming to the fore felt his heart miss a beat.

Suddenly, a voice from just outside the door came to them, 'Are we 'aving roast beef with all the trimmings as usual tomorrow, Mum?'

James waited in the kitchen, not wanting to intrude as his dear friend was being smothered with love from his family. After all, they had four years of loving to catch up on. He made use of his time by putting the kettle back on the stove. Soon, good hot strong sweet cups of tea would be welcoming to them all, including him.

Much later, as they sat round the table drinking it, Joey, with the help of James was able to give his family an insight into the lost years. He couldn't keep his eyes off them and they had to keep touching his hands or arms as proof that he was indeed back. Annie was on her third handkerchief. James thought it wise if they try to take it one step at a time, not fill his head with too much news in one go. But Joey desperately had to know two things, apart from being assured that everyone in Eynsford was safe, the first was, what had happened to Linda?'

'She's never stopped lovin' you, Son.' His Ma told him the news that he longed to hear.

'She'll be here for dinner tomorrow, but you won't be able to see her until then, cause she's gone with her mum to see her sisters new baby.' Annie could have gone on to tell him, that Peg had signed the shop over in Joey and Linda's names back in '45, when she had upped sticks and moved with her family to Maidstone in Kent where she opened up another shop that sold ladies clothes. But that would be for Linda to tell.

Joey, sighed, he desperately wanted to see his beautiful fiancée. But, if nothing else over the last few years of wanting to know who he was and where he came from, he had learnt how to be patient. Tomorrow was only hours away, seeing his Linda, was only hours away.

'And before you say anything else, Joey, let me say something to you. You certainly gave me a bloody hard job, asking me to find Jonny, Violet and Lily.' Georgie knew this was going to be Joey's next question. 'Good job I'm a bloomin good detective isn't it.'

It took a few seconds for what Georgie had just said to sink in. 'What, you mean you found them?'

'Course I did.' Georgie felt so good.

'I don't believe it. Where were they? How are they?'

'You'll get to see everyone in the morning, Son. You know what your mum's like, she always makes a big thing of the ninth of September.' They all laughed except poor old James, he was at a loss about what they were talking about most of the time.

Joey took James to the kitchen on his own. 'Can you give Georgie and me some time together James? Don't think I'm pushing you out of my life, cause I'm not, and never will. You and Louise and the home are special to me. I'll be back there one day soon to take up my duties, if you still want me that is. By then, I just might have another pair of hands to help us, if Linda really still feels the same about me.'

'Sam, cor this is going to be hard calling you Joey,' he laughed. Look, Mate, you go with Georgie, I'll ring Louise if your parents don't mind, then maybe your dad.' Joey loved hearing the words, mum and dad, James smiled reading his thoughts, 'As I was saying, maybe your dad could come and show me where the car is because I know I'll never find my way back to it by myself. Then I'll see you back here later.' James knew it would give him the opportunity to talk quietly to Joey's dad, whose head must be filled with questions.

Joey told Annie and George that he wanted to spend some time alone with Georgie, before the world and his mother heard the news and arrived on the doorstep.

'Don't get me wrong, Mum, I can't wait to speak to the rest of the family and see them, but me heads spinning at the moment. I just need to get meself together.'

'Cause I understand my, Darlin'. As your Doctor friend, James says, one step at a time eh?' Annie held her sons face between her hands, kissing him lightly as she spoke to him.

'Mum, Rosie should be here in about forty minutes, I'll make sure we're back before then. Don't say anything will you?'

'We won't say anything, Boy but you can bet your life Rosie'll know something wonderful has happened.' George smiled at his long lost boy. 'Don't think for one second your mum and me can take these silly smiles off our faces.'

'Rosie,' Joey repeated the name.' You don't know how good it is to hear all these long forgotten names of the people I love, Georgie. I can't wait see them again.'

'And I can't wait to see their faces when they set eyes on you.'

Georgie led Joey in the direction of the Avenue school, he'd picked up his mums set of spare keys to let them in. He took Joey and showed him the memorial plaque on the wall.

'I wouldn't let our old Headmaster add your name to it. I just wouldn't accept that you were gone. It didn't feel right, I thought that I'd have felt it if you were. Anyway, the Head made me promise that if you hadn't come back within a year and a half of the war ending, then I'd let him put your name up there with the others. You made it by the skin of your teeth, Bruvv.' They stood paying their quiet respects to those whose names were listed.

There was so much that they wanted to say to each other but for now, both were just content being together again. The war was over and time was something that they had on their side.

George started the walk back with James to Manor Place where James had left his car.

Annie went into her front room and opened the window, she leant out as far as she could, just in time to see 'her boys' with their arms thrown across each others shoulders walk round to the back of the Avenue school.

Some young boys were playing a game of football in the school playground, with a nod to each other, Georgie and Joey wasted no time in joining in with the game.

The End

Acknowledgements

My sincere thanks to Roy for allowing me to use his family name of Arments. Arments was a big part of my childhood years growing up in Walworth. I now live on the Kent Coast but still get to eat my pie 'n' mash as I have it delivered from their shop in Walworth, in bulk!!

Thank you to George Nye, who served on The 'SS Santa Elisa' and was part of 'Operation Pedestal' in the convoy to Malta. His detailed memories and further research allowed me to tell the story. George was one of the lucky ones in that he was picked up by one of the other ships in the convoy and taken to Malta where he had to spend the following two years.

My thanks also go to Joyce Wells for telling me her story of how she witnessed the aftermath of a bomb landing on a nearby school and to Pat Trott who shared her evacuation memories and was sent to the Country where she spent a happy time. And thank you to Josey Moseley who spent many happy weeks as a child in the Hopfields of Kent and shared those memories with me.

Printed in Great
Britain
by Amazon

31209718R00113